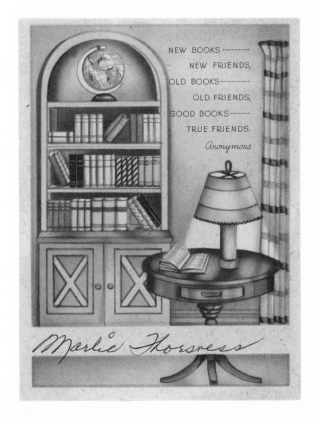

NEW BOOKS----------
NEW FRIENDS,
OLD BOOKS----------
OLD FRIENDS,
GOOD BOOKS-------
TRUE FRIENDS.

Anonymous

Marlie Thossress

The Limner

Books by Paul Darcy Boles:

The Streak
The Beggars in the Sun
Glenport, Illinois
Deadline
Parton's Island
A Million Guitars
I Thought You Were a Unicorn
The Limner

The
LIMNER

Paul Darcy Boles

Thomas Y. Crowell Company
NEW YORK / ESTABLISHED 1834

ISBN 0-690-00559-8

Library of Congress Cataloging in Publication Data

Boles, Paul Darcy, date
    The limner.

    I. Title.
PZ4.B688Li   [PS3552.0584]   813'.5'4   74-13959
ISBN 0-690-00559-8

2   3   4   5   6   7   8   9   10

For Dorothy,
as ever was

The Limner

One

THERE SHE WAS. I sure wish you could have seen the old sun flooding down around her. I painted a blue wash in the back of her, using the cerulean—prettiest word, and it looks just like the word says—and then highlighted the hill down past her father's place with a kind of fringe of willows.

Then I sketched her in and worked on her when she wasn't there. She couldn't be there all the time for sitting, had too much to do in the kitchen. Matter of point, I stretched out the sitting as long as I could. I was working better than I'd ever done, but she stayed about twice as lovely in the afternoon light as she was when she came onto the canvas. That was a nice piece of canvas, about four by three, and I'd paid six bits for it which was too much. But then it was the best Philadelphia'd had to offer at that time. Everything was high since the war, but they didn't have it half as bad here, in the East, as the South had. Nobody'd had it the way the South had it then.

While I worked at first, using charcoal, always do because it flows like a woman's body, I told her about how I'd been just too young for the war. Even if they were taking drummer boys for Chickamauga and Spotsylvania and Bull Run at ages eleven and twelve. Told her how I'd started moving around later, painting for my bread. Told her about the masts in the harbor, at Boston, how New York was with the horse-cars, the slow beasts pulling them in winter, how the Blue Ridge mountains shone in spring's light. How I personally wouldn't paint the dead from tintypes, because they'd never really look right to the relatives living.

Told her a lot then without telling her the real truth, which was how I was starting to feel about her.

She had a brown small face, like a hickory nut, but very smooth, with a bright head of hair like fire flickering on tallow, and the way she sat forward, hands bunched in her lap, made you think of the figurehead on a Yankee clipper, except of course I put clothes on her. Thinking it best to do so.

She had these greeny-blue eyes like looking into little watery reflections of leaves. A small woman. God knows, I don't admire small women any more than I do big ones, both can give ultimate pleasure, but there was a lot of riches about her for the size of the package, and legs so trim—which you could see stealing under her gray linsey-woolsy—they made me think of the tail of a mermaid, with that sweet flicker about them.

She never did talk much, but I could tell what she was thinking, and I knew it was along my lines.

Once at night, the second week I was there, I took a long walk through the side woods before bedding down, and when I got back there was just one primrose-yellow light shining in the kitchen from a lamp, and I looked in there from the outside, and she's there—in a tin tub, soaping her back. Her back had the loveliest curve, like a living temple with the columns springing from the water, that fine hollow between them, and when she stands up and turns, her breasts were sleek as warm wet small melons, and I watched them, and that sweet hollow where the backbone swept down, watched her hair tumbling and her belly curving down to her fine fleece. She looked out of the window square at me, I realized she could see me in the shower of light. I just stood there. I'm not a man who ever peeped before. She didn't flinch. It was just like it had been when she was sitting to be painted. She stood like a rosy flower, all there, in the old tin tub.

So I knew then, and knew from other things as well. Such as the time I was sitting on a hillside above the pastures, looking down at the late spilled light, and heard something behind me—thought it was a rabbit in the long grass. Then something touched me on the nape and I didn't even have to turn around to know what it was. It was just two of her fingers there. She kept them there for a space of seconds, then turned around and went off. I looked after her but she didn't look back. I stayed there long then, till shadows built in pools around me.

I'd liked to have gathered armfuls of roses for her except they wouldn't have been a novelty, the whole side yard was full of them, but it was pretty strange too because I'd never in my life been a rose-collector for a woman. And her father would've wondered what they were doing in the house, smelling up the place.

He was that kind.

I'd got to Jerseyville two weeks before, I don't know why they called it that except maybe because that was the kind of cow they bred most. Some Herefords too, and a couple of Guernsey herds, but mainly the Jerseys. Her father, Mister Einsner, had about a hundred of them. They'd splay themselves around by the creek and clump up under the live oaks and make the whole acreage look fertile as a cornucopia. I'd got there mid-July of 1874, when the heat lay over the land like water you had to press against to walk through, and the Einsner hired men, three of them, looked wet through even in the early mornings when they left the shed where they slept behind the barn and went to the barn to bring out the Jerseys and start sloshing out their runways behind the stalls and feeding them and slopping the hogs and doing whatever other not-so-odd jobs Daddy Einsner had ready for them.

That old plug. Einsner, I mean. I sized him up the second I'd showed my wares—the portrait of the little girl, the one of

Senator Margate, with his right hand stuffed in his vest, somewhat like Napoleon, and the boys bathing in the creek in
Virginia. The last was my favorite. I wouldn't have sold it any
time as long as I had enough to fill my guts. Daddy Einsner,
he was taken with it too; he had a cute eye for value. He said,
"We'll board you and you can sleep over the hired hands'
shed. Give you four dollars, straight, for my daughter's portrait. We want it to hang over the mantel in the front room,
and we want it done with no skimping."

"That's cheap," I says. "I can get ten good dollars for a
thing this size," and I tapped the good canvas, which I already
had stretched.

"Not from me." He looked around out the window. We
were in the front room, or parlor, he had been talking about.
There was just the place for the portrait over the mantel. His
bright little eyes—not green like his daughter's, but black as
pitch-balls—took in what he could see of the meadows. A couple of bees were working around the flanks of the house.
They *broomed* like gold machines in the sun. I could see his
daughter, this girl I've been talking about, Letty, moving back
and forth on the brick floor in the kitchen. All was cool as a
fist of cucumbers in that solid house.

Einsner cocked his head like a marveling robin. "You're
clever, but cleverness don't paint windmills."

"I never painted no windmills, nor barns neither," I told
him. "I'm a limner of the human face, mainly, with now and
then a thoughtful landscape."

"Four dollars and found."

I caught a glimpse of Letty again. I wondered if she looked
like her mother, who I'd gathered was dead. At least nothing'd been said about her, though there weren't any pictures of
her around. And you missed that feeling of clacking talk you'd
have had if there'd been another woman handy. As I mentioned, Letty herself didn't speak much. She'd said hello and
fetched me in and called her father. She'd looked at me in
sidewise glances, assessing and solemn. And quick as a squirrel. She paused in the door of the kitchen and gave me a look

right then. She'd a blue cup in her hand, a marvel of light against her apron in her little hand.

Then she moved on. And something in me jumped; I'd been waiting for it to. And I said, "All right then, Mister Einsner, done."

We shook hands. His hand felt like he looked. Solid and ugly and shrewd and tight.

He showed me around, slightly. Showed me the space above the shed, which he claimed was ratless because the cats slept there too. Showed me where I could ease myself and wash up—the outhouses weren't much on looks, but weatherproofed. That evening after supper he introduced me to the hired hands. Not a one of them spoke much except to look at me like I'd dropped from the moon—guess they'd never seen an artist before. It just didn't have a place in their limited lexicon. One, Arthur Fillitch, asked me if I traveled much. I could have told him of travels from Florida's strands to the Canada woods, but I let it lie and just told him, "Plentifully."

At night it was nice in the loft over the shed. First the moon would come up, grand as a seeking face, with a silver bleached cast in this weather. Flooding all the pastures and putting a touch of light to every grass blade and lift of wheat. I'd lie there on my belly, happy-tired from the day's painting—I was stretching it out to just a couple of weeks, doing a neat good job, not too many inches per day—and remembering how I'd gone down to the pond the creek emptied into and washed off after supper. I did that every night. Made me whistle-clean right through. I'd think how it had been, naked, in that secret water, and how I'd halfway expected Letty to show up on the bank and watch me. But she never had.

I'd recollect the day's work, the exact way her flesh-tones were, the way the flange of her left nostril shadowed her upper lip in the light—and then I'd even think with some joy of the supper. She was a superlative cook, the kind that thinks about food in dainty ways and serves it with forethought; she could make a boiled egg stand up and smile.

As the moon came up I'd rustle in the alfalfa—dry as punk—up there, and the cats, four of them, would move near me, all through with their hunting in the barn for the night. They were sleek as grommets in a sail. Big belly-swagging cats, with whiskers that felt like silk wire, and muscles you could feel like ropes under their slick warm fur. They'd arranged themselves around me the first night, like friendly guards, and except that you had to shift them when you moved in the night, it wasn't bad company. They hummed like hives when they were happy.

The night of the day I'd finished the painting—I'd known it was all done and there wasn't a single thing I could add to it, about six that evening—I was lying there figuring out that, come morning, I'd present the portrait and get my small money, and travel on, doing all this after breakfast, for I could do with one last Letty Einsner meal. And I was damned near asleep in the moonlight through the window, with the tail of the biggest cat, Job, about half-obscuring my vision, when I heard a creak from the outside stairway. It was just a jury-rig staircase that ran up from outside, to this place which they used for gourd storage and herbs and such. A nice-smelling place, with herbs and gourds scenting on top of the old alfalfa.

I jerked my head up and craned to the window. I had forced it open to let the night winds in. In this weather you needed them and I've never been one to hold with tales of night air killing you. I've slept out too much for that to be true.

For a while there was silence. It was that rich aching silence of after midnight with the moon holding the sky like a great nail-head. I could see over to the barn and I could hear a couple of the work horses in their stalls, the *clock-clock* of their hoofs on wood as they stirred. I could hear a hog moving in the pens flanking the barn. Below me I could hear one of the hired hands, I don't know which, snoring. It was a gentle snore like the moonlight itself. Then I could even hear a cow chewing—a faint sound, far away. Wasn't any wind.

There was a breath of coolness near the window, was all.

But I knew somebody was on the outside stair.

I hunched up on my elbows, not disturbing the alfalfa straw much. Then I see this shadow, soft as part of the indigo blue of the dark hiding from the moon, stretch up the stair and then here comes Letty. I know right away it's not just passion and love that's driven her out here. It *could* be passion and love, with Letty, I think, because still waters race very deep in her case (I'd made up my mind to that all right) but when I see her I know that's not on her mind now. For she's dressed in a rose-burgundy velvet gown, with a little ivory ruching at the high throat and a bright gold brooch catching the soft light; I can see her plain now. It's her face bothers me most. It's set as a statue's, and sort of Greek-looking; and those clothes don't suit her.

Not for a night prowl and the satisfaction of passion and love.

For that she'd have worn maybe just an old slip thing, or maybe only an apron.

She was so close outside I could smell her clean skin.

Smelled of lemon verbena and grass and, faintly, of cooking. But good cooking.

In a voice so easy I don't think it woke one of those masterful cats, I said, "Letty?"

There was a pause. I had the wish, watching her in it, I could have painted her now. Not in full sun as I'd done, with artful enough but simple day-shadows, but with this web of night around her and her face emerging from it like a haunt.

She answered me just as easy, only her throat moving. "Mister Applegate?"

"What's wrong?"

In what little talk we'd had, she hadn't volunteered anything astounding. She'd only smiled once, to my recollection. I hadn't cared; some sitters talk your forearm off, but it's better when they stay silent and speak only with their eyes and chins and noses and foreheads.

And their leaning bodies and their hands, most of all their hands.

"I'm running off, Mister Applegate." There was no wait between that and what she said next. "I'd admire you to go with me."

I was standing up, which I had to stoop to do, the ceiling being so low; I could've touched her through the window, over the sill.

"I'll reimburse you for the portrait, I'm taking it with me." I could see, now, she had it wrapped in a linen duster-affair under her arm. And in the other hand she had a traveling case, a little velvet-starred bag with a mouth like a purse. "We got to be quick, Mister Applegate."

I thought, I bet she s got a man friend waiting around the pike in a buggy. But then, if that's so, what's she need with me?

And there was something about that little face, so blanked out and stiff and set. Like you think of the old Greek goddesses, the Furies. Professor Allan, in Virginia, whose house I stayed at all one fall the year before, showed me pictures of such Furies.

It wasn't odd I should think of them now.

All at once I remembered I was naked except for my cotton drawers. I said something, "Ugh," or something like that, and even while I was reaching back for my pants and my paint and canvas bag—which weighs about thirty pounds but which hikes on the back very nicely—and my shirt and my shoes and other near essentials, I made up my mind, what there was of it at the moment.

Hell, I could trust her to pay me, couldn't I, and it wasn't any spit in my eye to fool old man Einsner.

I turned around, buttoning up and then reaching for the paint and canvas bag.

"I'm comin'," I said.

I went out through the window, not down the loft ladder to take a chance on waking up any of the hired hands. There was a door up here too but I didn't want it to scritch. Out between the barn and the sheds in the moonlight it was quiet as stone, with the shapes of everything moon-bothered and reckless.

She went a little ahead of me. She cut away into a patch of black and then into the mooniness again and I could see she wore high black kid shoes, elegant. She was heading away from the house. Then I stopped.

"My swimming boys," I said. She'd stopped also.

I meant my painting of the boys bathing. I'd left it, as a kind of lagnappe—there free for the viewing while I worked on her portrait—on that mantel in the front room.

"You can paint another, Mister Applegate," she said in nothing more than a fierce whisper. I had the feeling she wanted to fling me on her back and carry me.

"No—I'll be a minute, no more "

I dumped my paint and canvas bag down in the grasses with a soft thump. I ran toward the house through the silence-making grass. When I looked back, from the side porch door, she was still standing there but I could hardly see her in the shadow from the nearby oak. I opened the porch door, it didn't make more'n a mouse noise, and stepped in and went over the brick kitchen floor where pots and pans and the black coal-fired range all stood taking little edges of moonlight that wavered just a trifle, like being in the galley of a ship where the water reflects.

I made my way into the front room along the short hall. Same sort of shadows were in here, probed by the deft light-spears. If after I'd lifted the painting of the boys bathing down from the mantel and turned, I'd gone around the Dutch chest—the painted chest with its fine-tailed roosters—under the window, instead of the other way, I'd have missed what was there.

As it was, I stumbled and then looked down. There was just a patch of soft light here but my eyes were as used to the dark now as if I'd been one of the big cats.

It was Einsner. He was sprawled on his face, arms out. I could see well enough to see the pewter candlestick beside him and the place where I figured it had hit the back of his head, a mushy star-shaped wound. I bent over him, deep, and took up his wrist, but it was already cooling.

The painting of the boys in the water under my arm, I went

out the way I'd come. When I stopped out on the side porch and shut the door softly behind me I couldn't see her under the oak.

I walked fast that way, and then ran. I could hear animals moving in their places quite a distance off. But nothing in front of me. I cut down through the side yard past some sharp-smelling be-resined cherry trees and then went over the old stone wall there, lifting my paint and canvas bag which had been where I'd left it, up to my shoulders again and getting the straps crossed right for carrying.

I didn't want anywhere but away. I wasn't even thinking of her now.

But when I got into the tangled shadow of the road—big elms and oaks leaning over it and almost meeting and dripping light between their boughs—there she was, stepping out at me from where she'd been waiting beside the wall.

Both of us started running, the sounds of our feet making soft puffing spurts on the air, covered a little by the singing of tree frogs as we got nearer where the creek went under the road.

Two

PANIC WAS IN US, needles in our veins. She could feel mine and I could feel hers. We might've been children running from ghosts. But mighty bloody ghosts, I thought. Out in a field to our right, away from the creek which was bubbling now under the road and pouring down to the south, a mare nickered. It was a bugle noise in the night and then nothing came after it but tree frogs and the sound of running water again. Her left arm in that pouchy dark red velvet burned in a strip of moonlight like blood. I took hold of her shoulder and sort of shook her to a stop. We were spang in the middle of the road above the creek now.

Over the sound of that rushing water—it's hard to paint water such as that, it's like a million human faces and bodies curving and bouncing all at once and you can't pin it down by just wishing—I said, "Letty! Miss Einsner!"

She was straining forward. Her arm under the velvet which I had a handful of was firm as a sapling but more tender.

She was listening all right, but not wishing to.

I edged her over aside the road. There was a lot of fiddle

fern here with its pungent smell, and dock weed and jim-
sonweed.

I sat down, pulling her with me. I had my painting of the
boys swimming under the one arm and she had the portrait
I'd done of her under one of her arms. For all I wanted to ask
her, I asked her a sillier question now. Something I didn't
really want to know as much as I wanted to know all the rest.

I could feel her left ear near my mouth. "How'd you know
your portrait was all done?"

I could hear her plain enough over the babbling water.

"Wasn't any more you could do on it, was there? Mister
Applegate?"

"No," I said. But, I figured, it took smartness to see that.
Most people—old man Einsner included—would have wanted
extra buttons put in, maybe a couple of cows peering in the
background, and a tufted couch for her to sit on. They like
their money's worth. This was a woman to be watched and
weighed and not to ask everything at once. If she'd killed her
father then got me to go off with her she'd done it so cool it
astounded the very blood in the body, stopping the mind the
way a shock of earthquake will stop a clock.

She wasn't anybody you could figure quick and put in place,
like a wooden-nutmeg salesman.

We sat there listening to each other and to the night. It was
all around us, choiring. Ten times it almost leaped to my
tongue to come out with a tail of bubbles, like there was a river
or a creek inside me too, to say "You killed that old man." Ten
times at least. But every time I didn't say it. I even figured my
thinking it was so strong it made an image in the air.

But after a split of time she said, "If you don't want to travel
with me, you don't have to, Mister Applegate."

I watched a daddy longlegs come out from under a roadside
stone and dandle himself across in the wavy moonlight.

"Looks to me like you need me to," I said after another time
that could've been everlasting. Yet it was only a few mere
breaths. "Young woman out in the nation, abroad with only a
picture of herself and a small carpetbag."

She was looking straight forward across the road, the way I

was. But I could see her from my eye-corners, plain enough. "Suit yourself, Mister Applegate. I'd like your company."

Under all the words I was thinking, my God, she's a cold one. But then there was something not cold, too.

Right then we heard over the creek-stumble and the frogs the sound of wheels. They came racketing down this road from the Jerseyville side. I jerked her up and we stood there dumb-coddled as eggs. That was just for a moment, then a feeling came over me as if I was dropped right in the middle of a turbulent ocean and would have to grab at any chips that came by, let alone spars. It was a gambling feeling which I'd had before. I'd thrown in my lot with her for the time being even if she didn't know it. I worked my hand down her arm and squeezed. "I'll travel with you," I says quick. "For a time, but there's a lot has to be squared away between us. You know that?"

I caught her eyes looking at me, those green-leaf brilliances. They were fleering from the corners. She nods, quick too. Then it's been settled between us. It's nothing steady and forever but it will have to do for then. Because by then the wagon is upon us.

It was a lumber wagon, one of those old long carts might have been Conestoga born to start with, but loaded to the edges with slabs of oak and pine with a smell so rich it was like a traveling sawmill coming at you. Above the creek where the road tumbles down a bit the driver didn't even brake. There were four horses, lean nags in the racing light, stretching themselves, and somebody swinging a whip from the high front seat. I stepped to the road's center, letting go of her, and stood there with the moon blazing around me. Held up the picture of the boys swimming like it was a sign.

The driver slewed to the left. Then braked. Could hear his heel coming down on the brake-stop like a short tree ramming into earth.

All the horses back-haunched and their eyes moved like flashing marbles, taws rolling in the half light.

He cursed like a fool. "Goddamned tarnation idgit of the world!" He was fairly drunk. I'd walked to the off front wheel.

There was a jug twice the size of a Stoughten bottle beside his right boot. He stank like a tannery.

"Admire if you could give a lift to me and the old lady, the wife," I says. "Our cart busted down back of Jerseyville and the horse died. Now we're traveling upstate New York, or thereabout."

His nose, a high-arched object, seemed to be trembling the way the horses were. They steamed in the night-cool.

"Shit's fire!"

Something else too. He was scared. You could get it in a wave. Something had bothered him a lot of late, I thought. Like the devil imagined at his tail. In those parts you get edgy people come nightfall, believers in nixies and kobolds and night-blooming monsters.

I hadn't helped the scare, he probably thought I was a Tarrytown ghost or such-wise. I spoke gentle enough. "We'll pay you for the favor, mister."

He blinked and for a breath I could see him lift the twisted reins and debate whether or not to slap them down and let go of the brake, but I expect I looked flesh and blood to him now and the mention of money had firmed me in his mind.

All the front and back lanterns on his wagon were out, not a sign of light from them.

By this time Letty'd come out of the fiddle fern and was standing there too. He gulped her in fast like she was a draught of golden bitters. Even if he couldn't see too well in shadows.

"Jist the two of you?" I nods. "All right, you'll have to horse yourselves up there where the load's got a back-bulge in it—and there's a tarpaulin if it gets cold. I'm on my way to Mullin's Gap. 'Bout fifty mile along and I'd like to make 'er with no halts." He belched a lot and it made a gasping hook in the air. A big man, but loose-moving.

I could see the blue veins in his arms above the clay-colored sleeve-rolled shirt and they moved like free worms.

"We won't be no drag to you." I turned to Letty, she was already close. We walked along to where the load made a sort of cave. I could see now that it was lashed in with good stout

rope and had been tied by a seaman or anyhow someone who
knew the knots that'll keep lumber from shifting when it's
banged around. The driver turned around and craned after
me. His nose seemed to be following me like a hunting dog's.

"What's that airy thing you waved to me?"

"Painting," I says back to him. I was boosting Letty up. She's
solid but she rises from my cupped palm like a boy into a
saddle. I held the painting up again so the light could catch it
and so he from his place could see it better. "Them's my little
boys," I says, "and a traveling painter done it for me and my
wife last year."

"My, my," he says. There's the sound of the traces chinking
just light on the air above the creek's noise. The off lead horse
stamps. "My, my, now if a body could paint a picter like that
he'd be happy as a bull-pup all his days. Mister, my name's
Gondy. Rafe Gondy. Drive for the Clamber Trust Lumber."

I says, "Mine's Lester. J. P. Lester. I farm. M' wife's called
Rose."

"Well, Mister Lester. What you say to fifty cents? Cent a
mile."

"That'll do me. You want 'er now?"

"Nup. I'll trust you. Well, hike up."

I took hold of the wagon's rail and vaulted, pack, picture,
and all. Letty was already snugged back in the socket beside
the lumber, knees drawn up and those slim kid shoes shining.
I landed just in front of her. Hadn't landed two seconds before Rafe Gondy—was sorry I couldn't have given him my real
name, or hers, or took credit for the boys swimming, either—
cracked out a "Geeraaaap!" Then the whole wagon jolted and
the lumber jounced in spite of its tight roping. Between the
raw swarming smell of the fresh-cut lumber and the steaming
of the horses and the smells of Mister Gondy wafting back to
us it was a good thing, I figured as I sat back, that we were
going lickety-cut—because this brought us enough fresh air
streaming by so's we wouldn't quite expire.

We were squashed together so tight, eels in a barrel, there was
no modesty about it. After about a mile of the racketing flight

with the road streaming behind us and the tree boughs flicking over us like switches and the hoofs drumming in that long roll they get, I was getting uncomfortable the way you get when you are jostled against a woman's thighs and the front of her body and get to feeling you'd like to be even closer. But this wasn't just any woman. I sudden-like put my arms around her and tipped her back, feeling her wiry and wild under me, and then she was kissing me in a long drowning kiss like a kind of night-fire.

Jesus, I'd never had that. I'd had it with a lot of women, I mean, but not in that style and with that current of dragging down. I was hot as fire now, feeling as if I happened to be a rod on fire with grace, and I was leaning into her again, close as a pigeon covering a roost, and trying to see the flicks of light in her eyes, and sort of covering myself with that smell of her skin and her very pores, when all at once a jug cracks me on the side of the ear. It's Gondy, holding it back to me.

"Help yourself, Miz and Mister Lester! I always travel with plenty of juice!"

Through the mad I felt I felt, too, maybe it happened just in time. Maybe Gondy is an instrument of God, working on my behalf to save me in the nick from this Jezebel. I still wanted the Jezebel, mind, but I figured that other way too.

I sings out, "Thanky!" and took the jug in both hands and tipped her back slow, to balance against the jouncing.

It was old Pennsylvania lightning. Bug-juice that's stood about three days to mellow. The crock-texture jug was cool though, and I laid it against my cheek when I'd taken a snorter.

I got everything solidified again between the tonsils and the brisket, and polished off the mouth of the jug with the heel of a hand.

Letty says, her voice sounding ropy and up-and-down because of the motion, "You don't have to wipe it off for me, Mister Applegate."

"You mean you don't drink?"

My voice sounded the selfsame wavery way. Instead of starting to sponge out things you maybe don't want to remember in a flash, the way such rot-liver will usually do, the one drink had somehow brought up before my eyes that picture of old man Einsner slumped on his belly with that hole in the back of his skull. It just came sudden, like a pain.

"I mean you don't have to wipe it off." She took the jug. She handled it brisk, though I'd have sworn she didn't know the trick.

Then I had another and held it to her and she shook her head no, and I raised up careful and swung the jug around to Gondy again. He was singing "Buffalo Gal," in a voice that no cougar would have been proud about. But it seemed to go with the hoofs of the horses rattling every stone in the road and their withers sending steam in pale clouds up to the sky. Farmhouses black as India ink, covered and melted down for the night, folded their shapes against the sky and barnsmell from their barns rolled down the slopes to linger along with the stench of Gondy himself.

I sat down slow, and reached for her. This time it was all slower. I could hear and feel the wagon come out on a clear stretch, away from trees. There was just the light flickering across our bodies and my hands working down into her, and around her, and then she was slipping away the dress, the neckline of the dark red and rosy velvet slithering down and catching points of sudden light and then her breasts, lovely and pointing straight at me and the nipples tight as pennons in a wind, and above us the night wind rocked and swayed, and Gondy sang, unseeing us, drunk and also drunk with the joy of his driving, while I moved in her, and she moved around me, and we rocked like waves in the sweet hot blind darkness.

Christ, a woman like that—I've not known many, maybe none like that—like her—she is so close to you you want to lap her up like cream from the pans in a dairy floor, and live in her so close each knows the sweet stink of the other's cool sweat, and afterward, or between times, you just lie there and let her look at you. But she was a secret big as the restless world. She wasn't going to tell me anything that wasn't dragged out of her middle like a child.

You don't even think of fucking as a word, with such a woman; you just think you have to have her. Everything that went on under our flesh in the time I'd been painting her roiled and lived in me now. I knew one thing. I knew why I'd painted her, for that four dollars, as good as ever I'd painted anything on earth.

I says, the tones still wavering and even seeming funny like a flute in a storm, "You got a little baby birthmark on your belly." I put my finger on it.

"My mother had one right there too."

Her voice quavered too with the motion, but under the wavering was strong as a cyclone's.

"Your mother passed on?"

"No. She ran away."

Well, that was something; if she didn't want to talk much I could be grateful for halfway favors. Just looking at her, I was getting hard again. She knew it and reached for me, and took me and came down over me; I reached up around the fall of her hair, seeing only the faintest sparks of her eyes, and pulled the tarpaulin down over us. So there was only us in the whole running dark, or maybe even in the entire earth.

Three

IT WAS A GOOD WHILE LATER. I was sick of being jostled around. We'd both been asleep but I'd kept waking with the motion of the wagon. Once and again my head got snugged against a lumber-edge and I thought, This will rub all my hair off till I'm balder'n a snake. I figured Letty was having trouble slumbering too.

Now I'd waked again. A jolt threw me against her. She was dressed again, sort of. I figured this trip hadn't done that fine velvet party dress any good. I could just see her in tiny chinks and dollops of light through the tarp's edge.

I says, wobbling-voiced still, "You awake?" Though it sounded like "Yooo—ooo awa-aake?" Like an owl talking toward the morning about all the mice he's missed in the night.

I threw out an arm and ruffled up her hair. As if it wasn't already ruffled. Thin-feeling in each hair, but bushy and luxuriant, it was. Fine-haired she was as a lovely beast.

"Uh-mmmmm . . ."

I could feel the wagon slowing. Gondy wasn't singing now.

The wheels came on some kind of cobbles and rumbled like I suppose guns did in the Wilderness in the war.

I sat up a trifle and cast off the tarpaulin. I pulled myself higher. I felt a little lightheaded and hungry, but not much. Just the easy drained hollow way you feel when you've been loving all night, off and on, and you don't think there's another breath of loving in you. But yet you know there will be. It's marvelous the way a man fills up, like an everlasting well, when he's got the woman for it.

The sky to the east was lightening. There was a wash of rose madder and mazarine in it. Low to earth the shadows were still piled deep. The land here looked rich and smelled of wet morning earth. Sometimes a low hill close by cut off vision but you could tell it was fine tillable soil. We were on cobbles that hadn't been laid too straight or smoothed off too much. We'd slowed to a fast walk. Horses were breathing like grampuses. Gondy's neck sagged forward and bobbed and I figured he was asleep while driving.

While I watched, she sat up, shrugging closer into her nice dress and sort of smoothing out velvet wrinkles down her thighs. Just as unrumpled inside, she was, as a madam in a good house. But she didn't look like the product of any whorehouse. She was too fresh and rosy for that. Her face looked like a little girl's. I bent to her and kissed her light as a feather touching the skin of a frog pond, maybe an angel's feather falling.

For a flash she smiles at me, then the smile's gone and her face is locked in again. All shut up and sealing me out.

Then while both of us watched, we came into this village. If you could call it that. Some sort of town. Low buildings and a saloon, and a kind of inn over on the north and a circle of cobbles widening out and a town pump. Was a goose marching slow around the pump as if it was guarding it. Like one of those Hessians in the old days when this country fought the British. It was a goose that tickled me, for some reason; just the way it poked its neck out and walled its dandersome eye.

I'd liked to have sketched it.

Gondy wakes up with a jerk and calls, "Hooooah," but the

horses were ready to stop with no calling. They drew up before the inn. There were four wicker-bottomed chairs drawn up with their backs tipped against the wall of the inn porch and they looked like square-bottomed old burghers taking a rest.

Gondy was just about reeling in his seat. I thought how he'd looked on fire with fright the first time I saw him, and he saw me. "Sleep good, Mister?"

I razed the bad taste out of my mouth by running my tongue around my teeth and croaks back, "Fine as can be, Mister Gondy. This it?"

"Mullin's Gap." He nods. I expected his jug was dry; if he had a second jug even that was dry, I thought. His eye rims were red as the coming sun.

"I change horses here at the livery stable," he says. "Then I got to git on."

Letty was already picking up her velvet-starred carpetbag and the wrapped portrait of herself. I was going to help her down but she made it with no bother. Then she propped the portrait in its wrapping against a knee and put down the bag and stood fluffing out her hair with the first light catching her. I saw Gondy perk up. He did it visibly all over. Hadn't had a chance to really see her in the night. "Morning, Miz Lester!"

"Good morning," she says with a kind of absent tone, just flicking a glance at him sidewise, and still busied with her hair.

"Now I could wish I was headed upstate far as you're going, folks," says Gondy, wheedling it a little. "But I got to cut off west down the next road. If you want accommodations at the inn they'll serve you." He couldn't keep his little eyes off Letty. It amused me but truth to tell it bothered me too.

"We'll make out," I says. I'd jumped down with my paint and canvas bag on my back and the picture of the boys swimming well tucked under an arm. I strolled up to him and eyed him. "Fifty cents, believe you said."

He nods. Thoughtful.

"Well, here you go—" While I skinned the money out of my right hand rear hip pocket—I didn't have much, staying at Einsner's had been the end of a poor road of late—I thought

how I'd like to sketch his head; it was a cragged head like a
prophet's, and that nose made it interesting. It was like a bluff
overhanging sheer air.

I put the money in his hand. He sat there a second more.
Seemed like he was thinking up a speech.

"—an' ten cents more for the likker."

I looked up at him as if he was pure stone.

"The likker was offered to us in friendly spirit," I said. "I
didn't ask for it and neither did my woman."

"I'm a pore man, Mister Lester. I got to cut them corners."

I just looked up at him.

"Tell you what—" All his looseness leaned toward me.
"Gimme that painting you got, that you said was of your boys,
and I'll call 'er even."

I said, "That painting's worth a packet of gold, Mister
Gondy. You'd make me smile if I was in a mood for smiling."

I sure didn't like the way he'd said, "you *said* was of your
boys."

Now he murmurs, soft and sloppy-mouthed, "You sure are
a young strap to be farming way upstate. And to have them
boys in the picter. And your wife, she can't be no more'n six-
teen if a day. Ten cents or the picter, Mister *Lester*."

Then he winks and his voice slurs down even lower. He's
still dumbfounded with drink but he's got that shrewdness
about him his kind were born carrying around.

"Mister Lester, a lot's been goin' on in this here wagon bed.
I don't aim to dip into what's none of my business, nor my
pleasure neither. But I'll say for a old married man you got
some peculiar strength in your loving . . ."

Almost, I jerked him down from the wagon. Could have
done it by hooking my free arm around one of those boots.
And I was too nettled for comfort. I knew that, that I was getting madder than I should have, and was going to state something I'd regret later. But it was out like a toad in the air
before I could pull it back.

"I painted that picture, you flop-eared ignorant man. I'm a
limner and proud of it. It's just I didn't want to get in any long
conversation back there near Jerseyville. I'm a kind man by

nature but I don't like questioning talk. Now, since you want a
ten-cent piece for your likker, or a couple of handsome five-
cent pieces, I'll give you somethin' worth more." I'd sailed too
far to stop now; I'd dumped the paint and canvas sack, with
all its bulk, in the road and propped the painting of the boys
swimming next to it and ripped open the pack and was searching for a couple of pencil stubs and a piece of decent paper. I
found them. I straightened, mad as a bobcat, knowing I'd
think about this later and regret it, but doing it anyhow. I was
way overboard.

"This," I says as I steadied the paper on the wagon-flank
where in the undimming light I could see the name of the
company, CLAMBER TRUST, painted in curly but fading letters on the wagon's side . . . "this'll pay you for your belly-
wash, Mister." I sketched him fast. Back in Virginia Professor
Allan had showed me books written by a Mister Charles Dick-
ens, and in them were engravings of people by a man named
Phiz, illustrating the stories. Sometimes he could bring out the
meanness in a person in about seventeen hard-cut lines. I did
that with Gondy now, watching it grow under my fingers and
finishing off the nose with a spurt of heaviness that damned
near drove the pencil through the scrap of paper. Then I
started to sign it, and nearabout wrote "Lucius Carolus Applegate," then stopped that and just initialed it, "J. L." for Lester, but if you looked at the signature on a slant you could see
where I'd started the other. I put the goose in the background, turning around to get a quick flicker of him as he
marched around the pump. He was the stupidest-looking
gander-goose I ever clapped eye on.

I handed the whole shebang up to Gondy, whose fingers
shut around it and who then opened up his hand and canted
his head and looked at it.

But he wasn't mad.

"Sure now," he says admiringly. "Sure now, that's me, and
that old bird behind me. Sure now, Mister Lester, you're a
smart-handed man. No hard feelings."

And he belched one of his large ones.

I nods, quick, and watches him while he lifts the reins again

and raps them over the backs of the sick-tired horses, damned
near slumped in their harness. Letty and I stood watching
while the whole wagon got itself together and went on past the
inn porch and around the half-circle near the pump and then
down a side street, the last we saw of it the unlit lanterns
dangling like earrings from the tailgate.

Then I knelt down in the road and hooked my pack
together again, and picked up everything, including the picture of the boys in the water, and felt foolish.

I walked over to Letty. "I shouldn't have done that," I said.

"No, maybe you shouldn't, Mister Applegate."

I looked at her a spell. "You can call me Lucius," I says. "Or
even Luke. I expect we're acquainted now, Letty."

A little soft flush came climbing her cheekbones. They were
wonderous cheekbones. It wasn't just the sun that did it.

"There anything you want to tell me, Letty?" I said. "Seeing
as how we're cast together on a tight raft in an angry world?"

Those green prideful eyes just kept on looking straight.

"—because now's the time if you got something to say," I
went on. "Before we move out from here."

But she didn't answer me or say word one in any regard.

So I said, "Come on, then," and she picked up her rig of the
carpetbag and her own portrait and we went up the porch of
the inn, me going first. Out at the pump the goose ruffled his
scraggy feathers with a soft sound like wind in fern, and I
opened the door of the inn and held it for her to step into its
morning shadows.

There was a man asleep, a slimsy thin man with sleep all blur-
ring his eyes, and his suspenders loose over his shirt and
drooling down in his lap; he came out of his chair beside the
table and stood up and I says we'd like accommodations for a
time, here. I didn't know what else to tell him for a name so I
used J. P. Lester again, seemed I was burr-stuck with it. He
grins and I writes the name down, in a kind of backhand I
learned when younger, and put my "wife's" name, Rose Lester, and then he says it'll be four bits apiece, bed and we can

eat at the table which will open in an hour soon as the rest of the place is fit to start moving.

I swear I didn't have that.

But right behind me, Letty was already opening her close-lipped bag. I could hardly see over her shoulder but there seemed to be plenty there; her hand shut over a bill, a good enough bank certificate, and she shoved it at me and I shoved it along to the man. The man says, brisker now, "If you're staying long we could make a price," and I shakes my head. He looks at the bill. It had good paper, and was new, and snapped a bit as he drew it through his fingers. "You folks got a place for your rig?"

"We ain't got a rig," I says. "Aim maybe to get one later. We were brought here by a friend."

I was some ashamed of having lost my temper with Gondy. But I sure didn't want any more queries than had to be made, now.

Out of a till, which he unlocked by turning around to it, till only his belly was snugging at it, and him using a key on a rat-leather string attached to his belt to open it, the man made change. There was a fistful of bills coming back. I shoved them along back to Letty and didn't turn around then but heard her stowing them away. The man was waking up more. "We set a good breakfast table; and all the townspeople come for supper," he says. "And if there's any exters you want we'll be proud to have 'em."

I grunts, "We'll let y'know."

"Name's Tatum, Abraham Tatum, Mister and Miz Lester."

So I shook hands with him. I felt tarry and sticky and bunged-about and whiskery.

I thought of that four dollars, good dollars, still owed me by old man Einsner. Couldn't help thinking of him back there fifty miles gone and dead as cold fish. The shadow of him clouded around my head all the time we were climbing the stairs. The stairs creaked like they were full of dry rot. She went up ahead of me and I watched her hips just swelling that pretty dress nicely, and thought what was under the dress,

and yet I hated her too. I have to tell the truth about this or it
doesn't mean a thing, and now I hated her, wanted to be shed
of her. I was rinsed through with a kind of shabby dark feeling as though I'd once been a good man and now had something in my being that was so foul I'd never get it out. But she
swung up ahead of me, pretty as a mare even needing sleep as
she did, and then we were beside the door at the head of the
stairs that Abraham Tatum had said would be the door to our
room. We went in. The bed was good and it had a deep
feather bolster. More light was sneaking in under the near-
drawn blinds.

I put down my pack and propped up the boys swimming on
the bureau and went to the jug of water and leaned over the
basin—the china in it had little pictures of forget-me-nots
around the brim—and poured water over my head into the
basin. That felt better. When I raised up I could see her, half
in the mirror, putting away her carpetbag and putting her
wrapped portrait against a wall. She sure moved quiet and
nice. She caught my eyes in the mirror, which had a tarnish
spot like a long wet stain, and I saw her there as though there
were two of her, dancing in the first sun spots across the glass.

Then we both looked away. And then back.

I said, "Since you got nothing to say, Miss Einsner, we'll just
sleep a spell. No fooling around."

I was still looking in the glass; I thought she winced, but it
might've been a sun-bobble.

"All right, Mister Applegate." Her voice level as a plumb-
line.

No Letty and Luke or even Lucius.

When we undressed and slid under that puffed vast bolster
it was as though we were full strangers, apart from each other,
not even touching legs to get warm in the early cool of the
room.

Last I saw before I went to sleep, like a dark wave washing
out my brain, were the round tar-ball eyes of old man Einsner,
staring at me. He was alive in the vision, but just as ugly and
hard and tight and swelled with his own Dutch importance as
ever.

When I woke up she was wearing another dress, a gingham quiet thing, and fixing a rent in the burgundy velvet gown, the needle and thread going in and out like young rabbits in a hole. She didn't see me. Her hair was flax waterfalling over the job of work. She sat in the window seat with the blind rolled up.

I got up and stretched. Then I stirred up soap and water in the basin and made a lather and shaved with the long razor I'd bought one year—two years before, come to think of it—in Lexington. It was a good razor, could cut your flesh with it easy as pressing just a trace. I felt somewhat better but still dark and mad inside.

When I turned around, feeling my chin—it's like doing a small good sketch to shave well—I was looking straight at her again, this time in no mirror.

She says, "Mister Applegate, I've got twelve thousand dollars in the bag. It was my mother's. You can count it if you wish."

"It ain't mine," I says. I walked over and sat down beside her. I was buck naked but we might've been old married hands, J. P. Lester and Rose, as ever was. "You take it from him?"

"Not 'take,' " she says. "It was rightfully mine. My mother's, she left it for me alone. No doubt about that."

"You said she ran off."

"She did. Mister Applegate. She couldn't stand him any longer. He was a runagate skinflint, Mister Applegate. He beat her badly."

She might have been a little schoolmistress, hands folded over her sewing. And just as level.

So, I thought, you bided your time. And it got too much and you killed him and ran off in your best party-dress with a painter who might help you get along in society. I couldn't bring myself to say any of those things.

A lot of things roiled around my body and brain. She, looking so innocent. But the small tidy hands were fit to swing a pewter candlestick.

Then I shut my eyes and says, sort of fast, wanting to get it over with, "Look, let's not talk about this no more. I like you, let's leave her there. I'm named Luke to you, you're Letty to me. We won't talk no more about—this." I opened my eyes. "We'll start new as a bayberry leaf when it first comes out. We'll just begin."

It was one of the hardest things I'd ever had to get out, and it felt like I'd birthed a calf.

She gave one of her seldom smiles. Behind it I knew she'd stay shut up and close-locked as ever, but this was a bargain. A truce. She was taking it my way. I'd had to take it hers.

This time she kissed me. Then I stood up, starving, and dressed and then we went downstairs. We'd only slept an hour.

There were about a dozen people, some of them drummers, some farming men in town to buy flour and such, at the trestle table in the dining room. Hadn't been for the flies, and Mr. Tatum's hired help—big black women who smashed down the grub as though they just wanted to get rid of it anywhere—the food would have been more joyous. The meat wasn't as leathery as some I'd chewed, and the coffee made you sit up and blink and feel to see if you had a throat left. Some of the drummers wanted to make talk—about a storm up the Hudson that'd wrecked whole fields, about robbers and murderers on the upstate Pike—but Letty and I just nodded, and got a mute reputation, right off the bat, for being close-mouthed individuals.

After the breakfast, which we ate with Letty keeping her carpetbag right down there between her ankles, we excused ourselves fast before the drummers started to smoke after-breakfast smokes and the farmers started to occupy the porch chairs and chew, and we stepped out into the morning. It was new-washed as a wealthy child's cheeks, and the goose had stopped guarding the pump. We walked around the pump and made for a side road; it was the road down which Gondy had turned with the tired horses.

We found the livery stable with no trouble. I recognized

Gondy's horses in the stalls. I chaffered with the horse-and-rig hirer for a time and then settled on a nice neat-hoofed bay with fawn fetlocks. There was a good small buggy in a corner, too. I didn't pay in advance, not knowing how long I'd keep the rig.

When we mounted after the bay was harnessed up, the carpetbag sat right down there between Letty's feet. She'd changed from the kidskin shoes to something more fit for a speck of travel.

Clapping down the side road the direction we'd entered it by, we drew into the morning like a couple of kids. I'm not saying the darkness was gone out of me; I felt it would come back. But it was tamped down now like a smoldering fire covered with a drift of ashes. All around us, as we got out of Mullin's Gap, we could see the hills begin. First they were low like the rumps of grazing big beasts beside the road, and still a little touched with haze, though it was now about nine by the old clock back there in the inn; then they started to take on longer, spinier shapes in the air. I remembered the hills of the Smokies, how they went into those secret mountains where a man could die and find himself even more alive in the pure and searching air. I clucked to the bay. She splatted along smartly. After a time I took one of Letty's hands in mine. The hands weren't constructed for anything worse than making a deep-dish pie or studying the crust of bread or lining a cobbler dish with peaches.

All at once, soft but plain, she says, "I'll cook better for you than that tumpish inn can offer."

So she knew what I'd been thinking. It would've scared me if I hadn't been getting used to her by now.

"I know it," I says.

But there was more I didn't know. There was the wall rising behind all this front. I just kept things even and nice, and turned the bay up a side path. Pretty soon we were climbing. When we came to where the buggy wouldn't go any higher I tied the bay to a young chestnut and we went up higher on foot, she swinging the bag lightly. The path went crooked and climbed and climbed, getting steep. We passed cattle lying down and they were so thin and wild-eyed they looked like deer. Nothing like the Einsner Jerseys back at what now seemed a long way off. Pines made the air tonic and sweet-sharp. It was strange up here. We grunted and strained up one last curve in the path, not even a bird singing ahead of us now, everything silent, and came out in the clearing.

I'd never seen such a fine or lonesome place in all of my wanderings over the land or water.

Four

FIRST POINT ABOUT IT, it was a masterful place for being by yourself. Yet at the same time it had the lost feeling of a place that's known many people at one time and that's been left to itself to wonder where they went.

Ahead of us in the lacy light streaming through the long heavy pines—I never saw such big pines, even in the Smokies—was a green carpet of moss, like flowering interconnected great beds lying under that light that touched so easy. Above us the pines whispered in the morning and there was still dew on the grass tussocks alongside the rich old moss. And around us were four stone houses, small ones, a story and a half, but neat-built, you could see how careful the stones had been placed, you could make out the tightness of the doorsills and the strength of the small wide chimneys. And then there at the end of the clearing, overlooking the sky and the hillside that sloped down to a small but quick river, or the branch of a river, was the main house. It was of stone too, monstrous but not ugly at all, all in nice proportion, with the stones slightly blackened in the sun and the real slate roof—a few slates busted and draggling—and the door open halfway and facing us. Two steps, slabs of stone, led up to the door.

You could tell there was nobody home. Hadn't been, maybe, for a dozen years or more.

Birds once they got used to us being there started to talk. They talked above the slight river-noise. I started walking to the door. She followed me. I could see her shadow and the little shadow of her bag swinging. I thought of the money in that bag. It was more'n I'd ever dreamed about.

I'd said it wasn't mine. But if I took Letty in the circle of my ongoing being, wasn't it part mine? Even if it'd been stolen from a dead man?

The thoughts churned a little in me. Meantime our footfalls weren't making sounds on the moss. I got to the steps first and went up. I peered in the door. It hung back on its hinges. It was made of mahogany; had a quiet design on its front, you could just see where it'd been cut and the wind and rain had dulled it. A couple of sheaves of wheat, crossed.

I opened the door a tad farther and stepped in. Again on the dark flooring inside I could see her shadow following, printed in the sudden sun.

All at once a woods dove went by our heads so fast it made my heart zoom. Flew right out of that old ivory-walled front room. Out into the sun, just missing her bright easy hair.

We stood looking around. I didn't have the notion anybody would show up; all the same both of us walked slow on the old well-laid floors, out of some kind of respect. Dust was thick as ropes on things. There was the full furniture everyplace, some of it ruined, the red plush seat-bottoms of the tall old arched chairs looking neglectful and solemn, the harpsichord in the next room—light blue-painted, and pretty and delicate as a mourning woman—giving off just the taint of a sound as we passed it, like a sigh. In the same room there was a harp, or the skeleton of a harp, with the strings mostly gone. You could tell there'd been a fire, two of the back rooms were gutted with it, but the fire hadn't reached the heart of the charred overhead timbers and there was still plenty to work with. Funny, I kept thinking of how I wanted to work with it. It was a feeling in my wrists, beating there, and in the tips of my fingers—a yeasting, you could call it. It was the way I'd felt when I went to paint Letty, the first time, for that rotten four dollars.

Standing in a back bedroom, close together, we could look out the marl-gray window and just see a millpond down where the river-branch emptied. And above the pond the grist mill, the wheel covered with moss now but looking capable and ready, for all that, and the slabby but well-built mill house leaning and shadowed in the pond's nearly still water. A bunch more doves were flitting around above the pond, their necks stretching as they took off, their blithe little heads looking as though they supped the air, and their wings clean and potent in that skimming water-light.

We moved back farther to the kitchen. It was a great low-ceiled place with windows galore but they were darkened too. I rubbed away the grime and dirt and stale of the years with the heel of a hand. The sun came leaping in to touch the slate floor.

There were two mammoth ranges and pots all about the walls and cupboards standing ready. And a table solid as a brewery horse in the middle of the room.

Letty says, "Oh," and then she was picking, off a peg, what had made her say it. It was a long old light blue apron, dusty as flour, but it was hemmed with lace. Seeing her there I could see her working in this kitchen, maybe even singing as she moved.

I just looked at her. She put the apron back. She stayed at the foot of the stairs while I went up. It was a long dark staircase whose newel post was built like a jewel, and so were all its treads. There were four rooms upstairs, bedrooms I expected, and two connecting halls, and then a little room with round windows looking out on the quick-sparkling river branch, which I figured for a sewing room. Because even dusty and beaten-down and lorn, it had a woman's look.

Down below again, in the very front room above the stone-mouthed fireplace, I found a rifle hanging. Was so dust-touched it couldn't have worked, but it was one of the old

Kentucky kind—a Boone rifle, the barrel so lean and beautiful it was as if the metal had come kicking alive in the fingers of the gunsmith, the stock like a horse's cheek as it tapered back and the butt asking to fit the curve of a man's shoulder.

After a time we went soft as slow-walking night animals into the sun again.

We worked our way to the north side of the clearing this time, the house on our left. The pines sent a smell of peace over everything. I thought, What if I'd never stopped there in Jerseyville on the chance of getting a painting project? Well, I wouldn't be here, would I? But would Einsner be dead? Such questions you can't answer just simply. I'd always lived the simple way up until meeting Letty.

The noise of the river-branch pouring into the mill pond was louder now, and you could see the pluming race where the water came down. I was about to jump for the platform from the bank not far from the path—I'd have had to pick my way down the partly limestone-stepped path and felt like a bird that doesn't want to walk—when behind me, Letty says, "Ah, look!"

I held myself sort of still in the air and turned. A man was standing beside her. Of course the water sound had covered up his steps but all the same he'd been quiet as a leaf.

Beside him was a dog about as big as a good-sized pony, with a woolly pelt and a high head and handsome black eyes. A dark dog with hair like long feathers. The man and the dog looked like brothers. He was in rags, which made him look just as woolly. He was about sixty-five or seventy I thought, and his face was the stain of walnut; his hair was white and fairly long. Didn't know what else to do, so I nods.

"Heydy," I says. "You startled me."

His voice came out thin and dry. Didn't seem he'd used it much.

"If you jump—and land on the mill platform—she may bust through. Wood's mushy as pumpkin rind down there."

"Thanky," I says. I stood back. He didn't have any visible weapon. "You live here?"

"I do, young sir. But it ain't mine. Used to run the mill."

"And the mill hands lived in them small houses?"

"Yes, sir." He inclined his head, courteous. His eyes were smoky old blue. "I was foreman. Right-hand man. Mill was owned by my employers, Mister and Miz Carroll. That was long ago . . ."

He let all the long ago-ness lie on the air, as if he peopled the whole clearing with life. The backs of his hands were leathery but hard; not bulgy the way old people's often get. "I stayed on after the war and the fires—I trap and do a good bit of fishing; I keep to the first house down there as you come up from the path. I'm Seven Phillips."

"Severn?"

"Seven." Faint lines worked around his dry thin lips. "Long, long ago, young man, when my mother and father were whimsical and young and fresh from England, they named me for my place in the progression of their children. Yes, they had seven children and were still young. Laughed a lot."

"Who set the fires?"

"My people, the Carrolls, weren't popular, young man. They believed in no war at all; they didn't think the cause of the North was any more just than the cause of the South. Mobs came, trying to make 'em think different—they were burned out, driven off—I stayed."

"Ever since?"

"Ever since. No one comes up here."

He turned to the dog, which didn't whine a smidgeon; it just stood there looking at us. "Barabbas came to join me years ago. He was starving . . . it's appealing, this countryside. Plump, fat, joyfully giving. But its people can starve an animal."

I stepped closer. Barabbas let me. "Mister, I'm—" Then for a second I thought, Jesus Christ, do I have to make up a new name? I'd been J. P. Lester too long anyhow—a second was too long—and I never did like it. I flicked a glance at Letty, who stood there with her bag in one hand looking as young and new as Seven Phillips looked old and wiry and hard but unkillable; then I turned to him. "I'm George Rose," I said. I'd caught the spark of crimson from a rose, a woods rose, just

on my right up where the trees began. Maybe, I think now
looking back, he *knew* that; he was a man who always recognized urges from nature.

"And this here's Mary Rose, my wife. We were just traveling
through, kind of. Dunno what made us come up here from
Mullin's Gap this morning—"

Nor did I. Something had pulled us this way. I'd just
wanted to get away and get my brain free of webs and worry.

We shook hands. There're times when you do that you
know it's going to lead to something. Letty shook hands with
him too. We all wandered over back where the moss grew, so
green it was like lush old velvet under our feet. Seven wore
moccasins that looked as faded and supple as though they'd
grown around his feet for half a hundred years, as though
they were flesh. After a time, as we spoke, Barabbas let Letty
stroke his ears, then me. We didn't talk of ourselves. We
talked about little things, not of the past, but there was a probing in it too. It wasn't so much us testing Seven as him testing
us. Shadows pronged long across the moss. When we'd sat in
the shade of one of the oak's great boughs—there were oaks
among the pines, fringing the clearing—for a time, we got up
again and all strolled along again. By now Seven was dropping
little hints of how the Carrolls had left this place for good,
how it was anybody's who wanted to live up here but how he
wouldn't want anybody to share it who didn't care for it and
who would be rowdy and careless with it. He didn't seem to
believe we were rowdy movers and shakers.

He said once, "Pleasure to have people to chat with
again . . ."

He took us to a point higher above the path than I'd stood
when I'd been about to jump, and pointed. "Down there—see
it past the haze? That's Solomon. Nice quiet town. Better'n
Mullin's Gap; not so inquiring. Good stores there, if any man
ever wished to stock up this place again—" Shyly, he says then,
as if he's not saying it to anybody except himself and the dog,
as if Letty and I aren't even there in the bodies, "A man could
start the mill; a man could glean a reputation for being a good
miller. It'd take work, youth, money, knowledge—not so much

on the money, unless after a time one wished to fix up the
great house . . ."

It was long after noon when we said good-bye and started
down. I was a whit worried that livery-stable keeper would
start thinking we'd made off with his horse and rig and go out
for us. I'd told him all I wanted was a whirl. He'd seemed to
trust us all right; we didn't look like shameful people. Even to
somebody who lived in Mullin's Gap. On the trip back down
the long curly-roaded hill when we'd got under way I didn't
say a word. Not for a long time. We passed the lean rib-staring
cattle that looked like deer. We were near turning into the
side street of flat punky little Mullin's Gap when I says, "All
right, Mary Rose. You want to go live there?"

"I'd like it, Luke."

I sighed with my whole being. I clipped the bay over the
back with the reins. "Best call me George, soon's we start living
up there," I says. "And now dig down in your tote bag and get
the smallest bill you can find and we'll pay for this here rig.
No—no—" I touched her wrist. It was sun-warm and friendly.
Death and murder and damnation seemed a hell of a distance
off. "No, give me a bigger shinplaster. We'll dicker with this
man for the whole rig. From now on we need to stay clear of
this town and we'll do our trading in Solomon."

Five

I'D NOT MEANT TO FIND the clearing and the houses and the mill. For that matter I'd not meant, deepest down in me, to stay with Letty. At least I didn't think I had. Looking back, I can see you never know how affairs get firmed; you never know with people like Letty and me, when it is you both start growing like trees that've been side by side, into each other. There was something sour at the roots, something dead; there was a plague of guilt; but all the same, we were both set to move on the way we'd started and now it seemed we'd been flung into a long time of it.

That's looking backward. Right then, it was easy as just breathing; just taking one lungful after another. In the back of my skull while I chaffered with the livery stable man— name was Soames, and he was a better man at cinching a bargain than I'd took him for; it cost us more'n I'd expected to buy the little bay outright, and get the buggy thrown in, along with a commonplace but serviceable saddle I thought could come in handy—in the back of my skull I kept wishing this Mullin's Gap was more than fifty miles from the outskirts of Jerseyville. I could've wished to be a thousand miles off. Finally we got the papers signed, which of course to my chagrin in this dump of a town I had to sign "J. P. Lester" again; we drove out of there, sun slashing across our eyes, into the space in front of the inn again. It was a Saturday. Was considerable polite and neighborly drinking going on at the saloon across the way. But five or six good stout suspicious citizens, both farmers and drummers, still sat on the porch, the square-bottom chairs all filled.

I left Letty to be what they call the cynosure of all eyes—I got that word from Professor Allan one time—while I hiked in the inn and up the stairs and picked up my pack and her portrait and put them together with the painting of the swimming boys, and poured myself fast down the stairs again. Abraham Tatum's in the door, holding it for me.

"You ain't availing yourself of the company of our fair burg, Mister Lester? You're moving on?"

"I'd judge that's true."

Letty's sitting looking straight forward, the carpetbag at her feet, in the buggy. She looked proud enough to lick all those sour-nosed, chew-lipped individuals on the porch with just a wave of her fingers. But too haughty and unconcerned-seeming about them even to lift the fingers.

"Drop by again and spend some time with us. We're a sociable lot."

"I've noted it," I said.

None of the farmers, drummers, and such was moving a whisker. They were just stiff and drinking in with their red-tipped ears what we had to say. I recalled what Seven Phillips had said of Mullin's Gap, as compared with the town you could make out from the clearing, Solomon; from all he'd said I'd picked up the idea it was the Mullin's Gap good citizens who'd driven out the Carrolls up there, in that gone time. You can feel when there's ugly smoke in a town; when people are ingrown and snoopsome.

I went on across the porch, none too careful about not brushing against any one of these sitting mighty citizens, and threw the stuff in the buggy and got up and clicked to the horse. The bay mare had good hoofs that looked dry and tough, which argued Arabian blood somewhere. I'm no horse expert, or wasn't then, but Professor Allan was a student of them and he'd had a few. We drove smart around the pump and down the side road to the livery stable and past it. Then the low buildings ended and the bush grass began.

"Heydy," I says. "Glad to get shut of that. They were crazy to find out where we're headed."

"It's upstate, far as they know," she points out.

"The whole earth, far's they know. But that Gondy, I bet he gave the livery stable man a earful. Folks make other folks their whole livelong business here. I someway hope I never have t' touch that town again with even the toe of a boot."

She settles closer to me. After a time her left arm comes around me. It just rests light there and doesn't even seem to mean much. At first I don't care if it's there and then I'm glad it is. Just resting above the belt on the spine. At least it's not discomfortable. I don't ask her to take it away. We start climbing up the side road and the air gets winey again and I feel in my veins in a homing rush that I'm coming to a place where I was always meant to be.

This time when we got to the chestnut tree I took the horse out of the shafts and pushed the buggy back farther onto the hill slope, alongside the steep road, and looped some vines and leaves of the tree around it. Wasn't hidden but you wouldn't see it sudden. And I put the saddle on the horse, not cinching it, just laying it there, and with Letty carrying her portrait—dogged if she didn't seem glued to both it and the tote bag—and I with my pack and that other boys-swimming painting, and me leading the horse too, we climbed the rest of the way. The horse's hoofs slipped a little in the pine straw of the road but it came slugging up all right.

Then when we came into the great clearing it was just as soft and easy—with a tightness under the peace—as it'd been before. An old, remembering place; a place holding out arms.

Maybe now's the time to tell that I never knew my mother or father. Maybe that doesn't make a difference in everything that happened, but maybe it does. I don't even remember the orphanage where, so to speak, I was shot from. I remember the Clagberts all right, the people that took me out for a bound-boy when I was six; I remember running away from there with about the same rotted dark feeling in me I'd had, times, while running now with Letty. Missus Clagbert had been a great one for Bible reading—it was the one book she owned, and it was worn clear through so some of the pages would fall out. It was about all she had, I think; for the rest she was a wisp with red staring eyes and the bones of a scrawny fowl. Thomas Clagbert had beat her a good deal, just without any emotion the way he'd beat any animal. The way he'd beat me. Hell, I got so used to it, it didn't even seem to be happening.

All those things were back of me now, too, like shades from trees that you've sat under in your past life. We came out leading the horse in the clearing's center, and there's the main house ahead and the four houses around us. Then Barabbas lopes down the steps of one of the smaller houses and Seven Phillips comes striding after. He knelt down beside the horse and started feeling its legs; his hands went up around the cannon bones. "Good," he says. You could hear Barabbas panting and the river branch chuckling. "Not too old either," says Seven, straightening, and prizing open the horse's lips. He got the whole mouth open and looked at the teeth. "No, not too old." He stood back. "I take it you folks are putting in your lot up here?"

It was so simple, as he says it. So simple and it would move into so much in every day ahead.

"Yes sir, and we got a buggy. So we can go down shopping around in Solomon this afternoon." I'd stepped back; I looked at everything in the clearing. My woman, my horse, my partner if you could call him that, the place where I was going to sink down some roots and by God, survive. And at Barabbas. Seven had told us he was of wolfhound blood; he had the patient grizzled expression of land that had stood proud ever since the world was made.

"We've already shook hands," I says. "So we don't need to

do that again." The horse stamped. A soft thoughtful stamp on the moss. "We've sure got a whale of a lot to do," I says. "For now we'll live in one of the little houses. Maybe we'll fix up the big place later on." Maybe, my foot. I knew we'd fix it up and I already had an image of how it would look, and I could see the great deep-pegged mill wheel turning too.

Seven just nods, and that's all there is to it.

We were all sharp-set hungry and when we'd all admitted it, Seven asked which of the houses we preferred and we took the one next to his—for neighborliness, I guess. We left Letty there in the sun of the low stone windows, she'd already rolled up her sleeves and was starting to make inroads on the floor dust with an old besom broom that still had some stubs left in it. I let the horse loose in the shade under the oaks and pines where there was thick tufty grass. There were plenty of lean-tos beside the small homes and it could stay in one of those, nights, and I aimed to fix a trough for it in one. Seven and I, and Barabbas, hightailed down to the river branch, at the end farthest from where it came into the pond, and he handed me a fishpole—a narrow one, but whippy in its action—and some grubs and a hook and line. We sat in the long tawny-sunned grass of the bank and pretty quick we had three chubs. He told me there were chub, bream, perch, and along a way, under the stones, big trout. The chub we got were firm-bodied so you could almost already taste the sweetness.

He told me he used his own gear, he hadn't touched the Carrolls'. "A body could clean that rifle," he says. "And there's nine or ten good rods; there's all you'd need to work with."

"How's come those folks who routed the Carrolls didn't plunder the place?"

His voice was low and sweet, with flint around it.

"Mister Rose, any mob is ashamed. They came and left by night. They didn't frighten the Carrolls, it was with sadness the Carrolls left . . . but they left for good, and their hearts were cracked. There's a portrait of them both in the storeroom off the kitchen. I put it there so it wouldn't fly-speck."

"Well now," I says, and then nothing more, because I had another bite.

All the doves were swooping around the mill, down a way, and a woodpecker was hammering at a beech back in the woods.

I pulled up the fish—another chub. It flopped a second after I got it off the hook. That was enough to stay our appetites. I rolled over and stood up. Barabbas looked at me in a melancholy friendly manner. "We'd best make out a list of things we need first. We'll do that after we've et. I'd like to see that portrait of the Carrolls—maybe we can do that this evening. We're going to have a long and fruitful time up here, Mister Phillips. Seven."

He waggled his pole, his back to me. "We are that, Mister Rose. George."

We strung the fish through the gills and climbed back up in the long grasses.

When we got back to the house next to Seven's, Letty already had the fire started in the range. There was dry wood handy. I stoked it up a mite more for her, then after I'd watched her put a skillet on and reflected to myself that I'd swab out the whole house with river-branch water in the morning, and watched her spine the fish and lay them in the skillet where they were fat enough to fry in their own grease, I noted the carpetbag wasn't around. I went back into the single bedroom. There was no bed, but a shuck pallet on the floor and she'd dragged it to the center of the room where the sun hit strongest, so it could air some. But when I looked under the teetery bureau in there I saw how she'd dragged it out a way and put the bag under it and then pushed it back.

When the chub were fried we took them out in the clearing's middle and sat there eating out of the skillet with our fingers and drinking pond water from a jug of it Seven had scooped up. It tasted forty-five times better than Gondy's liquor. Seven fed Barabbas some dried deer meat; for such a monstrous animal he ate easy and meditative.

Then we started making out our list for the town of Solomon.

We must've been a queer crew to light on the eyes of the Solomon ladies and gents, but nobody acted like it. Seven said it was a highly religious community, Quakers, and if you wanted to like them, that was fine, they wouldn't skin your back with the idea they were saving you from everlasting flames. I liked the white paint they used on the houses on the main street, not too much of it, just everything trimmed up like a quiet doll's house. It was a trim place.

We bought kegs of nails and grease by the bucket and a good supply of oats and bran mash. Letty bought calico and thread and more needles and soap—they had hand-made soap that they'd scented with cedar bark, she held it up for me to smell and I wanted to tell her, right there, it didn't smell better than her naked self, but it was no place for that kind of talk—and we picked up a couple of newspapers, one from a press over near Jerseyville, another a Philadelphia paper that was about two weeks old and going dry. We bought ball and powder and bullets—some of these for the fine old rifle Seven had, which wasn't a patch on the Boone rifle, but, he told us, accurate—and an axe and three saws; we bought lard, flour, and a smidge of tea because Letty said it was nice to have. That was a long list, for a starter; I didn't want to have to add to it for a week anyhow.

It's strange; I knew twelve thousand dollars was so much it'd have set most folks up for life around there, and I was feeling a little strutty about it; then I'd come down to earth and think "blood money" and then something in me would go cold as a slab with a body on it.

And I felt admiring of the clerks in the stores, and at the hay and grain and feed place, because they were just doing a clean-fingered job and they were so helpful. Not cheating, either. I stood there across at the grain place smelling the grain that filled the sack from its spout; it was like pure raw gold to the nose. It seemed to lodge in the chest and speak about a long time of progress here; nothing big or famous, but just the days folding one into another and everybody being kind. I guess there must've always been a good deal of pettifogging

and thievery and meanness and that, in Solomon, but I sure
didn't feel it. We got everything in the buggy it could hold,
and I was thinking we'd have to get a light wagon later on, but
that could wait, and just driving along in a dream on the
way back. Seven had a mouth organ and he played it easy and
lonesome while the shadows built up around us going back up
the road. All the smells of the lonesome clearing welcomed us.

This time we didn't leave the horse down a ways, but got out
and walked, Seven and I helping the horse; Seven was as easy
and slow with that mare as if she'd been a babe, and finally we
made the full clearing, with the shadows coming down like
lovely water and the whole place full of the first whippoorwills
of night and the darting of bullbats and the playing of rabbits
up through the woods paths.

Nobody said much. We all started to unload.

Before we turned in for the night—we'd made a small fire of
chunkwood in the little fireplace in the front room of that
small house next to Seven's—I stood in the open door, it was
going to be a mild night, but not too hot for sweet sleeping,
and looked over at the main house. Such a house might be
haunted, I thought; I'd felt that while we went through it. But
it wouldn't ever bother me. They'd be gracious ghosts.

I was standing there remembering I hadn't yet clapped eyes
on the portrait of the two Carrolls; it was one of the many
things that'd have, now, to wait till morning.

Behind me I heard Letty's feet husk over the flooring. She
stood alongside me.

Jesus, I thought all to myself, it's like a land of wonder; a
man will never get sick of the ways of people up here. He can
just fold into the land like the grasses, the leaves, the water.

Beside the little house I could hear the horse chomping a
mite of fodder.

Letty says, "I don't know what to call you . . . Luke, J. P., or
George."

"George, like I said before," I says, turning. She was all
naked and blue and white and dimpled in the light. When she
turned and went back across through the front room and

kitchen and then the bedroom, moon rippling over her, her flanks were so fine it stopped your breath in your brisket. There were small dimples just above her haunches; she was made as beautiful as a bird, and I felt certain-sure she could fly.

I walked back to the bedroom, where the light was now climbing one wall. I drew her to me. We both of us flew.

Six

I EXPECT it was on the third day I told Seven all about us.

It just seemed I had to. All this business of having other names than the ones we did—matter of truth, I'd taken my own name when I was nine or ten from a lawyer's board that hung in a town in Alabama I was traveling through then; that was about the time I was starting to do portraits for enough to live on, though they were pretty bad portraits and nothing to what I could do later on when my balls filled out to maturity and my hand got its full drawing size—all this business was sneaky, and you didn't sneak with Seven. Least, I couldn't bring myself to.

We'd been cleaning the big wheel. It was full of years of leaves in its wooden cup-buckets and stuck in the water so's what appeared to be tons of leaf drift had gathered around the pegs, along with rubble that'd floated over the little dam where the river branch came splashing down. I'd been diving, the water was pretty deep around there under the wheel, and coming up with handfuls of the black soaked leaves and bringing them to a bushel basket near shore and then Seven would pull up the basket on a rope, hand over hand, and tote it a way off and drop it in a hill of wet leaves we were building. He said later it would make good mulch if we sought to truck-garden.

Now when he came back from dumping the leaves I looked up at him on the bank—really a steep short cliff—and half-shadowed in my eyes from the wheel towering above me, I says, "Seven, my name's not George Rose. It's Lucius Carolus Applegate." Then I hooked an arm around the wheel and clambered up its slope, and perched up there in the streeling sun and dripped off. I was wearing only pants.

He nods, and waits, the bushel basket of wet tangled dark leaves at his feet. Barabbas had gone back in the woods with Letty, who was searching for wild strawberries. She said she'd spotted some that morning.

"Sit down, Seven," I bids him. "I want to talk a little."

He sits, and I looked out and down over the slanting sun at the clearing and over the sound of the dam-rush, just soft as a baby prattling, I tells him everything. Or at least what'll count. It came to me while I was doing it that the reason I hadn't, even yet, taxed Letty with the killing of her father was because I was afraid to. I just didn't want to do it. I'd rather keep it unsaid, as if what wasn't said couldn't have happened. So it was an easement to tell Seven, and I did it with hardly a flicker of one eyelash.

When I was all done I cut an eye at him. He didn't look troubled. I figured he'd had years of all the hell of the earth rub off on him, here and there. His hands are clasped around his knees and he just nods.

"It seems an awful burden to you now, George—Luke," he says, smiling. "But you've been around the country a great deal. Did it ever come to you in the quiet times of traveling—the times when you had a chance to look at life—that what matters isn't time the way we think of time?"

"What you mean, Seven?"

"I mean we clock it, and tell our own lives by it—but maybe there's lots of times and they're all one. Maybe we live in what a poet, John Keats, called a vale of soul-making . . . and what happens to us is just a realizing, until we're finally all realized into it."

"I'd like to read that poet." I'd told him a good deal about all that had happened to me—the taking of the name of that lawyer from that lawyer's signboard, because "Applegate" and its ring appealed to me, and I sure hadn't wanted to be called Clagbert after the people I'd been bound out to when I was a little sprat; the ways I found how I could draw better than most people, and how it was in a way a necessity to me, like breathing; and about all the reading and learning I'd done in odd spots, especially at Professor Allan's in Virginia, the autumn before.

He went on and told me his belief—I don't know if he'd got it from books, or just visioning it in the sun, the way an old hunter can hear quiet voices—and I never did find out, or want to. But it was a belief, rooted in him as ginseng into a mountain slope, that one life is nothing, that we all live a lot of lives. But that the decisions made in any one life are of terrific importance, like rings linking together an entire chain from life to life, and so we have to make every minute count like gold in this life. It was something like that, and it sat lightly on my ears and went into me through the listening silence deep inside me rather than just through the ears to the brain. I didn't know if he was right or not but I had an idea he was. It had a better range of possibilities than the hellfire and damnation I'd heard springing from most churches. It seemed more to the point than those. Seemed to fit with the whisper of the pines and the rustle of water.

When he got through I says, "You know, Seven, you make me feel finer. Not glorious, but finer. Maybe you've pulled me closer to something I got to do myself—and not be so cowardy about." I stood up, took a grip on the sun-sere old stout boards of that part of the wheel where I was standing, and swung to the bank. "I know how much we got to do, and I know we got to hump to get the wheel turning and get the bedstone and the runner stone ready by harvest time," I says.

"But it comes to me you still haven't showed me that portrait of the Carrolls. Anyhow I got a streak in me to see the big house."

He dumped his leaves on the way over—the pile was getting pretty big but from the ache in my back and shoulders I felt there'd be a weighty thunder of more leaves to dredge—and we walked across the clearing toward the big place. We'd swept it up just a bit—Letty had red up even more in the kitchen—but we hadn't made a dent in the dust. We kept the front door shut now, though there was no lock. We went up and in, and from a back-room closet he got the portrait. To me, it was a little stiffish, but the painter'd got a nice expression in the thin, tall old man's eyes and the woman, though her throat looked dumpy and probably hadn't been—he just couldn't put in perspective, that painter—had a sensible mouth. When he was going to put the portrait away again I told him, "No—let's put it back over the mantel in there where it should be." We did that, and I thought I'd add my portrait of the little girl, and of Senator Margate—he was a friend of Professor Allan's back in Virginia, and even though he was a squashy man hog-bit with his own self-importance, I'd made him kick alive—and the one of the boys swimming.

I did that, that evening; and in the late light they looked wonderful, all those four portraits side by side on the wide mantel in the great house. I didn't put up the portrait of Letty, yet. Some way I felt a badness, a darkness, about everything that picture had come to mean. It was back in our little house next to Seven's, over its mantel in there. Once or twice I'd looked under the bureau and the carpetbag was back there. All Letty'd done was take the burgundy velvet gown and the kid shoes from it, and hang them in a closet in that smaller place where we lived. Besides that all she had was the one work dress and the sensible shoes, but she was doing considerable sewing.

I was so tired that night—and I knew I was going to be wearier, my muscles were going to have to do a hell of a lot more before they were through with this job—I didn't study any love and passion. Or even plain lust. I read the book from

the Carrolls' library Seven had handed me. It was Keats's letters to various people, and it was bound in calf that'd started
to flake and that I put some neat's-foot oil on to protect. In
the light from the coal-oil lamp we'd found, with Letty sewing
and her hair looking burnished and quick in the flickering of
it—the wick smoked some—and looking up at her from time
to time from the pages . . . oh, he could write like a man
always wanted to paint, that Keats—it didn't seem Letty
could've ever hurt a fly or a flea. She just nestled down next to
me and went to sleep, after the light was out, while owls called
and you could smell a late-walking predacious skunk, like she
was a child slumbering in the planet.

But two, three days later—we didn't keep track of time, those
days, just stunned ourselves silly with work, and I was starting
to hate the mill house and the mill and my flesh was getting a
permanent pucker from the water—on a rich still afternoon,
I've been diving again, and even as I break water with an arm-
ful of slimed leaves for the basket, I hear Letty calling up near
the small houses. I was up the wheel and out of the water like
a flash, Seven streaming after me. When I got to the slope
behind the house, there's Letty, with an old hoe in her hands,
and, thrashing about in the skift of leaves and needles on the
ground is a monstrous rattler; I couldn't see his rattles while
he flapped about there, but later I counted nineteen.

Barabbas has made it ahead of us, and he's dancing on his
forepaws like a dog on wicked coals, and darting in—but the
head's already off the snake. Seven told me later Barabbas was
a good snake-killer, quick and lithe for his weight, but of
course Letty'd got to this one first. With Barabbas whining and
Letty shouting, it was a real mixup, and she kept hitting and
cutting at the body of the snake, with blood going in all directions, and her eyes were like they'd been that night when she'd
climbed the outside stair to the sleeping loft at her father's
place—that Greek, wide way. Finally I got behind her and got
a lock on her arms, and she's still twisting and heaving there,
and arching herself to hit again. Then I made her drop the
hoe and then there was nothing but her breath lifting and fall-

ing and making that rasping dark sound in her throat. Her
hair was all over her eyes. I stood back.

"Get a hold of yourself," I says, soothing. "It's only a snake,
and he's sure dead now if he wasn't a twinkle ago. Letty. He's
a snake, is all."

She brushes her hair back with a hand. Her eyes come back
to the earth of the whole clearing.

"I heard it rattle," she said, "and I ran and got the hoe—
and—"

There was blood splashed on her legs. It's hard to tell what
she looked like, but I could still feel the muscles in her arms
and back twitching—like the snake's—when I fondled her.

Seven scooped up what was left of the body and threw it on
a burning pile we had at one side of the clearing, off the moss.

Then he went away, I expect to wash up, back toward the
millpond, and Barabbas launched alongside him, and I stood
there in the singing sun with Letty.

But hadn't I promised her we wouldn't speak of her past
again? I'd done that, all right.

It was the mean coward in me. The not wishing to spoil the
present, the being of right now, by speaking a single thing
about what was past.

It wasn't just keeping a promise.

I knew that too, while I led her back toward the millrace
and made her get her clothes off and swim in the easy shallow
part, with sand coming up in watery clouds around her legs,
like soft smoke, and with her looking so calmed and smoothed
and wet when she got out, it was all I could do not to take an
hour off and lay her on that bank and pump myself into her
full of all the joy and the bells of quiet that could ring in her
when she wasn't wrought up.

But later that night in the moon-hush of the lateness I could
feel she was awake while we were lying on the pallet, and I
unlocked my hands from behind my head and started kissing
her—the way she'd touched me so soft on the nape at the
farm that time, with two fingers—and parted the tendrils of
her hair at the back of her neck and went on touching her

there with my lips. Then when she turned over, her legs going apart and inviting me in, I says soft, "No, let's go out in the night."

She raised up and looks at me through her falling hair and I smoothed her breasts and made them tingle to my finger-tips. We were both bare and when I led her through the small house she looked dappled with power as some kind of night goddess the professor back in Virginia would have liked. But I liked her more than just as any dimpling sleek smooth statue. We went out and the night seemed to take us down whole, as if we folded into it, and we walked around the house and slipped down toward the creek. An owl was talking, but it stopped, then went on when we got past. On the bank of the creek where I'd wanted to have her that afternoon was another bed of fern, and little yellow and blue flowers, and when I drew her down there with me—didn't take much drawing— she gripped me by my root and touched its tip, and said, "I think you are beautiful, Mister Applegate or whatever you want to call yourself and us." Then she kissed me there. I took it very slow. Turned her over so we both lay on our bellies in the fernery—smelled bright as all the seething, chirping, call-ing nightfall—and stroked her haunches, then put my hand under, in her Venus fur, which had the tenderness of fern. She was swelling with want and need. I lifted her up like that, one hand swooped under her and stroking and going into her, and turned her over again, and then went home in her step by step like a welcoming, a saying, I love you with all my breath.

It was a shoring that felt it sealed us after all bitter voyages.

Then, gradual as the clock of the night tolling its secrets, we kissed each other all over and had to do it again, in various and secret ways, while the leaves looked on and the stars wheeled and the water of the creek sounded quick and low as our breaths mixing in peacefulness.

Yet in all those first days I'd stop working for a time with the sun-dazzle over my eyes and think, It's been nice, but now they're coming for us. Somebody is coming up that path with a gun. And they're going to stuff Letty and me in a prison and then we'll wither like dried leaves and there'll be nothing left but a dust-puff on the floor of the prison.

Always that threat around through the murmuring pine needles, and the soft motion of the big-leaved oaks. Then it'd go away when I went back to work. There was just so much to be done; it'd all been easy to feel that swelling of triumph in the chest and belly, and say, This place is mine; but it wasn't; not yet. You don't make a place yours until you sink sweat and blood and faith in it, and we were just starting to do that then. Were just getting into the rhythm of it. My muscles were just starting what they'd always known they could do. And there were other things, too.

For instance, I quizzed Seven from time to time about deeds to the place, and such. He said they were registered at the courthouse in Solomon, which took in the county where this place was, but his attitude was also that with the Carrolls gone—and they'd been fairly old—it didn't matter much. "Don't roil the waters," was his meaning, though he didn't quite say it. Yet I figured I would.

"How's come," I asked him, "nobody from Mullin's Gap *or* Solomon's taken over the mill? For any fool'd know it could pay; you yourself said there's not another for twenty miles."

He looked at me from his old blue slow eyes. "In Mullin's Gap," he says, saying it as though the name was a slur, "they don't have the gumption, Luke. In Solomon they've got the gumption, but they're contented people. And it's all walled out of their remembrance now, in both places . . . and of course there's all the work involved."

"Work, work." I looked at my blistered, water-puckered hands. When I wasn't diving I was working on the bedstone. It was so clogged in there it was like stiff rust. During times in there, staring out at the web of joists and supports coming up from the water, you'd feel like you were caught in a vise and could never get out to the sun again. And both of us knew running a mill this size was no two-man job. I walked off, then.

Sometimes Seven and I didn't talk all day long. Just laid out the work in the morning and then did it. Seeming to make about as much progress as a pecking hen could make in a hill of iron.

One morning when the air the night before'd been tight-packed as though it didn't want us to breathe much of it, and we'd gone to sleep stunned with our own tiredness, I woke up before sun. I could feel storm coming. I didn't know if it would be a personal storm, or natural. Seemed I hadn't had time to sketch so much as a line since this had started. It was about a week and a half since we'd gone down to Solomon for supplies, and we'd have to be visiting again soon. I decided to drop in at the courthouse when we did.

I lay there, watching the weak not-yet-quite light steal through the window and over the stone and around Letty. She was on her side, and the curve of the hip that was raised was something tugged like a rope at me for a pencil and paper, and even, maybe later for paint. I hadn't even looked at my canvas and painting sack. I looked from the portrait of her, blind-still and shadowy, over the mantel, back to the creamy-still and sleeping body of her, herself. Then I kissed her hip, very soft, and got up and walked around, also softly, and looked down at her face. It was both woman's and child's. No trace of bad dreaming on it.

I got dressed and went outside and made water and then went over to the main house; licks of first sun were just touching it through massy clouds. It was going to be a sulphurous day. From the two steps—I stood on the top one—I could see the damned mill wheel, rising so pretty in its build and so hard to tangle with if you ever wanted it to move again. I went in and got down the Boone rifle from the mantel, snuggled now, as it was, between those three portraits I'd done and the one of the Carrolls. Felt to me as though the eyes of both the Carrolls followed me while I stood blowing dust off the rifle and holding it in my hands. I had powder and ball for it but I wanted to use it, the first time, with Seven handy. His own hands were born for such a piece.

I walked out. In the newspapers, the fairly local one and the one from Philadelphia, there'd been nothing of any murder in the Jerseyville countryside. But news gets to the papers late, I'd thought.

I felt all full of the kind of needles that'd plagued me on the night we ran down the road from the house.

It was going to be a heat-stunner.

While I stood there I thought I saw a flicker in the ivy down near where the path started. Probably a bird. I thought I'd step down that way anyway. I went easy. When I got halfway across the clearing here came Barabbas, running like a dark streak of woolly cloud across the clearing, a fast lope and low to the ground—he wasn't a dog barked much. I started running, but by the time I got to the path's edge Barabbas had stopped there and his eyes were just staring down into the foliage. The ivy covered everything. After a bit he whined, just a bit in his throat. I could've wished I'd had the rifle loaded. I thought I saw just a touch of motion farther down along the path side. But it could be just being on edge, I tells myself. There wasn't any breeze, and wouldn't be. I went back to the main house and put the rifle back and Barabbas came with me, only, once or twice, looking back at the edge of the path.

Seven

THAT SAME MORNING at breakfast—Letty had hot biscuits and some sorghum we'd found in the mill loft; the sorghum hadn't soured because it had been well stoppered—I kept mulling about how I'd like to have just started talking to her about all my past. And then listened to hers, like I was drinking good water. But there wasn't any saying those things.

For one thing we couldn't say them because we'd got in the habit of having Seven share breakfast with us in our house. I suppose he hadn't had good cooking in all the years he'd lived here by himself after the Carrolls had been driven off. He was appreciative. Of course he hadn't told Letty anything of what I'd blurted out to him in confidence. But he never did look at her as if she happened to be a red-handed murderess either. He was a man for reserving judgment. He just kept it balanced in himself, being your friend and not pothering up the crystal water of friendship.

I was going to tell about the something I'd thought, or felt, at the edge of the path, too. But I didn't. We just sat and ate.

After a time I said, "We need a lot more things. I've made

another list. This time I'll go down to Solomon by myself—try to get back before noon."

Seven nodded, a bite of biscuit in his jaws. I fed Barabbas a snibbet of my biscuit. I sat back.

Oh, Letty, I said inside myself. I want to tell you of all the wanderings I've had in my life. I want to take up from what I was saying when I first sketched you. I want to tell you about the black seals off the California coast, with the waters creaming in. I want to tell you about the prospectors I've met in the West. About all the faces and arms and hands I've painted since I learned I could keep soul and body together that way. About all the longing I've had in my belly and heart for someone like you who'll listen and not just smile and nod like a whore. I want us to lie still in the nights, after loving, and tell each other all about our inmost selves. And there's this father of yours between us. Dead, he's bigger than he ever was before. He rises up between us like a demon on the air.

All that I kept in my head, while we ate the good breakfast.

Then I brushed my clothes down a bit, took one of the small stogies I'd bought on our first trip down to Solomon, bit off the end, lit it on a horse-match, and conferred with Seven on what he would be doing while I was gone. Though he knew, even better than I did.

Letty walked with me across the clearing, swinging a basket she was going to gather some cress in, from down around the cool of the millpond in the morning. There was a light dew still on the grasses and even on the tiny green flowers of the moss, but the sun was heavy on our backs and necks. Every step you took on such a day, you'd sweat.

Sometimes, those days, I could feel her wanting to tell me all she thought, so badly it was like an ache between us.

But both of us kept the promise of not talking about it.

I looked at her brown shoulders under the dress. All of us were getting to look gold brown, except Seven, and I suppose he'd always looked that way. She smelled of her baking and of the mint on the air.

"Be careful, now," she says to me at the lip of the path. I

took her and held her close and said I would. "Keep a sharp
eye out—"

I grunted something. The mare which I'd let out of the
lean-to—we often let her just graze around the clearing during the day—came near and I took her by the halter. Then I
pulled out the buggy which we'd pushed over by the path's
edge, and made a to-do about getting the beast harnessed and
between the shafts and ready to go. The mare was sleeker,
even in the week and a half since I'd bought her, than she'd
been then; she was fairly dancing with the need to be off and
down the hillside. Letty stood watching for a time. Then she
moved away. She had a few blue flowers she'd found in the
woods, shining in her hair. She made a habit of decking herself neatly.

She was still watching there when I clucked to the horse and
went down the start of the path. Last thing I saw. I felt a need
to stop and jump out and run back and say, "All right,
woman, let's forget all this stubborn foolishness and tell each
other what we truly think. Have it out, once for all. You know
I'll stand by you in any case."

But the stubbornness stayed. Like a rock you can't move. In
a way, like the stubbornness of the locked-in, time-stilled mill
wheel. I could hear Seven banging at the shaft now with a
sledge. The sounds echoed all over the clearing. Barabbas
would be up there with him watching the work. I thought how
I couldn't even call Letty *Letty* around Seven because she
didn't know I'd already told him everything about us. And
how, around him, she still went on calling me *George*. It was
like the flick of a burr at my flesh every time she did that.

I was in a towering dark mood. Part of it was the sulky
weather.

Going down with the buggy was tough, too, because the
mare had to strain and hold back to keep from crashing down
the steep overgrown pathway. All around us above the creaking of the wheels was the chirring of insects. Locusts starting
their daily tide of noise over the fields and in the trees rimming the fields. A smell of summering, ripening wheat hang-

ing deep to the air and so heavy it was like eating chunks of it.

Going down, I had to keep myself so busy with the driving I didn't have time to think more about my slight scare, or instinct, or whatever it had been, earlier that morning. And I didn't see anything out of the way. Just the stitching of insects and the heat holding the horse and myself in its core.

When we got down on the flat, going along to Solomon, it was better, so I let the horse out in a spanking trot. After a time we passed farmers in their fields, a couple of them striding down some corn rows. The corn had been way above knee-high by the fourth of July in these parts. Then there'd be a long easing stretch with no farms, no buildings at all, just the land rippling out forever, green and sometimes toasted brown toward the hill-flanks, and once at the junction of roads—one leading back toward Mullin's Gap, the other to Solomon—I heard the voice of a train whistle a long way off.

Then, later, I saw the train coming a long distance down from me, in one of the valleys. It looked so small down there against the thick green. Four cars, it had; its stack was like a church bell upside down. Heavy smoke maned back from it. It made a miniature puffing from here that you could barely hear though. I thought, Letty and I could be on you, moving across the nation, many miles from here where there is danger. But I'd thrown in my lot with the mill-clearing, with Seven, and with whatever tomorrow the clearing could give.

My soul, it was hot. Too hot even to smoke another stogie.

I still shaved every day—I like the feeling of that—but the first morning at the clearing, I'd started to skip the upper lip. Now there was a furze growing there. It was faint dark red in the mirror in the house where Letty and I were staying. It prickled considerably. I felt it with two fingers, and sat back under the buggy roof's shade and clucked harder to the horse. She went sweet as a patch of good paint and before long here came the same Solomon you could see from that one point in the clearing. It looked new-washed in the dayshine but as though not much would be moving all the day. The church was a plain white building with a simple spire. I marked the courthouse in my mind, and went along past it and turned in at the line of stores and tethered the horse. I left her with a short nose-bag and went in.

There weren't any customers this soon in the day, except myself.

This was a general store, and when I'd bought what I judged we needed—and some more of that good-smelling soap for Letty—I wandered around a bit, and came to a stack of buffalo boxes on a counter in the back. Most of them were just nice boxes, like small coffins, well made and worth whatever was asked for them—in Solomon they didn't handle much trash—but there was one that drew my eye especially. It was dark green and made of metal: steel, I judged.

The store man knew me from our previous time, at least he knew my face, and he says now, seeing me finger the box, "That's a safe. Got a key that goes with it. Yes, sir. Strongbox safe, you could keep any manner of valuables in it." He wasn't trying to sell me it, any more than he was being proud of its workmanship.

I said, "I'll take it."

I added it to the heap of things in the buggy.

I bought a couple of more newspapers. This time the Philadelphia paper wasn't so dried out as the last one I'd bought.

Then I stood teetering on my heels and passing the general time of day with the man, in the slab of sunlight heating up the oiled floor in front of his door.

He wasn't snoopy. We talked wide-open things such as crops and weather and both of us hoped when the rain came it wouldn't be a flailer that would mash down the wheat and strip the corn. He was the sort of man who wouldn't pry and poke and bother you. His name was Felton, Jas., from the curlicued lettering on the store window. I finally said there wasn't anything more I wanted, and he figured up what I owed. I gave him one of the bills from Letty's carpetbag. He didn't even ask how far I was going or where I lived, though he now knew it had to be near. And, it came to me, maybe he,

or some others who'd seen us come into town for the first
time, had recognized Seven—there must've been quite a few
people in Solomon who knew that Seven lived up there, or
who'd remembered him from his days with the Carrolls at the
mill.

But we were nice and courteous and unprying of each
other. I took my change and left the horse nibbling and patient where she was and went over to the courthouse. Had
quite a time finding what I wanted, in that sleepy place. The
man who finally got out the deeds and plat for the mill-clearing found them under a whole lot of old papers at the bottom
of a drawer in a wide cabinet, and I studied them awhile. He
was a round-faced white-haired red-cheeked fellow who kept
wiping sweat off his forehead with a fat bandana and making
pools of more sweat on the counter when he leaned there on
his elbows.

"Reverts to the county," he says, "for taxes—but I hardly
think anybody wants it, or'll buy it up. There's land lower
down a sight easier to work. And nobody'll ever get that mill
to turn again."

"Be a bounden difficult task," I agrees.

"You could have it for the tax. Just to hold it a time, or see
if anything builds up around it and it hikes its value."

"How much is the tax, Mister—?"

"Prescott, Claron Prescott. Clerk of this county. Wait now,
I'll figure her up—been a long while since anybody's even
thought of that old place . . ."

It turned out it was a small amount; I says, "Here we go,
then."

He took forever, with a squeakily pushed pen, to make out
the papers that went with it. All the time he was doing that I
thought, What will I sign? I was so sick of not being myself. It
was the self I'd been ever since I took the name Applegate,
you see. It was fixed and groined into me. I surely didn't want
any more Lestering or Rosing. So when the time came, I just
wrote out the whole Applegate name, and no backhand
either—the regular signature I'd put on any portrait if the
people who'd bought it didn't mind me signing it, and he

sanded it and blew on it and we grinned at each other as though we'd both done a stroke of lucky work.

I folded that batch of papers up and stuck it in a back pocket with the key to the safe-box and went back across and climbed in the buggy. Before I started up, I read through the papers. The one from near Jerseyville was full of the news of a plight of hog cholera that'd visited the vicinity in the past few weeks, and some things about barn raisings in the community. It had nothing whatever of a Mister Einsner and his demise. That made me wonder a good bit. I went through the Philadelphia paper too, with its important city news, but there wasn't even a squib about what I was looking for.

I folded the papers and thrust them in the back, on the top of the provisions and such.

He'd sure been an important man and you'd think the local sheet at least would have put that in large black ink.

It gave me chewable food for thought while I urged the mare homeward. I didn't urge her too hard, though, because her flanks were shining and it was no day to push anything. I wondered if Seven had managed yet to unfreeze the main wheel shaft and thought that no, he wouldn't have, and I wondered even more, with the base of my being, about Einsner. It was a mystery hanging like a dark shadow that you could only see out of the corners of your eyes in the sun-soaking, sweltering day.

Heat waves danced ahead of me on the hill. I passed the wild-looking cattle—they hadn't yet been out on my way down, I figured they must belong to some slop-fingered farmer grubbing out a living lower on the hillside, who just turned them loose to forage at will by day. Then it was harder going and just about time to get out. I got out, threw the reins down over the horse's head, and started pulling and walking up, urging her along in careful low tones because it was a terrible grind. I called her a pretty piece of horseflesh and a lovely animal in all respects. She was, too. Her flanks strained with the muscles standing out like ropes on a sailing sheet in a gale, and her legs dug into the shale and sand and dirt of the path and her shoe-plates dug like broad knives. I stopped to breathe her. That was when I heard something behind me. When I looked around here was this man standing with his arms folded.

Everything I'd felt that morning came flooding back and made my cock and my belly draw together like wrinkled ice.

I didn't have the soul of a firearm on me.

I says, "Heydy. You mind moving on so I can pass?"

He was any age you wanted him to be, but for all that, for all his Indian-smooth face, young, with blue-black hair. Bare-foot, and standing not like he owned the earth but as though he would like to get back on it. A shy-looking man, with black eyes that were four degrees blacker than old man Einsner's had been, and a washed-out blue shirt nearly in the shape of a bag, looking thin from use, and cotton-thin pants. A hat on the back of his head with a crow feather sticking up sharp. Kept his arms folded.

"Because I got to get on," I points out.

The horse snorted.

Maybe I could call out from here, I thought. But the path took too many curves ahead and sound would get lost in the long bush-grass and the rocks on this hill slope.

Besides, I didn't wish to appear that bothered.

Then three other men stood up from the sides of the road. One had the stupidest-looking, crazy-butted rifle I ever saw. They all looked just about like the first except the one with the rifle didn't have a shirt. I thought, the law minions of Pennsylvania are sure sending out strange deputies.

We all just stood there, sizing each other up, in the blazing stillness.

Eight

"ALL RIGHT," I said finally, when not one of us had talked for about twenty seconds. "If this is a robbery, say so, and we'll get it over with."

I didn't see what else it could be, with them just standing and staring steady at me. Although the one with the odd rifle held it canted down toward his feet, and I kept getting an itch to warn him that if that instrument was loaded he might well blow one of his toes off. A butterfly went sailing over the bushes near us and I watched it move out of an eye-corner, already envying it because it didn't have the responsibilities of mankind and could go frittering away time while I had to stand here sweating. I resolved if I ever got out of this to buy myself a palm hat with a wide brim like a Kentucky tobacco planter; it wasn't so bad working in the shade up at the mill, but down here in the open it was fierce. I still felt scared and chilled through, though I didn't want to show it at all.

I breathed in deep, and took a step toward the first man who'd showed up—not the one with the rifle. "State your case, mister," I says, low.

They were all about the same height; I was about an inch taller.

The man who'd rose up first says, low, "We're the Darlings."

I heard him plain, but didn't quite believe it. I swallows, and for some reason I wanted to laugh.

He goes on: "Jase Darling, that's me. This here over here's Peter, and that's Paul. And that's David."

The ones he pointed to made ducking motions with their heads. The one called David held the rifle.

"You mind poking your weapon in another direction?" I says to this David.

He looks down at it and then he says, muttering, "No ammunition."

"What's it for then?" I asked. "You swat flies with it?"

"It shoots all right," puts in the one who'd spoke first, Jase. "He just has to hold it a funny way. Otherwise it comes apart and sprays the shot."

I could see the rifle was a point of tetchiness with all of them. They were all Indians or I never saw one. There's a lot of leftover remnants of tribes around that part of the country. They are what is left of those who went up and down the Mohawk Valley long before I was born. There's still a funny feeling in the people roundabout there, about them. As if they can still vision in their bones what the word "Indian" used to mean in those parts. The British used them and the French used them and we robbed them clear down to the gum in their toenails, but there's still what they used to be hanging like fire and flint on the air.

Was getting tired of this arguing and fencing.

I folded my own arms. "What's on your mind, boys?"

"Well," says Jase after a second, looking that straight way at me—they didn't smell bad, anyhow, didn't have that pine marten scent some Indians always had—"we thought you'd like help."

"What kind?"

"With the mill," puts in the one called Peter. He had a headband made of an old diamondback. It fitted his head well.

"How'd you know we were at the mill? You been spying?"

"We live down there," says Jase, who'd took over now as their accredited regular spokesman. "Down to the west." He points.

"Them your cattle down lower?"

"Ugh huh," he says.

"Figured they belonged to somebody let 'em out to forage," I said. I was feeling some easier. I still had some stogies with me. I took them out and passed them around. They each took one, David laying his rifle, if you could call it that, down to light his while I passed around a match flame as well. The one called Paul was stroking the horse's nostrils. Over a puff of smoke Jase says, "We'll work good. For the grub."

"I don't aim at holding slaves," I says. "You live down there by yourselves?"

"Our mother too," says the one named Peter. "Our old man, he died last winter. Ain't no place for a man if he's got our blood to get work on the farms. Cows don't give us much—we raise a little corn."

We stood there in the sun and fixed it all up. They looked like solid workers to me. I told them they could share in the profits, if there was any profit, after we got the wheel moving and the stones working, if we ever got them working. It was a pretty tentative arrangement we came to but it wasn't far-fetched. It just sort of kept dazing me to think of myself employing anybody. I'd worked in cotton rows with that damned long sack filling up so slow and the bolls coming off so hard—you have to give them a flick of the wrist or the five prongs of the boll don't come out right and you lose the staple—and I'd worked on lumber gangs and I'd shoveled cow shit aplenty, in the times when nobody had the wit to want a portrait; I thought I could estimate workers when I saw them. They said, one at a time, nodding at one another as well as to me, that they'd work for the terms I offered—and I saw them looking sideward sometimes at the stores in the buggy, not like they were going to steal them but wistful as children. I knew they were hungry.

We didn't even make a pact or smoke a calumet pipe on the deal. We just took it all for granted and there we were. Soon as I'd said yes, and Jase had pointed out they'd stay up with us in one of the houses and work from first light to no light—can till can't—and go down and see their mother was all right from time to time, it was fair-settled. Without anybody saying much further, they started unloading the stores from the buggy and carried them, and that lightened the load considerably and made it easier for the mare to haul the buggy up the rest of the slope. Soon's we came clambering into the clearing—there's the deep clanging sound of Seven attacking the wheel shaft with the sledge, like a clock striking forever—Barabbas scented them and came running, then they stood still, as I bade them do, and he sniffed at their legs while I told him it was all right, that they weren't come to harm anything. Letty came over from our small house and I introduced her—just said this was my wife—getting each name connected to each man after a bit of hesitation. They were wonderful in their shyness. Then Seven stopped his banging and came over too and I told him what we'd decided.

He didn't bat a lash, just nods. "They can start right in," he points out.

"They'll start soon," I says. "Right now, I'm peckish and I'd say they are too. And you, that sledge must've grown to your fist, Seven. Letty, whatever you got to eat that's good and quick, boil or roast or fry it up and we'll all set down to table in our place." I unharnessed the horse while the Darlings—I couldn't get over their name, but it was sufficient for their purposes—helped stow away the merchandise I'd bought. Letty kissed me, quick, and then she went to cook up a cloud of smoke. When I'd unharnessed the mare and let her wander, and the boys were walking over to the mill with Seven—I could hear his level flat voice showing them what had to be done—I stepped into our house and went through the kitchen, giving Letty a rump-pat as I went through and marveling how she was built of sweet flesh with just the right spring to it, like a wonderful bow that'll shoot straight, and then moved into the bedroom. I picked up the metal buffalo box and got down on my belly and hooked the carpetbag out

from under the bureau and tipped the cash into the box. Letty
was cooking fast in the kitchen. I patted down the cash—it
sure looked like enough to set up the world of hungering folk
forever—and shut the lid over it, got the key out of my hip
pocket, and locked it. Then with it under my arm I strolled
out through the smells of slab-meat frying and buttermilk biscuits coming to the rise, and though Letty looked at me as I
went through—I've said she didn't smile much, but you could
tell when she was happy and the thing between us wasn't roil-
ing her—I'd have bet she hadn't noticed the box under my
arm.

I cut across the clearing, away from the path, through the
flickering shadows—if it was this hot up here you could tell it
would be terrible in the shadeless fields below—and went
along through the long grass till I'd paced quite a way above
the river branch. Air was cooler right here with the water
smell mixing into it. I looked around for a likely spot. It wasn't
my money, maybe it wasn't Letty's either, but I wanted it in a
place where I wouldn't have to fret about it between times of
using what I had to of it. Finally I spotted a stand of birch,
over the branch and leaning twinned in the water—so it was as
if two birch stands grew there, one staring up from the dark
glass of the water and the other looking down into it. Professor Allan, who liked the Greek legends, had told me about
Narcissus.

I leaped the branch, with the box in one hand. Then I
parted the small shoots sticking up from the base of the
birches, smelling wild cabbage on the air near the water, and
thrust the box down deep into the space between birches. I
stood back. The green of the box was a dull finish and you
couldn't see it a foot away. In fact, you'd have had to be seeking for it to find it.

I nods to myself and marked the spot in my head. It was
sufficient in its height above the branch so even high water
wouldn't touch it. I could see old high water marks on the
birch boles. From this side of the branch, or across it, even at
night you could mark this place with that moony glisten of the

bark, and yet a body could've stepped an inch from the place and never been wiser.

I leaped back across the branch and went back to the clearing.

That was an odd meal all right, with Jase and Peter and Paul and David so skitterish at first you'd think they weren't trembling to eat the food Letty had laid on in abundance, and with all of us crowded around the table in the center of the room and sun swashing over us like a benison. After a while I managed to get David to let go of his peculiar rifle and let me prop it in a corner for him. I thought while I did it that it wasn't strange he clung to it so, it must've been the only thing he had that attested to his being human and a man. From scraps of what they said, then and later, I got the built-up knowledge that they'd teetered on the edge of starvation, like pariah dogs, for some while. In Mullin's Gap it must've been the worst, though they told me sometimes they got work helping with the harvest over toward Solomon. But now it was just dig in, which after that first hang-back time they did—it was a joy to see them eat when they got started. I let them know there'd be plenty of scraps to take their mother whenever they wanted to, so to speak, send a runner down with them.

Made me feel in a small way as if I was a father without the worry of hand-raising four young men. Yet they weren't so much younger'n me.

When they'd swallowed all they could—I swore in myself I thought they'd faint when they stepped out in the strike of the sun again—Seven and I walked ahead of them back to the mill, and I strips my shirt off and we all got set for a time of true work. Right off, it was better having them there; they weren't born mill workers but they were handy and so willing it oozed like the sweat out of their coppery bodies. They all shucked down naked, pretty fast—it was the quickest way to keep from sweltering to death unless you were working under water—and while I dived, still leaf-clearing, with Seven pulling the rope and the basket, they swarmed in among the beams and timbers and joists and shafts, and pretty shortly all you could hear was that clang as they took turns with the sledge trying to unfreeze the big shaft.

But it didn't come loose. I sometimes, then, didn't figure it ever would. A wheel that's frozen gets its own ingrained stubbornness, like a mule that hasn't worked for years. I just went on diving, not being able to see much in the dark water when I was under, sometimes brushing a turtle—which always swam away through the mote-cloudy water—and then rising up toward the dancing surface and seeing it get lighter and gasping and blaffing when I got out; and whenever my head surfaced, with a ring of heat sudden around it, I could hear that sledge striking the shaft.

I'd put the key of the box careful in my pants; I thought of the box sometimes, both hating it and glad it was there so I could keep on working with these people until the wheel started, and afterward. But sometimes I'd feel that snaggled-down way, as though all we were doing was just child's play in the teeth of the job ahead. I'd put the deed papers for the place in the box too. No use bothering anybody about that right now. I couldn't have told, clearly, in a month of Sundays why I'd wanted the deed; it was just that all this was the first place I'd ever come near owning, even if it was Letty's money, or even if it wasn't.

We went on all that day, killing ourselves in the close, still heat. When night came down there weren't any stars. We worked till good dark. Then I took one last dive—the wheel cups were getting fairly cleared, but that wouldn't mean a lot if the wheel would never turn—and climbed back up in the guts of the lower floor of the mill. There were shadows webbing all about, great spiders that reached to wavering heights above me. All the boys were working, David shoving pieces of rust and frowsty scale from the shaft—the main shaft—with the blade of an axe, Peter up farther tightening some bolts in the wood, Paul cross-legged on the floor whaling away with a hammer at a board patch in a place where the floor had worn through, and Jase swinging the sledge at the iron shaft so deep and hard it made your brains rock to hear it, this close.

Between strokes of his sledge I hollered, "Come out of it!"

Streaming sweat, they all looked around.

"Best get the house you want to stay in fixed up. There's two left to choose from. Then we'll have us supper."

Jase says, his muscles slick as a beaver's hide, "We c'n go on a bit."

"Shach!" I says. "You don't have to prove yourselves. You've started doin' that. Tonight we'll have supper same place we et today, then I'll give you some staples and you can fix yourselves something when you want to on the range in the house you pick out."

I got a lot of lip from them. Wanted to go right on working. Finally I got even a shade mean. "What I say goes," I says.

I guess they'd been waiting to hear it, for they started dropping out of the beams nimble and yet tuckered out. At supper, they sat there dressed and wearied out, sweat-patches large on their skimsy clothes, even the feather in Jase's hat—which I sure never told him to take off at the table, he was a guest, wasn't he?—seeming limp and downcast as a much-used pecker. But that didn't stop their appetites.

After supper when I'd given them bags of staples, and seen they were fixed for the night in one of the smaller houses which they chose, right across the clearing from Letty's and mine and Seven's, Seven and I sat on the step, the top step, of the main house, which we'd come to do in the evening, and in the thick dark with only the lights of the houses making the clearing alive, we smoked, Seven his short-stump pipe, with wild tobacco he cured himself, I the last of the stogies. I'd forgot to get more at the store.

"They'll work out good," I observes.

"If we can move the wheel," he says.

"Yuh." I could hardly see the smoke from his pipe in this darkness.

"Tell me more about there bein' more than one life," I says after a spell.

"Oh . . ." He took a last draw, then emptied a speck of dottle and fire and ash on the step, and then blew it carefully away off into the black. "They could tell you better, son. The boys. They could tell you how their god gave all men everlasting life, many times of being alive all wrapped into the single soul."

"I been reading that Keats," I points out.

"Well, then y' know," says Seven, hunching on the step. "It's all there in him and others. But you don't have to write poetry to know it. I expect millions've known it, through all there is of time . . ." He shifted, easing his bones. "I kind of have the feeling you were meant to come here, it's part of what your certain destiny is—"

"Sometimes I don't feel like I've got one."

"You've got one, all right. Stronger'n many." Then after a time he says, "I, I'm comin' to the end of this body. There are strengths in it yet, but sometimes toward the break of day I can feel the end nigh."

I says, "Well, kindly don't go dying on us. If that shitepoke wheel ever unhitches itself you'll be sore needed to show me and the boys just how the mill is supposed to grind for best results."

I could tell he laid his hand on Barabbas's head because the dog gave a low grunt of pleasure.

"I'll do my best," he says.

It was so hot that night I knew Letty couldn't sleep either. I'd thought it would be just as it'd been other nights, that you'd fall into sleep like a stone falling down endless chasms, but no.

I lay there looking up. She was naked as was I and her body flowed like a candleflame and glistered in the very little spackling of groundlight coming in back through the front room and kitchen from the open door to this place. I couldn't see her eyes but I could picture them green and looking up at the unseeable ceiling.

The horse which I'd put in its lean-to for the night moved just a hair. I could smell night flowers opening around the woods, and a squirrel took a leap to the roof, up past the loft, and then went off the roof. It was a dark dripping stillness. After a time I couldn't stand it any more, all that was between us, and I said soft as a puffball, "Letty—"

"Uhm," she says. Just a ghost of saying.

"—you feel bad? Like hell and dark is around us?"

She thought that over a lot. I could tell. I remembered how she'd been with the rattler. Felt that way about her father, and I knew well how she could, it wouldn't have been a moment's work to slay him.

"Not if you don't."

I reared on an elbow beside her. Now, faint as it was, I could see her eyes. Those greening glints.

Why, I thought, maybe she suspicions *me*. It was something had never come in my head before. I thought how Professor Allan had told me I was a fine egotist. It meant I just couldn't see myself giving way to get on a level with folks I disliked, or doing things I hated with my gut.

I could have talked then, but I didn't, and it was too hot even to think about loving her up, though I knew she'd have been open to it. After a while, when I'd lain back, I found myself asleep, in one of those half-trances when you aren't awake but can't wake up. In it a round man with tar-black eyes strolled into the room, shreds of flesh hanging from his rotted lips, and says, "Four good dollars for a portrait of my daughter." Then I struggled out of that and there was nothing in front of my eyes. But there was first thunder. It came from far over the hill, and as I sat higher and then got to my feet I could feel the touch of a wind bowing down the trees around the clearing.

Nine

ON THE HEELS of the wind came more thunder. Just one crack. It was so close it seemed to shake the flooring. I dragged on my pants and went to the door. The clearing was full of excitement. When the gusts came they blew the leaves, not much yet but enough to prove there was something huge coming. Then there would be a pause and in it you could have heard a fish flop in the millpond. Then the wind again, in a bigger push. I watched the oaks and the pines. In this new wind some needles came slanting down to the clearing. And a few fresh green leaves whipped off the oaks. Their darker green looked like deep emerald on the cushions of the moss.

And when the next gust came I could feel it on my chest and arms. I stood there touching the doorframe. When I looked back, Letty was still on the pallet. Just a tinge of the low light touching her hair back there. I walked out in the clearing. There was a brightness in me that kept opening up, like doors. The moss was soft and cooling under my foot soles. I looked straight up at the sky and could see the fringes, the underbellies, of those heavy clouds moving around us. The whole woods around the clearing gave a sort of community groan. It was as if one tree was warning another tree to bend low, if it could, and to cower to earth in the face of what approached.

The wind this time was so heavy it blew my hair out, stringing around my head and like to picked me up. I stepped away to the house Letty and I slept in, again, but I didn't go in.

I couldn't have. Something like that coming after such a time of work and sweating and frustration is like a gift. It is a thing that gets under your skin like a knife. I wanted to hold out my hands and tell the storm to come straight down. Fact, I wanted it to wipe out all my dreams and half-dreams of the back of old man Einsner's head.

Now another clap of thunder came, and if the last had been sharp, this was so deep and gut-shocking it had to wake up everybody.

Letty came out, wrapping a dress around her as she ran. We didn't talk. She stood with me looking up and out. Across the way I saw the shadows of the Darlings, those boys, gathering in their doorway. Seven and Barabbas showed up on the doorstep next door. All of our faces were little pools of pearly light raised against the tossing green of the trees. The horse gave a nicker. Then the first drops were coming, big and heavy as if each one was a bucket of god-juice from heaven. They were so cool when one fell on my shoulder and I rubbed a finger on it and tasted the fingertip it was just like ice. And sweet as a kiss. The big, fat drops came faster, rushing down into the clearing and reaching for the dry ground and rubbing the moss with beauty. Everything suddenly started to smell like a pocketful of brimstone. But as clean as waking up when you're a child and know something that's going to get sponged out later but that right then you *know*.

"Heydy!" I says. I was laughing. Letty looked at me and her mouth went the way mine was.

Around across the way the Darlings were milling in their doorway. Lightning came in a ripping flash that filled the clearing and in it I could see them, Jase with his hat still on—I wondered if he slept in it. Expected he did. Barabbas's eyes in the same flash were like black stones with quartz shining in them. Letty gripped one of my wrists.

Seven calls out, "It'll raise the millrace!" His voice wasn't loud through rain-drumming. He was standing there with his head cocked like he was one of those old shamans, the Indian wise men, knowing the spirit of the forest.

Over at the mill I could just see those heavy dark dry boards now soaking up the rain. It fell faster and faster. At the main house it boiled and bobbed on the slate roofing. More wind came and blew it all out slantwise. It was like leaning from the deck of a ship into crosswise waves. Just the silver of it around us and plastering us. Letty's hair had gone dark and hung in long tendrils. Then everything was coming down so heavy, no seeing anything in it, that I took her by an elbow and steered her into the front room. Everything had waked up; there couldn't be any going back to sleep in this. We stood there by a window and looked out for the glimpses we could get of the things the rain would let us see. This wasn't much. The rain was like a solid body of brilliance and the drops lashing down the panes were shadowed in Letty's eyes and lifted face so she looked as though she happened to be running under sliding shadows even though she was only standing still, like me, and watching.

It went on for what I'd have judged was an hour. We didn't say much. After a while I looked up the lamp and lit it. The forks of the flame made the rain-shadows through the window jump even higher in here. It wasn't only a goose-drownder, it was a cataclysm. But I wouldn't have given up one drop. I was relishing them all. I says, "Hope she stops before morning."

"You happened to be going to ask me something, earlier, George." She was standing just in front of me, her eyes flared into by the lamp-glow.

I can't quite tell how mad that made me. It had cost me enough to stop my tongue every time I wanted to talk about what overhung us; if she couldn't keep her part of the bargain then I was going to throw away my skin of coward-acting ease and speak out too.

I felt myself stiffen up, as though I happened to be a rooster firming himself up tall for a fight, and I said, leaning to her across the lamp, "You're right I was, Letty. Yes, Letty. And from now on you can call me Luke. And no pretending to be something we ain't, around Seven or around anybody. I'm sick to death of play-acting." I was leaning close above the lamp, we could both feel the lamp's heat from its chimney.

Her eyes were that cold green and she was as ready to fight as I. Maybe readier. Outside, the rain boiled down as if we were on an ark and would be found in the dayshine high above the world floating on dancing waters.

I took a deep breath right from the core of the system, and I says, just loud enough to make it clear over the rain, "I found your daddy, Letty. He'd been killed with a candlestick. He was in the front room when I went back to get my painting."

"*I* found him there," she says just in the same tone I was using. "I'd got dressed and took the money up from under the plank in Mama's old bedroom where I knew she'd put it. I knew you'd finished up the portrait and it was time to go and you'd seemed to me the kind of fellow who'd be a wonder to travel with until I could get well rid of Daddy. When I came out of Mama's old bedroom there through the parlor I came to him on the floor."

"How—tell me how he looked, Letty."

"Head toward the door. Both arms flung above his head. On his stomach."

"Somebody laid for him and killed him. He sure hell didn't get there by himself. It's an odd way for anybody to commit suicide. Impossible."

Our noses were nearly touching. I could make out every little fleck of green in her eyes. Her dress came open and I saw the tiny strawberry-colored butterfly mark on her belly, just over the navel.

Her head was raised proud as a lily stalk to mine.

"It'd been easy for a man to swing the candlestick. Easy for you. If you did it, I'll stick with you. I'll call you Luke or George or J. P. Lester or Beelzebub or General Grant, what-

ever you want. I made up my mind to that before I came to
get you from the loft to travel with me. But I was dead-scared
inside you'd already have gone. I mean, you'd been scared of
what you'd done and gone kiting off in the dark."

"I wouldn't soil my hands hitting anybody chincy as him."

"Maybe you would and maybe not. Point is, Luke, somebody
did it. I didn't hear anything, no noise. I'd been dressing in
my own room, taking the only dress I ever got I liked, that I'd
kept back enough to buy out of the egg money, and then I
went to Mama's room and lifted the plank and put my money
she'd left me in my bag with a commoner dress. Then I came
out and found—him. Dead. Then I went to you. That's the
whole story, and if God wants to strike me dead with a thun-
derbolt coming down the chimney and a fireball running
across the room to utterly consume me, He is invited to at this
given moment."

No fireball came. It was as though both our tongues, and
our very inmost beings, had been loosened the way the rain
was torn out of the heavy sack of the sky.

I shakes my head. "So you think I did it. All this time
you've—"

"What else am I to think? You acted like it."

"Would I 've gone back to get my painting of the boys
swimming?"

"You know in your soul you would, Luke Applegate. If you
were red with his blood you'd still save a picture you'd done
you favored."

"And I know in my soul you've got the dander and the hate
for him to've met him when you came out of your mama's
room with that bagful of cash money and before he had a
chance to say Bo to a goose, gather up that candlestick and hit
him."

I'd reached out and took her wet shoulders. I'd shut the
front door and rain was crashing against it like a white tiger
wanting in.

I shook her slow. It was like shaking a young tree that's not
going to be uprooted no matter what.

"You, Letty. All this mortal while I been living in a kind of terror of you, though loving you too if the truth's all told. Not just with my cock and balls but loving you and wanting to know you better my life long."

"And me with you, Luke. You're hardly a refined man, though I don't know as I want a refined one. One time, I nearly went off with a preaching man who had a protracted camp meeting in the west meadow. But he was too nice and he stuck out his finger when he drank the camomile tea I offered him and I doubt he'd have had any gumption in existence. I vowed from the time I was eleven, and Mama'd run off, to wait and hope and then go when the time came . . ." She stopped. She was breathing hard as though she'd been racing, which, when you think of it, for a time we both had. I could feel the warm of her breath on my mouth as she talked up to me. ". . . charity's not in it, what I feel for you, Mister." She shook her wet hair. "I didn't want something like *she'd* run off with, either."

"How'd she come to?"

"He was in a circus, playing other side of Jerseyville. He juggled plates. Wasn't a very good juggler, kept dropping the plates. She'd took me to the circus—of course Daddy didn't know—in the daytime, and that night he came to the door and she kissed me like a smothering, and she was crying, and she went off with him. Little bit of a man with wide shoulders and a peaked face. Name of Harkins. He'd a moustache like the one you're growing, but scraggier. They'd talked to each other at the circus. That was when she told me about the money that she'd inherited from Uncle Dexter Follope, and said where she'd hid it. *He,* Daddy, never did know—"

"Why didn't she take the money with her?"

"She took just a bit to get along on until she started life with Harkins—I don't even know Harkins's first name—and she left the rest for me. She thought I'd be able to get along on it the rest of my days. I was the apple of her very eye. Don't know why, I was a wispy little child."

"Why didn't you start off earlier?"

"Why, why, why! I was waiting for the right time. That night, the time seemed ripe."

I nods. "So," I says. I'd let go her shoulders. Tell the truth, I could just as easy have made love to her right then. I mostly wanted to. But I was trying to get everything else straight in my none too nimble skull. Seemed everything had come to a kind of peak; honesty seemed to be laid out like the naked heart of the night before us, and in the rushing rain-sound something had come good and clean. All the same I was still confused. I could see her, in the eye of my mind, a little, peak-nosed child with her mother bidding her good-bye while this Harkins waited. I could see how she would have gone to the hiding place of the money, later, and pried up the board and looked upon it as her key to freedom. I was even seeing how she'd have been scared, likely, to set out on her own until somebody came along she could put trust in—or think she could.

Then, if she hadn't killed old Einsner, it must've been a mortal shock to her to find him sprawled and believe I'd done it.

She still didn't believe I hadn't.

I didn't know if she had, or hadn't.

Both of us wanted to believe the best and it was like two spirits struggling on a cliff to see if they'd both stay on it and keep from falling, or if one would go over the edge and go tumbling to hell.

For some reason I strokes her cheek—that lovely cheek-bone—with the tips of my fingers. "Poor Letty," I says. "All this time thinking I done it. Girl, I don't have a speck of proof I didn't. But somebody did."

I kept pursuing this. Almost to myself, I goes on, "Somebody had to do it—somebody maybe who knew there was money around, who was seeking it out—the hired hands?"

"You know how they were, Luke. They hardly ever came in the house except when they'd slicked up for their evening suppers. They were scared of Daddy."

"So it's not likely they'd know about the money."

"Far as I can see, nobody knew except me. Unless Mama told somebody about it in the six years since she's been gone. Or somebody who knew Mama before she left, knew she had it there. Or knew she had it *some*place. Oh, Luke, I've studied all that in my mind. I've thought, Why, if somebody like that killed Daddy, didn't the somebody *take* the money?" She breathed deep. "No. It's got to've been somebody who didn't even know about it."

"Don't be too sure," I said. "Maybe this somebody just got scared as hell after the killing and ran off, the same way we did. People don't just do things straight the way they've planned, even if they've got a map of a robbery in their minds. Maybe when you came out of your mamma's room and found your daddy stone dead, you scared somebody who was hiding there waiting to ransack the house for the money. Money's just shit at times like that. It's a magnet drawing people and it makes them not even people, it makes them fools."

"Well, Luke, all I know is, for all that time since Mama left and while I was growing up, I didn't tell anybody about it. Didn't even look at it very often, and I was always sure the blinds were down and everybody was far outside the house and I was on my lonesome when I did take a look. And Daddy didn't know a breath about it or he'd have had it in the bank with the rest of his pile long, long before. I kept it locked like a secret in the middle of my soul."

"But you'd trust me with it—even thinking I was the one killed your father."

"I'd trust you with all."

"Schach!" I shakes my head hard. "Letty, I'm doing my best to swallow all your story, and I know you're strainin' to gulp down mine. Leaves us still at the mercy of the law, even if we didn't either of us do the deed."

Then she says something that made my bones start to melt. As if they all wanted to run together with affection for her.

"What we've got to do, Luke, is try to believe each other with every ounce of hope in us. Because we're locked together, now. And we can't let anything rise up and give us the tumpish doubts any longer. If we do we might as well be hung already."

I put my arms around her and drew her in close. Her breasts were cool wet against my chest. Her whole length leaned in to me but it was a strong being as well as a willing one. She'd laid it out the way it had to be.

I murmured into her soaked hair, "It's got to be so, Letty. By damn, it's got to."

The rain roared on the roof of the small house as if it wanted either to crush it to the ground or to let out all the devils of doubt in it, in a rush that would go up and join the atmosphere and go hurrying and sighing across the night.

We went back to bed and just plain fell asleep to that sound, that crystal rushing. Didn't even make love, much to speak of. Just held onto each other. When I waked I blinked and then disengaged from her, slow, not to waken her, and stood up and walked out to the front room and then opened the door against the patter of slow rain falling. It had all leveled out to a noise like the harpsichord in the big house would sound, in my head, when it got to be in tune and somebody dexterous played it.

I walked onto the doorstep and then down into the clearing.

It wasn't yet morning.

Rain fell on me cool as cucumber skin. Then while I walked over the squashing moss, seeing when I looked down that it left deep footprints which started straightening up as soon as I'd gone a few feet past them, I could hear this other sound.

It was a deep heavy gurgle. Thinks I: the millrace is full. Slopping over, I bet.

I started running over to the mill. When I got there the sound was tall as a tent around me, it was like I was living in the middle of a roar of waters. The millrace, and the pond, and the whole branch was running white.

I looked up at the body of the mill. It was soaked black. But there was something else besides its appearance. There was a feeling, shaking the earth a bit, that wasn't either millrace or rain. It was a raw, dark, big, stony sound. I recollected how we'd left the arm—the big wooden bar—that brought the bed-stone and the runner stone together, locked in. I climbed up as fast as a squirrel shinnying to the second floor, with the white water whipping under me, and then all at once I was damned near hit and swept around by the wheel. It was moving, and the extra sound I'd heard was its motion, those timbers that hadn't moved for a great weight of years, now moving, and the cogs inside turning, and the raw dark coughing steady working sound, the noise of the bedstone and the runner grinding one upon another.

Seven got there then. He was a sight but there was no time to remark on it, even though he looked like the eldritch spirit of the woodland. He hollers, "Help me, boy!" We went around, teetering on the timbers and the half-rotted floor, and put our shoulders to the lifting bar, and I thought I felt my balls and back break together as we pushed. I know he was pushing just as hard.

Then we'd unlocked the stones and the sound stopped, and the great wheel of the mill moved a bit faster in the push of the hungry water in the race.

"My God," I says in a gasp.

Below us the Darlings all showed up, their faces like brown peach petals gazing.

"The Lord may have something to do with it," says Seven. Barabbas was with the boys below, I could hear him panting over the darkling, wonderous sound of waters around us. "She's working," Seven went on. "She's turning, oh, bless the fates. But the stones would have ground the good out of each other running without grain." He sighed and leaned on a dark post. "My boy, we're going to be milling this autumn. I wish my old friends the Carrolls could have seen it."

The sound of the turning wheel came around us with a steady grace that didn't stop. After a while Letty showed up below and I jumped down, not even able to talk much yet, and put an arm around her, and we stood so, gazing up at the rolling and gulping majesty of the wheel.

Ten

WELL, I'M NOT GOING to say everything went smooth as bear grease from then on. But it did seem that with the wheel turning life was better. It was also as if Letty and I having spouted off to each other that night of cleansing rain had cleared our personal atmosphere so that now we knew where we stood. She was right; we had to cleave to each other, had to believe neither of the other had murdered, because we were caught into the event the way two people could be locked together by invisible chains.

As for the wheel, in the days that came then, after the air cleared off and more of the real work started—for there was so much to do to get the mill ready it seemed each day's labor only made more work—in those days, wherever I'd be, in the main house washing the floors and oiling them and cleaning up, or in the mill helping Seven and the Darling brothers to repair the floors and fix up the loft ladders and firm up the uprights, and so on—wherever I'd be, I'd cock an ear suddenly and then I'd hear it: that steady moving, that rolling, gulping clutch of sound that was like something you'd hear a long way off, from an enormous beehive; a sound of running water, a working of the wheel through the days and through the nights.

It made most of the worries settle down into your bones and life move as sweetly as a bee roving through a set of clover.

The morning after the rain stopped I'd gone across the branch again and inspected my hiding place of the strongbox. It was perfectly safe. Water had come within an inch of the high-water rings on the birches, but it wouldn't come any higher without another cloudburst. There was also the great satisfaction that the cloudburst we'd had hadn't hurt the wheat and the corn in the surrounding countryside. It had all come upright again—it wasn't the sort of storm that lasts for days and sours the roots of grain and leaves the farmers walking their rows and wondering why the Lord has deserted them. You could fairly smell the richness of the fields lying for miles all around Solomon; sometimes on the evening air the scent came up here, so spermy and thick it might have been a cloak you could touch and draw around you. The Darling boys took turns visiting their mother down below, and sometimes brought Letty and Seven and me news of the farming world; they reported that there was going to be a bumper crop this year, that everything now pointed to it.

Of course they didn't know anything about what Letty and I—and Seven maybe a little because I'd told him—feared; they were putting on a bit of weight, in spite of the terrible work they laid on themselves. They laid it on themselves even when I didn't parcel out chores. The wonder of a good worker— and it's true in painting as well as with any labor—is that the good man sees it's there to be done, and aims at it quick, and doesn't wait to be urged, or to consult a map.

I'd stocked up enough with the last trip to Solomon, in mid-August, so we didn't have to add anything now. And the rest of August went by with hardly a division of hour from hour, let alone a division of days. Letty showed up in a new blue calico dress she'd stitched all for herself, in spite of everything else she had to do—for she was helping red up the main house now, too, as well as doing the bulk of the cooking; she'd

polished the old harpsichord till it shone like easy glass—and
she looked grand and cool in it. She'd put up her hair, too, so
it glistened like a cap of faint gold.

And, sitting on the steps of the main house with Seven, long
after the light had gone out of the sky over the ridge of hills—
the sky shining Rembrandt old gold through the pines, then
deepening to burnt umber, then laying cobalt shadows over
the whole clearing, then welcoming the owls and the bullbats
and the other nightbirds, and showing the stars clear and keen
against the spears of the pines—I'd just commune with him, so
to speak, in what for the most part was silence. I'd read a good
many more of those books from the Carrolls' library now.

They worked in me like clabber in a pan. They were full of
ideas. What Seven called the "Lake Poets"—all those said
things I'd felt in the human faces I'd tried to limn. I realized
how even the portrait of Letty—which I still hadn't put over
the mantel of the big fireplace in the main house—wasn't what
I'd wanted of her. It was too pretty-pretty lovely, even though
it was a good likeness. But too—well, dandified. Still too much
what the world might want but not what was truly there.

Came September with the Big Dipper high and the other
belts of stars—the Little Dipper, the Archer—shining like they
wanted to pull the soul out of you when you looked at them
long enough. And on this night we're sitting there, I'm smoking a short pipe like Seven's, which I'd found in the Carrolls',
and I says, "Harvest's not so plumb far off now, Seven. We got
to start noising it around a little, that the mill's going to be
operating."

"You'll only have to tell one or two," he said. "Gossip travels
fast in Solomon. And it's the only commodity Mullin's Gap has
to offer."

"I'll inform that store man in Solomon," I said. "And maybe
the court clerk over there. But I'm damned if I'm going to set
shoe in Mullin's Gap again."

"You won't have to. Just make a couple of hand signs and
send one of the boys to put 'em up in both towns. They'll
rouse plenty of interest."

The old mill wheel was turning steady and even in the

night. We kept the shaft greased deep. Everything in there was looking better.

"What'll we call the mill?"

"I don't think it signifies much, one way or the other," he says. "Call it the Old Carroll Mill. You don't have to be like God naming the animals. It's been here a long while."

"I'll make the signs tomorrow," I promised.

Then after a time I said, "Would it bother you a whole lot if Letty and I moved into the main house, here?"

He took a pipe-draw. "It needs somebody in it. All the while. It needs laughter and talk and the rub of humanity. I'm not its keeper any longer, Luke. You've taken over now. I think it'd be right for you to take over the full distance. It's a pleasure working with you, boy."

"It'll go right on being the same with you, Seven." I'd told Letty about telling Seven about the truth of us. She hadn't minded. In bits and scraps I'd also told her about my own past. It was a patchbag past, but I'd told her things such as how I learned to read, when I was about eleven, in Wisconsin, from the revivalist who painted signs on rocks, such as REPENT OR FRY, and DAMNATION TO DISBELIEVERS. He was a cracked old man but he'd shared his bread with me and he could certainly teach somebody his letters. He'd been in the Civil War—or as Professor Allan always called it, the War Between the States—and he'd had one leg shot off at Chancellorsville. Thinking of him, now, put me in mind of Professor Allan; I'd told Letty about him, too. In limning through the land, you make friends sometimes; not often, because you don't often stay in one place long enough. But Professor Allan had been as true a friend as any I'd ever had. I really should have written him a letter, I thought; the only point was, I wasn't much for letter-writing; seemed I'd much rather paint a picture.

So next day when I could take time out I made a couple of handsome signs, lettering it out clear in some scarlet lake and lampblack black from my paint and canvas bag, it being the first time I'd truly lifted a brush since coming up here. I made the signs simple and plain in essence, inviting all farmers to do their harvest milling at Old Carroll Mill, which was now again in operation, and after consulting again with Seven, I put the prices clear and bold.

Then I sent Paul, whose turn it was to go down into the world of farming and such, with the signs and told him to put up one in the general store in Solomon and the other on the wall of the inn over at Mullin's Gap. I told him to be cautious, though I didn't have to do that; he was born cautious. He was gone down the path like smoke.

That same day I started moving Letty and me into the main house; we chose a front bedroom that overlooked the clearing with a view from the side windows of the mill.

Along about sunfall, Paul came back and I saw him join the others—his brothers and Seven—over at the mill, where the job of repairing all of the upper loft was going on. I strolled over from the main house, where yellow light was already falling from a few of the windows against the coming dark, and where Letty was trying to get a spinning wheel—an old rosewood one, a Saxony wheel—she'd found, to get working. I got to the mill and climbed to the loft. The ladder was firm now and didn't sway and creak underfoot the way it had before. The place smelled of oil and old wood and useful iron now, too, and not nearly so rat-ridden and owl-pestered as it had. I summoned Paul over to me and he squatted beside me at the mouth of the well while I stood on the ladder.

"Everything go all right?"

"Sure." He nods. He wipes sweat from his upper lip. "Except in Mullin's Gap, that man runs the inn—"

"Abraham Tatum."

"Yuh. He asked me who'd took over the mill. I said, 'The man I work for,' and got ass out of there. All right, sir?"

"Don't call me sir. You did right."

"Thanks, Luke."

On this matter of names, all the Darlings called me Luke now, and Letty, Letty. That was the way it was going to be. I still couldn't figure why the law in all its majesty and glory hadn't come after us, but since spilling everything to Letty, and having her spill what I was immortally hopeful was everything, to me, I wasn't going to question fate any longer.

Next day, about four in the afternoon, Jase Darling came to me in the main house where I was trying to wrestle a bureau up the staircase without scarring that lovely staircase rail, and says, head back and hat with its crow feather making a sharp shadow on the wall in the sun, "Men out here to see you,' Luke."

I like to dropped the bureau, which was a small one from the little house where we'd been staying. Women are always wishing to move things, I'd found that out too in my travels, and I'd argued with Letty about moving this piece, but then I'd given in. I settled the bureau down on the landing so it wouldn't fall and came down, wiping my hands and all at once going very still, still as a hawk, inside. Because this might be it. This might be the whole thing come crashing down.

I was breathing without seeming to breathe when I stepped out in the sun.

But right off I saw I'd never looked upon these men before. They were puffing a bit, being heavy-built individuals in farming clothes and not used to climbing young mountains by steep paths. There were four of them, and they diddled around a bit when I came up to them. I realized that with my moustache, which was now a caution, I might not be familiar to them even if they'd seen me before; I'd bronzed up a good deal too.

They kept on diddling, hemming and hawing, and then the front one thrust out a hand like a Pennsylvania smoked ham that'd hung so long it was dark red and going black.

"Offans is my name."

"Applegate's mine," I said, throwing my cap over the windmill just as plain. But I wasn't going to have it any other way now. Too much had happened not to be honest with whatever of the world wanted to ask me questions. I knew what deviltry this could play in Mullin's Gap, where I was still known as J. P. Lester, but I tell you, I'd crossed a line and wasn't going back.

We shook awhile and then he introduced me to the others.

They were Apfelhizer, Greinding, and Bull. Bull stuck his chin out and says, stiff, "We come to see your milling. What you got to offer."

"Stroll over here a ways and you'll see, gentlemen."

The wheel was moving easy but firm in the latening shadows. Everything was still except for that underthrob of noise. They came into the mill careful, not men used to climbing around but men used to plowing and walking the rows, and they looked with keen eyes in the murk of the mill. I showed them how we'd rigged a loop of rope, a kind of net, to lower the bags without doing the whole thing by hand and passing them down hand to hand, and how the bedstone and the runner were clean and ready to lock together.

All the while the wash of water being taken up by the wheel and spilling from the cup-buckets made a soothing noise in our ears.

They didn't come up the ladder with me to the loft where the boys and Seven were hammering, but Seven looked over the edge.

He recognized the men and called a good day to them.

The one named Apfelhizer calls up to Seven, "Just like in the old days, verdammdt! Grosse Gott, Mister Phillips!"

Seven's silvery-copper face looked pleased. He went back to work.

It was like his being there put a seal on the fact that the milling would be good.

When they'd gone—I gave them some of Letty's biscuits and a little elderberry jelly she'd made while we were in the small house—I waved them down the path and came walking across the clearing. They hadn't seen her but she'd seen them from the windows of the big house, it turned out. That night Seven told me they were large bugs in the Solomon community, slow-moving but once they'd made up their minds, set as stars in their courses.

That same night, too, I started to sketch out another portrait of Letty. I used the back of the canvas of Senator Margate to do it. I'd never liked him but he was a good come-on for other work, and the technique was careful. She sat at the harpsichord in the lamp's light in her new blue gown she'd made herself and even though she happened to be barefoot at the time she looked like a great lady. A great, small one. The sound she got out of the harpsichord when she plinked the keys wasn't too musical but I figured that, later on, I could find somebody who was fit to tune such a fine instrument.

A moth flapped in the slightly open door, which I'd rubbed with beeswax till that design of the sheaves of wheat sparkled even in the moonlight. The moth circled above her head and distracted her, and she batted at it, then saw what I was doing and came over to look at the sketch, standing a bit behind me.

"But you did one, Luke."

"I know you better now," I said.

She watched my hand work with the charcoal.

Then when I turned around she was smiling one of her only-now-and-then smiles.

"You do, at that, Mister."

We just left the work and went upstairs. In the dark night up there, on an old feather bolster that was aired and clean as a cloud, we made love fast as though we were finding it out for the first time, then slow, and between times, not knowing what o'clock it was, looking up at the ceiling and feeling the strength of the house, the clearing, and the mill, around us, and hearing the even deeper strength of the wheel turning, I thought, Applegate, you ought to remember this all your days. For it will never be quite so again.

But it kept on being so. And the mill was nearly in shape, though now and then we'd all—the Darlings and Seven and Letty and I—find something else we needed to do. We were all living a lot more off the land, now. Letty'd never asked me what I'd done with the money. I'd told her it was safe as churches, and knowing some churches, probably fifty percent safer. Seven and I had loaded the Boone rifle and tried for wild turkey on the slope of land rising up from the east of the clearing. We'd almost got a gobbler. I thought we'd get one later. He was better than I'd ever be with that rifle. But with his small rifle we got some smaller game, rabbits and squirrels and such; there was no dearth of game for the pot.

I like to bring that time together and roll it in my mind, now. The time when September slid into October and in the mornings when you'd get up there was the slightest rime of frost on the moss in the clearing, and the sumac up toward the mill was starting that delicate turning that would in a short while come to flame.

Eleven

I REMEMBER THAT LETTY and I had been talking, quite a bit
lately, about her past; that I'd tried—without seeming to be
probing—to bring out more colors and shades of colors of that
past, so I could get straight in my own head how it had been
with her and with old man Einsner and this money. "Daddy
never knew about it," she kept saying. "Had no more idea
than a hen has of being a hummingbird."

"So," I'd say. "So far so clear. But how's about this point that
so far nobody's been chasing us—or seeming to? It just irks
my mind, Letty girl. Sometimes I'm willing to accept fate, the
way Seven says he wants everybody to do, but other times I get
the feeling of a big fist ready to crack down on us, through
these smiling days."

They were smiling, too. There'd been some rain but nothing like that first burst. Just enough to keep everything growing. Harvest was starting now in some fields. Out of the
corners of my eyes while I was busy about the main house and
the mill, I kept looking toward the path, expecting the first
customers any day. Seven said there was no doubt about them

coming. The reputation of the Carrolls' mill had gone on through the years since the war; a farmer's a practical man when he's nothing else. We meant money in the pocket to these folks. I looked out the window now, as we talked; I was starting to fill in the outlines with paint, in the second portrait of Letty. But there was nothing out there but the leaves of the oaks changing color, like so many headdresses of relatives of the Darlings come back from the old days and flaming through the sun. Sometimes a bit of a wind would rain down leaves; they lay on the moss through the clearing and crackled like snakeskins when you brushed through them. Everything in the air had a bound and lift to it like a buck deer stepping the earth in the bounty of his prime.

"Your daddy have any special legal counsel?" I asked her, while I painted in the tip of one of her eyebrows, as soft as the down flickering in the sunlight on her arms. She'd got the Saxony wheel to working and was treadling it. The flaxen thread came out of the small light wood cradle as easy as honey out of a hive. The spinning wheel made a noise that was a soft buzz under the always-turning of the water wheel down at the mill.

"Oh—" She shrugs. "Had an ol' family friend, name of Wayde Mitchell. Wayde with a y. Puffed-up soul. He commiserated with Daddy considerably after Mama run off. Called me 'pore little Letitia,' stroked my hair a good deal. I wouldn't trust him to shoe a horse, let alone with me alone in a room. Soft-soap and goose grease. But he was just about as greedy as Daddy, so they saw eye to eye." She bit at a piece of thread which had turned to a tangle. Spat it out.

"He stood to profit by anything Daddy did. When Daddy wanted the west sixty from old man Ringleknapp, Wayde and Daddy connived to snap it up. Wayde's a political man. Kind of thinks he's another Daniel Webster."

"Got his finger on the community pulse," I says. "And is a lawyer. So he might know about your mama's legacy even if your daddy never did."

"Might." She studied me. "It'd have taken a lot of foxiness on his part, but he could. I never thought of that." Then, treadling along and not missing a stroke, she says, "Mitchell had an itch to marry me. If you'd never come along and I'd not made up my mind to run off maybe things would have gone along, so, and I'd've married him."

"And he'd have got your daddy's acres and money and cattle and whatever by the time your daddy died a natural death," I says. "And maybe he knew he'd have got the money your mama had left you in so-called secret as well. I'm just wondering about this Wayde Mitchell. With a y."

She laughed. "Luke, he's not the kind of man would lay for and kill anybody. Not that way. Might have it done and pretend even to himself he didn't know about it."

"You paint a picture of somebody I'd want to meet for the first time in open sunlight," I told her. "Not in a dark room."

She nods. "He's like that. There's the other thing, too, though—he wanted me for more'n any money he'd finally get out of us being married."

I looked at her. "Most men would," I says. "I've no doubt you've had more'n evangelist's offers."

"My, yes," she said. The spinning wheel was going a little faster. "I just beat off suitors with both hands, Luke." She shook her head. "No, it wasn't like that. I guess I got a reputation for being a cold person. Tried making love once, last year, with—name doesn't matter now—fellow took me to a strawberry sociable. I didn't like it while he was doing it, and didn't like it when it was over."

"Ah well," I says. "Some men don't have the sense to touch joy without spoiling it. Or the guts to take it all the way, so I ain't blaming him."

"You're the least modest body in the world sometimes, Luke Applegate."

"I got a lot to be unmodest about," I says. "Now sit still, and pull your face just a twinge more around in the full sun."

I painted, then, though I still couldn't help—far in the back of my thinking—mulling all these things over in my mind.

But then I thought, Don't force it; let the day ride out with its own blessings and just take it slow and soulful. That is a good way to think—or to stop your mind from thinking at all—when things are going fine and you're engaged on a portrait. Already this portrait was better than the other one. I didn't suspicion that people, most people, would think it was as pretty-nice as the first one, but the people whose judgment I liked, such as Seven and Professor Allan and a few others I'd met in the course of my life, would like it better.

It was just the next day following that we had our first customers. Quite a body of them. Offans and Apfelhizer and Bull and Greinding, to be sure; but they brought with them others, and when the first wagons came up off the down-path, their wheels digging deep in the loam and brushing past the sumac that was now turned and flaring that sweet deep red, I thought it looked like a western wagon caravan, with the horses—and one wagon was pulled by deep-muscled oxen, their horns shining pearl in the new light—straining and the whips cracking and the body of all making more noise than a party. There were little children who'd come along, and quite a few dogs and even a tortoise-shell cat held in one of the little boys' arms. Barabbas, he walked around solemn and good-tempered, not picking fights even with the feisty farm dogs that were spoiling for it and which he would have gulped in one brief swallow, had he been so minded. Seven stood routing the line of march, around and to the mill-path and each wagon to take its turn and the grain to go spilling down the great chute that we'd fixed up till it was right and tight. Nothing smells so good as grain on the air while it's being milled. Seven and I pulled the bar down to lock the stones in place, and when the first spill of grain came in it was like a lifting wild wave of smell on the air and the stones got their heavy sound, different from when they'd worked together and not been chewing any grain; a lusty, juicy sound that made you, made me anyway, want to whoop and holler for the beans of it. Seven nodded at me, satisfied.

Neither of us had to say anything; we couldn't have been heard above the sound, at any rate. The Darlings helped, nimble-handed with the bagging, and when that first stream of flour, medium-grind, poured into the open mouth of a bag, I couldn't help sticking my fingers in it and then rubbing them together and tasting and smelling the result, the way Seven and Greinding were doing. It tasted sweet and full, leaving a chalky back-taste on the tongue and something else that was like sizing glue. "Gluten," says Seven.

Greinding nods and hollers above the noise. "Sweet and big! Dot's a good mill, Mister Phillips!"

"Got good wheat, sir!" says Seven.

The line went on all that morning and afternoon. I moved among the people, free and clear, and so did Letty, serving cold water in big buckets to anyone who so wanted it, and at noon she brought out bread she'd baked on a main-house range, about twenty loaves of it; I've said she was a good cook but I like to remark on it. We didn't have butter for it but there was wild honey. The women remarked on how good the bread was, to Letty, and she explained how she thought it'd been better if we'd milled our own flour for it, but that it would just ordinarily do. They were all farm women, most of them running to fat where they didn't look undernourished from so much work on the tidy farms they came from; she got along with them just famously. I expect they all thought we were married. I felt a swelling pride in her, and a pride in the way the Darlings worked too, quick to jump when jumping was called for and keeping everything flowing in one good stream. The trick was to keep the grain going through and not let the stones run dry—or to let them run dry as little a time as possible without lifting them apart—in other words, to use the bar as little as you could, because that took time. We got the thing down to a flowing science after a few hitches.

Among the people from the farms around Solomon were others, from Mullin's Gap way, and I thought to myself from time to time, with a tiny flick of foreboding, that I recognized some of the farmers who'd been at breakfast on the one morning Letty and I'd spent in the Mullin's Gap inn. But it didn't signify. Hell, I thought, if they remember me it'll only have been in passing, and likely, with this moustache—it was a big sprouter now—they won't even do that. I felt neighborly and watchful at the same time.

I don't paint scenes with a flock of people in them as a rule, but someday before I keel over from age and wickedness and lovemaking I'm going to get a canvas full of all those people in the clearing, and at the mill, and the women trailing over with Letty to the main house and sitting in the cool of the big ivory-walled front room and blowing snot from their children's noses, and clacking with talk, and the men in little knots around the fire-and-gold of the oaks and the tall green of the pines and the leaf-patched green of the moss, but how to get the sound of the flour being ground is something I haven't yet figured out between me and God.

Or how to get the taste of the chaff in it, and the dusty dryness that caked on your arms and got down your lungs and made you hawk a little and feel bottled up; when you took a slaking drink of the cold water you were all right then.

I tell you, when the last wagon had gone rocking down the hill in the dusk I was glad to see it go, glad in my bones. "There'll be more tomorrow," says Seven. He was sitting in the front room with us, in the main house—which I sometimes, even though I didn't feel it was, all the way down to my marrow, thought of as *our house*—in the night. All the day sounds that the foofooraw of people had made had died down and the sounds of the dark were around us. Down at the Darlings' house there was light playing on the stone of the doorstep, washing it with yellow like butter, and through the trees the nightbirds went moving, some of them the big snowy owls that hang around come fall and feel winter coming in their mouse-hunting selves. The crickets were making their fiddling, a rise and fall of sound, and as Seven said that, about there'd be more people coming tomorrow, he and Letty and I and Barabbas all sat forward. For there was a calling in the darkness that swept under the stars. We went to the open door—I had a fire in the fireplace but it was a good night for smelling the openness of the air, washing the last flour-and-dust patches out of our lungs—and stood there, the dog too, looking up. Above the oaks, some of whose boughs were stripped now and angling toward the sky like twined thin arms of imploring old men, we heard the sound again.

It tugged at me like a voice from both within and without. It told me while I tasted the wind that I'd always been an exploring, rambling man. What was I doing here good as married and settled with Letty? But it was only a wisp of feeling, gone then, only powerful as the wild geese came over, honking and barking high, heading deep to the south, and just seeable in their wedge as they rushed with the cold air streeling around them and them cutting it in their ship's prow progress.

When they'd gone we turned back. Seven says, sitting down in the high-backed rocker he favored, "As I said, there'll be more people on the morrow." He fondled the plates of bone on Barabbas's head; the dog looked up at him, its throat leaning. "There's still passenger pigeon flocks coming," he remarks almost to himself. Looks down his nose, as if remembering. "They don't blacken the sky like a continuing storm the way they once did . . . too many men have shot 'em. But when they come we'll get our decent share of them and not kill for killing's sake."

Then he went on to tell of how when he'd been a boy before he'd ever come up here to work for the Carrolls, he'd been West. Well, so had I, but in a later time than Seven's. All I recalled was the gold fever in the people, and the stink of the camps. And the women who'd get feverish with the kind of gold they made putting out for the miners, and who couldn't tell one body from another even when it was between their knees—good women, I'd always thought, but drawn into being part of a mob. I'd seen the buffalo, too, the herds with their heads like shaggy flowers, and the hides lying swarmed over with green-bottle flies and thick with maggots; you'd think the very air would quit allowing itself to be breathed after such a sight. But that was no slaughter to the things Seven had seen. He talked about it in slow bursts, like hoofs dragging down a trail, how he'd ridden with the scouts who had just fired at random into the herds, till their Sharps rifles burned in their hands. Men towering with the blood lust and then falling like trees from the exhaustion of killing.

He didn't say a lot but it had weight, the way it had when he spoke of one life being more than one life and all moving in a progression of being. When he'd gone Letty says, "I hope we can stay here a long while, Luke. So much to be done here."

I went to work on her portrait again. I was taking it just as slow as I'd taken the first. Except this time I wasn't trying to fool anybody at all, just bringing out the way the hand had to go to capture what she was. I thought as I worked, I don't know her yet; but I'm getting to, and isn't that a thing?

The lovemaking was a swarming necessary part of it but there was everything else running below it. In the wells of time, the waters under the earth, moving us and the earth like the millrace moved the old wheel.

Both of us, sitting there, were listening to the wheel creak and roll over in the boundless night.

Next day they came again—the whole day shaped up like the first. And it went so that whole week, with a rest for Sunday— nobody from Solomon, or even from Mullin's Gap, would've dared to mill their wheat on Sunday, and I was glad for the rest. But midday of Sunday, when I was lying on my back on the slope above the pond, a good rod—bamboo, and with jewel-like line-runners in it, it had been Mister Carroll's— arching from my hand into the water, I felt somebody sit down beside me. Clears the sun out of my eyes by blinking and rolls over.

"Luke." It's David Darling.

"At your service."

"I just got back from Solomon."

Could tell he was worked up, under his face's flat calm.

"It's a quiet burg to see on the Sabbath."

"Yeah. Luke, they got a whiskey-cup contest coming up down there. They got a fair, the harvest fair. They run it every year. The prize," he goes on, hugging his knees solemn and looking out over the shine of the pond waters, "is a new rifle. For the best performance at the cups."

"Whiskey-cupping is an old-style thing," I says. "In Revolutionary times it amused a lot of souls. Well, what's the point?"

"My brothers and me, we'd like to go down. We shoot good."

"Good God," I says. "You're not going to shoot that—" Then I shut up; the rifle they had was all they had.

I'd given them ammunition for it. I'd told them, not to

make them mad or cut the skin of their sensitivity, not to
shoot it anywhere near the clearing. With that cockeyed butt
and the wire wrapped around it it was just as likely to bust as a
cow is to bellow.

I'd implied, I guess, that I'd hate to see one of them blown
apart and spread all over the clearing because of it.

"We been practicing some." His voice was low as a loon's off
across a marsh. "We shoot good."

"Well?" Then all of a quickness, I understood. Being Indians and low in the scale of mankind even in a town as quiet
and fairly biddable as Solomon, they couldn't just go down
and enter the whiskey-cup shooting. They had to have somebody notable and reputable to speak for them. I says, "When's
the fair?" in a different kind of tone.

"Next Saturday night."

Oh, I could've given him a rifle to use—not the Boone, but
another from the big house. Or Seven would have loaned him
his. But that was hardly the point; they were so prideful it was
chancy even to suggest such a thing. I stroked my jaw a bit,
and nods, and finally I says I thought it might be a good idea
for us all to get shut of the clearing just for one evening out,
and that we'd go in a body down to Solomon on the coming
Saturday night.

I figured two ways: I figured the coast might stay being
clear—after all, it'd gone on so far without trouble—and that
all together, we'd put up a forcible front against anybody trying to put down David and his brothers.

He smiled even a lot less then Letty. But I got the feeling
when he grunted "Thanks" that it meant a good deal.

He shadowed himself off then, and later, while I was still
fishing—caught two trout, so sleek-wet their rose-stipples kept
showing strong for quite a time before they expired and
paled—I heard shooting going on in the woods above the
birches where I kept the strongbox. It was fatter with cash
than it had been. There were even a couple of gulden from
the old country.

By next week, Friday, the customers had thinned out; I'd figured there'd still be a lot more coming, but spaced a little dif-

ferent now as people in outlying communities, farther away than Solomon and Mullin's Gap, got the word. On Saturday they were still stringing in, but not steady at all; we had to lift the bar disconnecting the stones quite a few times, and it was marvelous hard work, binding the muscles for half an hour after. I'd got Jase Darling to stand in, sometimes, for Seven, while doing this work, and Seven didn't seem to mind the rest.

Early Saturday night, with the air snap-cold around me and the tops of the part-skinned oaks rustling against what was going to be a sharp night wind, the kind you like to take into your lungs with a sharp pleasure as though the long knives of the year are coming and you're hale and ready for them, I went in the shifting shadows down to the creek and jumped it, as I'd done most every night since we'd started milling in earnest, and took the strongbox out of its hiding hole.

I snugged it to me and jumped back across the water and went to the main house. Letty was reading one of the books I'd recommended to her, after it being recommended to me by Seven. This was Keats again, but this time his poems. Her forehead was a trifle wrinkled. We had the one thing in common even more than anything else: we'd both read every scrap we could find from the time we were puppies.

I knelt down before her and opened the box. Then I counted out all that was in it. Sometimes her bright green-blue eyes looked up at me over the pages. Again, she'd just keep reading.

The money made a soft rustle. When I'd counted, and re-counted—a little tickled because she was so stubborn she wouldn't beg me what I was doing—I held up the box.

"There's your twelve thousand, all of it," I says. "And I'm putting it back now . . ." And I told her just where. "The rest is mine and yours together and I never want us to touch the other again, and sometime we'll return it—if we can, without getting arrested on account of it. It's all blood money, as it turns out . . ."

She just listens, her hair taking the light like new-mint gold.

". . . we'd not used much of it," I goes on. "And I'm sorry we had to use airy a dollar."

I went to the mantel and put the rest that remained from

the milling fees, and from paying back into the box, up there under the Boone rifle and between the portraits of the little girl and the swimming boys.

Shut the box, walked out, jumped the creek, put the box back between birches, jumped back across, and stepped through the rustling leaves of the clearing to the door of the main house.

"You're a man so full of justice and duty it'll break your skin," she says from her chair.

"I just feel good," I says. Then I lay down beside her, watching her read, the way the light went over her hair, down her arms, across her lap, across her gold-downed legs that showed under the blue skirt. I told her about going to the fair. After a time she starts reading to me. " 'Great spirits now on earth are sojourning.' "

I figured they were, along with all the others that weren't yet quite as accomplished as to be even middle-sized.

"Bring along the book if you want," I says, pulling her up. "But now get dressed while I harness up. We're on our way, I promised the boys."

Twelve

I'D ALREADY TOLD Seven we were going. I'd told him during the week. I'd wanted to save it as a surprise for Letty. Didn't seem to me it would do us all any harm to have an airing off the clearing and rub shoulders with the multitude.

In the clearing after I'd harnessed the horse, which was getting very fat and impatient from so much idleness, I held a kind of council of war with everybody standing around.

Moonlight picked out the Darlings in flashes; their black eyes never looked eager, but they didn't appear to be dull either.

Felt like I was Noah giving orders to the crew just before stepping ashore.

"Stick all together, bunch close," I said. "There's a lot of temptations at a fair and we'll have to stay one unit."

The Darlings didn't say a word. Then with the Darlings walking the first part of the way down the path and only Seven and Letty and I riding, to save wear and tear on the horse which had to set its forehoofs and strain back against the steepness of the pitch, we all started out. Barabbas was a shadow in the long grass at the path-lip. We could have left him to watch the place but I trusted there'd be no more customers coming up tonight, and it wasn't an easy point to reach from below, as most customers already knew. I thought that in the coming spring, if everything worked out and we were all still here and doing business, I'd start leveling off the grade of the path some, to make it easier for the wagons. Seven had told me it had once been more level than it was now, but that rains over the years had eroded the edges and they needed smoothing down.

Only thing that bothered me then, and that only in the back of my mind, was that Letty was wearing that burgundy-rose gown again, and that bright small brooch, and the kidskin high-ankled shoes.

They just kept reminding me of the first night, which now seemed long gone, when we'd fled from the Einsner farmhouse.

But I hadn't told her not to wear them; they were still the best she had, and I must say she glittered like a prim diadem.

Halfway down the path where it leveled off was easier going, so I told the Darlings to get in and then we all came out on the road to Solomon. Was a plump moon showing the fields that had been harvested, with a lot of the wheat already in shocks and the corn cut too, farther along. Barabbas trotted along at the heels of the mare, right under the buggy. After a time we started seeing other rigs; wagons from surrounding farms, and now and then a surrey owned by a well-to-do farmer, and once in a while a buggy like ours with the horse sleek as oil and with its ears a little back and on its mettle.

When we got to Solomon itself we could see the torch-flares lighting up the strip of land on the street between the courthouse and the general store and the other stores. It made a flaring that poked up a bit into the sky. When we got even closer we could see the buggies and wagons and such, all drawn up and their horses at the hitching rails and we could start hearing the blustery rumble of the crowd. It was a real fair, with pumpkins—prize ones—on display, and squash and prime pies, and the torchlight flaring on all that food made a sumptuous sight. Letty was sitting straight as a bolt. Could feel her straightness at my flank. I swerved in to a place where there was room for horse and buggy, helped Letty down from the step just as if I was Prime Minister of England, and waited while Seven and the Darling tribe got out. Then I spread a light blanket over the mare against the chill and tied her to the rail and we assembled again. Barabbas kept sticking close to Seven's heels. I noted that the stores, general and all, were open; no use not making a dollar, I thought. And over in the strip of land in the center were a couple of tents, and alongside them, stands where thimblerig men were collecting crowds. Then down to the east were the men with their rifles and a long section of snake fence that loomed against the dimmer shine of flares set up there, which I thought was where they'd be setting up the whiskey cups. I cast a glance at the Darling rifle, which David was as usual carting in his arms as though it happened to be a badge of distinction.

I could have wished I'd risked making him mad at me and at least offered him a decent object to shoot with.

Around us the good burghers of Solomon jostled and walked and gaped; among them I sighted a few more who looked more like Mullin's Gap residents, more foxy—I thought I could tell the people who lived in the two towns apart, though probably I was just making internal judgments—and shifty-shouldered. I did see Abraham Tatum, at one point; with him was a man with a wonderful belly in a flowered vest, and a fawn clawhammer coat falling in its flaps halfway to his heels, and a flowing tie. Letty didn't look around where I was looking and I didn't tell her that there went Abraham Tatum with his curiosity and his smile that I didn't believe was too well meant.

We walked down the line past the tents, Seven and Letty and I in the lead, then the Darlings, Barabbas pacing very close to Seven's right calf.

When we got to the tents we all caught a glimpse inside one whose flap was up; there was an elephant in there, and people were crowding to see it. It looked a tired elephant, the flick of a glance I got. I'd seen one before. The Darlings all looked at each other as if they'd witnessed, in a flash, the Behemoth of the Bible; they couldn't help it. I felt an urge to pay some coin and lead them in for a look, but we couldn't waste time if we were going to geꞇ to the whiskey cups in time. I promised myself that after the shooting, which I didn't expect they had a chance in hell of winning, we'd have a little educational inspiration with the elephant.

The elephant was part—the main part—of a small circus which also took in the thimblerig artists and, farther along, a man who was yelling that he was about to swallow a sword. Against the background of the pumpkins and the prize pies and the cakes—they looked like twenty-five-egger cakes—over in the booths, all this seemed blasphemous and from another earth, as though the torches painted it in the tones of hell. I felt the cash in my pocket—I'd taken it off the mantel, the surplus from the twelve thousand all safe in the box—gripping it like a yokel; but then, I figured, I might be right to do so, for you could never tell if there mightn't be pickpockets connected with the meaching circus.

Some of the onlookers were Quakers, some of them wearing the dark garb; they didn't go very near the circus and its attractions, but stuck close to the food and cider and such.

After a bit we all arrived at the whiskey-cup place. Were a couple of men, cheekbones scarlet in the light of the nearby torches, taking admission money. Cost two bits to enter. I stepped forward a bit apart from my group. "Two bits, Mister," says the money-taker, and "Thanky!" He looks me over. I couldn't recall seeing him before, but then I couldn't tell. I'd already had a couple of the farmers—Apfelhizer, Bull, one or two others who'd been our customers—wave to me and say hello. I reaches around to usher David and the rest of the Darlings forward, and the man—he had a speckle of blue dots over his cheekbones, I figured he'd been buckshotted sometime in his life—says, "Now, there. That's an Indian boy."

"That's right," I points out. Had my hand on David's shoulder. "He'll be shooting, and that's his entrance fee. Him and his brothers work for me and he's a good man. They all are."

"Don't make a damn," the man says, and the other man, red-haired and taller, whispers in his ear.

"Oh," says the first man, turning back to me. "You're from the mill? You're—what's the name?"

Felt myself keeping down my mad, and my alarm, in equal quantities.

"Luke Applegate." Just behind me, Letty stood haughty as a princess.

"Well, Mister Applegate, I think with you being a responsible fellow and all, and doing a good deal for the whole community, what with opening up the old Carroll place—"

"—don't have to give us a speech," says somebody else, rolling up. Then I recognized the round-faced white-haired Claron Prescott, the county clerk. "Mister Applegate's a landowner, he can have anybody step in and shoot for him, under the rules."

He grins to me, and I to him.

I couldn't see that Abraham Tatum anywhere now; or that tall self-important fellow with him, in those rich duds. I steps back, thanking both the money-takers kindly, and doing the same to Claron Prescott, and I pushed David forward. Seven leans on the near fence, Barabbas standing so close to him his head seems part of Seven's leg.

There's a whole slew of men ready to shoot for the cups, now.

Down at the end of the strip of shadowed grasses between the side fences the cups, four of them, show up pale gray and clay-dull on the end fence. It's a good distance down there and, thinks I, Seven could do it, and I might, with a decent weapon, but the Darlings don't have the chance of a lightning bug in a bonfire.

You've got to hit all four cups in one round of four shots, or go back and pay again and try again.

Men started stepping up to shoot. Watching them take their time, steadying their pieces and drawing them slow, then squeezing off, I put them down for fine shots, but not one hit a cup. They eased back into line, except for one who walked off and laughed that he'd never be able to hit a cup. The rifle everybody was shooting for was a fine new Winchester, standing on a box and propped up by a broom handle sticking up through the trigger guard; looked new and gave off a smell of newness when you stepped near it. People were lining the fences on both sides and a lot were clustered around at this end.

More shots went, spanging off into the darkness past the torches at the whiskey-cup end, and you could hear them ricochet off into the town bushes down there. Then a lanky man taking his time, trying, I supposed, to wall out all the chuckling noise around him, hit a cup—the clay of it went flying and he throws his rifle in the air and catches it and says, "I done it! Done it!" But it was just one cup; the rest of his shots—close but not close enough—winging to dark.

He goes back to join the line again, paying his two bits for another chance. Somebody ran down to the end fence and put up a fresh whiskey cup. This brings up David.

He was wearing a shirt tonight, I was surprised he had one, but I expected he'd bought it in Solomon out of what I'd paid him that afternoon. I'd divvied fair and square among the boys and Seven and myself. That that had been left over, and was in my pocket, was all Letty's and mine. As I've said, the Darlings took turns going down to see their mother and see their stock was all right, and sometimes they would buy things for themselves. Even so, it was an old shirt, loose and bagged like his brothers'.

He holds that terrible rifle like it's a golden cannon.

Somebody laughs, just a nickering, and it makes me want to yell out, "Shut up now!" but I grips my teeth hard and don't say a syllable. Letty has her hand in mine, and she squeezes hard.

David takes aim, even slower than the men who'd preceded him, and then squeezes off as if he's just touching something so fateful it can make repercussions forever in this town and in the night and in the ends of the aching earth.

As he does so he's holding the rifle so light-fingered it looks as though it's going to fly away like a laughing bird.

Funniest way I ever saw to handle a piece.

The cup on the right explodes, fair and square. The people around rustle and laugh and a man slaps his knee and says, "Fluke!"

Jase steps up and confers, just a few words, with David. They reload together, and I'm marveling that the rifle ever held together the first time, let alone through all the others they must've used it and through all those practices.

Paul and Peter move over and *they* confer with David.

Then David is reloaded, and the other boys step back, and he lifts the rifle, and this time it's as if he's holding it much too high; as if the barrel will spew out something that'll strike a star.

But still, nobody's so amused now. He takes all the loving time in creation, and it's all I can do not to shut my eyes and kind of pray the whole shebang won't go to smithereens, killing innocent women and children and animals. Angle he's holding it at it could have wiped out a multitude if it'd blown up.

He shoots.

Second cup goes away as if somebody's dragged it down from the end rail so fast you couldn't even make out the motion of the hand, with a *sping* like stones busting.

A whoop and a halloo from the crowd. Lady in a pokebonnet near me, with more stumps than good teeth, cheers as though she's going to throw her basketful of yard goods at the heavens.

Then just a flat silence from this whole part and pocket of the fair, and in it, David and Jase and Peter and Paul all reloading together. Could hear David's feet on the bare ground as he walked back to take position. He shifts, muscles moving in his legs. You can hear the grass grow. He shoots. Third cup that was there just isn't there, and shards of it seem to float in the air before they come down, appearing for a second against the moon.

And Jase and Paul and Peter pulls forward again, to have another fearsome conference with David.

They steps back, after a time of talking low, and David's by himself again—I know how he feels; I've so often felt that way, out in the beyond with no one at your flank and nothing to help you but the strength of your hand. In a way, I think strong, he's got a gift good as mine. Because if he can handle that horrible instrument this way, what could he do with a true one?

He's holding it *low,* now. Looks, I swear, as if it'll shoot under the railing by at least a yard. I look around at Seven. Seven's not watching anything but David, and Seven's lids are half-hooded.

The trigger is squeezed. The last cup vanishes with a clicking of clay shards.

Then there's such a noise you hardly ever heard. And the man who didn't want to take my money for an Indian, at the first, is smiling and nodding and getting the new rifle, and bringing it over to David. And Letty and I and Seven are with the Darlings, and Letty leans forward and kisses David.

David isn't smiling. Takes the new rifle, in this ring of people, and smooths it with his fingertips; then gives the old one to Jase, who cossets it firm in his arms; he's the owner now.

Rules being, the first man to get all the cups in a row gets the prize. I kept looking for some sign of glee on David's face but there was nothing, not even wonder. He knew all the while he'd win it.

He looks up at me, and then holding the new rifle careful as rare glass with his free hand, reaches with the other into a pocket of the shirt and brings up the two bits I'd paid for the entry fee.

"Thanks," he murmurs. "Want to pay you back for your favor."

I nods, and pockets the money. With a rush I'm glad all through that the Darlings and I, and I think Letty too, and sure enough Seven, all feel the same way about staying free.

On the crest of all that, like a wave, we all went to see the elephant. This time I did insist it was my treat. It was in a mashed-grass place under the tent, which was none too new and didn't look to me as though it would have stood up in a moderate hailstorm, but folks were very reverent around that beast. It looked pretty old and weary-eyed, but intelligent, as they all are. After a time I whispers to Seven, "Keep an eye on them," meaning the Darling brothers, and he nods, knowing what I mean is keep them quiet and together, not that I think they'll move off now. I'd just remembered a notion I'd had earlier about buying myself a broad-brim hat. I takes Letty by the hand and moves off, looking back with the flicker of a glance at the Darlings, who are staring sober as young judges at the elephant, and at Seven, who is standing just behind them in the crowd, with Barabbas. Maybe Barabbas has never sighted an elephant before, either, but if so, he's not about to show any dog-ignorance.

We cut across the grasses in the torch-flashing night. Up above the stars are so clear it's like they're signals of good to come. That winey late autumn feeling, all the juices it puts in the veins. "Too elephant fusty in there," I says as we head for the general store.

Her hair is painted bright by the torchlight and she looks rosy as a young child. We go into Jason Felton's, and he's behind the counter. Nods to me as though he's known me forever. I look over a stack of hats and find the one's just right, that'll keep the flame of the sun off for years to come. Letty tries on a couple of bonnets, and finally gets one sprigged with pink and almost the color of her rose-burgundy gown. She goes to the storefront to try it on in a mirror there next to the window, and people are passing by, some of them turning their heads to see her cock her own head in the mirror. I come up behind her, wearing the palm hat. We're both looking into the mirror which also shows us people in the street.

She says, "Like it, or is it too dauncy?"

"I like it," I said.

Then she went straight as a poker. I followed her eyes around to the street. Outside are standing men, their eyes plastered, so to speak, to the glass. One is Abraham Tatum, the Mullin's Gap innkeep. The other is the tall, double-chinned, bright-vested, hammerclaw-coated importance-fuming man I've seen with him before. Another, and my heart turns over like a deep-diving fish when I see him, is Rafe

Gondy. Has the same fouled boots on, same hat half-hiding his cragged face, same bent big nose.

And behind him is yet another man who I can't tell is law or not. But looking the same way all the rest were, as if they were about to crash in through the glass and ruin the gilt name of Jason Felton painted there.

Then they all wheeled and started for the door of the store.

Letty and I had no more than time to turn about, when they were facing us.

Thirteen

I GOT A STERN GRIP on myself. I remembered how, in many times past in my wandering ankle-loose life, when people would start clamping down on me—and it happens a lot, you can't help getting tied into people's foolishness, even though you wish to be cool and icy-apart from it—the best thing to do would be to stay calm. It's a hard trick but useful.

In those few seconds I put my mind to the Darlings. I was responsible for them now. And for Seven, and Barabbas. And of course for Letty. I reasoned how David had just kept calm and taken those shots at the cups as though he was by himself, on a cloud, being so purely himself he shot the way he'd always known he could.

All these thoughts, or resolutions, went through me in less time than a few ticks of a grandfather clock.

Abraham Tatum and Rafe Gondy and the little bead-eyed excited man with them sort of stepped back to make room for the powerful-gutted man in the fancy clothes. He had a face smooth as a flitch of bacon, kind of yellow under the fat, but groomed like a prize shoat's. Big, loose-hung mouth a bit like Gondy's, but not tobacco-stained.

Beside me Letty straightened so quick the hat she'd been trying on nearly fell off. One of her hands went up to steady it.

She says in the top of her throat, "Wayde M-Mitchell!"

So, I thought, struggling to keep the same calm; this is the friend of her daddy's. The Daniel Webster aspiring one.

The one who probably knew all about old Einsner's finances and maybe knew as well about the money Letty's ma had left her in supposed secret.

And the one wanted to get married to Letty.

Just as easy as putting a hand under a hen, Mitchell rears back his head, which gives an extra cant to his well-fed stomach as well, and says, "My—little—girl!"

Then tears fairly shoot from his eyes, and before she can move he has his arms around her, and is sobbing like a whole waterfall. He could have, any time of his life, entered a crying contest and won the golden teacup. He turned it on so easy it made your nose wrinkle. It made my gut freeze.

He nuzzled his chin on her shoulder, and shook her back and forth—this time the hat did fall off—and his voice is a jug of liquid sloshing back and forth, and he said, "Lost, lost and now found! Oh, the miracle of life, the losing and the finding! Ah, the nights of heartsickness, the staring into the dark for a sign! The prayers!" He went straight on in this same vein, holding her close and juggling her as if she happened to be a feather bolster. His hands were fat, with two or three rings that looked ponderous. I saw Jason Felton, the store man, standing to one side as if he didn't quite know what to do but wring his hands. But the little man with Abraham Tatum and Rafe Gondy was sidling close to me and giving me a shrewd look on fire with interest.

I straightened up a trifle, as if I had nothing to do with all this loud blubbering going on at my shoulder, and says to Felton, "How much for the two hats, hers and mine?"

He stuttered a bit—it didn't seem to him a time to be buying hats, what with this reunion going on, and all, and then figured up the price.

I gave him a bill to cover it and waited for my change. While he was bringing it back this Mitchell reared back again and, hanging on to Letty as though she was the key to the pearly gates, bellowed out, straight to my face so I could feel his cow's breath surrounding me, ". . . and this is the young man who's rescued you! This is the marvelous painter of whom I was told by the employees of my departed friend!"

Which means, I thought, you talked to the Einsner hired men. Who wouldn't know a painting from a sour apple, even if they tasted both.

Kept wondering why the merry hell he didn't just turn to the small law-looking man and ask for me to be arrested. Under all this blustery, bawling surface he was smart, there was a lot going on there the uppermost words didn't say. All I could do was wait.

"Sir—" He swung to me now, thrust out a hand that seemed it would be a pulpy job to squeeze, "Sir, I give you my heart and hand!"

I took the hand, couldn't see the heart. I wanted to plain blurt out that I sure hadn't rescued Letty; the way Mitchell talked you'd think some gang had killed her father and tried to capture her. A little flash way back in Mitchell's eyes kept telling me he wanted things to appear this way, so I stayed shut. After he'd pumped my hand a bit he said, "We must all adjourn to the inn for a talk, now. These gentlemen with me"—he swung a hand to take in Tatum, Gondy, and the small man who was starting to appear to me, more and more, connected with the law—"are laboring under natural misapprehensions. They believe you and Letitia might have done foul play! Of course this is ridiculous. I am Miss Einsner's counselor and friend—ah, Letty, the roses in your cheeks, the wonder of finding you . . ." He swung to me again. "Sir, I shall take on your defense, and vouch for your appearance in court, and get to the truth of the matter, post haste. I know in my heart you are innocent."

I noted he kept hold of Letty. Now, as if his left hand had a life of its own, he was running it up and down Letty's right arm. As if he might be guessing her weight.

"And," he booms on, "there is no doubt whatsoever about

Miss Einsner's innocence. How could she, raised in fear of the Lord, by a father whom even now I cannot think of without a shudder of horror at the method of his going, and a need to see his slayer hanged higher than Haman and justice done— how can or could this blossom of purity have had aught to do with his death?"

The blossom of purity gave me a look just past Mitchell's obscuring shoulder. Her face under the gold tan and pink was a shade white but she was bearing it all well.

Mitchell goes on, "We will find the truth in calm, in amity, in love, in peace, and in earnest."

Jason Felton had come back and he gave me my change from the hats. I put it in a side pocket.

I says to Mitchell, "Mister, I'll tell you the truth and so will Letty. Right now I'd like to know whether or not I'm in any sort of custody, or she is either."

"Moot point," says the little man standing with Tatum and Gondy. It's the first time he's chirped, or had a chance to stick a word in. He had mean eyes and a tired hump to his back as though he'd been around jails a long while. He put a finger alongside his nose. "Lawyer Mitchell vouches for you both. He's been on your trail for some time now. Kept everything out of the papers, did his own seeking out—has his own way of doing things, and since he's an important body, and has high-up friends, we respect his wishes."

Things were coming clearer. Let's see, I thought fast as light: Mitchell wants Letty and the money both. And he'll want me out of the way fast as he can do it. He sure can't think Letty and I've been living like brother and sister, he sure must hate my guts down to the last red rag, but he's got to make things look this way on the surface until he can pin everything on me, and leave the coast clear for him to take Letty.

I realized, in the flash, that Mitchell didn't give a green damn even if both Letty and I had murdered Einsner; all he cared was for how affairs were going to look, how he could make them look. But right now I still had to go slow and keep froze as far as any outward signs went. So I went on, jingling change in my pocket, "Then as I see it we're not yet in irons. But all the same we have to go along with you. That it?"

Mitchell nods, slow. The little sheriffy man nods.

Mitchell says, "Mister Applegate—" I noted that when he called me that, he cocked his head a trifle, as though to see if I might deny owning the name. I didn't. "—Mister Applegate, you must accept me as your counselor and good friend, as I am Miss Einsner's."

I didn't have any large choice so I could see. I didn't say anything.

"Then we will repair to the inn and hold a conference."

I says, "Where's the inn you want to have this conference in, Mister Mitchell?"

"At Mullin's Gap. I have headquartered there."

Jesus, I thought; he's followed us all this time. Getting in touch with Tatum, at the inn; with Gondy, through the livery stable. He's got high stakes.

"So," he says now—he still had hold of Letty and it made my belly curl to see it—"let us hasten. Sheriff Wheelman"—he jerked a thumb to the little man—"has his duty to do. He is bound to view the whole proceeding in a less understanding light than I. He has not known Letitia from the time she was a fair-eyed, darling babe, has not watched her grow in sun and rain and love of the Lord . . . does not realize, as I do, that her soul is a flawless pearl."

I couldn't help it. I said, "And you don't know my soul's exactly a flawless pearl, either, do you, Mister Mitchell?"

Was a pause you could have hung a midget in.

"I have faith, my boy. I am certain that in some manner as yet unknown to me you had the decency to save Letitia from the killers of my dear friend—Carl Einsner, agrarian prince—and to spirit her out of harm's way. Perhaps they intended to kidnap her, perhaps they intended—" He shook his head. "But this is no place to discuss it. Come along, now."

He had my story all set. What a mass of oil he must have spread around in the months he'd been following us.

And I didn't have any choice. Felt everything was crashing

in, that my ribs themselves were cracking, but I know I didn't
look that way. All I could do was take Letty's arm, sort of jerk-
ing it away from Mitchell's hand. She snuggled her arm in
mine then as though I happened to be the one rock she could
hold to.

Wasn't any chance to talk to her now. I hoped there would
be. We'd have to keep our stories straight. Abraham Tatum
slid his slimsy eyes to me. Gondy sidled a bit closer. His breath
was heavy. Same whiskey, I supposed. I remembered how
he'd looked ghost-struck the first time I saw him back on that
road over the creek in the night.

I thought of that night in his wagon, me drowning myself in
Letty, her drowning herself in me in turn. But there're lots of
ways of drowning.

Outside in this night touched with its jolly flares I could see
people going by.

Mitchell handed me a card. Felt cool to my fingers, with real
engraving. On the front it said, Wayde Mitchell, Counselor at
Law, Family and Estate Representative. I turned it over. On
the back it said in blue ink: Wills Drawn and Probated.

He said, "Trust in me, my boy." Again that flash in the wet
eyes, meaning a lot more than the tears.

I slid the card in my pocket with Letty's and my supply of
cash, and pressed Letty's arm harder.

Rafe Gondy said, "Hear you tuk over the Carroll Mill, son."

"That's right," I said.

He licked his eyes at Letty. "Sure fell in a bucket of honey,
didn't you, Mister Applegate?"

"If you call honey running a mill and busting your ass for it
and priding in it," I said.

I wondered if maybe Mitchell had his eye on the mill too, as
well as Letty and her inheritance and the hidden money he
might or might not know about. Expected he did, expected he
wasn't a man who would ever miss a thing, down to the last
sop of molasses.

Sheriff Wheelman, in his dark clothes and with his
squinched look, wiped his nose with the back of a hand. "Well,
let's git on."

"Indeed, Sheriff Wheelman, indeed we will," says Mitchell. "Come," he says, including me, and Letty, and Abraham Tatum, and Gondy, and Wheelman, and everybody in fact but Jason Felton the store man. "Come, we'll move along to the next village, and talk it all out, if it takes the night through." One of his pudgy soft-coated arms curled around Letty's shoulders and drew her to him, though I kept hold of her arm and she kept hold of mine. "Ah, my child, little Letitia. So flowerlike, so dazed by the evil of circumstance . . ."

She looked about as dazed as a whalebone rod. Rattled, maybe, but also holding herself ready, as I was.

We started out of the store. Sheriff Wheelman slouched close to me. Right back of him were Gondy and Tatum. I says to Mitchell, "Mister Mitchell, I've got some people depending on me. Outside Letty. They're along here and I'd like to have a word with them before I go off."

Behind me, Sheriff Wheelman says sharp, "You can't—!"

And then Mitchell whirls all the way around and holds out a hand, like Moses commanding the sea. "Wheelman," he says, cold as a bullet. I can see then where the real Wayde Mitchell stands, and how he'll be when it's his own coonskin cap he's protecting.

Then the oil came back. It spread like a yellow hot sun over the big face. Face as pear-shaped as the tones.

"Of course, Sheriff, the lad may speak with his colleagues. Let him talk to them. But you must go with him, in performance of your duty."

I figured he was paying Wheelman pretty well, and that Wheelman was the kind of small-town priceable sheriff who'd keep getting all he could. Figured Gondy and maybe even Tatum to be on this payroll, too.

Sheriff Wheelman dogged my steps even closer then. When we'd all walked a short way out into the bracing night—oh, I wanted to be back within sound of the mill, with Letty somewhere close by and the air smelling of brightness as though the stars themselves made the scent—we got to the elephant tent. The thimblerig men were still at it, shifting their walnut shells on their tables, but the crowds around them had thinned. Down the way the sword-swallower was starting another performance. Mitchell and Gondy and Tatum—Mitchell still hugging Letty to him, which made me want to shut my eyes and turn to stone—stayed outside the tent.

I went in with Sheriff Wheelman hugging my shadow.

Seven turned around before I reached him. At his flank, Barabbas bared his teeth at Wheelman. Didn't growl, just showed his teeth like ivory and diamonds unsheathing.

Sheriff Wheelman stayed right behind me, out of bite-range.

I could feel Wheelman's ears cocked like nets to catch the breeze.

The Darlings were still inspecting the elephant. The elephant stood tethered to its stake, sometimes shifting from one foot to another, just as patient as a mountain wanting to sleep.

David held his rifle close. Jase held the crazy old rifle, and Peter and Paul stood close-bunched to their brothers. None of them really saw me, they were still drinking in the elephant. Yet I had the notion that all I had to do, now, was call out the word, fast, that I was in trouble, and lightning would have struck in that tent.

But I couldn't do it, not with Letty out there in the hands of that powerful sobber and planner.

Keeping my eyes on Jase's hat with its feather standing up stiff and cocked, hardly even looking at Seven, I said, "Seven, I got to go with Letty over to Mullin's Gap. Seems there's been some sort of ruckus. If I don't get back in an hour or two you'll be so kind as to take the boys home and see to things around the mill. We'll try to be back soon, but I don't know."

He could tell from the way I didn't look at him that something was far out of kilter. He had noted Wheelman with me, too.

I turned my eyes full on his, finally. Didn't want him to see anything like desperation or blind hoping in them. I wanted all to go well at the mill. He was awfully old.

"Just keep things moving," I says. "And no need to alarm the boys."

If they hadn't been so intent on studying the very secrets of elephanthood I expect they would have looked around and seen me, and I even expect they would have guessed something about what was wrong, and started to inquire, and then to act. They weren't ones for useless words—you hardly ever hear of an Indian orator—but they could sure read eyes. So could Seven, but he kept his counsel and I could feel him looking after me when we'd turned around again; I would have liked to say something great to him, but no great speeches came to me then. When I went out through the tent flap again, Wheelman shadowing me, the back of my throat was dry and I was starting to shake somewhere deep inside.

I kept recalling, as I hadn't for quite a time of nights, that body of Einsner lying there cooling. We walked up to the bunch waiting, and I saw Mitchell look toward Wheelman as if to read whether anything I'd said was revealing, so I knew then—I'd already known in many ways, but this just seemed to cinch it—on whose side Mitchell was. His own. I doubted that he'd ever been on anybody else's since the day he came out of the womb and started crying.

I walked close to Letty, and with the hand she had free—the other was all touseled up in one of Mitchell's swampy fists, he was still holding her half to his bosom, so to speak, which made for hard walking—she gave my hand a strong hard grip. Keep gripping, Letty, I thought; something tells me you're going to need all the iron you got. We came to a big barouche sort of buggy, with fine black horses and a black boy, no older than Paul, the youngest Darling, waiting by the horses' heads. Tatum and Gondy and Wheelman waited till we got up in back, then got up with the little driver. The springs creaked and the horses started off good with the black child moving them, and above and around, the night was clear as a bell. A funeral bell, thinks I: not one for a wedding.

Fourteen

I SUPPOSE IF YOU'D JUST MET, or been exposed to, Wayde Mitchell in a casual way, and if you were an innocent person impressed by the salve of his voice, and listened, so, with your ears more than with your sensibilities, you'd have swallowed all he said whole. At least I could vision a lot of farm people and drummers doing it. I know Daniel Webster, when he lived, had been an *honest* man, dulcet-toned and blustering by turns, but meaning right at the core; yet it's always seemed to me there's a tendency for people to listen to the organ music, and not the sense, of a man like that. So if he's a bad man he can get away with anything at all.

I was most of the way damned sure I had him pegged as we spanked behind those good horses through the dark-bright night—the fields were flushed with moonlight and all the trees, those with leaves still on them, stood carved like bronze in the light, and the shadows were deep beneath them and projecting like lakes of black from the hills—I was sure I had him pegged in my feeling, if not yet entirely in my mind. Came to me I could be wrong; might turn out, I kept telling myself with a flickering of hope, that my *feeling* was wrong, and all he meant was well. But every nerve in me said the opposite, and I kept sliding my eyes to Letty, who just listened to Mitchell spout, and who didn't say a word herself. Now and then she did catch my eye again, and there was a power of trying to communicate in those glances.

I wondered, Had Mitchell killed Einsner himself? Even if Letty'd said he wasn't that kind, but might've had it done and then pretended, even to himself, that he hadn't—well, Letty was the kind of strong person likely to underestimate what a creature could really do. She knew him too well, you could say, to know him. He was the sort of slitherer you couldn't just put in a hole in your mind and say, This is what he is.

If you play checkers with such a man he'll wait till your back is turned and change the board in his favor. Then when you tell him he did it he'll deny it so hard you'll start believing he didn't, and that your eyes must be going bad. Because, you see, such a man—and there are women the same—can convince himself he *is* innocent. There are a million kinds of evil, but that's the hardest to combat, because it doesn't even know what it is. It was birthed without being able to see itself. It's hard as Vermont granite and soft on the outside as Michigan sand, and it didn't step on the earth just yesterday.

All this I felt dark in my middle. I watched the back of Rafe Gondy's dirty neck, what I could see under the hat's shadow, and the stiffening of Tatum's shoulders, and the stooped, bloodhound-packed readiness of Sheriff Wheelman's, and they spoke louder than all the words Mitchell was spilling.

The black boy, name of Andrew, was a smart driver. We scudded into Mullin's Gap in no time at all. Once, as we slowed, I had the crazy idea of vaulting right out of this conveyance and running across the road to the trees, but I'd seen glimpses of the pistol Wheelman was carrying under his belt, and I didn't know how his marksmanship would stand up, but didn't actually want to test it.

Mitchell was patting Letty's hand. Telling her about the grand funeral he'd given his murdered friend. Describing how it was well attended and how he'd given the oration himself. I'd bet he had. I'd bet there hadn't been a dry eye or an unwrung handkerchief in the place. I'd bet he did well at Fourth of July orations, too, and that when he gave the blessing at mealtimes it went on while the warmest mashed potatoes got cold.

He told her, too, that in the interval before she'd been found—he was rubbing her hand brisk, now—he'd watched over her affairs with honor, stability, and care, and that the farm was in good condition and he had kept the hired men on and was paying for all that himself, pending, as he said, the settlement of the estate.

Her name would never be sullied, he said, or smirched by appearing in any newsprint in connection with this horrible crime.

He talked like I was her honored defender, some kind of watchdog which had stood by and kept her from unknown dangers in all the time she'd been missing. I wondered if he really thought we'd been playing patty-cake all the while.

Here came the Gap; the tawdry blistered-paint inn and the circle with the town pump, and the saloon standing across the road. Weren't any people on the porch of the inn; for one thing, the night was growing sharper, and for another, most would have gone over to Solomon for the fair. Only an old man crossing the road from the pump looked our way, then stopped for a better gaze. The gander-goose wasn't anywhere in sight. The three men in front got out first, kind of fast and watchful—and then I got down and Sheriff Wheelman stood close to me. Then Letty, with Mitchell handing her down as though she was made of rare porcelain.

He put an arm around her again as soon as she'd lighted, and I wanted to tell him she was a strong body, didn't need his steady attention, but I swallowed that too. We went in and all climbed the stairs, except for the driving-boy, Andrew, who stayed down on the lower floor looking up after us. We came to a room near the head of the stairs, not the same one Letty and I'd slept that single hour in, on a morning seeming a huge stretch of time ago; this room was bigger and had some gold and red brocade curtains that had seen plenty of moth in their existence. I kept recalling how I'd been so put out with Letty for having got me into this, even maybe having killed her pa, that we'd slept in the nearby room without touching each other; I could nearly tell from looking at her green light-shining eyes that she was thinking of that.

Sheriff Wheelman, Gondy, and Abraham Tatum gathered in the doorway of the room. Wheelman was in front of the other two.

Mitchell turns and motions to them. "Now you can step out, gentlemen. This must be between my young friends and myself." He motions again, harder and meaning it strong to Sheriff Wheelman, who blinks and backs up. I had the notion Wheelman's salary was going to rise again, on the Mitchell roster. Start paying people to keep hushed and you can go on forever. I could feel the message between the sheriff and Mitchell with my nerve-ends. I sat down in the window seat, hands on my knees, waiting. After a bit Letty joined me. Lawyer Wayde Mitchell lifted the tails of his hammerclaw coat, neat, and took a chair opposite us and close. "Be comfortable, be at ease and fearless," he says to us as though he had just laid us, like eggs. "Now we are united and the terrors of speculation are over and done. The voice of justice will sound in the land, for the Lord has seen fit to bring us together."

"Seems you've had a lot to do with it too," I says.

"I am but an instrument. Jehovah is my keeper."

"In the long run, mine too, and Letty's," I said. I wanted to take her hand again but couldn't seem to, time being, with him sitting there fond-glaring at us. He was a pillow sack full of intestines under the fawn coat and flowered vest, the flowers little forget-me-nots.

I said, "Mister Mitchell, where in hell's name do we stand, and what's all this about some gang of robbers or such having murdered Mister Einsner?"

He shut his eyes. Seemed to quiver, as he might do just before presenting a summary of a case to a leaning-forward jury. While he was sitting that way, a Poland china hog about to rise from massive thought, I heard a board creak in the hall. It was real close to the door. Those were old boards. The gold and scarlet curtains behind me hung a smitch open and I looked around that way. I saw Tatum standing down just off the porch, in the moonlight, looking up at this window. And the two others would be guarding us as well. When I turned back Mitchell had popped his eyes open again and was smiling all over. Professor Allan had a little figure he called a Buddha, made of china, and it was like that, except that Mitchell was harder to take in all at once.

"I'll ask your indulgence, Mister Applegate, while I hold forth."

"You got it," I said.

"First of all, when I say we are united, I also mean we must remain so, presenting a solid face to the world. For, alas, it is a skeptical world, and the circumstances of your flight are highly suspicious. I reason—ah, we must apply reason above all, and you must keep my reasoning uppermost in your thoughts—that some low felon visited the house the night of July twenty-eighth—Carl was not found until morning—and that, having slain my old friend"—there was a suspicion of moistness again, but not near as much as before—"having foully despatched him, searched the premises and then departed. I reason you, and Letitia, or both of you, discovered the body and fled in pain and horror—the girl, my dear girl, too shocked and benumbed to speak, perhaps, for days, you taking care of her, nursing her . . ." A tear did come out now, and slid down the well-fed cheek and trembled on a jowl.

". . . bringing her back to health and sanity, so to speak, until such time as she was fit to brave the world again."

"Poppycock, Wayde Mitchell," says Letty.

He turned to her as though she'd wounded him sorely, and she said, chin lifted, "You probably think we killed him and then ran off. We didn't, so I'm going to tell you just what happened."

His smallish eyes got bigger, they couldn't have got wetter, and he gave me a look as though to ask if Letty was all right and all there after her ordeal.

I said, "That's right. Tell him, Letty!"

She looked at her fingertips which were held stiff along the knees of the velvet gown. Then she started to talk. In a quick, low and easy voice she told her story the way she'd told it to me, but this time—and it was a gap as big as one in a hedge you could have driven a wagon through—she didn't even mention the plank in her mother's room or the lifting of it or the taking of the money. She just said it had been time she ran off and she favored me for running with.

When she got to that point, Mitchell wasn't smiling, or near-sobbing; he was sitting up straighter and his boar-hog look was deeper fixed. His mouth had pulled down to a small wrinkling in the pudding of his jaws.

He opened his lips to drop in a word, thought better of it, and then his eyes got brighter when she spoke of finding her father dead on the floor in the front room, and of going to get me from the sleeping loft.

He kept shut, though; as she went on, telling about the inn here where we'd stayed, and the mill—but not about us being together as we were, though he could take that for granted in her attitude—he slumped back and only batted his eyes from moment to moment, but when she finished up and laid a hand on mine and said, "And that's it and nothing'll shake it, Wayde," he gave a jerk as if hornets bothered his ears under his loose and puffy locks.

His jaws were working; he started to talk a couple of times, again thought better of it, and finally said to me, "Now, lad, you tell the story. I counsel you to be forthright and plain-spoken."

"You're a fine one to counsel that!" Letty gave a little wriggle that moved her all over. "Seems to me, Wayde Mitchell, all you've been doing is setting up a kind of smoke-cloud in front of us—so I'll be spared. Well, I want Luke spared too!" She tossed her head and the hat bounced. "Go ahead, Luke . . ."

I gave her the ghost of a mouth-corner smile, saying thanks for what she'd said, and told my own story of the night. Same as hers in all respects, and taking her cue to leave out all mention of the twelve thousand she'd put in the bag from its hiding place. And like her, of course, I didn't mention the love-making or the fights or the talking on that night of the rain, or much else beside the mill and my own puzzlement as to why nothing had been noised around in the papers, or otherwise to us, about the murder.

I got done, and he was leaning so far forward it must have pinched that wonderful corporation quite a bit. Breathing deep, too.

"Do you realize what you have told me?"

"The truth," I said.

"Perhaps. But the truth, Applegate"—I noticed he wasn't calling me lad, now, or boy, and was glad of it—"the truth is a strange element, when it reaches a jury it requires illumination, it cries for evidence. As affairs stand, I have myself—in the interests of friendship, protection—created a little legend to account for why you and Letitia disappeared after the crime. I have softened edges, I have spent much time in quashing rumors, I have—"

"You've paid off everybody you can and swung your influence like a mop to clean up after us," I said. "Because you want Letty for yourself and you want the estate and you want—" I'd just about started to say, "what's in a strongbox between a couple of birches," but I pinched it back. I was on my feet. I was ready to curve one from the frayed carpet and lay him low. Yet I guess I still sounded calm enough, didn't hear myself as though I was yelling. "You want those things and you don't give a cuss in Goshen about my hide."

He gazed on up at me. "Applegate, all I know of you is that you have gone to and fro in this land like the prodigal son, selling your little portraits for what the tariff will bear. I have word of you from the Einsner hired men, they say you are remarkably taciturn and moody, close-mouthed. You are to me an unknown, a mystery. Yet because I will cede to Letitia's wishes, I will still undertake your defense. I will try to keep you from hanging."

Now it was out, the whole spillage of it. He'd dropped all the oil and sand and under it was the old granite, and it was showing scarred and ready. "Yes," he says, soft now, not a suspicion of any tears shooting or crawling either, "yes, I'll try to keep them from stretching you with the coarse hemp. God in His wisdom has given me a talent for touching the hearts of

my fellow men, and I can probably get you off with a jail sentence. And . . ." He fishtailed around in the chair, and looked
thoughtful out the window through the curtain-chink. "And I
think Letitia will agree that such a conclusion would be better
than simply turning you over to the authorities now and letting them do what they will. For she thinks well of you—and if
she has a mind to your welfare, I believe she'll think this over
and look upon it with my eyes. If she decides otherwise,
then . . ."

He wheeled back around, body creaking the chair, and he's
looking right at Letty.

Letty's eyes flashed. I swear they gave off a green instant of
lightning. She was up now too, the way I was, the soft velvet
hanging handsome around her and a mite tight at the bosoms,
and I had the feeling, still as mad as I was about Mitchell—
and maybe even madder for that that he'd said about my
"little" portraits—as though they were dried grass I'd tried to
palm off as asafetida—that I'd like to paint her this way sometime too. I knew that like her or love her, I'd never get tired
of seeking her out in her inmost being.

She said, "What's keeping somebody from hanging? What's
that, Wayde Mitchell? Suppose I tell you to go ahead and turn
us both over to some jailer—"

"Then both of you will probably hang."

She stopped. He was looking at her with his little eyes burning like secret lamps and just seeable, pouched in flesh.

"But I doubt you'll do that, my dear. Because you do perhaps think you love him, and you won't see him hang. His fate
hangs on you, really. I'm asking you to let me handle all of
this as I have planned it, to have him taken into custody tonight. I can keep you out of it, I can even be a character
witness for you myself; but as for Applegate, if you want him
to stay alive I advise you to go along with me. It's wonderfully
simple."

No, I thought, it wasn't. But it would work. If she loved me,
it certainly would.

She took a step forward. Then she slapped him. "Melon-
mouth!"

He only sat there.

She took another step, quivering almost all over. Good solid quivering.

"You mean you'll throw him to the wolves! You mean, you—"

"Ah, my dear, my dear." The tears were back. Not only back, but springing. He reached into the tailed coat for a handkerchief, got one up, I could smell its scent, and it was a silken affair, and he dammed at his eye-corners. "How you wound me. At great expense I have handled this, I have kept the minions of the law from performance of their duty, I have—" He buried his eyes in the handkerchief. "No matter, though. You wrong me. All I have ever wished is your good, your—I'd have vouched he was about going to say love, but he held it back—your wonderful, womanly esteem."

Letty was sitting again. I did too, and this time I did take her hand. Was all I could do. I could feel a noose tightening around me. It couldn't be seen with the naked eye but it seemed to rise and loop itself all over me, in webs that covered me. I squeezed Letty's hand hard. She mine. But I wondered in all that no-time instant if I wouldn't be rotting in some jail, forever; and I even wondered, again, if she *had* killed her daddy and if she was, to save her own neck even if she wanted to save mine, holding back that one thing that would save me. I couldn't blame her, but if she was, there was a rift a mile wide between us, and even though she gripped me as though I was the last spar in a hurricane, there was a frozen place that spread and spread.

Went all through me as though I'd never be able to really move again, even though I seemed to be doing it to the eyes of those who looked upon me.

Letty said then, so it almost exploded, "If I was sentenced for Daddy's murder, the farm and everything'd go to the state! That's so, isn't it!"

Mitchell was still sniffing. Took a last sniff, and nodded.

"And you want 'em. You want me, and everything else with me. And you're telling me if I don't play right along with you, you'll see both Luke and me damned and flung to the law together. Right, Wayde?"

Took him longer to nod now; he hated bare facts.

So raw like that, and sounding so bald.

But he did sure enough bob his chins slightly.

Everything was clear and out of the bag now, with a feeling as they say, like veils ripping. I've said he could have fooled some people real easy, but they weren't Letty people. They'd have to be the kind—there are plenty—who entrust their life savings to a gold-brick salesman. Or who buy the kind of lightning rods that wouldn't keep off a summer flickering. Or who trustingly put their hands in a preacher's and vow they'll will him all they've amassed during their lifetimes, including the outbuildings, sheds, and chattels.

I grabbed Letty's elbow. I says, "I'm not guilty, and neither is Letty." Didn't know she wasn't, but now it didn't make a whit.

I leaned deep to him. "We're in your hands. I'll go along and do what you want me to."

"That's for me to say," says Letty.

"No," I said. "You think it is, but it isn't. There's only one way this can go now. If you go with me to the law and we give ourselves up, there's no protection. They'll just have us both for something neither of us did, but this way you'll be kept from jail . . ."

Mitchell was eyeing me strong as a sparrow, a large one, looking at a moth-worm.

". . . and who knows, I might have a chance," I goes on. I was trying to look him straight in the eye, but it was hard. I don't mind spiders. Some people can't stand them but I reason they have their own life and besides they're made beautifully. It's the humans who can spin such complex webs they are amazing, who make me go cold. Now I was keeping my voice as quiet as I figured David Darling might. Or Jase, or any of them. All the time 1 could see, in my imagining, Letty holding him off for a spell, while he did what he could for me, but finally going under to him, the way a blade no matter how sharp will wear away under the working of a whetstone. Could see her married to him, a community pillar—her being the funding for the pillar. And in her older age wondering why she hadn't spoken up and confessed to the killing—if she'd done it. Oh, Jesus God, I thought, why do I have to have these doubts that go on even though I know the rest of her almost as well as a man can know a woman?

All the cards were on his side. I says, level as smooth water, "You got us, we're playing with your deck. What happens now?"

He heaves a plump sigh. I doubt he'd ever missed a meal in his existence. I like food too, but it needs valuing in a different way. "Why, my poor boy—"

"Just Applegate'll do."

"—Mister Applegate—" He's looking at the floor, covered with that threadbare turkey carpet, but the best this inn had. "You'll have to spend the night in, well, incarceration."

"Jail. Why don't you say things, Mitchell?"

"Jail, then. And in the morning I'll start bringing the case together, notifying authorities—"

"But you'll keep Letty out."

"Yes, I can do that. It is no idle promise."

"Certain-sure you never made an idle promise in your life, Mitchell. Now, what happens to Letty in the meantime? You going to smarm around her, tamper with her, what they call try to molest her?"

"Applegate! I'm an elder in the church, I—"

"King David was mighty high up in the sight of God, too, if you want to be biblical."

"He couldn't touch me," says Letty, "with a host of angels on his side to hold me down." She turns and kisses me. Square and fair and clean, her tongue flickering a trifle during it. Then says out to Mitchell, "Where'll I be spending the night?"

"Right here in the inn, my dear, in your own room, with a guard on the door."

"I'll lock it from inside too, 'f you don't mind. And I want to do a lot of talking to you, tonight, Wayde Mitchell. Now, what happens to Luke in the morning?"

"He'll have to be taken, arraigned on suspicion of murder, held in another jail at the county seat, and you, you will be released in my custody . . ."

His brow knitted, like wax cracking, while he thought all that over. Was sure he had it all planned out well, but was just going over it, holding all the strands together, everything working the way he wanted it to so far. I knew if I stayed in this room with him much longer I'd do a true murder.

Plain as a pikestaff I knew it.

Looked out through the curtain-chink again. Thought for a second of crashing out and down. Didn't fancy a broken leg, it was a whole floor down there; Tatum was still standing below.

Watchdogs all around, watchdog master in here with us.

I said, "I'm ready." He gave me one more look, let out a whuffling breath like a fart from the wrong end, nodded, rolled himself up, and went to the door. Sheriff Wheelman almost fell in. Mitchell muttered to him. Wheelman nods, steps to me, and then Mitchell frowns at him, as much as to say, "Not here, not in front of Miss Einsner." So Sheriff Wheelman backs up, and I steps out after him. Looked back at Letty. That face so proud and still, that hickory-nut face with its own joy that'd been so near to me for such a time, that face I was still trying to get down on canvas as it should be, not prettified but whole and shining. I says, "See you soon, I devoutly trust." It was even, part way, as though I was berating her for not telling that she'd killed her father, if she had. All that in that flickering jumping instant. Then I went on out. Wheelman took my hands and lifted them and then here came the handcuffs. Black, iron, and they felt like the world's heaviest. They snicked to, and we went along the hall and downstairs, him snugging sharp to my back.

Fifteen

HALFWAY DOWN THE STAIRS I jerked back a bit and Wheelman almost fell onto me. He had a hand around his pistol butt. He didn't quite poke me in the back with it.

"Where's this jail?"

"Right across the way. Git along."

"How's it feel to be the pet dog of a big bug lawyer?"

"Feels like you better move on 'fore this thing goes off."

It was chilly down below the stairs but I was sweating. That black boy who drove for Mitchell, Andrew, was asleep curled up on the table. Tatum stood out below the inn porch. Weren't many people on the street, though some had come back from the fair and as we crossed the street, Abraham Tatum catching up with us and jogging alongside, we got quite a parcel of attention.

I stopped again. This time the pistol did give me a dig in the aft ribs.

"Cut that out," I says. "I'm not fleeing or attempting to flee." Out here it was cool and the moon was considerably farther down the sky. It yellowed that little dusty street and sent

a curious shine to the roof of the saloon across the way. I
could hear glasses chinking from there, and there was a drunk
sprawled on the low porch. Mitchell's horses and his splendid
rig weren't anywhere to be seen. Turning, I could see through
that curtain-chink up into the room where we'd all had the
palaver, and as I watched, in the instant, I saw Letty's new hat
burning against the light like a little red and pink-budded cabbage. She had her head close to Mitchell's and in the instant
sight I had, she appeared to be taking him by his coat lapels.

Sheriff Wheelman rammed me along. I moved, just about
steered by his pistol-end, up beside the saloon and then
around in back of it; then the noise of the Saturday night
saloon died down and we were crossing a little yard at the end
of which was a small building, not much more than a garden
shed, it looked.

Gondy was sitting under its one window, on the south. He
rose up like a loose thundercloud, all tatters and sprawling,
and Tatum, who'd dogged our steps all the way, says soft,
"You want me to help guard out here too, John?" He says it to
Wheelman.

Sheriff Wheelman scratches his head with his free unpis-
toled hand.

"Hell, you two are sure strong on guarding," he says. "All it
takes is the one. Rafe," he goes on to Gondy, "you stay, and
Abe," to Abraham Tatum, "you git along back to your inn and
see to it that when that young lady repairs to her chamber for
the night, she stays inside it. Unless I say different. These are
both customers slick as slippery elm."

Tatum says, "Been a sight simpler to apprehend if it hadn't
been for Lawyer Mitchell."

What he said irked Wheelman.

"Ain't the point, you fool. He's got his own ways of arrang-
ing things. You, you'd a-strung 'em up to a pine first chance
you got; and you, Rafe, you'd a-done the same." He nods to
Gondy.

Gondy says, "I've already lost a good time of driving, and
I'm a pore man."

I'd heard that mealy mouth before.

Wheelman said, "You're compensated a good deal now, and there's more coming. Better'n you'd make driving for Clamber Trust Lumber in a month Sundays."

Rafe Gondy smiles a shade. I see he's got a jug beside the bench where he's been sitting. Abraham Tatum starts loping back across the yard and around the saloon and across the street to his hotel.

Gondy opens the door of the shed-house. There is a candle burning inside, on a bench. And that's all in the livelong place. The floor is dirt, hard-packed, and it smells of sourness and acid-like soil. Couldn't grow manure in such a place. From the one window, which doesn't have any bars, but which is tight-shut and has two big panes in it which haven't been cleaned since the town got built, I can make out old dandelions growing in a field out in back, their puffing white soft heads looking like the heads of tow-haired tiny children.

Sheriff Wheelman unlocks the handcuffs. Made my wrists lighter.

I have to stoop down to enter. I straightened inside and turned around.

"This what they offer for a jail? This is where I spend the night?"

Wheelman says, "You be thankful you're protected. If these citizens of Mullin's Gap knew about you and that pert-nosed bitch and your killing, they'd stretch your neck like a swan's."

I says, "Maybe if they knew Lawyer Mitchell was figuring out the whole thing for his own ends they'd think about stretching him, and putting you in a jail too."

Wheelman goes a little red, I can see it even in the dim light.

"You'd ought to get on your knees and thank him, Applegate. You know you done it. He's an educated man with high-up friends and you can thank Christ he's handling it."

"From what I hear," I says, "you and Gondy here, and Tatum, can be thankful too. Puts more lining in all your pockets, don't it?"

He kept on glowering, but Rafe Gondy didn't glower. He

says, "The jailhouse is bigger over in Solomon. Where you'll be durin' the trial. It's got chamber pots and all."

"I'm real happy to hear it," I says. "Let's see, that's three of you Mitchell's paying, ain't it?"

Before Wheelman could cut in, Gondy says, "Four, the way I reckon it. There's Soames at the livery stable, he's helped us get a line on you too. See, we knowed some time you was up at the mill, but Lawyer Mitchell, he didn't want no stir-up fight going on with trying to take you up there, what with them wild Indian boys you got and all. But you walked into our hands nice as could be, and no fuss about it."

"Rafe." It was Wheelman. "Just put a bung-starter in your mouth, you idgit!"

I sat down on the bench. I'd noted the door had a good heavy lock and several chains. The shed was thick-walled enough to keep a grizzly from getting out.

The candle was about four inches high, and sputtering. The bench was nothing that was going to be good to the spine for any long time.

Sheriff Wheelman stepped back and shut the door. It crushed shut and then there was the business of shutting up the lock and fixing the chains. I could hear Wheelman giving some last orders to his great deputy Gondy, but I couldn't make out the words. I prized the candle loose from its tallow dripping and lifted it high. This sent my shadow, strange in the palm-leaf hat, wavering and shrugging over the walls and ceiling. Somebody who'd been thrown in here at one time or another had tried to draw a picture of a man hanging, with a black pencil, on the west wall. I reflected that I didn't even have real sketching materials with me, but for a pencil stub I always carried around. If worst came to worst I could do some sketching, though; the walls were old pine and that'll take pencil.

I felt sticky with being in that room with Wayde Mitchell and now so shut up and locked in and icy I wanted to shut my eyes and breathe deep and just hear the mill wheel turning in my dreams.

I sat down, putting the candle back in place. Pretty soon I
saw, through the crusted window, Gondy's shape come
around under the window; he sat down on the bench out
there and leaned back against the window frame, cutting off
all but a little moonlight that fell around him into the shed.

I did shut my eyes. I didn't sleep but I mulled over a pile of
things.

As I've said, it doesn't do any good to let anybody else know
you're not calm at a time like that. Through my squinched-
shut eyelids I could see the yellow-red candle flame and it was
like a kind of sun.

I held on to myself to keep from pounding on the walls. It
was a struggle but after a time I'd made it. Then I must have
gone really asleep, because when I woke up I had the feeling I
was back at the Jerseyville farm and those belly-swagging cats
were cradled all around me, and in front of me, bending low
in the velvet dark and rosy dress, here's Letty.

It was the clanking of the chains and the fooling with the lock
and the opening of the door that had wakened me.

The candle had burned down to an inch. Everything felt
late and small and intimate.

The door's shut.

"Hello, Letty," I says hoarse.

She put a finger on her lips. She sat down beside me. Was
just room for both of us and the candle, on the bench.

She whispers, "Talk soft, Luke."

I didn't think a soul could hear us through these walls, but I
whispers too. "How'd you get here? Who allowed you?"

Her fingers were gripping my arm. "Wayde allowed me.
Knew I could do it, easy as falling off a log. He's mush where
I'm concerned."

I could see her eyes like green-blue lovely grapes with that
bloom of glory around them in their glistening.

"Good God, woman," I says, and it's hard to keep it to a
whisper. "Don't you see he can do what he wants with me?"

"Not while I hold some power," she says. "I made a deal
with him. Remember, Luke, he needs me for his purposes 's

much as I need you and want you. I'll be at the trial and I'll testify for you, and he'll fight to get you off completely—not with just a jail sentence, but off all the way, whole and free."

"And what's the other flank of the deal?" I was hardly able to swallow. Didn't want to hear it, but I had to. "What'd you promise him?"

"I'm coming to that," she said. She touched my neck with her fingers, just the fingertips.

"For your size I expect you can do some tall string-pulling," I says, still dry-throated. "And I guess it's better to do that than to have either my neck broke or be in jail from now till I'm eighty-five. But—"

"Not while I'm around, your neck won't break, Luke." I recalled what she'd said, with all her soul it seemed, the night of the heavy rain, about us having to believe each other. I believed her now all right, but about her being guilty I couldn't tell, any more than she could tell about me. There was always the strength of *wanting* to believe, but then she had that for me, too. We might've been swinging from the stars out in space, here in the wavery light.

She goes on, the smell of her, that grass and flesh and quietness, making me long for her; yet I didn't touch her now. . . .

"Luke, I promised Wayde I'd marry him the day you're free."

It was like being hit on the head with a block of dark wood.

I swallowed all the bile it made come up in my upper belly. I said, still soft, aching soft, "That pussle-gutted soul."

Then I sat real still and tried to figure; I wasn't doing well at it because I was so mad. "I take note you didn't mention the strongbox money."

"Didn't, Luke. But I got a notion some way he knew Mama had it and figures it's someplace."

"And the mill, I expect he's after that—"

"Yes, he mentioned it."

Could feel everything passing like old smoke out of my hands and away in some dim corner, and it made me ache through the held-in iciness.

I says, "Well, I'd rather die." Then I changed that. "No. I'd not rather die. But I'd damned to middling near it. There's times when life, valuable as it is, isn't anything you want to keep just to go on living."

I was a lot louder now. "Couple of things. One, if this has to be, it has to, to keep you from maybe hanging straight along with me. Two, I don't quite see how even the flummery of somebody as good at it as Mitchell can keep his skirts free forever. I mean, suppose we went to a—oh, a judge or somebody, and spilled the whole thing, all about Mitchell's part in shadowing it over and working on our fears, maybe then we could get at least a fair trial."

"It's an awful slim maybe, Luke. At this late stage, with us having run off and stayed so long. I've thought of that too, but I'd say in that case the judge, or whoever, would look on us with mighty skinned eyes. It's easier this way, and anyhow, there's no chance now unless *I'd* go to somebody else . . ."

I shakes my head. "Another point. You, Letty, you think you can handle any man 'cause you're a proud woman. Now, suppose I was to crash out of here some way, what'd you do then?"

"You couldn't think of it. They'd hunt you down like a fox and—"

"Would they, girl? Mitchell's got too much to lose after all he's put in this so far. I bet he'd—well, he'd try to get me back in his own hands, by hook or crook, and maybe he'd put out a reward for me, and maybe it'd have to hit the newspapers and so forth—but don't you see he'd have to keep it kind of in the family, like?" I stared at all I could see of her; I could feel the rest. "And suppose I did get out, well, what'd you do then?"

"I'd still have to squash anything I could—about anybody else knowing about us—and play along with Mitchell. But shoot, I can play Wayde like a fat fish, I said."

"Think so, do you?"

She birded up and bridled a bit. Then she did more. She reared herself up as tall as she could for such a small person who's sitting with her feet drawn under the bench, and I thought, in the flash, how at the first times in our acquaintance she'd only have made me laugh inside, at being so sure of her own power, but how now, for the first time in my own life, I felt green and riddled with jealousy. "He knows I'll not let him touch so much as the hem of my skirt till he's kept his part of the bargain. I got him going and coming, Luke Applegate, and it's the one thing'll set you free."

"You may not be as powerful as you think, Letty," I says, "and all this makes me the pimp of the world, too. You can din-dangle yourself before him till he slavers, and I'll forever live with that over me, like a cloud. Shit! And I suppose you'll go through with it when I'm a free man? Through it with him?"

"Haven't thought that far. Might have to sign everything over to him, and—"

"D'you offer to do that now?"

"Yes, I did, if you must know. But he's wanting *me* too. Not just everything else."

"No matter how you look at it, he's got the aces," I said. "But I might be able to cold-deck him a little, even yet."

She was staring up at me with her whole body leaning up like a red tree. I was off the bench, leaning over her. Her breath came around my face. "Don't you try a thing now, you sit tight, Luke. Mister Applegate! I've got it stitched up, and don't you pull out all the basting!"

I says mostly between my teeth, "All this is like pulling the skin off me, flaying me, goddamn it. I don't want to think about anything more to do with it."

Cold as a gravestone in December, she says, looking up, her hair mist-gold under the bobbing hat, which I recalled she'd scooped back from the floor in the general store after it had fallen off of her when Wayde Mitchell had slobbered over her at first—leave it to a woman to save something pretty—cold as that, she says: "It's all we can do now, however it turns out. It was in the deal I made that I might come here and talk to you one last time by ourselves, too. But now—oh, no, Luke Applegate, you're so set on your own overweening selfishness, you don't even want to save your own neck when the chance is there! Well, you've got to! This time I'm running the show!"

She stands up. I suddenly reached out and scooped her to

me. So hard she'd bear the print of my chest through her tits.

"All right, but it's against every bounden wish I've got. I think the less of you for it and I always will. It'll go on flaming in me till I'm an old man. Now get out. We had some good times but the rest seemed all poison, and I rue the day I promised to paint your portrait, the day I saw Jerseyville and you and your father. Go on, get out!"

I wrestled her over to the door and yelled, "Open up!" After a second Wheelman opened. I pushed Letty out of the door and she stumbled but recovered fast, mad and rosy and spitting like a cat.

She stood out there in the thinnish morning-making moon-light.

Then she straightened and said, low, "Luke, I wouldn't do it for anyone but you, and you know it, and I'm doing it."

All the saloon noise was gone now. The night was frail with its light ground fog. Cold, too.

Sheriff Wheelman slammed the door in my face. Gondy had come around and was standing there as well. The business of the lock and the chains started up.

I sat back down on the bench. Held myself in to keep from blind raging, howling like a dog, trying to set the shed afire. But after a bit I couldn't easily have done that, either, because the candle flame went long and then went out, with a string of stink from its going.

When I figured I could move again without lightning playing out of my nose and ears, I got up and looked out of the window. It was considerably later; now Gondy's shoulders, returned there against the window frame above the field of old dandelions, showed around them the creaminess of first day.

I tapped on a pane.

Cumbersome, Gondy turned around and showed his face. "I'm hungry," I says loud so he can hear it through the dirty panes. "Comfort me with apples, for I am sick of love!" It was something Professor Allan might've said. I meant it.

His nose was like an old hawk's beak.

Fairly squashed against the glass.

"Food," I says, making the motions of eating.

I saw his big hands come up and then he's heaving, and then the window's coming up and open. It came hard.

"Well, Mister *Lester*—" I see he's armed too. His pistol's bulging at his belt. "Now, I don't recollect any orders to bring you food, or even water. I expect in time, they'll keep you enough alive to go through with the worry and wear of a trial, but . . ."

Enjoying himself, he was sure doing that.

I didn't cotton to him any more than when I'd first seen him, full of scaredness.

"You know my name's Applegate. I'll pay for the food." I reached in a pocket and held up a bill.

His lips just about watered, but he shook his shaggy head.

He was being real dutiful and torturing.

"All right, then." I put the money away. "Tell you what I *will* do, if you got a bit of paper around you, I'll draw you a better picture of yourself than you had last time. With more character in it. You got a great deal of character, Mister Gondy."

He thought that over. He was a big loose pulpy man, yet that made it even tougher because he was used to drinking and that kind are hard to figure in a scrap. Breath was rich and teeming.

"And I'll trade it to you for just a mess of greens, anything."

He kept thinking. A slow process. I could see him get drawn into the idea by degrees. "I haven't got no paper," I said, "but you must carry *somethin'*—"

When he brought up a bill of lading from Clamber Trust Lumber, I could see everything was working. It was fairly wrinkled. But steadying it on the half-rotted sill I was able to make a fair likeness; better than the last time, from his standpoint, not so mean and hook-nosed. My pencil shaded in the background, made it look as though sun was rising around him.

While I worked it was getting lighter. Heard a cow bellow not far off. Birds were starting to twitter. I figured they twittered even in Mullin's Gap; birds are forgiving creatures.

I worked with only my hand doing it for me, inside I was so battered and beaten I couldn't afford to have a thought. There's a thin edge where only the body works, the brain doesn't even have much to do with it. But the instinct does.

Then I was through; I pushed the paper to him. He took it as he had last time, and a smile started going up around his slack mouth and he starts saying, "My, my, now that's worth a mess of greens or even poke salad—" And in the same second I was out of the window, all of me.

I swarmed over him square and knocked him over and then we're both rolling in those squashy elderly dandelions and then I'm on top. He's got a deal of weight on me but I hooks him around the belly with my legs and then while he was still scrabbling for the gun in his belt I hauled off and hit him. Did it left-handed, hard as I could in the short space. He'd been in many a brawl, but I connected right enough to make his head go back and the blue-gray balls of his eyes show as his lids went back and he breathed heavy. I rolled myself off him, hearing nothing around me but the birds. Then I was gone down across that little yard fast as I could, and after a bit I saw the furze of young willows ahead of me and came to the creek that went snaking along back of the Gap, thinking, This is probably the end of the millrace where it comes off the mill clearing and goes all the way through Solomon and on down south.

I went along there, feet half sloshing in the cold water, feeling my way but running as hard as I could against the rising sun. I figured I had at least a few breaths in which to take cover before the alarm went up. Gum trees showed ahead, then a stand of maples. I cut off to them and found myself in a field, where sheep had been sleeping all night and now were starting to crop. I cut through them, their cloudy shagged shapes moving aside in a flurry, one or two baa-ing in fear and wonderment as I went. I could feel and see the sun higher; it was about to spread all across the land. After a time I made my way over a fence and up into a good little wood that smelled fresh as Letty, in the early-going light, and then I had to crawl against an oak trunk and take breath.

I found while I gasped there, being as silent as I could about it, that I could think about Letty again without starting to rage like a mad bull. I picked up some cool long grasses from the base of the roots of the oak I was leaning back against, and chewed them for the good taste and the cool they gave my mouth. I thought when she heard about this it would give Miss Letty Einsner a smart surprise.

Sixteen

I GOT TO KNOW that little woods real well. As the light came up
I left my personal oak tree and, going low and stepping light,
moved over to the outer rim of the woods where it hung on a
bluff about twenty feet high above the road. From here,
kneeling my way through the bush grass—everything smelled
of dew, earth, and quiet breathing—I could see out and along
the road. All the way back to Mullin's Gap one way. And a
good distance along to Solomon on the other. I reasoned
they'd found Gondy by now. Or he'd got up and spread the
alarm. How strong an alarm it would be I didn't know.

If when I came up missing, Mitchell would play down the
search for me or set it up in a loud alarm, depended on how
strong Letty's hold on him would be; and how long he could
hold off the real law—I mean the law outside this part of
Pennsylvania, the kind he couldn't control in its operations. I
could fairly guess at how much he had connived back around
Jerseyville to keep affairs as quiet as possible. I was still half
cold-mad at Letty for playing him like a mudcat on a worm—
and on her sweet-shaped line—because in my book, I just
didn't want to have her have anything to do with him.

Thought of her the way I'd last seen her there in the wash of morning-coming moonlight before she'd gone back to the inn. Thought of how just before the jail door had shut she'd said all the truth as she knew it.

Well, she was practical. Letty had a lot deeper practical streak than I did. I admitted it, and felt a mite sorry about getting so mad. Just a mite, so far; figured that sorriness might grow in me.

Didn't feel sorry about Gondy; he wouldn't have brought me turnip green number one; he'd just been playing with me and getting another free drawing of his own self-prized face into the bargain.

I resolved these affairs in my mind. My palm-leaf hat hadn't come off in the quick rolling fight, I'd had it jammed down pretty far. Was going to be glad of that in the day's sun heat. For October it was going to be a sharp-starting but warm Sunday. I wished I had some of Letty's warm-baked bread, a hunk of it in one pocket.

I wished I had a pair of binocular glasses, too. But by squinching my eyes, hard, I could make out the inn and the town pump. And even, now, that goose coming out to walk its beat around the pump. From off in the direction of Solomon came the ringing of church bells, carried on little gusts of wind. There were the stalks of dried daisies around me, and farther back, a stand of mushroom. I debated about testing the mushrooms against my hunger—I was really hungry now, after thinking I'd been fooling Gondy with that tale—but decided I didn't want to be discovered next spring as a skeleton up here in these grasses. Still, I eyed the mushrooms with a near drooling fondness.

In back of me as the woods woke up all the way a bluejay started calling "Thief! Thief!"

Then another one answered. It didn't sound to me as though they meant anybody but me. I lay low and kept peering.

Shortly, out of a side road, there far and tiny in the distance, came the smooth-running rig of Mitchell's, appearing from the mouth of that lane where the livery stable was. So I figured affairs were starting to pop down there. Then against the sun-wash in my eyes I saw it pull up and go out of my sight near the inn. Shortly after that, here it came again, swinging out into this bigger road. I watched until I could make out Andrew the black boy, driving, and Mitchell and Gondy and Wheelman and Tatum and now one other man—I reckoned it would be Soames the livery-stable man—in the barouche affair. They were making good time even though they seemed to snail along in my sight.

In a little, I warped myself back among the tall grass and melted into the cross-hatched shade of the woods again. I heard the rig go down along the road below the bluff. When it was well past and the wheels were making their slurring noise from the west instead of the east, I crawled back to my lookout point and saw it fairly close, drawing away with a boiling of road dust behind it. The other man with the rest was Soames from the livery stable all right.

I plucked some more grasses and frowned, thinking. Didn't seem to be any general hue and cry. So that meant that— probably with the outlay of more of his cash investment in my future, and mainly in his own future—Mitchell was still keeping the hunt generally quiet. In what I'd seen, and heard, the night before, I'd got the impression this didn't sit any too well with Sheriff Wheelman—I'd felt he was uneasy, no doubt frightened for his job if this ever came out, and I wondered how long it could go on. But it was good for my purposes. I doubted if any of those intrepid hunters could find me if I put my mind to it. But a whole body of aroused and alarmed people, scouring the countryside, would have been able to put the wind up me pretty fast. Wherever Letty was—I supposed back at the inn, probably sleeping the sleep of the just, and recalled how nice she looked when she slept—I wished her fairly well. I just didn't want to think of Mitchell too close to her. My own roiled feelings about her still worked in me.

I went back to my tree. Was like a brother to me now. Curling myself near those broad roots, I dropped off to sleep. The jays would wake me if anybody else came up here. I slept

sound and deep and when I woke up the shadows were different. All stretching far and pooling over the fallen leaves
and with small castles of bunched-up color, and seashell-
shapes, dancing among the leaves in the light, ruffling breeze.
I'd been sleeping with the hat over my eyes. I woke up to see a
badger that had been watching me look startled as an old gray
city clerk and turn around and waddle off with portly dignity.

It was a long day. The sun went down so gradually it was as
if it had decided to admire the very day it lighted—to linger
the way a child will linger when it's a perfect day and he
doesn't want to lose a breath of it. The rig of Mitchell's didn't
show a sign of coming back. My left hand, at the knuckles, was
swollen a little where I'd cooled off Gondy. But it would go
down after a time. I found some mint—a little unfresh because of the time of year, but still with some healing in it—and
wrapped it around the bruise. I held it there and studied
about people who knew all about healing, and milling, and
making-do for themselves, such as Seven. From there my
mind slipped to wondering if what he said about having many
lives was true in every man's case. If it was I figured that in his
last incarnation Wayde Mitchell had been a tub of marmalade.

I thought about the Darlings. It had come to me that since
Mitchell's rig had been going in the general direction of Solomon, he might well have pressed on up the side road and the
hill to the mill clearing. In that case the Darlings—God knew
what they could do with two rifles; with three they could have
been Napoleon—might give him and his minions, or myr-
midons as Professor Allan would have said, quite a shock. I
hoped Seven kept them well in hand and didn't allow any
mayhem. I was already too involved in a dead body to suit me;
I'd had enough of that to last a good many lifetimes.

Came the night, so gradually all you could see was the coat
of pearl the sky got and then, through the rags of the pink-
washing sunfall, the first star coming out so easy it might have
been grown just for your own wonderment. I edged out to
above the road again for another look. Nothing on the road.
Far behind me, in that low field the way I'd come, a noise of
sheep.

Far back in my mind, joggled as it was by recent events, was growing a kind of plan. It was as rough and hazy at the edges as a portrait might be if you wanted to take it very solid and slow, just letting it come by degrees of feeling and not pecking at it too much.

It got dark and the sweat that'd collected around me during the warm full day, a day as round and silent as a peach taking the sun on all its curves, started cooling. And the shy wind grew up and talked in the brittle hanging leaves of the oaks. I couldn't see a hair of Mullin's Gap now. The road was getting duller in the rising shadows. There was that smell of time and earth and the joys of evening all about. It's strongest in October, it pinches in and dies away just a bit later. In the fields over on my right I could make out the shocks of wheat and some corn cribs beyond them. The mill would be turning steady right up to winter's tide.

I wished Wayde Mitchell hadn't ever known Letty's father. I wished old man Einsner hadn't ever been killed, whoever did it, and we'd just run off, Letty and I, in freedom and passion.

Wishes weren't horses. At least not my bay horse.

When it got good dark and the moon was up, with only a few clouds floating between it and the earth from time to time, I started on, out of the woods, heading across fields and through other copses, toward the side road that went up to the mill clearing.

Above in the cooling night I heard geese honk. Didn't see them this time. Thought well of them, though. I thought that that flock Letty and I and Seven and Barabbas had seen glinting in the moonlight, not so many nights before, must have been the first of this season. They call creatures who move first harbingers.

I figured as I sneaked along through the dark fields, over the stubble, that I'd be a harbinger now.

Was going to have to be to carry through the plan that was swelling below my ribs and partly in my brain cells.

There was some late traffic on the roads but not enough to bother about. After a time I was going faster. When in the shifting light I got to the side road and started up the hill I went quick and tidy. There were some horse-droppings on the path but they didn't look fresh. I figured if Mitchell and his loyal crew had come this way they were still here. I could smell the pines now, as if they were waves beating around the nostrils in the down-moving night wind. I came up the path side like a ghost, not even, I thought, making as much noise as the Darlings had in that time just before they'd made their proposition to me.

But I'd reckoned without Barabbas. From the edge of the path as I parted the sumac and looked over its ragged bright leaves, I saw him, then he must've seen me, or sensed me, for the wind was away from him. He gave a short bark, just gruff and quick. Then he came racing down. I reached up and touched his grizzled muzzle. He didn't make any more noise. I shifted position and leaned up higher, studying the lay of the land.

From the house where the Darlings lived fell rays of lamplight. Also from the Seven's house. Mitchell's big beautiful rig was in the clearing's center. The horses were trying to get nourishment from the late grasses between the moss beds. Andrew the coachman was standing beside one wheel. I heard the voices of men from down the line near the mill. The sound of the turning wheel, running slow and free in the race, covered what they might be saying. Otherwise in spite of the sometimes-rattling breeze it would have been a still enough night to hear.

I didn't head for them. Stooping low, going from oak to oak and pine to pine, Barabbas pacing me but acting decent and not drawing attention to me, I made for the main house, whose windows were blank and still.

Seventeen

I WENT AROUND the back way. Couldn't hear any of the men's voices now, even a waft of them here. Barabbas stayed outside when I opened the kitchen door and went in. I worked without a light, and fast. In the kitchen I stripped down and washed at the pump, then I spied a wooden vat of Walnut juice that Letty'd been using to dye some of her bolts of cloth. It twinkled dark in the half light through the kitchen windows. Stripped, I got in it and spread it considerably around my body; I hadn't meant to do all this when I'd come in here, I'd just meant to get my canvas and paint sack and be going as fast as possible, though I'd have liked a word with Seven too; but now I thought, If a man's going to travel while he's hunted, he better look different as possible.

Outside the kitchen door I could hear Barabbas panting. He would sit patient and wait; I didn't think he'd draw any attention to me right now unless Mitchell and Wheelman and Gondy and Tatum and Soames came back in here. I could tell, in the part darkness, that they'd been here; a lot of things were misplaced. Letty's pots were misarranged on the walls and somebody had even spilled out part of a sack of flour. I figured they'd already gone over this place as hard as they could, had spent the day doing it.

It just firmed up my judgment that Mitchell knew about the missing money. I splashed the dye over me, heavy on the face especially, and then prowled through the front rooms; in here everything was hunted through and not in its accustomed place, too; but my portraits, all except the first one of Letty, were still on the mantel. I was drying now. The dye felt sticky and gummy but it was glazing. I went up the stairs. More confusion up here. Made me so mad to see those rooms that we'd labored over so hard, interfered with. I got my paint and canvas sack and carried it downstairs. Didn't have any new canvases but I would have to use what I could find while I traveled. I remembered hearing that Raphael painted that round-framed Madonna and the baby on the end of a barrel. I'd often painted on what opportunity offered. It could be just a tidy board that would take the color smooth. In the kitchen again, pretty dried off now, I made a cold lather of lye-soap at the pump in its sink and rubbed it into my face, including the moustache, and shaved it off with my long razor from the paint and canvas sack where I always had kept it. Then, looking at myself in a little mirror garlanded with wooden cupids that Letty had found upstairs in a closet and kept down here, I saw there was an undyed place where the moustache had been. Made me look tolerably naked and strange around the upper lip. So I had to slap on some more Walnut dye there and wait for it to work into the skin.

I spent the time waiting for this to dry by checking, mainly with my fingers, everything that was in the paint and canvas sack. I had some pretty full paint tubes and some handsome brushes. I thought I was dry enough to wear clothes again without them sticking to me and mortifying the flesh, so I dressed in the oldest clothes I had. Left the ones I'd had at the fair on the stone floor. I stuffed the palm-leaf broad-brim hat into the carrying sack. Then I rummaged in the larder. Was some bread there, and I wolfed off four or five chunks of it, chewing fast; then stuffed four loaves down in the paint and canvas sack. I got a piece of jerky from the tin chest where Letty kept it and put that in too. I'd transferred the money I'd taken to the fair—it wasn't a huge amount—to the pockets of the pants I was now wearing. Had a couple of pencil stubs too.

Then I slung on the pack and stepped out of the door. Barabbas glinted his eyes at me and came padding along behind me as I crossed around toward the mill. I went very light-footed now. The clearing was full of shadows and stripes of light. I could hear the men's voices again. I went down, moving soft as I could, clear to the end of the millrace and jumped over the race and got to the birches. Barabbas stayed on the other side but I didn't like the jolly way he was staring across at me; anybody for a breath or so there could have spotted him and seen he was looking at somebody across the creek with eagerness. I knelt down and felt for the strongbox between the birches. It was there, and that's all I'd wanted to know. Mitchell and his men wouldn't find it for a terrible long time, maybe never.

I didn't want any part of it. I just wanted to keep it out of Mitchell's grip.

When I straightened I could see across the murmuring water that Barabbas had paced down a short distance and was sitting, waiting for me to come back. I didn't. I crept along downstream until the noise of the mill was filling my ears, the wheel turning and the water cupping up slow in those great cups and then sluicing down the other side like the grand great wheel of a clock that told time for the world. I lay down on my belly in the skin of old leaves and pine needles on this rim of the millrace and waited for what I could see and do before I departed. I sure wanted conversation with Seven.

I'm lying there, barely able to see out, when Andrew, Mitchell's driving boy, comes there on the other side—giving Barabbas plenty of leeway, not that Barabbas would have touched him—and looks across. I swear he sees me.

There's just a touch of alarm in him. Then I thinks, But he won't know me. And maybe he wouldn't whisper a word to his employer even if he did. Maybe I looked to him like one of the Darlings, though I didn't feel very Indian. For about the beat of two seconds all this took place, and then he turned around and sauntered back, kicking through leaves. I hadn't alarmed him much to speak of, then; he'd figured I went with the place.

Which I sure did.

After a time the men talking across the way, I couldn't see them but I could hear them at their corner of the mill—after a time they broke it up and moved off toward the clearing's center. I could see them go when I stood up again—Mitchell was laying down law about something; the four men with him were following along, and Seven was the one Mitchell was yammering at. It would have been so simple—the way it would have been in the circus tent the night before—for me to jump out of my hiding and call for the Darlings and raise a general alarm, and rush all these usurpers off the hill. But it wouldn't have done any good.

When all of that bunch with Mitchell, including Seven, were out of sight I jumped back across the water again, damned near losing my balance, what with the sack's weight on my back, and falling backward, but saving myself from a dunking in time. Then I trailed them in the pines and oaks at the clearing's rim. Barabbas had decided I wasn't going to be very talkative or playful with him, this night, and had gone trotting after Seven. Light from the Darlings' house sprayed out comfortable over the green beds of moss and I still kept wishing as I stepped around in back of their house that I could have roused them to action, but all that would done would have been clap them in jail, and then what would their mother do? If the mill was going to run while I was gone, Seven needed them.

After what seemed a dragging time of years instead of minutes, Mitchell hoisted himself up in his barouche, and must've ordered the top put up against the night breezes because Andrew hopped to it and raised the braces, and Soames helped with this. Then all the Mitchell crowd was in the rig, and Andrew was on the seat to drive; the springs sagged quite a bit and I had a flash of hoping that when they came to the path's lip they would lose control and go crashing down that path all

spread galley-west; but they were strong capable horses, even
with that load. Besides, I didn't want anybody really hurt bad.
I'm not the kind of man goes around choosing fights to be
engaged in; hitting Gondy that crack had been necessary. It
was as I'd told Letty, I didn't even choose to hit the chincy
people of creation. Not unless I deeply had to. Besides, you
can't always use your left hand and with a crushed right hand
I wouldn't have a trade.

They went lumbering off, then there was a lot of noise at the
path's edge, a lot of hollering from Mitchell to Andrew to hold
the team back; then they were making their way down, with
enough noise to herald an army marching. When the bushes,
the sumac and the willow sprouts and the oak shrubs and
such, had done snapping and the noise was farther down, I
stepped forward. Seven was just standing there with his
shoulders sloped. His hands were a little clenched. He heard
me and turned, and Barabbas looked up at me too.

I says, low, "Step over here, will you, Seven? Don't want the
Darlings to get roused up; what they don't know won't hurt if
they're questioned again later."

He nods, and we move off closer beside the creek. This far
from the mill we could hear each other pretty well even when
we talked softly.

I says, "I know I must look like the wrath of Jehovah. Do I
look like I did before, though?"

"Not much, Luke." Seven smiles slightly. "Guess I'd recognize you in any form, but a usual observer wouldn't."

"All right." I sat down on an oak stump. "What's happening
with Mister Wayde Mitchell and his followers?"

Seven bent his head. "Now he's searched the houses and
grounds, he's going to rouse the countryside, Luke. But I
gather he wants you delivered to him personally, and he said
there'd be a reward for you. He says there's a matter of thou-
sands of dollars stolen—as well as that you're a murderer most
foul, which you've proved by your jailbreak, and a poisonous
influence over Miss Einsner . . ."

"So," I says, sighing. "Well, I got a notion she's just as much an influence on me. Though I don't think evil."

"Nothing is evil when there's courage and trust in it."

"Sometimes we got that, and sometimes not," I says, staring at a withered fern stalk. "I mean trust. As for spunk and sand, she's got the earth's supply in her craw."

As if I had a lot of time—which maybe I did, I didn't think they'd come back up here right away—I told him, step by step, about what had happened in Mullin's Gap. Told him about Letty's so-called deal with her old friend and mentor Mitchell, too; didn't tell him where the money was, but indicated that I knew, and that Letty knew.

It was as it was with the Darlings; if he didn't know where it was he could say so with an honest heart. He wasn't a lying man but he'd have lied for me; didn't want him to have to do it.

He'd just have to half-lie if they asked, in the coming days, if he knew anything about my whereabouts.

I didn't even tell him all of those, just said I had a plan and was about to travel.

He sat down beside me, after a spell, and took out his pipe and we chewed over matters and for a bit it was just like it had been before, when we'd communed in the nights after the heavy days of working.

I told him more about my doubts of Letty than I'd ever done before, and about my getting mad when I thought of her in the flabby claws—but claws for all their flab—of Mitchell. He says, ". . . Mitchell is a poor man, for all his influence. Hard to pity men like that; but they're pitiful. You ought to trust Letty."

"Yeah," I says. "But it makes me boil when I think of her having to deal with him, at all."

"And yet you admire the spunk she has to do it."

"Sure! Jesus, she's got enough courage to lick anything!"

He nods. "Growing up's a painful, awful process, Luke. Some never get there. Whatever happens now, you'll have to cultivate trust in her. Keep it when the going's muddiest."

I blurts out, "But deep in my mind I still don't know she didn't kill—"

"No, you don't. You'll have to take it on faith."

"—the way she killed that snake—"

"Well," he said, "from what you've told me your temper isn't exactly dull-edged."

"Always thought of myself as peaceable."

"Within some bounds. If whatever puts us on this earth meant us to be smiling and simpering idiots he wouldn't have put natural rage in us. Or they—they wouldn't have. I can't consider the Deity as a single being."

"More like a law?" I says.

"Yes. A law everybody is still attempting to fathom—sometimes even succeeding."

I got up and scuffed in the leaf-mast. "When I think of her not caring a cuss about me to the extent she'd even marry that waddle-assed legal spider, or if she doesn't marry him now I've busted jail, getting some other kind of concessions from him by dangling herself before him like a side-road whore, maybe even giving him a piece—" I slammed a hand on a tree. Barabbas looked at me interested, as if I'd spotted a 'coon in the tree and was drawing his attention to it.

"Growing's hard," says Seven.

I waited a breath. Then I leaned down and we shook. His hand was hard as an oak plank, but the bones in his face looking thin as if you could have seen a lamp right through them. His blue eyes looked like pieces of good old cloth.

"I'll be back," I says. "You'll know when."

"I'll try to be here. Nobody'll take over the mill, or bust things up, Luke, and as you say you've hidden the deed to the place. The Darlings will help me. I'll make out. So'll they."

"Good-bye," I says, starting off.

"Good night," he says.

This time Barabbas didn't follow me. They both sat there very quiet. He looked silver in the light; Barabbas looked black and hunkering, like a major prophet.

I skirted the clearing. The lamp had gone out in the Darlings' house. All was dead silent there. I got to the path and slid down it. There were deep wales where the barouche of Mitchell had gone down, mixed in with wagon-wheel tracks from customers. The last I heard, about fifty feet down the path, was the rumble and purr and splash of the mill wheel. I looked out and down. The roads were still in the moonlight. In the morning I thought they'd be buzzing with peril. I got a lump in my throat I'd never even had when I'd skipped out of the orphanage all those years before. Fact was, then, I'd been glad to see the end of it. Glad, later, to see the tail-end of the Clagberts. Now, I was filled tight with a sadness and a need to see Letty and to know we were on our own and free of even the shadow of her old man.

I'd not taken the bay mare, though I'd looked upon her fondly over in her lean-to; she'd been spotted now and was too noticeable an animal.

But I wished I'd brought her, by the time I got down off the hill. For one thing, I'd done a devil of an amount of traveling this day already, and for another, I needed to make some time.

I knew I looked different, but soon as the alarm went up that wasn't going to stop people in the near community being suspicious of any man tramping through and strange. Felt sorry for all the tramps this would bother. I got to the main road into Solomon and took its curves with caution, smelling all the moist earth scents and the barn smells drifting along. Once I passed a farm and dogs set up a racket high up the clifflike hill where it rested above me. I could make out the hex signs painted on the end of the barn when I could see it, a trifle later; that was good artful work. That was barn-painting far out of the ordinary. The dogs shut up and I was on my own again now, getting a fair stride. Cattle were feeding in a field close to a fence on my right flank. They stopped and followed me with their eyes. They were Jerseys, like Einsner's. Their dumb solemn eyes glittered as they watched me as though they were tranced. Then they started walking along beside me on their fence side, as if they'd elected me their leader. Their breath made bright lazy plumes on the quickening air.

About that time, I heard the train whistle. Remembered seeing the train come through here some long time ago in the high heat of summer when I'd been driving to Solomon. It came again. I perked up my ears like a rabbit hearing the snuffle of hounds, located the noise and vaulted over the fence, the cows trailing after me for just a spell then not coming any farther as I ran through foot-plucking stubble. In a trice I was climbing a hill toward the trestle bridge, hearing the whistle on my east in the curves of these hills, and wishing I could climb quicker but hampered by the paint and canvas sack. I got up there breathing hard, right at the end of the shadowy trestle bridge, and waited.

By reaching out, I could feel through the timbers, which seemed shaky, standing here a long way above the bed of the creek which tumbled smoky and blue-bronze below, the thrill of the train shaking the tracks. I remembered how trains were always crashing down through bridges in this part of the country, wreaking havoc and maiming innocent passengers.

The noise got louder. The whistle blatted again, seemed right in my ear. Then around a curve came the train's light, probing against the light of the moon and the lamps of the stars through the darkness. I held my breath and got ready. Could see now there were two cars besides the coal car and the engine. I didn't look down, because there was nothing but a stony creek bed under me, and a good long drop before reaching it. The train came on.

Eighteen

So my travels had started again.

I thought this even as the cowcatcher just missed me. It was a wide thing and nearly swept me off the bridge. Then I grabbed onto the next car and swung up. The engine was going slow on the bridge, not trusting its timbers. The engineer was spending so much time poking his head out of his cab and concentrating on his job he didn't see me. I clung to the rattling car. It had slats along both ends and the slat I was holding to kept jiggling like a crazy dancer with St. Vitus disease.

When I'd sucked in a couple of breaths I climbed up and over the edge of the slatted car. By now we were off the bridge. The train was picking up speed. As I came to the top of the car I saw the monstrous shape looming its back above the car. It was an elephant. In the moon-glints it looked strange as an underwater sea beast swaying hard to the rackety car's motion as speed picked up.

I dropped to the bottom of the car. The elephant gazed at me. It lifted its trunk a bit and swayed it like it was groping around for a thought to express. I stayed as far at my end of the car as I could. I was pretty sure it was the same elephant that'd appeared to the Darlings' wondering eyes down in Solomon. You don't see more than one elephant in a year or two as a rule in this countryside, even if you're searching. I expected the rest of that small circus would be moving along in the other car.

Hay was wisped all over the car's floor, like yellow gold in the moon's sliding light. The elephant smelled the same as it had in the tent, but maybe a little less confined.

I sat down, back against the end of the car, and looked up at the animal while it looked down at me. After a time I took out one of Letty's bread loaves, from the pack, and busted it in half; offered half to the elephant, tossing it over, and the elephant nosed it for a moment, then conveyed it to its mouth and munched.

I ate the other half.

We rode on like that through the night. After a time I stretched myself out, head on my packsack, and looked up at the clouds and stars and moon. The rails sang their clicks under the wheels. Cinders blew back in gusts and streamers. The elephant looked like a cliff of shale just barely keeping its balance.

Thinking about Letty, wishing I had her here on top of me, or beside me, or under me—I didn't particularize—and thinking too that I'd forgive her all her muleheadedness about Wayde Mitchell if only we could be clutched together, I fell in a light sleep. In it I had a dream about Mitchell and Letty in bed together. It was like a walrus or an octopus smearing a flower. I woke up mad and tense. Elephant was still there and morning was showing in its raw yellow and whited rose madder to the east of us. We were still traveling south. I sat up and fed the elephant another half loaf of Letty's bread, which it accepted gratefully. We were both just finishing up the crumbs when a short man with a bucket of water sloshing in one hand came through to this car from a door into the other car and caught sight of me. He most dropped his bucket.

"Who're you?"

"Just a man riding along."

He came closer. "Thought you was Indian at first. Or Nigra. You don't talk like it."

"They talk any special way?"

He said, "You'll have to get off in Maryland. Don't mind hoboes riding, but that's where we stop."

"Thanky," I says. "You the circus that played in Solomon?"

"That's correct. Magnusun's Amalgamated Illustrious Entertainments. I'm Magnusun."

He took the bucket to the elephant, which started trunking it up, and came back to me and kneeled down. "You a circus man yourself?"

I told him, a painter; a limner. Might as well always tell the truth about that. I didn't have a whole lot of cash left from the fair and square mill profits and was going to have to earn my living while I beat my way south. I said no more about any other subject.

"We might use a painter for a time. Signs need refreshing. Day or so's work. I'm the sword swallower. Got two card-trick and walnut-shell men with me, and the elephant, and that's it. Used to have a larger organization. Had a bareback rider and trained dogs. Dogs run off and the bareback rider joined up with another outfit. You could water the elephant and help shill the crowd too. Can't pay a cent but you'll eat."

"I'll join you, temporary basis."

He didn't ask more questions, but asked me to come back to the other car. We went through the door and he introduced me to the two other men who were just rubbing sleep out of their eyes. They looked something alike. They were both swarthy and dressed in checkered suits, and while they poked around getting themselves some breakfast, mostly hard-boiled eggs and cold peas, they kept showing each other sleight-of-hand tricks, taking cards and bunches of wizened paper flowers out of each other's pockets, trying to fool each other and not succeeding. Names were Tad Ainslee and Sir Alpheus Merry. Sir Alpheus said he wasn't honestly an English lord, it was just, so to speak, a cognomen.

"Solomon was a goldmine," says Magnusun, scrooching himself up against the bulk of a folded tent and drinking some tea Sir Alpheus Merry handed him in a tin cup, "—but Greenport won't be that rewarding. One thing, it's not a farming town and there ain't so much coin around during the harvest. But it's a fine place to winter and the town bulls wink their eyes at circus folks."

I liked the way they didn't ask me ten thousand questions. They just rambled on, living and let living, Tad and Sir Alpheus now getting out their walnut shells and, every time, the one who was doing the guessing figuring out exactly where the pea was under the shells the other was manipulating.

While the afternoon showed gold and free past the slats of this car and the fields slid by and the whistle called out banshee-quavers from time to time, I got nice and casually acquainted with them all. They found some paper and I sketched them all, not signing any sketch; they liked my work and suggested I set up a tent booth alongside them and split the take with the main pot, in case I was interested in making some money outside my keep while I was with them. I said I surely was.

During the long riding time they all chatted about the other circuses in this part of the land—those that were rivals, those that had done well this past summer, those that had busted up.

"Farley's Balloon Ascension, that's the money-taker," says Sir Alpheus Merry. "It's got the novelty and the draw. Rest of it's not worth a hill of dry beans. That fortune-telling rig and that juggler lives with Madam Fortuna—the one drops the plates—what's his name, Mag?"

Magnusun says, "Harkins."

"Harkins, correct, Mag. They're no good. But when Milt Farley blows up his balloon and hovers above the rooftops it just naturally brings everybody within a radius of thirty miles, tearing to see him and to spend whatever loose jingle they can break loose from their mattresses."

I sat up quite a sight higher. "Harkins," I said. "Seems I've heard that name—"

"Well, he certainly ain't celebrated; him and the Madam, they're just hangers-on to swell the mob and skin off a mite of extra take."

"And he drops his plates?" I says, laughing slightly.

"Don't hold on to one in eight," says Magnusun. "Pass the tea, Alph. Nooooo—there some men born to juggle and others who can learn it, but he's just naturally butter-touched at anything to do with the art. If he's famed at all he's famed for that. Madam, though, she tells a fair fortune. But as Alph says, the balloon ascent holds the outfit together. Farley's just good-hearted about the others, he could work without them any day."

I asked a few questions. It seemed Farley's Balloon Ascension was playing around the south somewhere; had been as far down as Mobile, Alabama, the month before, and was probably working its way up over the land now. Circuses, even little ones like these, tried not to overlap one another's playing grounds, if they could keep from it. They kept a kind of grapevine of information going as to where they'd be playing next. Tad Ainslee put in as his opinion that Farley's Balloon Ascension was probably on its way into Georgia by now, from which it would move on up through the Carolinas. He said he didn't think it would go any farther up than Virginia, though, before the real winter set in.

I rolled these pieces of information between the hands of my brain as though I happened to be working a mill wheel inside my head.

Harkins was the name of the little man who'd run off with Letty's mother. Would there be two of them in this part of the world, especially who juggled and who weren't too good at it? I didn't reason so. And was Madam Fortuna Letty's mother?

I'd make it my special business to find out. Sometimes when you're looking for information it's like you're a magnet to which filings flock. I hadn't been looking *especially* for Harkins but it might be instructive to take a look at him soon. I joined in a game of slap euchre with the three others and would have been cleaned right down to the bones, save for the fact that we were playing for straws. Toward evening I went and watered the elephant, this taking about ten buckets of water from the barrel they carried for the purpose while in transit.

It was a fine if ancient elephant, name of Sara. When you gave Sara a hard firm slap on the forehead, reaching up to do it, she seemed to smile in approbation and joy. She felt soft-furred over the wrinkled leathery hide, like some people's consciences.

Came into Greenport, Maryland, in the cool dusk of that Monday night, and were let off at a little side lot that lay beside the tracks on the edge of town. Cars would have been empties if Magnusun hadn't made an arrangement to use them, and the engineer and his fireman watched with a lot of fascination while we set the ramp and urged Sara down it into the gloaming. Then she was off, and the big wheels of the engine were churning away, and already, as if they were magical creatures with mouse eyes which appeared from the ground mist, dozens of children, mostly boys, had showed up and had their attention riveted on Sara, just the way the Darlings had done. There's something so mystic and rib-tugging about an elephant.

Magnusun and Tad and Sir Alpheus showed me how to go about setting up the much-weathered tents, and I joined in with a will. I can swing a sledge with anybody; heaven it knew, I'd had enough experience trying to unfreeze the mill-wheel shaft. It was rich dark before we got everything solid, with a small tent for me as well, and by torchlight—Magnusun always traveled with torches, said they appealed to the caveman instinct of a crowd—we scoffed some cold supper, I thinking of Letty's cooking with solemn regret while I wolfed cold stringy meat, and still studying about this Harkins as well. I tucked him into the back of my mind for future reference. Then by the same light I commandeered some more paper—they traveled with scrolls of it—and did a few posters, calling myself Andreas Artifact, the Quick-Limner of the Human Countenance, and hung them on the tent they'd given me.

I slept good. Almost had to, what with the work of carrying

hay and more water for Sara and all the rest. Didn't dream of
a sight or soul.

Come morning, Tad Ainslee and Sir Alpheus Merry
mounted their respective stands on each side of the tent holding Sara, and I set up down the line from Merry, and Magnusun was farther along on his stand, in front of his tent, with
his sword glittering and the tights he wore showing a lot of
muscle.

When the crowd had gathered we all worked hard. Tad,
along with his gambling with the multitude—or with any who
had a ten-cent piece—also took admission to see Sara. Magnusun stuck his sword down his mouth, which he gaped up to
the sunlight so far it seemed he'd stretch its corners and boil
his tonsils, and then worked it all the way down to his vitals.
Made me go chill in the gut to even cut an eye that way. Then
he worked his audience into the tent for more sights of mystery and wonder, including a lock of hair from Abraham Lincoln's scalp, supposed to be, and the original sword of Robert
E. Lee, and other such joys. Between times of painting quick
portraits of anybody who had one dollar—it was a skimpy
price but they were just accurate paint sketches, and not so
many people had a dollar so I made the sketches real good for
those who did—I'd jump down from the platform in front of
my tent, where I did the actual posing of the model and the
painting, and run around flapping my arms and bawling for
people not to crowd, to step up one at a time, to see the elephant from the wilds of equatorial Africa which could pull
twenty times its own weight and had killed fourteen bush natives being captured. Or if Magnusun was having a quiet
stretch of time between gulping his weapon, I'd draw attention to the condition of his esophagus, which I said was cut to
Mecklenburg lace from having been assaulted by that keen
blade in his stomach walls.

I used swatches of ordinary tent canvas, of which they had
plenty for tent-patching, for the portraits.

After a time the last visitor straggled home, the final buggy
and wagon made their way toward outlying homes and farms

and under the torches we counted up our take. It was fine, and Magnusun says it's going to have to be because the next night will fall off considerably, and from then on it'll be slim plucking in this place. He and Tad and Sir Alpheus didn't seem to mind a bit paying me my share of the division from the central pot.

I woke early next morning. Dew was thick on the flattened grasses of our pitch. I went out to make water and I see a man over at a fence beside the lot. Then I heard a noise I'd thought was a big bull woodpecker trying out his beak on a maple.

The man was pounding a nail into a poster. Poster said, WANTED FOR MURDER. $100 GOLD REWARD. The name on the poster was Lucius Carolus Applegate, may be going by the alias of J. P. Lester. The description was me, including a moustache.

They were working fast. I'd guessed the posters had been dropped off with some bags of mail the night before, maybe by the very same engineer who'd brought our train here. Or maybe by the mail riders. I didn't care from where. I felt mighty odd reading the information. I thought, Letty hasn't made much of a deal this time. Felt glad of that. But then, knowing a good deal about her indeed—among which was the fact that I couldn't ever anticipate the way her stubbornness was going to rise up—I really couldn't tell how she'd be acting with Mitchell.

The poster called me "heinous."

Even made me feel that way for a twinkling.

It said I was a capable limner and smooth-tongued.

The maple holding the poster was just taking the first light like a golden crown—maybe King Arthur's, on the first morning of the world.

Man says, "Fine, fresh day, sir."

"It is that," I says.

I went back to the tent I'd slept in, gathered up my canvas and paint sack—adding a few tent-canvas swatches for later use if necessary—saw everything inside was tidy, and sloped out of there. Last I saw, Sara was looking out of her tent after me.

"Good-bye, old lady," I said in my head. I went on through Greenport, most of it still half-asleep in the morning, without anything else happening. When I came to a side road I took it, and when I found a small body of pond water beside the road I shaved clean, not even bothering with lather but just using the water there. I was just patting my face when the red cart came moving along.

Nineteen

I'D BEEN ABOUT TO DUCK back in the bushes, but the cart held my eyes. It wasn't only red, it was trimmed with green and a doughty affair. Drawn by a couple of donkeys with shining hoofs and long ears, though they looked not much bigger than oversized rabbits in the new light. On the driver's bench was a man with a plug hat, beaver-furred, and a stock of yellow, and a gray coat, and long sideburns held up by a face so shrunk to the skin it might've been a skull's until you looked at the clear soft eyes.

He clucked the donkeys to a halt. I was fixed and caught now.

"Looking for a ride, stranger?"

On the flank of the covered cart, where I could now see a girl's face show up in a window, with a sunbonnet shadowing her dark eyes, I read the words: *Dabney the Phrenologist.*

Seemed I'd been meeting odd people, but interesting kinds.

"I'll take one."

"How far?" He was looking me up and down now, without truly seeming to study. Wondered if he'd read the poster about my misdeeds. I felt cool and clear-headed, but none too talkative.

"About Virginia. Actually, Richmond."

"Ain't that a boot burner! Well, climb up and we'll cart you some way."

"Yes sir," I says, hoisting myself and the pack to the cart seat. I decided he didn't want to vouch himself for my company till I'd proved myself not a robber or waylayer. He flipped the reins and we started on up the draw. He says, "What you do for a living, if it's not too nosy to inquire?"

I took a quick think. If he hadn't read the poster, or one like it, he was going to. They'd be up in plenty of places. Folks would be double-locking their doors against the murderer and shuddering, happy, beside their fires all winter over it. The poster'd said that the reward of one hundred gold was offered by the notable lawyer, Wayde Mitchell. Nothing had been said on it about Letty.

Made up my mind, post-haste as they say, and said, "I'm a limner. Name's Luke." It was a hell of a risk but sometimes you have to take them. I hadn't ever told Magnusun and Tad and Sir Alpheus what my name was. Sara the elephant hadn't seemed to care.

He squinched his eyes. "Hello, Luke."

We clacked on a mite farther. We were rising up the draw now and I could see the whole countryside sparkling. The donkeys didn't make great time but they pulled with ambition.

Then he said, "My name's Jericho Dabney. My daughter's in the cart fixing breakfast. She's Penelope . . ." A little pause came, that you could have dropped a hayload on. "—and I know you're hunted and chivvied. Did you kill somebody, son?"

"No," I said real quick. Then, in bits and pieces, slow but thorough, I told him about all I thought he needed to know.

He nods. "Girl did it, then. This Letty you tell me of. A woman is unfathomable. They ought to have different names for women than just women. Every one is an entity of its own, and you cannot fathom it even if you live beside it for generations. Ain't they wonderous, though?" He smiles. His cheekbones were sharp but not wizened. "Might as well make up your mind to that. She'll shake you in time and enjoy the fruits of her ill-got gains. You'll figure in her memory, when she is an old and powerful matron, as a feisty interlude in extreme youth. She'd see you stretched higher than Mount Ararat and still justify herself to herself, but still wishing you well if that could be arranged."

I didn't believe that.

I says, "I think you got her wrong."

"I play the Devil's Advocate because I find, so frequent, the Devil's got the primest arguments. Yes, son, I saw the poster back in Greenport, early this morning. Plastered on the side of a corn crib. You've heard my considered opinion after listening to your tale. Don't make a rat's ass, however. *I* didn't expect you were a killer, *I* suspicioned right off that there was a female at the root of this particular herb cellar, and *I* wouldn't want no blood-money gold reward on my conscience. I'll give you a reading soon as we've et."

"Thanky," I says, not yet knowing what a reading was but glad enough, I supposed, to receive it.

"Here's a good stretch," he says, a bit farther on, and steered the donkeys out into a clear patch where there were still wild chrysanthemums, that had come here blowing from the seed somebody had once planted, bushy along the fence side like ruffled bronze heads. They smelled fresh and noble. There was a good space here to browse the donkeys. He got down from his seat, and I did too.

"Tell you what," he says, looking at me critical. "Your Walnut dye you told me about is running. Won't stand up, hasn't had a chance to get sun-baked. And I like your style, Luke. Seems if you've got a talent I could commingle with my own—I'm studying about that. Have the result for you shortly." He turns to the cart. "Meet my daughter, Penelope as ever was."

A door opens in the cart side, a step flies down, and down onto it steps this girl. A mite older than Letty, with dark wild hair, a thin face, bright black eyes like a quick-minded bird's, and a figure that just went in and out in all the right places, jiggling a bit too so you could tell she hadn't ever wasted any money on whalebone. She's dressed in yellow, with the bonnet shadowing her eyes.

Jericho introduces us. Calls me Luke. She looks at me and gives me her fingertips to pump. Then she laughs, slightly, as though all to herself, and starts spreading out a cloth on the grasses, and adding to it plates and knives and forks and a bottle of wine, and jugs of potted meat and various other viands.

I think I'll go help her, but she's so efficient it would simply bump her out of her accustomed ways, so I don't; I stand there wondering if I haven't been the fool of the earth to spill my guts out to this Jericho Dabney, and decide that this point is still in the balance. After a bit Jericho, who isn't much taller than his daughter, steps over and while she's still setting out the food, chats with her, too soft for me to hear.

Once during this she looks up at me with her head cocked and the dark wild hair falling and gives me a clean-cut once-over. Then she nods to Jericho. Something's been sealed and set.

Jericho comes back to me. "Seegar?"

"Don't mind if I do."

They were pretty fair cigars, though I'd have bought different.

He tips his head rearward. "All right. Here's my offer. I'm a phrenologist, and if you don't know what that is, it's head-readings. I can run my fingers over your skull, son, and tell you where the lump of sensitivity is that makes you an artist, where the particular point in your cranial cavity occurs that makes you partial to seegars, even—and give you an insight into your future by just touching this pate-knot and that. It's a true science, I sometimes think, though naturally I embroider it a trifle. But say we put together our feats of derring-do."

"How's that?" I says.

"Say you stay in the cart, during our pitches, and just peep out that side window enough to study the individual I'm phrenologizing. Don't let him, her, or it see you. Then when I'm through head-feeling on this special subject, I duck in the cart and offer the subject, not free, but at a considerable extra expense, the wonderous and exact replica of the subject's face which I've just been able with marvelous dexterity to draw from feeling the head with my fingers. I'll call it"—he squinted up his wool-soft eyes to the sky and a few floating clouds—"I'll call it Phreno-Portraiture."

"Ought to be able to charge a packet for something so amazing," I suggests.

He tickled me and I was feeling easier.

"A packet! A five-dollar gold piece every time! And I'll split right down the center with you, with allowances for food, drink, and seegars."

I said fine, and about that time Penelope Dabney straightens from her work and says, "Ready to eat!"

We strolls over and sits, cross-legged, and buckles down to it. She wasn't any Letty cook but she set a decent repast. While we ate I cast around for some subject for conversation, and finally says to Penelope, "You've got a very good profile."

"Thank you, Mister—"

"Among ourselves, Applegate," says Jericho, biting a sandwich. Then he explains to her the situation, about as I've outlined it to him. Of course I'd spoken nothing about the twelve thousand, and neither had the poster said anything about that whatsoever. But from what he's dropped earlier about his opinion of her, Letty's, "ill got gains" I'd gathered he thought there was money connected in this somewhere. Most folks would. He was what Professor Allan would have called perspicacious. He tells Penelope what he has in mind for us to team up with, and she nods and plays with some sprigged flowers on her dress.

"I'm sure it'll go well, Father. It has all the elements. And it's new."

From the look she was giving me she might as well have been saying, "And you're new, too, in my life, Luke Applegate."

"We'll keep you somewhat quiet and stashed away," says Jericho. "Down out of sight and hid while you're working, naturally. But maybe when we get your appearance changed again—a little spruce-up here and there—you can take the air with some freedom. Till we get to Richmond."

I sat up stronger. "You're going—?"

"Didn't want to tell you till I'd made up my mind about you, but I certainly have, and we can just as easy as not detour a bit. Then we'll drop you off, after our venture together, and mosey on down toward Alabama. Montgomery. We stay there, winters."

"Lord, yes, I'm so homesick for that place," says Miss Dabney. "We've got the darlingest little house there, you'd just adore it. Magnolia tree in the back, and swings and all, and you're welcome to come on with us, if you'd wish—"

She was putting out a slew of welcome for one she'd known only half an hour, and for one who might be a born killer at that.

I told her, though, I'd think it over after we'd traveled together a time.

Couldn't keep my eyes from moving to her. Girlflesh was taking the sun like the giving earth. She wasn't a raving beauty but when she stood up the dress, I think muslin, was so thin it printed her through it like a young sapling feeling the touch of spring. And here it was well into autumn.

After we'd filled ourselves and she was clearing up, Jericho Dabney takes me off to the side of the cart, gets a chair, sits me in it and works over my head with his fingers. Massaging my head as though it was a new and important discovery man had never set eyes on before.

"Bump of knowledge! God, hanny, I have never in my life touched such a swelling. Boy, for one who's had no formal schooling, you are a wonder!—and feel this, would you? No, put your hand, here, closer under the temple. That's the memory bump. I'll show you on the chart, you'll see it later today when we set up in Collinsville."

"That where we're headed?" I was trying not to feel swelled up over what he was telling me. Figured there might be some truth in it, but not a lot.

"There, and then on down through northern Virginia. Same route Penny and I've been on for years."

"Penny's ma departed?"

"Her ma and I split up. Tilla went with a medicine show, though for a time before that she was with Milt Farley—he happens to be an aerialist, flies a balloon. Tilla was the fortune teller till Madam Fortuna took over. That was a long time back. Penelope was just a little slip."

Here it was again. Slow, I weaseled out a few more things about Madam Fortuna from him, with careful questions. It was like bobbing for carp on a day when you want to keep them interested but not jerk the hook too fast. I figured I'd been lucky twice, after all the no-luck in Mullin's Gap, and that God, or whatever Deity Seven Phillips believed in, some way wanted me to know more about this Harkins that had run off with Letty's ma. It worked its way through my skull that Letty's ma couldn't have just forgot about the money, and that it stood to reason she might've mentioned it to Harkins somewhere along the line. Circus and roving entertainment people live well when the living's there, but there are times lean as Satan.

From the ends of my hair under Dabney's fingertips came a prickle, as I wondered if Harkins, or Letty's ma, or both, might've been playing near Jerseyville the night Einsner got murdered.

And from Dabney now I got the news, too, that no, he didn't know much about the Harkins man Madam Fortuna lived with, or much about her, herself. But like Magnusun and the thimblerig men, and, I expected, every other traveling show and shill-man and individual in the business, he knew where the shows were, and where they'd be.

According to his calculations, the Farley outfit, with its balloon—he was full of praise for the balloon—would work its way up into Virginia come the deeper winter.

He finished reading my head, and it was my turn. So I got out the paint and canvas sack and a swag of that tent-patch canvas and stretched it a bit on some willow wands from the stand of them beside our breakfast place, and sketched him in pretty well. Then I didn't make it a full painting, by any degree, but with just enough strokes of black and pure white and a bit of ochre for the jaws and nostrils to make it jump off the canvas.

"Luke, your hand is good. You've got the Power of the Hand."

"What's that?" He'd just taken a peep at the work. Penelope's shadow was near me on the grass. She was watching from behind.

"The Power of the Hand is what the craftsmen of medieval times, in Europe, used to look for in a man. And then set him apart from others and see to it he was skilled in his paint-mixing, and goldbeating, and so on. And give him time to work, to reach what he had to find inside himself."

"Must've been nice." I liked the words, Power of the Hand.

Kept wondering while I was working what Letty was doing now. Could see her in the eye of my mind, sitting up bold and stiff and above the multitude, on that front porch of the scruffy inn in Mullin's Gap.

I finished the painting, though it could have been worked on two more full weeks and really been a wonder then. It was like a cartoon for the finish, though, not bad in its own right.

Penelope clapped her hands. "You've caught him, Mister Applegate!"

Dabney shook hands. Solemn. "We will amaze the natives with our Phreno-Portraiture."

I put away my gear and buckled up, saving out my palm-leaf hat, and Penelope got back in the cart and her father and I mounted to the seat and he started the jennies. He told me to keep the hat low on my eyes, and act lazy and calm when we passed others on the road. He wouldn't have had to tell me.

We went along that road all afternoon, not halting for lunch, having had that hearty breakfast. The road was brown and sunned, and when we passed through the rim of a small town just before getting to the Potomac, the shadows on it were shading to darkling blue with sun-red at their rims.

Then there in the late light was the Potomac. While we clapped across the bridge, joining quite a bit of other traffic, wagons and drays and so forth, I felt a squeeze in my belly. It came from several approaches. One was hoping to God we'd make fair time across Virginia, another was feeling exposed and strange on the cart seat now. And another was thinking about Penny or Penelope Dabney, riding back there in the cart.

We got across the bridge and put up for the night in a saw-mill yard, in a wedge of grass there.

Dabney said he'd played this town, Collinsville, before, and that morning would find it a pretty fair crossroads for work-ing. He unrolled his head chart and got all ready for morning. He gave me a sleeping canvas against the night-damp.

Toward morning in that yard with the air fresh as a wet stone, I turned over and woke up. Miss Dabney was standing alongside me. I felt urges, moving around like ants that'd got themselves trickled inside the canvas. Didn't flinch from the urges, though. I could just see her legs, bare, and feet the same—they were well-shaped feet, with nacre-blue in the veins and with high arches.

I shut my eyes and played possum. I heard her go back in the cart and shut its door after drawing up the step. I had a hard time falling back to slumber then, and didn't make it until I'd pretended, hard, that Letty was sleeping sound at my side. I didn't know if I could perform this feat another time.

Twenty

THERE'S A LOT OF PEOPLE who still have those phreno-portraits in their homes, spread around from the edge of Virginia right down to Richmond. I didn't keep count of how many we made but I know my wrist and hand got tired making them.

Even this far south, you could tell a difference in the people; they were beat down and solemn with the hard living since the war. Lord knew they'd had every sort of rough time, with the North sending down the kind of politicians who couldn't pour piss in a boot without getting some in their eye, and lording it over "a nation of slaveholders." Well, I don't like slaveholding myself and never did. But the way they had treated the South was fearsome, and you could see it in the eyes of the men and women and even the children who came to get their heads read—if they had the money, and if not, to stand and watch and marvel.

Jericho gave a good reading for what he charged. A couple of money-dripping individuals, young bucks on their way down from Washington and empowered to tell the farmers how much they could charge for cotton and pay for side meat, started it off; Jericho charged them a good deal, and told them in the bargain that they had a mite of water on their brains. Then he brought up the phreno-portrait idea, and I watched all this from a side window with Penelope hovering at my back, dabbing out quick portraits of them as soon as they bought the notion and Jericho Dabney popped into the cart. They were fair likenesses.

When Jericho delivered the portraits to these two specimens, they were dumbfounded with the rapture of it, and all the other folks crowded around marveling as well. Jericho left it up in the air as to whether he had just abracadabraed the portraits out of whole cloth, or whether he'd painted them himself.

Folks flocked by dozens then.

I tried to give real value because I knew most of those people would be looking at their pictures for the rest of their lives.

All the same, sometimes I felt a little bad. Here were people who five dollars meant months of work to, spending it this way. For that money I could have given them the kind of portrait I'd always given mankind.

Dabney told me to forget about it, when we sat in the cart in the evening talking over the day's work. "If you didn't skin 'em, they'd be skinned by other knives."

"Don't like to give less'n full value," I told him.

Penny was smoothing out the muscles of my back, which had got kinked from sitting at that window with a bit of canvas in my lap and peering out through the chink in the curtain at whoever was being head-read.

Her fingers worked deep in the muscles and her hair brushed my back as she worked.

Jericho counted out the coins and bills. He divided them and pushed a heap to me.

I was quiet for a time while Penny's fingers worked.

"Well," I says presently, "wouldn't it be a sparkling world if mankind didn't have to mulct his brother in any way, just to get along."

His soft eyes leaned to me. "Boy, you've not even got any element of the killer in you. Didn't I say it the first time?"

"Don't be too sure," I says. "I've met men I could squash like a mosquito if the time came to do it."

I was thinking of Wayde Mitchell. It had often come to me that if I was going to be hung, might as well be for a real reason. That thought had crossed my mind considerably in the days since I'd been in that tight-smelling jail room, that shed they called a jail.

That night I couldn't sleep. We were going to stay in Collinsville three, four more days. Seemed we'd never start working our way all the way to Richmond. I looked at the cold stars and breathed quiet. But no sleep arrived softly. I had the sleeping canvas pulled up around me in the dark. After a time came a slit of light from the cart door and then a shadow down the step; then here came Penny. I could smell her.

The donkeys were asleep, heads butting against a fence over in a corner of the lot. I reared on an elbow.

Penny drifted to me and I could see her thighs through her nightdress in the ground light. I reached up and put a hand on one knee. It felt like touching a night rose, that skin in the darkness. Then I put both hands around behind her knees and she folded down beside me. She lifted her heels and snugged herself down deep under the canvas. I turned to her, putting my arms around and under her, and we lay warming each other's lengths in the freshness of night.

After a time I wanted her without the nightdress. I raised it from the hem, pulling it up over her hips and then her head. She helped wrestle the rest of it over her chin. When I clasped her again, naked, she was smooth as mother-of-pearl and wiry as a mare, and moist all over, and coming up against me with her fine hairs pressing like a loving bush.

I touched her, light at first, feeling the muscle in her belly tremble and then against my chest, close as satin purses, big, juicy, firm, her breasts warm up to hotness and the nipple-ends toughen and reach, tight and round as hawberries. She reached down and raised one of those breasts in her fingers, bigger it was than Letty's, but not too milchy, and says, in my ear wet-warm, "Eat it, hon."

It was good-tasting as the night itself, as all the grasses around us. I could hear a new fall cricket chirping while I nuzzled. She reached down deeper, and took my balls in her fingers, rubbing them, stroking around them, and says, again in my ear, "I wish I had these for me alone, Luke, I most surely do."

She couldn't have them for good, I was going to need them quite a few more dozen years, but I didn't say that. By now she was all moistened from crown to toe, wasn't anything I could touch wasn't needing and true-needing, and I thought how dear all women are, dearer than anything else they ever made in this world.

And I rolled around and got on her, sinking home just as sure and right as having trudged all night and seen a light in a window, and she was a hot light all through me, and I in her. Going down like nothing they ever have a name for, into balmy, hot, then fiery gracious waters, diving deep and deeper, so she moans and holds me, and laughs and holds me, and then she's motioning and rising and cradling me, and down again, and up, and her hands around the small of my spine and her legs locked. Then, finally, coming that first time with some kind of white light around us, like explosions of brother-and-sister stars.

When it was over the first time and she was saying in a soft quick untired voice, "Wouldn't care if we woke up the world, I'd go right on doing it," I wanted her again, but also knew I wanted Letty so much it made my bones ache.

"Luke," Penny said, so close her eyelashes were tickling my chin. "Hon, you're full of man-sorrow. Don't grieve about that girl. Just be for being's sake."

Christ, I thought, nothing wrong with just being, nothing wrong with two people needing each other and giving each other; it's the wanting somebody else. But I didn't think Penny had ever felt like that. So I started tracing her body with my fingers—blossomy it was now as a hill of soft-touching dark gold—and kicked off the canvas and crouched up, and took her haunches in my hands, and raised her to me, and parted her warm, wet bush-hair with the tip of my rod, while she lay back, arching herself on her elbows, and we moved together, and the spice-hot, rum-hot, fire-hot giving at last went straight down my spine and up and out of the balls and into her, and she came at the same second, making a noise like a great dove flying in air it couldn't live without.

One way and another, we spent most of the night like that. Till the donkeys were just about set to call for their morning corn, and the roosters of the town were crowing, and we could—feeling light-boned and happy—hardly stand up when it came time to. She slid the nightdress back on and kissed her fingers to me and I watched her slip across the dewed grasses to the cart and go in, then plunged myself into some kind of sleep till the sun woke me.

The days went like that, and some of the nights too. On the fourth morning we moved on. I'd spent the evening before pumicing off the rest of the dye from my face and parts of my body, which took some freckles and skin with it too; Jericho'd bought the pumice for me at a notions store in Collinsville. Jericho'd said that, now the dye was off, it might be better for me to ride inside the cart, so I did that, Penny sometimes joining me as cozy as though she happened to be my wedded mate. There were more of the same posters around and about, advertising the reward and noting that I was badly wanted. It was in newspapers too. They said the reward would be paid by Mister Wayde Mitchell, prominent citizen of Jerseyville, Pa. Said very little about Letty, daughter of prominent slain dairy farmer. Jericho said such sensations died fast, new ones took their place. I guessed he was right, because in the newspapers we picked up later the headlines about me weren't quite so sprawly, and later still I found myself kind of wistful when they started relaying my story to the back pages among the ads for plows and female complaint tonics.

Down we went, slow as cotton blowing stiff-stalked in the fields, through Manassas, then crossing the Rappahannock one evening. Then through Fredericksburg and then one morning, Spotsylvania. Right after that we put up for almost a full week in a town where the main attraction was trotting races; they were lovely, and the crowds made our business good. But I kept itching to get on.

Jericho visited the local stores again and spent some of my money on a long coat, not as loud as Mitchell's hammerclaw, and a shirt, judging me by eye and not carrying measurements, and a pair of doeskin pants and some new boots. Said I'd look like a young artist ought to look. And Penny trimmed my hair.

I didn't even look like Luke Applegate. Topped it off with my wide-brim hat too, even though I'd last been apprehended in that skimmer. But I figured there must be a lot of them.

I'd yammered a good deal more with Jericho about various kinds of circuses, but couldn't make him pinpoint any more'n he knew about the Milt Farley outfit. I was afraid we'd spend so much time making money and portraits that I'd be bereft of seeing the Farley aggregation forever. I wanted two things: a good long look at Madam Fortuna, and a careful look at Harkins. Not that their faces could tell me anything; this was just a feeling I had, which might lead to other things.

One night when we were about a dozen miles above Richmond at last, it snowed. It was just a light skifting but it made me feel even farther off from Letty while I watched it come riding in on an easy wind and cover the stand of cold oaks below our camping place. I didn't sleep out that night. Slept in the cart, on a floor pallet made up below Penny's bed, and Jericho snored so hard he couldn't have heard us if we'd shivareed him. There's a kind of sad fucking, I thought while we pleasured ourselves; you could cry a lot while doing it, if you were so-minded.

"You're moody as the weather, honey."

"True fact," I told her. "In the fairytale books everything comes out all right in the end, but it doesn't tell about how the people felt afterward and how they kept wishing it could happen over. Red Riding Hood missed the wolf."

I kissed her just a tad below the moist cup of the navel, and went on: "And just before he got made into meat, I know *he* missed *her*, terrible. Oh, people miss people such a lot in life."

She puzzled. "Well, I think you're bewitched!"

"How'd you know that?"

"I know it."

After a little she said, "You're not coming on with us to Montgomery, are you . . ."

"No, I can't," I said.

She cried a little. Not hard. Didn't keep us from loving each other up again before the winter's dawn came in.

Next afternoon, start of November, we rode into Richmond. I'd forgotten what a city it was, gracious even on a chill-touched day and full of pride and promise. Even the war hadn't cut that away from it. They let me out on the edge, they had to keep on going at a good pace now to make Montgomery and winter in their house there; Penny kissed me long and straight, and I felt real sorry to part with her. Jericho raised his high-cheekboned face and his sideburns flapped like leaves in the shrewd wind. "Luke, I hate to break up a wonderous partnership. If you ever want to get in touch again, simply ask some of the sojourners of the road; they'll have heard where Penelope and I are working."

I looked at his fingers that had felt out so much amazing fact in the shapes of so many heads. Melon-heads, pumpkin-heads, redheads and black and yellow and no-color.

"Schach!" I says. "We'll see each other in time. Have a good wintering and I'll write."

They'd given me the address in Alabama. As I said, I'm not much on letters—writing them in my head, maybe, but not getting them down and mailing them. But I made a pledge to myself to write them. Last thing I'd done, day before, was finish up a portrait of Penny. A small gift for all she'd gifted me.

She got in the cart. Raised the step. Waved. I waved. She shut the door. Its bolt went home.

Jericho got the donkeys started up at a quick clip and the whole cart disappeared down the cobbled street.

I swung off toward the house where I hoped against hope Professor Allan would still be holding forth. Leaned against the wind, carrying the paint and canvas sack with an air as if it happened to be a smart traveling bag.

After a time I hitched a ride on a dray going closer to Professor Allan's street, riding on its back and watching the cobbles disappear behind me in the gray light as though they were mileposts flickering closer to where something inside me told me was going to be either the right place, or a complete mistake.

Twenty-One

WHEN I GOT to the house, on its quiet street, I stood in front of it for some time with my hand on the hitching post and the paint and canvas sack at my feet.

Didn't want to burden Professor Allan with something that would just worry him. After all, among all my friends, he was the grandest and most fixed. I'd had the notion all this last month while traveling that once I got here everything would somehow come together; now I thought, Well, maybe that's simply overwishing it; maybe I'll just add to his load of worries.

And maybe, too, I was in a bad lorn mood from having just parted with Jericho and Penny. I mean, having gone along with them so long, and regretting even a tiny bit now that I wouldn't have Penny to look forward to in the nights, and she me. I mean, she was a well-meaning girl and she sure wasn't shy about knowing a man once she favored him.

In the late light the bricks of Professor Allan's house looked burning pink and fine; the sun was sneaking through the cold clouds now and it was the time of evening when Professor

Allan would be in his study, reading Greek and nourishing himself with a toddy. All up and down the street children were playing, rolling hoops and so on, and from the shine of the creek—which was a tributary of the James—down behind his house, the light rose up to gild the air and put promise into the evening.

After a bit I picked up my sack and made my way up the bricked front walk. I climbed the steps and gave a rat-tat with the knocker.

Miz Amily opened the door. She'd worked for the professor for I expect about thirty years. She was nearly as wide as she was tall and had a high hair-do and pince-nez glasses. She smelled of rosewater and starched gingham. At first she says, "You have an appointment? You from the university?"

"Why, yes ma'am," I says, since she didn't recognize me. I was wearing my yellow coat and the doeskin pants and the vest, and I'd brushed up a mite after dropping from the dray. "I'm a student of arts and sciences. And I thought if you'd let me in to see the professor he could tell me how many angels stand on the point of a needle, and other likely formulations of general philosophy. Hello, Miz Amily."

Then she opens her arms and gives me a hug like a ravenous bear. "Good lord! And where did you drop from? And aren't you—didn't I read a piece in the paper—" By this time I'd come into the hall, and she'd shut the door. She seemed flustered by what she was remembering, but hardly taken aback, as they say. She said so loud anybody could have heard it, "—aren't you a *hunted man?*"

"Not so hunted as I was, though I imagine most people'd be interested in the reward. Anybody but my deepest friends."

"Well," she says, "I don't think you could even kill a moth!"

"You know that's not true, you remember me butchering that hog for the professor last year about this time. You got any more hogs need butchering, or bits and pieces of odds and ends of work I can help you with for a spell?"

"Heaven to John, yes, Luke. The back stoop's in ramshackle shape and the help we get around here's not worth duck eggs." She was rushing me along the hall, into the front room;

I dropped my pack again and waited. It was as if all the room smiled at me. The silver candlesticks—but I kept remembering a pewter candlestick far down in my belly—and the portraits of the professor's ancestors and even the girl he'd been engaged to, who had died of the phthisic when he was but a youth. The sideboard with the tantalus for wine, and the chairs with their carved backs and the chests and tallboys and all the books that there wasn't room enough in the library for so they overflowed into every other room and crested up the walls.

She shook me a little by my lapels. Then kissed me. "You ornery, runabout child. Seems to me there's a couple of lines in your face weren't there before."

"You try escaping the talons of the law and see what it does to your skin."

"But I wouldn't have recognized you. Not in that getup. You resemble the lamented Lord Byron."

Was a little bust of him on one of the shelves in a knick-knack cupboard. With him was Milton, Shakespeare, Beethoven, Shelley, and Poe. None of them was a recent comer, but they were right around the corner as far as the professor went. So was every man who'd ever written or composed, right there to be talked at and argued with, fresh as fields of daisies. There were other cabinets full of the Greek philosophers and drama-makers, and Miz Amily hated to dust them because she always felt she might drop one.

She went along to the door of the professor's study. Gave a hard cheery rap.

Inside a voice rumbled, and said, in a kind of dark effect, "Be off, thou secret, dark, and midnight hag!"

"Don't screech at me for a hag, you rumbustious man," calls Miz Amily. "Come out and see what's waiting you."

"Tell it to come in," says the professor behind the door. "At this hour of my moulting and thin-threaded life I am Mahomet, and the mountain may arrive any moment."

So I steps to the door, opens it, and walks in.

A shaft of sun lay athwart my legs but my face wasn't too clear in here. There was the sharp scent of bourbon from the toddy, and in his big leather chair, which smelled of warmth and oldness, the professor sat with his book—it was Vergil, he was favoring the Romans tonight, I saw, though he never held that they were anything but conquerors and usurpers compared to the pure Greeks. He has a face that all bunches together in front and leads up to a haughty jib of a nose, and a quiff of hair like a cockatoo's comb. The hair is like cotton that's been varnished, in color and sheen.

I says, "It's Dick Turpin, the Highwayman, come from his haunts. Your good housekeeping woman says I'm Byron, though. I don't feel like either. Feel like Lucius Applegate."

I bowed to him.

He got out of the chair, no taller than Miz Amily but considerably lighter, and sprier on his legs, and comes to me and takes my hands. His eyes shone like topazes. "My boy. Luke." Then he says, "I've heard of your exploits, if exploits they are. And I've done a sight of Anglican prayer on your behalf. Now here you are, delivered, wrapped in light. Sit down!"—and to Miz Amily, swarming in the door, he calls "Bring the bottle and my silver stirabout!"

She clambered off. Then he pushed me, very agile for his size—I'd seen him tame a pretty ill-tempered horse quite fast—back into a chair near him, and sat again, this time perching on his big chair's edge, and quizzes me with all his being.

Soon as I'm through gazing at him, I starts in answering his questions. This was the fullest I'd told the story yet, starting with Seven and including Mitchell and going on to Jericho. I didn't leave out a grace note. Miz Amily brought a bottle and the professor used his stirabout and sugar and hot water to mix me a good strong toddy, which felt grand down the throat-lining after all the time I'd had nothing but some wine with Jericho and Penny. It warmed the middle of the stomach and made a ball of shining there. I took sips of it between times of telling the tale.

Told more about Letty than I supposed I'd realized, or my tone got different when I talked of her, and once I slapped my forehead and says, "I never knew such a woman for hurting a man!"—and I expect that gave him some insight too. I couldn't help that. I might keep my voice even and quiet while speaking of anybody else, even lawyer Wayde Mitchell, but I swear I couldn't keep it level when referring to Letty.

Not that Professor Allan wouldn't have understood anyhow. He took life in through his pores. I was recalling, with just a smidge of me, all the time I was being urged by him to go on, and he was mixing yet more toddies, and the sun was slanting in through the trees that still held wisteria—I was recalling all I knew of him, which was a sufficient amount. How he'd ridden with Jeb Stuart and then later, after the war, had started one of those vigilante committees they called the Klan. It was pure in purpose when he started it, and necessary as bread to ward off the fools and renegades and mistakes for men the North had put in charge; it was necessary for keeping men, women, and children alive. But then it had changed and weasel-brained men had taken it over, still calling it the Klan, as an excuse to beat the living tar out of any poor black child, woman, or man, in the order named, they took a dislike to. So then the professor had found himself on the other side of the fence, fighting the Klan. I knew he'd done it with a way and a will, he made me think often of a tidy small Moses cutting through a dozen or so Red Seas every day of his life.

All that, I knew about him; and about me, he knew everything there was to know except what I was telling him now.

He clasped his knees in their good black broadcloth and nods. I'm through telling, and it's darker in the room.

"I'll help you with every ounce of imagination and skill and capital I have, Luke. The whole case is fascinating. Who could have killed Einsner if your Letty didn't?"

"Don't know, Professor. Men don't fall like that and kill themselves. The chest he might've hit his head on—one of those old Pennsylvania Dutch things with roosters with long tails painted on it—was on the other side of the room. The candlestick was lying alongside him."

"Of course, of course." He strokes his jaw, shoots up, takes a turn around the room, whose books in their calf with gold along their spines look back at him, twinkling in the last scarlet light. Indigo shadows are building. Professor Allan has his hands stuck under his coattails, and he whirls around.

"You've opined, naturally, that it might've been Mitchell himself."

"Yes sir. Sometimes I think it was, had to be. He was the one with everything to gain—includin' Letty. He probably drew up Einsner's will. With Einsner dead he stood to gain even more by marrying Letty. He seems to live rich, but a man like that often needs money more than others."

"Again, that's natural. I've told you in the past you have a ratiocinative mind. Well, in the weeks to come, we'll study every angle of it. Tomorrow when you're rested up a mite from your Ulysses wanderings—I'm sorry I have no Penelope to offer you—"

"I lived pretty serious with one all this last month."

"Ah, yes. Tomorrow I want you to sketch an exact duplication of this front room where the deed took place. With the corpse in it, the position of the candlestick, anything else your inward eye remembers. You think with your fingers, and I believe such a reconstruction may have its value. Not the only value, but one that can fit into the total portrait with assistance."

"I'll sketch it tonight," I says, "when I've washed up. But I sure don't want it to be weeks I'm here. Here's Letty, and—"

I was leaning forward trying not to breathe like a pit bull with a mouthful of beef.

"My boy. Patience has never been one of your manifest virtues. Now, I'm afraid it'll have to be. After all, what can happen to Letty?"

My face showed everything I thought could happen to her, with Wayde Mitchell handy.

"No, she's a strong woman from all you've said, and I doubt that anyone taking her body could have any other part of her unless she desired it."

"That's true," I says, weak.

"Then be larger than your own jealous spirit. Rise out of it and see on an objective plane—the pure, strict, Greek vision. It will be difficult—like plucking out dragons' teeth—but it will hearten you, and it's going to be necessary. For we must put together a mass of threads, a veritable Minotaur's maze of wandering alleys—and as we do this, we'll stay here and enjoy the winter's delights. You have my promise to explore every avenue, which I'll delight in doing . . ." He walks over to one of the bookcases. Squints quick, then with a dart takes down a book and comes back with it. "E. A. Poe," he says. "The poor benighted and marvelous man. How he would have taken joy in your talk of a balloon ascensionist, a fortune teller, and a juggler so inept he drops the tools of his trade. That's a part of it which interests me. The huntsmen are up!"

I sat there figuring. There was everything in what he's been saying, he doesn't talk to hear his tongue whip; I didn't know about any pure, strict, Greek vision on my part, seemed to me I was going to be buffeted by the winds of wondering and puzzling and grinding my back teeth when I thought about Letty and Mitchell, for some time to come. But you can't faze logic. So I tried to tuck away all these churning thoughts, along with the impatience I'd felt building while Jericho and Penelope and I moved down across Virginia; I sat real still, and finally I nodded.

"Good! Now, for dinner. And during it—we have a fair fowl which Amily has trussed and browned as a sacrifice to the gods which brought you back; I regret we cannot offer a bullock—we'll plan activities for the times to come. Let me bring Mister Poe along with me and leaf through the complexities of Auguste Dupin while we sup."

We went in to dinner, me first excusing myself and washing up. Miz Amily had given me the room I'd had last time, the one overlooking the back gallery. There were lamps lighted in here and it was a room the professor would have called dulce, if he hadn't been too used to living like this to remark on it; high-ceiled, with a good pomander-ball scent about it and thick quilting on the cherrywood bed.

While I washed I stood looking out over the basin into the growing dark. All seemed like coming home, but it wasn't my home any longer. When I'd left here last I'd felt the road drawing me. The need to see many new faces and get some of

them down on canvas, for cash. Now there was a need twice as
strong as that. Was a picture, a sepiaed photograph I think, of
a frieze of horses, strung out together in a line the way they
appeared on what the professor had once told me was the
pediment of a Greek building. It hung on the wall of this
room and caught the light. I looked at it slow. They were marvelous horses. Looked like they could pull any man out of
darkness into sheer sun. Going downstairs to dinner, scrubbed
up, I remembered something he'd quoted me when he'd first
shown me them, "Run slowly, O slowly, horses of the night."

Seemed I was going to have to run slow for a spell of days. I
got to the table, the professor clasped my hand, and Miz Amily's, and said a grace, thanking God for returning me. I
thought about Seven and the way he looked at life, with many
times of living it. And did each time have to be so packed with
grief and hoping as well as joys and brilliances? I didn't know
that. The professor talked a streak of purple all during dinner, quoting Poe from time to time—though he said he didn't
think "The Purloined Letter" had much bearing on our case—
and made plans for the morrow. Last time I'd been here I'd
wandered the town and country, miles around, painting what
I could, and making some money, though not much, doing it.

This time, he says, we'll set up at home as a salon. I'd heard
of a salon before but I'd never set my mind to being part of
one. "Besides," he says, "it will create an image of you as a
gentle soul with no footloose tendencies."

"That'll sure be misleading," I says, pronging a chicken leg.

"And I think you can with good conscience charge more for
each portrait, assuming the mantle of the expert who is con-
sulted in his lair."

"That's more like it." Raised my head. Couldn't tell either
one of them how glad I was to be there without making a long
speech and I was already dried out from speaking. So I just
said, "You'll kindly let me pay as much of my own way as I
can, not that I'd ever be able to pay for what you gave me last
time and now."

He fixed me with an eye like a tiny gimlet's, that steely.

"That is the unforgivable, Luke, and you will kindly never

bring up the subject again. As to expenses concerned with what we must learn in the days ahead, you may help me there if you wish. For now, let us map out your future as a romantic portraitist. Considering well the point that romantic portraiture is not commonly associated with one who is still, even though the publicity is dying down, keenly wanted in Pennsylvania."

I could see how that would be useful too. We all talked till the clock in the hall, which had a small sun and moon and stars on its face and stood about as high as Letty, brought out one stroke. Miz Amily went off to bed, then, telling me she'd appreciate my assistance toward repairing the back steps in the morning, and the professor and I went up, bearing candles.

We'd had a good bit of his wine—the Madeira, he said it was—after dinner. I didn't feel anything swim though. I went to sleep in that easy air coming over the sill, and looking at the picture of the carved stone horses in their flying and charging through the world. Run slow, I told them as I dropped off, run slow if you have to, but please get me back to Letty soon.

Twenty-Two

RIGHT OFF, next morning, the professor got busy on his campaign of what he called enlightenment.

The night before while we'd sat at the table over wine and cheese and nuts, I'd sketched the outline of old Einsner lying face down with the candlestick beside him. I'd put in everything I could remember: the way the shadows were, moon peering in a side window; candlestick lying there near his head. It was a sketch gave me the willies myself when I'd finished it. He had taken it to ponder. In one end of the library—which was the room just off his study—he set up a desk and what he termed a working arrangement of deduction, the sketch I'd done pinned to the paneling of the wall over the desk. That morning he wrote half a dozen letters. One was to P. T. Barnum himself, of the Barnum, Bailey, and Hutchinson circus, Greatest Show on Earth; he told me he couldn't fathom anybody knowing more about circuses, tiny to lallapaloozas, than Phineas Taylor Barnum. Still other letters went to various officials roundabout the country.

He told me how he'd already been approached by some

marshals who'd been asking about me, having heard he'd had
a sort of hired man by my name the autumn before. But he'd
fobbed them off by saying he never expected to hear hide nor
hair of me again. That was fairly true, too; he hadn't. He
forgave me for not writing to him though; knew I wasn't a
man who liked to do that. Upshot of the whole situation now,
he said, was that I'd have to don a whole new personality; be
just as different as I could from what I'd been in the past.

He said the thing to do was be aloof and rapt, as though I
was always studying some inward sign of truth and glory, or
listening to a hoot owl only I could hear.

That, it seemed, was the popular way a poet or a painter
was supposed to look.

It came to me that all along, neither he nor Miz Amily had
even at one moment in time had the notion I might've killed
Einsner.

Which was a mighty warming thing when you considered it.

That morning, while the professor dashed off his letters and
got them sealed and sat figuring my future, I fixed up the
back steps for Miz Amily and went to say hello to the professor's horses in the stable around in back, and admired every
foot and inch of the place I'd left the fall before. Sometimes
the professor called me from his window. Every time, he
wanted to confer about a piece of information, such as how
tall had Letty said Harkins was—to which I answered she'd
said he was small and wide-shouldered and peak-faced and
had a little moustache, nothing more—and how old a woman
Letty's mother was, which I didn't know to save me, and so
forth. I stuck close to the house and yard and outbuildings,
doing small chores, all morning. At noon when Miz Amily
called me in for lunch the professor says, "This is embarrass-
ing. In the house I can call you Luke, but I'm afraid to outside for fear the neighbors may get on to it. So does fear dog
our shadows. It's not precisely conscience making cowards of
us all, it's simply fear of possible consequences." He looks at
me, sizing me up. "You'll have to change your name and we'll
have to call you by it."

I nodded. Didn't like the idea—I'd already had too many names to suit me—but I could see its necessity.

"How does Tobias Dalton fit you?" he asked.

I was going to say all right, but Miz Amily said, "Not enough weight to it. Not fancy and perfumed enough. How about Delevan O'Rion?"

"No, no," the professor says, wrinkling his forehead so his hair-quiff shot up like a white plume.

"No," he goes on, "I think Delevan is fine, but the Irish are notoriously bad painters. Excellent poets but they smudge canvas. How about . . ." He shut his eyes and breathed lowly. "How about Delevan Gainsborough?"

I said that was all right with me, but it'd take me five or six days to get used to it. So all the rest of that day, while I was puttering around and trying to possess my soul in patience, he would suddenly sit back at his desk and call "Delevan?" or "Oh, Mister Gainsborough!" and though I was hard put to answer once in a while, I started getting trained to it fairly fast. In a book he had I'd seen Gainsborough's paintings; he was a caution with fine line and color but I thought I could paint hands just as well. Most limners, which I'd noted when I was a young mole and starting out, skimp the hands; I never did. You can tell so much by them. Even in that sketch I'd made of old dead Einsner, the hands, half-clenched, couldn't have belonged to any other man.

I'm not saying anything bad about Gainsborough, mind. No limner, even one as choosy but low-down as I am, ought to even breathe harshness about another's work. Painters are lone wolves and go better that way than in packs, but even in packs they'd ought to keep their personal eye and spirit, and keep mum about all else.

Things went on like that, and I started to get used to the name, which Miz Amily called me too. So after a short spell it got comfortable to answer to Delevan, or Gainsborough. Figured if it was sprung on me for a test in public I could stand up to it. Without flinching. And in about a week's time I started riding out with Professor Allan in the afternoons; also started showing myself when his friends called. He had rafts

of friends and acquaintances, all of them having known him
for donkey's years, a lot having been his fellow teachers at the
university, some his students. Bevies of girls would show up
like flower baskets. First time he summoned me in to meet
them, introducing me as Delevan Gainsborough, from
Europe, I just kind of hung back and smiled and sometimes
practiced looking serious and in-turned, as though I was suf-
fering mild colic.

There was Miss Anne Raintree, Miss Sally Lou Loudermilk,
Miss Farleigh Nevins, Miss Gilda Lee Marchbanks—Lee was
always going to be a popular second name in Virginia—and
Miss Tora Will Simmons. These were daughters of his friends,
and friends of the daughters; and they were *his* friends too,
who looked on him as a kind of mountain of information,
which he was. He could social-chat like a steamboat churning
along to Memphis in a clear day, and he knew all the histories
of every family for miles around. Sometimes the young ladies'
young men came with them, and then there'd be a feeling in
the room as though they were just waiting to call me out and
spit me like a roast. But I stayed high and mighty and above
them. With the young women coming this way, we got the
paintings started.

I promised to paint Miss Sally Lou Loudermilk's portrait,
and she said she'd be so grateful for it. Since as the professor
had told her, I didn't like to even think about such mundane
stuff as money—I didn't, either, but only on account of running out of it often—Miss Loudermilk and the professor dis-
cussed my fee in private.

Turned out it was fifty dollars. When he told me about it,
after she'd gone that afternoon in a flutter of lace, bows, and
curtsies and laughter, I says, "Heydy! That's more'n I ever got
for even five paintings!"

"So you'll have to make it a good one," he says, smoothing
his hair back, and smiling. "Don't fret; some of these families
couldn't afford it, they're all coin silver and proper lineage
and pride. But Leonidas Loudermilk was a war profiteer and
I'd like to part him from more than that mere cash pittance."

So next day I started on her. That same afternoon we went

down to the best frame and canvas store in Richmond at the time—they also sold paintings, mostly flower pieces—and I found a couple of good canvases, already stretched. I managed to refurbish my supplies of paint, too, and was feeling good while we spanked home in the sun behind Jarhinda, the professor's best mare. It was gay being out in the light again, holding my chin up proud; I was set to give anybody who came after me a cool pace for his money, even though sometimes at night I'd still look quick out of the corners of my eyes at a sound of wheels in the street, or a tree limb cracking in the night's chill.

"Delevan," says the professor as we rounded the corner into his street, "I heard from P.T. Barnum's secretary today. I was right; they do keep track of all rivals. Not because they're afraid of them—Barnum's afraid of no competition—but because they constantly search for new acts and wonders to add to the Greatest Show. According to him, P.T.'s secretary, the Farley Balloon Ascension is due here next month. And they seem to have the habit—Farley's, I mean—of performing right up until the snow flies."

"Here in Richmond?"

"Such is the case." He swung Jarhinda around under the trees and up the brick drive and we came to a halt in the stable yard.

"Sure seems a long time of waiting."

"It does, but you're bearing it well. Remember, I'm not asking you to become a fine grammarian. Simply hold your distance, stay aloof, mumble a great deal, commune with your muse, and put up the same front you've been assuming. Grammar," he says getting down from the carriage, "is no great shakes when it comes to expression at any rate. I have the notion Homer spoke the argot of his people. In fact, I know he did."

In the house, he showed me a piece in the Richmond paper. It was all about how Mister Delevan Gainsborough, lately of Paris and Rome, was paying a happy visit to his old confrere, Professor Harvey Allan, and how the community was honored by harboring a man of such attainments as aforesaid Delevan

Gainsborough. "The tenure of Mr. Gainsborough's visit is as yet unknown," the article said, which I translated as meaning I was going to stay a hell of a long time.

Painting that girl was harder than I thought. She sat good, but she was a giggler. And I kept thinking about Letty, how she never giggled in all her days but just had that figurehead look. Sally Lou was a butter blonde, just a mite pudgy at the edges; I could tell when she got to her forties she was going to spread like a setting hen, oozing out at the seams. She had a mouth that was rosy and spreading, too, and about the hundredth time she giggled, at that first sitting, I looked back from the sketch I was doing and raps my hand on my brow and groans.

"What's the matter, what's wrong, Mister Gainsborough?"

I'd set up the easel, which I'd also bargained for at the paint and frame store, where the light hit it good in this old ballroom. She was wearing a blue-gray dress with a cloth rose in the V of the neckline.

"Please," I says. "I can't work with that skittish noise."

I did keep her down to the point where she only giggled about half as much as she'd done. But when each came out it was a buster, to make up for lost effort.

She got kind of to look at me, awed and wondering, after she'd busted loose; and in the air between us starts growing a little feeling like sparks. Next day I see the sketch is good for what I want, but instead of sending her packing I keep her there while I'm at work. I don't know what makes a man horny, and I'm still thinking of Letty all this time—the way I'd done with Penelope Dabney—but that doesn't amount to a hill of beans, for the urge is there. It lives and straightens and itches under everything, and the worst thing is, she can feel it too.

After a couple more sittings I get so I can hardly kiss her plump but shapely wrist when she takes her leave, without feeling myself a monster, as the professor would say, of deprivation and degradation. The two do go together, when you think of it.

Finally I start taking cold baths in the center of the afternoon, getting in a zinc tub up there on the second floor and blaffing away like a seal and chilling myself good. I finished the painting in about a week and a half, breathing a sigh of big gladness when the family came to get it, Leonidas Loudermilk turning out to be a portly soul with a meaching mouth—which somewhat reminded me of Wayde Mitchell—and the professor treating him like he was dirt, without actually saying so. By this time the professor's rounded up nine other portrait commissions, and I can see I'm going to be rolling in wealth.

Some way this doesn't matter. I sleep Letty, dream Letty, wake wanting her.

The next portrait is of Miss Tora Will Simmons. She's easier. She's skinny, all slats and vinegar and a dark face that's been born sad even though it has a wistfulness about it I like. I put her in front of a column the professor had, he said from Delphi, and graced the column with a lot of smilax running down its flank. She had a hand on the column like she was going to feed it sugar, as you'd do a horse.

Her barley-water expression got onto the canvas nice, and sometimes she talked of lost loves and children dying young and romantic lovers dying together and twining into each other in roses above their graves, and sometimes she recited poetry which she'd either written herself or clipped, careful, out of sad books; it sure lacked the spunk and fire of Keats or Coleridge or even Wordsworth.

We got along in good fashion. After her portrait came Anne Raintree's, but that was no chore because her brother came along with her and sat stiff as a jug in the corner, eyes on me as if I was a tiger might move on my prey any minute. My horniness went down a spell; I was feeling better, except in those pinching minutes when I'd think, Where's Letty now? Could she have run off from Mitchell? Could she go back to the mill and hide up in the days, with Seven and the Darlings seeing to it she's all right? Or could she have opened the strongbox and gone her way, leaving Mitchell to pant at her footprints?

I didn't know.

A week till Christmas. Miz Amily's got smilax all over the house, and is creating food you wouldn't believe unless you'd tasted it—nothing better'n Letty could have done, but marvelous. Sillabub in a great punchbowl. I took Jarhinda downtown, with the professor's second-best carriage, to get her shod. While I'm in the smith's I look around and see some shops where I believe I can get hold of a little silver box I've noted there before, for Miz Amily for Christmas; I'd already got the professor's gift, a small painting I'd done in secret, in my room, of him in his favorite chair reading Greek, just looking up, caught sudden, at the second. Outside the second portrait of Letty it was the best I'd ever done.

I dickered for the silver box, in the shop across from the smithy. The shops—even the smith's—were fixed up a bit for Christmas; there wasn't much money about, except in homes like the Loudermilks', but there was sufficient cheer to amuse a multitude.

In all the homes along all the streets that green feeling swayed and leaped. They all had their rooms of green, from staircase to ceiling, swaddling them close.

Out in the street when I came out, the box wrapped under my arm, I nods to the editor of one of the papers—he's been at the professor's to visit—and to several other citizens. "Morning, Mister Gainsborough; morning, Mister Evans." Walk down a way, see Jarhinda's still having her hoofs shod, move along, and then, sudden, over the housetops and the spindling winter boughs of trees, straight ahead, see a sign attached to a kite flying in the clean winter air. It says, Farley's Balloon Ascension, and I followed it up, keeping my eyes on it so careful I bumped into a number of other walkers, who in this generous season didn't appear to mind.

Twenty-Three

YOU MIGHT THINK by this time people would have recognized me—somebody would have, anyhow—from my having been here the year before.

But fact is, people accept you for what you appear to be. Say Lawyer, and they think, law. Say horse coper, and they think that. Say mysterious painter from over the sea, and that's what they think and see. Once in a time, I'd had narrow escapes; especially when I'd gone down to the creek behind the house and found some of the same boys I'd painted the year before in that picture I'd liked of boys swimming. But while they fished for little shiny wiggling perch and sprats and such, they had just looked at me sidewise, and I'd understood how different I looked now, dressed up handsome, and kind of aloof the way the professor had suggested I be. The year before I'd been hired hand, man-of-all-work around the professor's, and sometime painter. Now I was full-time painter. Didn't figure that unless Senator Margate, the one I've mentioned that the professor had me paint back then, heaved in sight, I'd be wholly pinned down and recognized. And Margate was in Washington, helping wreck the affairs of the nation.

I thought all these consoling things a dozen times a day. Thought them even now as I hiked my way through the crowds to the edge of the field where the kite-banner saying Farley's Balloon Ascension floated above our heads. It was a field with canvas fitted around it about to the height of ten feet, and posters on the canvas; there was a flap in the canvas where a man was taking money to get in. Cost a reasonable amount to get in, just fifteen cents.

Was a line of people, a good many with Christmas packages under their arms, all in a jolly mood, waiting to go through the flap. I got in line. Paid my fifteen cents. Went on through. The man who took my money was a trim fellow in a bright blue close-fitting coat and a good many mufflers around his neck; he had a bronzed, quick look and a steady set of eyes made me think of a less shy Darling brother.

I found myself along with all the others coming in, in a runway behind a rope which stretched around the field between the canvas and the pickets that held the rope, and out in the middle of the winter-dulled field was the balloon. It lay half-slumped on its side alongside a wicker basket which looked pretty commodious and handsome, with bags of sand in the basket and the whole basket-rig appearing as trim as the man who'd collected the entrance fee.

But it was the balloon that drew the eye and just naturally sucked you into admiration. It was monstrous, even slack and lying there quiet; made of silk, colored scarlet and blue and white in triangular swatches, and looking so bright it made a small child in the arms of a woman near me crow like a baby bantam and clap its hands. I couldn't help grinning at that child or feeling good all over when I looked at the balloon, either. It was a sight to my mind as handsome as the elephant of Magnusun's, that Sara, had ever been, and I'd got to feel real fond of Sara.

After a spell, having garnered all the crowd he can for this trip, here comes the man who'd taken our money, and I figured him to be Farley; the way he walked through the crowd

and ducked under the rope and rubbed his hands together
and went at his work like a beaver starting to build a dam,
made me feel he knew what he was about.

When you see a painter coveting the feel of his materials,
taking his time about paint-mixing and tasting the tips of his
brushes and his hands liking the feel of all he does—just as if
he's addressing a good woman who likes to be loved—you see
the same thing you saw with this gent now, as he hiked up the
balloon and spread it careful and smooth, moving around it as
though he'd been born to get it off the ground and had broth-
erly knowledge of its inmost workings. He whistles through
his teeth, and a short little man, with a doings of a moustache—if I couldn't grow better I'd never have done it, back at
the mill—came running out, and with ropy muscles standing
out on his wide shoulders, started helping the first man get
the lower end, the mouth, of the balloon up on edge. Then
the littler man with the fur-brush moustache also starts building a fire in a small iron stove that already had the coal
stocked in it, and that had a narrow gooseneck pipe slanting
from it. The mouth of the balloon, the lower part, was fitted
around this gooseneck pipe. I kept my eye close on the smaller
man.

For if everything I'd heard so far was right, and it looked as
though it was, this was Harkins, the man had run off with
Letty's mother. When he switched around to tell the crowd to
stay back of the ropes—some children were trying to scrooch
under—I saw his eyes were small and set a bit too close
together, like a fox's. But for all his muscle he didn't seem extraordinary as to agility, to my thinking.

Slowly, the bag of the balloon filled with the warm air. And
that was good to see, too. It was like a live animal taking in
breath. It wriggled and swelled. People hushed down now except for little digs at each other with elbows, and saying,
"Now, look at that," and other marveling sounds.

I thought of how I'd felt when Letty and I'd first walked
into that clearing and seen those houses around, and the main
house waiting for us, and the then-stilled mill with its silence
and its waiting.

Made a brief tug in the inside of you, under the skin, churning.

The balloon kept filling. Now it was starting to stand up, rising on its own and erect as a great handsome blob of color shadowing the field. The first man, Farley it had to be, was pulling on ropes to get it even straighter. It loomed up above the basket and wanted to escape into the sky. It seemed it had acquaintances up there in the clouds and wished to rub chins with them. Farley, if it was him, and it had to be, stepped in the basket, going over its edge neat as a rabbit into its accustomed hole, and then he ties off the balloon-mouth even closer to the stove's pipe with wire and string, doing it dexterous and tight; then he stands there, blue-clad chest filling with air and mufflers floating out around his throat, and calls out, "Cast off, Loogan!"

So the man I took to be Loogan Harkins untied the slip-knots of the ropes holding the balloon and all at once, in a sighing of the crowd and a raising of their heads as it went up, there goes the whole balloon with the basket swaying beneath. Went sharp, fast, straight.

We all craned below it. Silent, even the children—even the baby in the arms of the mother standing alongside me. Then somebody whooped and a tall cheering stood straight up, so pleased it must've puzzled the few starlings circling nearby in the air.

Pretty soon the balloon against the tempered half-sun-washed day is just a speck against the sky and looking so neat and brilliant it made you glad man could invent such a thing.

After a time up there we all hear the voice of Farley, small, crisp. Calling down: "Clear away!"

At this time Harkins—or Loogan Harkins—is running all around the rope, still bidding people to stay back and out of the central circle under the balloon. It's coming down fast. A sandbag comes squashing down like a plumper shot goose, landing in the center of the field and tearing up grasses. Then another, and another. The balloon rises. And then the balloon is coming down again. But slower.

Everybody sighed, and I sighed too, as it settled again to

earth and as Farley jumped out and began helping Harkins
haul on the guy ropes that kept it tethered. They left it tugging at its stake moorings there, alive as a horse fretting to
leave the post again; I figured they would have four or five
more performances this day. And now Harkins is waving and
motioning to a small tent, one of three over on the west of the
field, and calling for people to come have their palms read
and fortunes told by Madam Fortuna. He jumps up on the
platform in front of the middle tent and starts tossing plates
into the air. Wasn't as bad as Magnusun and Tad Ainslee and
Sir Alpheus Merry had said; while I watched him, and while I
pushed forward to the tent along with some others—but not
many—who'd decided to take advantage of this opportunity,
he only dropped two. They were iron or something; they
didn't break. He was sweating and keeping his eyes on the
plates while he exhorts the crowd to go in and see Madam
Fortuna. He bawled that she was the seventh daughter of a
seventh daughter, born with a caul; I doubted that, since
Letty'd never told me a word about having any aunts.

I took my place in the short line, shuffled along, noting that
Madam Fortuna gave very quick readings, for the line moved
at a steady pace. Stood behind a citizen who kept gawking at
the signs of the zodiac painted on Madam Fortuna's tent as
though they might mean something grave and great to his life
in the next few minutes; I supposed they might, in the hands
of a real fortune teller, but naturally I had some Fortuna
doubts. But I was afire to see Letty's mother. Finally the citizen ahead of me in line ducked in, as another one came out—
this last one didn't look too pleased, and mutters, "It's a sell!"
in my ear as he huffs along on his way.
    Inside I could just hear a soft voice talking, just below the
level where anybody standing outside the tent could make out
the words and get any free prognosticating.
    I breathes light, biding my time.
    Then the citizen I've mentioned, the eager one, comes out,
looking just a mite dazed and scratching his head before he
puts his hat on, and I ducked under the flap.

Was so dark inside, and smelled so of perfumed smoke from the sticks of Chinese or Indian incense burning in little braziers to left and right of the entrance, I both blinked and held back a sneeze.

"Sit down," says a voice in front of me.

I sat on a stool in there. Then I could make out in the flame of a candle beside a crystal ball, down at the end of the dark-curtained low table between us, the face of Madam Fortuna.

Well, it's like Letty's and it's not. There's the same forthright proud look and somehow the same stillness; but this woman's taller, and bigger-shouldered, with deep big breasts I can see even behind the purple-gray shawl that half-covers her body. She wears a silk cloth around her head and the hair I can see showing under it is darker than Letty's. The face is a kind of wonder of handsomeness, but there's a light of suspicion too in the eyes even in only the candle flame showing them. Suddenly all I felt was sorry. That didn't keep me from holding out the palms of both hands, as she bade me do. This close, the voice was Letty's in timbre and the way the words were spaced, but the face sure really wasn't. There was still fire in it—she was a woman you'd have turned to on any street in the nation, looking after her—but it had seen hard times, and was nothing like the hickory-nut smoothness and openness of Letty's. But the point was any man looking at her would have known her for Letty's mother if he'd ever seen the daughter. Came to me that *she* mightn't have recognized Letty, since she'd left six years before when Letty was so young. That seemed so sad it ran under all the words she said.

Her patter—she'd hardly looked me in the face, just took the hands—ran along, "You have a beautiful life ahead, they are young hands, they have seen much work but they are strong and well shaped. Now to trace the life line—ah, mmmm. Here we find troubles, young man, plenty of them . . ."

"That's always been a fact," I supplies.

Her eyes, darker green than Letty's but still with a flick of that leafiness in them, look up. She seems irritated.

"I'll do the talking, young man."

Then I think for the first time she sizes me up. Sees the vest, the good coat. Fixes me a bit.

"Might you prefer a longer reading? A full one, using the crystal ball of Astarte?"

"Astarte?"

"Love goddess of the Phoenicians. Brought from abroad, smuggled here at the first of the century—"

It looked fairly ordinary crystal, was flawed a bit in checks and patches.

"I give true readings. In the home, by appointment, or here by appointment as well. But they take time."

"I'll think it over," I told her. I was still feeling sad about her; sorry I had to do this, but needing to do it bad.

But I knew this was just the opening gun, this palm-reading visit. Knew if she and Loogan Harkins had anything to do with old Einsner's killing I was going to find out about it before many days passed, beyond these flickery feelings of sadness and anything else. Kept remembering *she* was the only one outside Letty, and maybe Mitchell, that could have known about the money.

Set my jaw, and says a bit rough, "Get on with this. If I do want a special thing, how long'll you be around?"

"All the winter long until March." She'd dropped her half-crooning Fortuna ways now and was just speaking to me. Was matter-of-fact and again somewhat more Lettyish. "You live in town?"

I debated, fast, whether or not to tell her. What harm could it do? She might've heard of the killing—whether or not she had a thing to do with it—and of me being wanted; but that didn't make a damn because she'd never seen me before in her days. Nobody had any pictures of me, I'd never had one taken, couldn't afford a Mathew Brady. Outside this darkened secret place with the tent canvas smelling of the incense and Harkins's voice bawling the suckers inside and the sound, now and then, of his plates hitting the soil, was the whole world of chance and change. I says, "I live at Professor Allan's," and gave her the address. "But I'll have to think about a special reading. There's some things he wants to know and maybe he'll be int'rested."

I can see her noting the address.

She went on reading my palm then. The right one. She'd dropped the other hand. Her hands weren't as handsome as Letty's but they were still nicely made. She told me I'd likely live a long and prosperous life, and that I was connected with something in the art line. She could've got that from the local papers. Connecting it up with the name of Professor Allan and considering that piece that had been in the papers about Delevan Gainsborough. I expected palmists and foretellers gave all newspapers a good going over for useful hints. She was brisk about it all, but says, as I get up when it's over, "Get in touch when you can, Mister. You won't regret it. I promise an interesting evening for you and all your friends."

"I'll think about it, ma'am." I paid her the two bits.

I stepped out in the air. Felt bothered and crawled on by something. Couldn't tell what. It sure wasn't that handsome balloon pulsing away on its ropes above the field and making the whole day quicken in this field.

Went back to the smith's and picked up Jarhinda and the second-best rig, and felt I'd see more of them all: quick agile Farley, to be sure, but even more of little-moustached Harkins, and Letty's ma. Felt it bubble along in my veins while we clipped our way home, Jarhinda moving smart as mustard but no better than my own bay in the past when I put her into a trot, through the Christmas-beaming crowds in the streets and the good feel of parties in the air.

Was a party that night at the professor's. Just one of the many semi-balls and gatherings went on all through this part of his city. I'd told him about finding Farley's Balloon Ascension. About, especially, Letty's mother.

He said, while we stood beside the small orchestra tuning up—five fiddles and the piano, in the ballroom which was smilax-dripping and fine, with the bowl of sillabub handy and the tables looking lush . . . said, "Delevan, we are homing in.

Maintain your patience and wait. I've heard from a good friend of mine—he lives in Washington. My inquiries were discreet, but they piqued his curiosity a great deal. He knows of my interest in you, although, quite naturally, he does not yet know I am harboring you. He may have to, before long. He may visit us here. We'll leap that fence when it arises. For now, let us study Madam Fortuna and her cohort. I'll go for a reading tomorrow."

He told me how the Romans, in their ignorance, had told fortunes with chicken guts. Seemed a waste of gizzards.

Then the orchestra struck up and he led the ball with Miz Amily on his arm. I stood aloof and broody for a time, till I couldn't stand it any longer and went and collared Miss Sally Lou Loudermilk from the stick with pants on she'd been dancing with, and I must say she cut a mean reel for such a plump girl, and that whirling her around got my mind off Letty and onto just general womanhood for quite a spell. At least ten minutes.

Twenty-Four

NEXT DAY THE PROFESSOR WENT by himself to see Farley's Balloon Ascension in the field.

I had an appointment to take Miss Sally Lou Loudermilk boating on the James. All that day I kept wondering in the back of my head what the professor would make of Madam Fortuna, and Loogan Harkins. Sometimes I'd think, Well, he knows what he's doing and maybe all his work on writing letters and figuring a design in all this will come to something; and then again I'd think, And maybe it won't.

Of course I trusted him more than anybody I'd ever known in my life. Wasn't he risking his own reputation as an honorable man for all this, and didn't he run the chance of being arrested for harboring a wanted man? Other hand, I knew he enjoyed the whole thing; there was a good deal of the small boy whipping up thick-meshed plots and hiding behind apple trees and pretending Indians, in his makeup. I suppose it's there in all really interesting people.

With me, it burned serious in the back of my mind. But I enjoyed that heifer-plump Sally Lou Loudermilk too. We boated around the islands in the river, it was a real clear day, though moving toward the cold side; in spite of the chill she had a bright little blue umbrella she kept twirling in her fingers while we sloshed along. After a time we landed at Belle Isle, where they'd kept prisoners during the war. She minced her way around the sights, and when we went back to get in the boat she slips, half on purpose, and falls against me.

I grabs her, supports her in all her lace and finery, and all at once I'm hugging her and her lips are open, so I bent her back farther and gave her a good rousing kiss.

When we straightens she's giggling, which was her way of saying she'd enjoyed it.

I picks up her umbrella and returns it. On the way back to town she's very fluttery-eyed and the giggles come along like a bird remarking on the beauty of existence, just a flood of clucking and snirting. Again I'm a trifle roused by her, but I really don't want it to move any farther—though it could; she's the sort of woman you could take while she was eating an apple and looking through a stereopticon machine—mainly because it wouldn't take any edge off wanting Letty; just make it worse.

That evening when I get home the professor calls me in his deducing room, the library, shuts the door, and says, hands spraddled on his knees, "Delevan"—for custom, he called me that even with the door shut—"we move apace."

"Kind of hoped we might," I says.

"Faster than you may like," he says.

I says, "Sir, nothing can be too fast."

"Excellent, then. Today I invited Madam Fortuna—or Mrs. Einsner, as you're convinced she is—to give a seance here the day after New Year's Day."

"Oho!" I says.

"It seems Farley's Balloon Ascension is taking a holiday on that day, and, learning of this, I also invited her to bring along her friend, Mister Harkins. She said she would. I promised a good emolument for her reading; I'm certain they'll both show up. The reading is scheduled for three o'clock in the afternoon. And I also made friends with their employer, Milt

Farley, and invited *him* along. If they—Harkins and Mrs. Einsner—were connected in any way with the death of Einsner, it's quite possible Farley might know about it—might, perhaps, even be protecting them; or, Zeus save us, have been involved in the murder itself. I doubt it—"

"So do I, just on the surface," I says.

"—but it isn't outside the realm of possibility. Still, I like him. It's not difficult to admire his art—and he *is* an artist, we had quite a talk about Montgolfier and other famous ascensionists—"

I might have known the professor would do all that; there was very little about the world he didn't know something of, in dibs, dabs, and smatterings.

"—in fact, he is a soul I enjoy. Not so Harkins—I spent some time with all three, and he's a suspicious and flighty man, although I must say I bent every effort to charm him. As to Madam Fortuna, of course she is a charlatan—but she also impresses me as a woman *capable* of carrying through whatever scheme she had set her mind on. I want to make plain that I asked no leading questions—merely set my snare. Three o'clock the day after New Year's, they will deliver themselves on our doorstep."

He took a full breath. Could tell he wasn't through yet, by a far shot.

"And now, my second point. Since they will be here, all together, I propose to inject another element—an element containing risk, perhaps—"

"It's all been full of that, sir."

"True. But this is greater risk for you than for me. The other day I mentioned having heard from a friend of mine, an official in Washington. I told you of his keen interest in my questions. This morning, after returning from the ascension field, I heard from him by post once more—and I find that he wishes to visit here, and wishes moreover to arrive on the morning of the day after New Year's. My dilemma is this: shall I telegraph him and tell him to come ahead, or shall I fob him off for a time? Luke—Delevan, I forget myself—Delevan, he is a very old friend. We were on opposite sides in the war, but I admire his courage and fairness and sense of justice; he's a United States marshal, Tom Prosser."

Could hear myself swallow, the click in my ears.

Professor goes on, "I don't believe he has the faintest notion that you are here, on the premises. But he wants to quiz me thoroughly and in person; perhaps unfortunately—perhaps toward enlightenment, who knows?—my questions to him have aroused his enormous interest. And, though he tells me little, I have the impression he is most conversant with the slaying of Carl Einsner and eager to know more of all I know."

I didn't answer yet. Professor says gently, "If you don't approve of his coming, just say so, and I'll make some excuse and we shall continue to move in other directions. But it might help bring affairs to a head. And Thermopylae was not fought by cautious men."

I waited, still mum, and the professor put his head back and shut his eyes and says, "My lord fool, from this nettle, danger, we pluck the flower, safety," and I nods even though his eyes are shut, and he goes on, opening them, "What's your decision, Delevan?"

I felt all the past ever since running from Einsner's house that night along the road in the moonlight, wheeling through my mind. But I'd already put myself too far in the professor's hands to back out. Having a U.S. marshal under the same roof would be a prickery feeling, but I'd stood just as bad so far without wilting.

I says I'm game.

"Ah, good, good. I'll telegraph him to come ahead. And now for the seance. I have some special plans for that. You can help. Let me tell you what you can begin doing in preparation for this excursion into the black arts . . ."

He started telling me about how he planned to handle the seance, and while he did I got the feeling it might work. It was as crazy as some of Jeb Stuart's riding around the whole Union lines just to get some fresh real coffee for his troops— which were sick of drinking stewed bark—but that had worked, and under his high forehead and cotton-silk hair the professor was a raging chance-taker who'd often in his career come through with triumph.

I still had some work to do on some of the commissioned portraits, and that night I worked on them in the ballroom for a time, then started on the special painting the professor wanted me to do. It was part of his plan for the seance. I got into a heavy working mood with it, and covered it up good after I'd got it well started. I was just strolling back to the front room, with the ballroom door locked behind me against this other secret painting he'd wanted, when there came a rat-tat on the door—the professor had gone out earlier to send his answer to Washington—and I happened to be right behind Miz Amily when she answered.

It's a black man from the Loudermilks, dressed in the violet and gold uniforms all their servants had to wear. He says, "For Mister Gainsborough, ma'am," and hands her a sealed letter.

She says thank you, gives him a small Christmas gift—she kept them in the hall for anybody who came by on any errand—and he skips back down to the Loudermilk carriage. She gives me the letter and I opens it. "From one of your young ladies?"

"Looks like from her pa," I says. "The young ladies don't write me notes, they just plague me till I've got blisters."

I slit it open. It requested me to call at the Loudermilks' the next afternoon for a chat with the father. He's signed it, flowingly.

Shows it to Miz Amily. I says, "You expect he wants *another* portrait of his daughter? Be all right if I liked painting young cows for a living. But I got to hump now to finish up the rest that's been ordered."

"Oh—" She scans it. "I think I'd put in an appearance. They're a vulgar family, but they can be tolerated. If you ever want to pink him, ask him where he got his wealth."

"Professor told me about that. War profiteer."

"—selling necessities for dear prices while the rest of us starved. Dealing with the enemy. But Christmas is nigh, and we must be charitable, the Good Book says."

The professor got home about nine o'clock, having sent his answer to his friend the U.S. marshal, and cussing the inefficiency of the people who handled its sending. He shrugged out of his going-out cape and took off his broad-brim hat, and was full of himself and his plans. "The die is cast, Delevan. Have you started the project I asked for?"

I took him back to the ballroom, unlocked it, and showed him what I'd done so far and kept turned to the wall with a cover-cloth over it. He says, "It's ghastly. Keep on."

So I worked a while longer, and later, when I went up to bed, sat by the window a long time, looking out. Rain was starting, silver on the green pines down at the back of the lot, and on the stable roofs, and glinting on the creek back of that. I thought about the night of the big rain with Letty; seemed if, in the rear of my mind, I could see the mill and hear that wheel moving and moving. Also seemed when I finally slipped into bed and lay there looking up at the picture of the Greek horses, that they'd started running faster than ever before.

They motioned in my sleep.

Next day, now only a handful of days before Christmas, I took Jarhinda again, riding her with a saddle now, and made my way through town and out to the edge to the Loudermilks'. They had an enormous old place Loudermilk had got cheap toward the end of the war when people around there had to sell off their nearest and dearest stuff for a few pennies. It rose sassy and bright on a hill surrounded by tall poplar and magnolia and weeping willows and all manner of azalea plantings, and glossy hedges that flicked rain-wet on Jarhinda's coat as we spanked up the drive. I rode her under the portico and a black man came skimming down the steps to take her. Even climbing the steps was quite a task, and by the time I got to the top I was sorry I'd come. I felt I should have just stayed on my European-artist dignity and paid no attention to any polite summons.

I didn't even have a chance to rap-tap on the door with my riding crop—which was the professor's—because it was already open, and the butler let me in. The whole place was bedizened for Christmas, but it wasn't like a lot of other houses in town because not so many attended the Loudermilks' balls. Not the old families, and sure not the professor. I felt a kind of pity for Mrs. Loudermilk and Sally Lou because of this; reflected that I hadn't told the professor I was coming here; remembered the meach-mouth way Leonidas Loudermilk had acted around me when he and his lady and his daughter had dropped by the professor's to approve of Sally Lou's portrait.

The butler led me into a side room, and Leonidas got up and came toward me. He looked so prettied up he might've stepped out of a New York store window, as a dummy. Reminded me just a bit of Mitchell, as he'd done before.

"Well, my son. My son."

We sat down, kind of edgy.

He hems and haws and I thinks, Why can't he just say it? The whole room, a gracious room in its walls, was full of little bird-wing china pieces, and the chairs were horsehair and not fit to sit on square.

I says, "Rain's chilling some. Snow for the holidays?"

He says, "Yes indeed!" as though I've just brought him several engraved tablets to ponder.

Then he says, looking at the ceiling, "Mister Gainsborough, what I have to say is of a delicate nature, and since you have not come forward with it, it behooves me to bring it up."

"Be behooved," I offers.

Then he looks at me, wambling-eyed, and says, "I'm sure you and Sally Lou will be very happy, and I am prepared to offer you a splendid position in one of my tobacco warehouses. I realize yours has been somewhat of a wandering life—unsettled—and I know you'll wish to give up painting, except as a social accomplishment, when you become part of a solid family. I—"

"Whoa, horse!" My heels came down on the polished floor with a whack and I sat up straight as Letty could ever sit.

Says, "You speaking of your daughter and me?"

"You have compromised her." It was hard for him to say that, and he says it looking at his feet.

"How? You mean I've tampered with her?"

"Tampering—" he starts to say.

"Fiddled with her, humped her, tupped her, had her, built a fire in her stove?"

"Mister Gainsborough!"

I tells him then that it was with some regret I hadn't fiddled with his daughter, or done any of those other things either. Says it was only because I willed not to, though. Says it's mightily apparent that when a man plays a so-called gentleman around the Loudermilks he's going to be held accountable for things he's never done. Says—remembering something I'd heard the professor say—that they order these things better in France.

Turned on my heel, then, and stalked out. I was partly wanting to laugh, too. But when I'd got halfway down the steps here came a waving hand from a clump of blossomless azalea down on the east of the steps, and I sashayed that way, giving a pat to Jarhinda who was standing hitched to a column-rail under the porte cochere.

It was Sally Lou. She pulls at my fingers and she's trying her best not to giggle, maybe because she knows it irks me. Says, "Down here in the summerhouse."

We went through the rain and here's this place with a domed roof and a little wicketed door and divan-benches all around inside, rain pattering on the roof like a song.

She steps in, I following. If ever she had fire in her, now she did. She says, "Are we engaged?"

"No ma'am." I takes her by the shoulders. "And we're not about to be. Nor am I about to be an official in the tobacco warehouse line and breathe dust all day and eat humble pie all night. What'd you have to bring this to a head for?"

She was a long way from giggling now. Looked better'n she'd done any time since I'd painted her.

She couldn't help it if her daddy had scoured up all his coin from grinding the faces of good noble thoughtful people who believed in everything their part of the war stood for.

Her eyes got big, and she clutches my coat.

"Oh, Delevan, Delevan—I can't lose you."

"Not a matter of losing, matter of never owning." I didn't want to be cold and abrupt though. We sat down on one of the divans, cool from the rain-feeling of the day, and I stroked her and told her I didn't love her the way she wanted it, with getting married and all; I told her everything about that. But not about Letty, though I'd just as soon have. And then I says, "Seems to me you've got your mind set on a glass-bubble life, where you'll show off your husband at parties and teas, but not ever knowing him and him knowing you the way people can. All I can offer is a little pleasure for a time, and it may not last long but it's kind in the memory. If you want it, fine, if you don't, that's elegant too."

She looks at me close for a spell. Breathing hard. I'm ready to be pushed away or stay, though if I'm pushed I resolve to take a long cooling ride on Jarhinda before I circle back to the professor's place. I'll need it, by now.

Then she says, "Unhook me," and I want to cheer a little for the bravery that took. I unhooks her. She sure had all manner of stays. More than Penelope ever thought of wearing, more than Letty would stand wearing. When they came off she was like a big half-peeled-back wonderous rose, petals too large for most life, but enticing and lovely for this.

I helped her off with some of the rest of those unnecessitous garments, and in the green rainlight she was better than I'd even thought she'd be.

For such a dumpling-built girl she had a mighty talent. I'd expected it was there, and I wished her well with it the rest of its joyful days.

Says, afterward, as we're parting at the door of the summerhouse, "Don't blame yourself, that's the main thing. While you're at it, don't blame me either."

Shakes her head, she won't. She smelled of warm powder and some perfume and herself, but not as nose-filling as Letty.

Oh, it's a good scent, a warm woman. They ought to bottle it and sell it in medicine shows.

She went her way, I mine, I thinking I'd like to paint her as she was when she was under me, the way some of the French painters who get the whole bigness of womanhood seemed to me to do. Felt sad but whole and lighter again. Hopped on Jarhinda and cantered out of there, she dancing at the bit and wanting to really streak, me holding her in with tight elbows.

When I got home I told the professor about answering the request to call out there, and the professor said, "And what did he want?"

I told him, and indicated that other things had happened between me and Leonidas Loudermilk's daughter. The professor saw it quick, I'd not needed to go in detail with him, then got to laughing and had to sit down in his leather chair. He shook his head, waving Miz Amily away as she came to the study door to see what the noise was. "I hope the girl is happy," he said when Miz Amily'd gone.

"I think she'll be," I says. A feeling of monstrous need for Letty Einsner flowed through me, bootsoles to eyes, as I'd known it would. "I hope so. I like her dearly."

Then he got serious and plotting, and says he's had the acknowledgment back from U.S. Marshal Tom Prosser, and that his old friend will be here the morning following New Year's Day. That night at dinner—he'd let Miz Amily in on all his plans for the seance, in fact, she was part of them—we sat up late, working out the details of the scheme, down to where everybody would sit.

The professor didn't seem to give a whit about Loudermilk ever making more fuss. He was above all that. Had been, his bright life long.

Twenty-Five

FOR A FEW DAYS after that, right up till Christmas and after, I missed the flint and fire of Letty so fierce I could hardly stand it. I plunged myself in work, finishing the last of the portrait commissions and getting paid for it. I finished the secret painting the professor'd had me do, too. But in between times I prowled like a bear in a pit, and glowered around and thought, sometimes, it would be better just to give myself up to the authorities if that meant I might soon see Letty again.

Miz Amily said I looked peaked, like Byron had in those days when he was dieting. She gave me sulphur and molasses, though it was a long time till spring.

It tasted awful but could be wiped out with a smidge of Madeira wine afterward.

On Christmas I was feeling especially let-down. Made all the proper motions, and gave Miz Amily her silver box, which was lined with cedar and had been made, the man sold it to me said, in Florence, Italy. Gave the professor the small painting of him done mostly from memory and from thumbnail sketches when he didn't know what I was sketching. They gave me a whole new outfit, medium-tall hat included, all in dove gray with blue facings like a rich mercantile man's. Wearing it to church with them that afternoon, for the professor liked going to church on occasion, said it cleansed him of rubbage, I felt like a smart citizen—but sad as stump-water inside.

In church, filing in, we all said hello to various friends and acquaintances; when we got to the Loudermilks there was a mite of coolness, and some held-back smiles on the professor's part, but Sally Lou gave me a considering, warm look and I figured the tumble in the summerhouse hadn't affected her permanent, or crazed her mind.

It was a nice church, where once on a time Patrick Henry had said that about liberty and death, plumping harder for liberty.

Then on New Year's Day we went the round of visits together, the three of us, with the bells ringing through town and people seeming to joy in the turn of the year. I didn't figure 1875 was going to be much different, in the main, than 1874 had been; all I knew was that 1874 would always be blazed somewhere in me like letters cut deep in a stump, because it was when I'd met Letty. Under what you might term odd circumstances.

The day after New Year's the professor was up bright and early and jumping about like a bird after juicy crumbs. Seeing that Miz Amily and me knew our parts down solid, as though he was rehearsing for one of those old Greek plays in those outdoor theaters he had models of. Except we didn't wear masks. I might as well have worn one, because I was so jumpy inside I didn't feel I even looked like L. Applegate, or, much, like Delevan Gainsborough. Kept being fumble-handed and going dry-mouthed and wondering what U.S. Marshal Prosser looked like, and if he carried handcuffs. He was expected on the morning train.

When it came time for the professor to meet him the professor had reached a fever pitch of excitement and planning, but this just made him cool and crisp. He gave final orders and buzzed off in the carriage; I went behind the curtains covering the alcove off the library, checked my painting there, came out, walked across the library to the other end, checked the magic lantern to see it had plenty of oil and could be lighted to cast a good clear circle of a beam where we wanted it cast for the seance, and then tried to settle down in the library and read a book till Prosser arrived. After a spell, looked up from the book—it was the Chapman translation of Homer, the part about Ulysses that goes, "The sea had soaked his heart through"—looked up because Miz Amily was standing beside me. She laid a hand on my shoulder. "He's here," she says soft. "They're just coming up the street. Be of stout heart."

Told her I'd do my best. The heart seemed all right. But I felt my bowels turn over a bit. She went out and after a while I heard the door opening and U.S. Marshal Tom Prosser and the professor coming in. Then there was a little old-friends talk among them with Miz Amily joining in strong. I sat still without thinking a thought or reading a single singing word. Then into the library comes the professor and Miz Amily and this Tom Prosser.

Prosser's a square-faced bulldogged-looking man with hair white as the professor's, but worn short. He's bigger than the professor—not a hard thing to be—and even a shade taller than me, but with stooped heavy shoulders. Dressed in black broadcloth which makes his frosty hair and frosty eyebrows— tangled like waterweed—seem to shine out against the black in the library. Flesh tones all white, and jaw a slab of bone and gristle, and eyes pale blue but searching. Doesn't seem at first look as if he likes me a bit.

He's got a voice like a boat run aground and warning off other vessels from the shoals.

He says, "How do you do, sir." Gazing deep at me.

Professor says, "This is the young man I was telling you about, Thomas. The gifted and redoubtable painter, Delevan—"

Professor stops, because Tom Prosser has just grunted. Then Prosser is lurching across the library to me where I've now got up in front of my chair. He sticks out a hand. It's a bone-crusher of a grip, but not holding on—just letting go after the first second. Then he turns around to the professor and points a finger and says, "Harvey. You're incurable. You're so romantic it will be the death of you. Or of me." He swings back to me. His belly is square-cut too under the black vest with its gold droop of watch chain.

He says, "Again I greet you. But this time I shall give you your real name. How do you do, Mister Applegate."

I stood there like I'd been hit by a rough tree falling on a calm day. Found, after a second, that I could still move. Enough to open my mouth. And when I opened it I could hear myself talking while the professor stood back just opening and shutting his own mouth—took a lot to make him flabbergasted—and what I was saying was, "All right, sir. Applegate it is."

Yet right through my guts-falling-out feeling was a kind of lightsomeness and relief. Came sudden and strange and I had the notion that whatever stood ahead now, it would come faster, and whatever it was, I could bear it under my right name at last.

"Yes. Applegate it is," says U.S. Marshal Tom Prosser. "I had a very large notion something like this might be going on. Knowing Harvey Allan and his penchant for foolery. Well, Applegate, let me say this. First, I'm perfectly familiar with your case. I have been for about a month. Now sit down. Let's all sit down."

Sitting down was the foremost thing I needed to do.

He, himself, sat square-bottomed as a bear looking over a honey tree, and combed his fingers through his short hair. Regarded me strong all the while. The professor wasn't saying anything, though I doubted his powers of speech had been stopped forever. Finally Tom Prosser said, quite quiet, even a mite sad, "Harvey will never learn. He dotes on plots and stratagems. They worked for him in sixty-two and sixty-three. They won skirmishes, and the same kind of tactics won battles. If Jefferson Davis had allowed the South to go straight through to Washington, when the path was clear . . ." He shrugged those big, bent shoulders. "There's even a wild ge-

nius about it. But it doesn't work in a case like this one." He
swiveled and said to the professor, "It won't do, Harvey." He
turned to Miz Amily.

"Amily, I'm ashamed of you for not getting in touch with
me the moment Harvey started this charade."

She said, tart enough, "Luke is our friend too, Thomas. Just
as you are. And he didn't slay a soul."

"I'm not implying that he did. That is not the point. You
know it isn't. Now, all of you. Tend to what I say."

Then he talked a little, in the soft rough voice hooting in
the back of his throat like a boat whistle. While I listened I felt
myself getting even lighter. As though everything that had
been pressing on me, for a month Sundays, now had a chink-
hole that could be letting in relief. Prosser's mouth was ungiv-
ing as a trap, but there was something else about him. I
thought whichever side he'd been on in the war his men
would have been lucky.

He said how he'd been very interested in the case, first time
he'd heard of it—first it had crossed his desk, as he put it—this
month or thereabout ago. And how it had come to his attention through some of his operatives, that the sheriff of Mullin's Gap, Wheelman, was working for a lawyer named Mitchell who hailed from Jerseyville, scampering around covering
up any true investigation of the Einsner killing. He said how
his men had discovered, too, that the innkeeper in the Gap,
Tatum, and the livery-stable keeper, Soames, and a lumber-
wagon driver name of Gondy, were in deep cahoots with—and
under the money thumb of—this same Mitchell, who was an
old friend of Einsner's.

He said he'd had the operatives ask around a good deal
more, on the quiet, and dig all they could. And they'd found
Miss Letty Einsner had been living with me up the hill at the
mill above Solomon and Mullin's Gap.

And one of his men had talked to Miss Einsner just a few
days before. Talked to her in Solomon, where she was living
by herself right now.

Right there was where I had to jump in. Didn't care if he
shot me for it. I said, "How—how'd he say she was?"

"In health, Applegate. Not under arrest. Though she is

being watched. And so are you—from this moment until the case is wound up. She made a statement to my man. I want you to make one for me in a little while—after I've had some breakfast, for the food on the train was unbelievable. Yes, she is being watched, and so are Mitchell and his men. And now we have you. We need just a few more. Then we shall be ready to close in and round up for the finish."

"You believe Letty?" I couldn't help saying that, either. Didn't care if he shot me twice and stamped on the body. "Believe neither of us killed her pa?"

His mouth muscles worked. Then: "I don't 'believe' anyone yet, Applegate. Both of you complicated the case badly by running off. Then it was royally complicated by Mitchell's self-serving machinations. It is true that from Miss Einsner's state-ment—it is very lucid—I have put together a few notions. A few ideas. If your statement agrees with hers, some of the ideas may become more than that. It would be well for you to speak the truth in every way."

"He's never done anything else, Thomas," says Miz Amily, with a sniff.

The professor holds up a hand. He'd had a stiff blow in the wind but was coming up for air with everything working and banners aloft. "Luke has told the truth, yes, Amily. He has, Tom. The idea of—of obfuscation, masquerade, was all mine. I do apologize—you are right, I should have told you every-thing, should have had Luke tell you everything, the day he came here. But I coerced him into the cloud-cuckooland of my own impulse—I thought, somehow like Auguste Dupin, I might solve this myself, even from a distance." He jumped up from his chair, white quiff of hair agog. "Tom, you mention that you are seeking 'just a few more' suspects. Could these be"—he puffed his chest up and looked sly and at the same time proud—"could they be Mrs. Einsner, Mister Harkins, and possibly a gentleman—a balloonist—named Milt Farley?"

Tom Prosser just gazed at him. There are looks that wither, but this wasn't that. It was just a heavy, patient, deep-set ex-pression that said without saying it that the professor might be intelligent but was also in the way, and that his in-the-wayness might never stop in all of time, and that Prosser wished to God he would stop it.

The professor sat down again, leaning forward sharp, though.

Prosser says, "All right, Harvey. Tell me what you know about these people."

So the professor spouts it all—all we know. And he tells, kind of rubbing-hands gleeful, about setting up the seance for three o'clock this afternoon.

When he finishes—with a flourish, all his flourishes were still there and I didn't think anybody could ever have changed them—Prosser says, shoulders humping even more, very quiet, "Yes, Harvey. We have a lot of information about Madam Fortuna—or Mrs. Einsner, and Harkins—and even Farley. We've had it for quite a while. And now I am here, Harvey, I am inclined, on careful thought, to let you go forward with your little plan of surprise. I should like to see these people under these circumstances. But Harvey, please don't think you were clever. If I had not come here today, in my capacity as an officer as well as a friend, your plan of attack might well have frightened them off and made my job even more difficult. Harvey." He stops and shakes his head. "You are incorrigible, but try not to be. Don't look upon it as a virtue." He swerves his head over to Miz Amily. "Now. Breakfast, Amily? My hand on my heart—I am starving."

Miz Amily gets up, smoothing down her dress, and starts for the kitchen. "You've been talking pretty Yankee, Thomas. Maybe you ought to starve awhile. But I might have some corn fritters and other food fit to eat, ready before long. Come along and help me, Luke." I got up and followed her, or started to. Then at the door she turns around and said to Prosser, "No, Tom, Luke won't jump out the kitchen window onto the shed roof and make his way across the land, murdering and pillaging."

"I'm sure he won't," says Prosser, looking at her and then at me. "I think he knows better now . . . corn fritters. You are still the gem of any ocean, Amily."

She went on out. I followed.

After the fritters—which Miz Amily naturally spread herself
on—Tom Prosser takes me into the professor's deducing end
of the library. Sits me down in a chair beside the desk. Sits
himself at the desk, opens an old rat of a valise with a brass
lock which he holds on his lap. Belches a trifle—which of
course makes him human, nothing unhuman about him, not
even that tired, cold, steady flaring look in his eyes. Says,
"Begin, Applegate. I'll interrupt when I want you to repeat or
amplify anything. Tell all the small things as well as the large.
Go on."

He made me go over parts of what I told him—–and I told
it all, even about talking to Letty the night of the rampageous
storm, though I did leave out that about the blind, hitting way
she'd killed that snake—made me go over them so many times
I couldn't keep count how many. While I was doing it he
keeps looking up pieces of writing on the pile of papers he'd
dumped out of the valise. I figured those were pieces of
Letty's own statement he was balancing against mine.

I'd just about got through—had to be through, couldn't
think of one thing else to tell him except maybe about Penelope Dabney or Sally Lou Loudermilk, and I doubted if they
had real bearing on the case—when I noted that in one of his
uplooking glances he'd caught sight of that first sketch I'd
made for the professor, showing, in charcoal, Carl Einsner
there on the floor in the front room just as he'd been. Sketch
was still pinned to the paneling over the desk. I see Prosser
look at it slow-eyed, then he reaches up and unpins it. Holds it
in his hand thoughtful, a big hand just as square-shaped as the
rest of him, just as snow-white.

"Is this accurate, Applegate?"

"Right down to the wool in the carpet he dropped on, yes
sir."

"Dropped," he says. "Now, that's an odd word, isn't it?"

"It's what they say in the West," I says. "When they shoot a
man they say they dropped him."

"In this case it's right. He looks—dropped."

I blinks, but that's all he says on that score. I'm sure as I can be of anything, he won't answer another thing if I try to ask *him* questions. Then he starts asking yet more.

So I go right on making noise like a mowing machine in high fall time, that earthy old clacking.

Some minutes to three, I'm in the alcove off the library. Curtains are pulled shut. Here's where I'm supposed to be for my part in the shindig the professor's been planning all these days, the seance. I'd brought the book I'd been reading in there with me. But I couldn't read it—a little too murky anyhow—so I laid it aside, soft, and just felt strange and tight in the dusky afternoon. Can hear Prosser and the professor and Miz Amily ready in the library. Time keeps on dragging, and I'd have sworn it was long past three when I heard the clock in the hall clear its throat and chime. And right on the heels of that the front door had a knock on it, and I clenched my hands and sat still as a thoughtful squirrel when an owl is floating nearby.

Then I heard a voice I made out to be Milt Farley's, fresh and brisk, and after it, the voice of Madam Fortuna—or to call her right, Letty's mother. Also heard the edgy voice of Loogan Harkins; so it had all worked out, they'd all come, they were in the library. Now the professor raised his voice, partly for my benefit, and says, "Please draw the window draperies, Amily." Could hear them being drawn. I risked a peek out of the curtains that hung over my station. I could see just a glimpse of the professor, sitting not too far from me, and Miz Amily at the end of the room where the magic lantern was covered by a velvet cloth, and the candle that'd been lighted in front of the crystal ball over which Madam Fortuna hunkered. And I could see Loogan Harkins sitting nervous, to one side, looking like something dredged up by accident when you were fishing for something else; and Milt Farley near the professor, and past him, Marshal Tom Prosser. I got all this in the swooping glimpse, then cocked my ears and waited.

Took just one glance up at the painting I'd done for this event; it hung directly above me.

"Conditions being right," says the professor, "—and are they, Madam Fortuna?"

"I believe they are, Professor."

"Then, that being so, I wish you to summon the spirit of an old friend. I think—I feel—he has been so near me lately, in thought, that he will come, answering your powers, almost without fail. I cannot give you his name; I think it fair to judge that he may have taken another name in the astral beyond, and I wish to put no earthly shadows in your way."

Madam Fortuna says, in a voice that's paced like Letty's, "It would help if I had his earthly name, Professor Allan."

I'd just bet it would. But he's stubborn. "No ma'am, I have the conviction that it would cloud matters. I myself feel him very near. I have dreamed of him three nights running."

"All right," says Madam Fortuna. I can barely hear her, though I can hear the professor as if he's lecturing. "Then it'd help to know where he lived in his earthly days."

"In the East, Madam. Toward the East. He was a man like a biblical patriarch, cultivating his vines and acres. His fat flocks. But further I do not intend to go. I feel it would only put a pall of earthliness between us. What he is now is not, of course, what he was then."

"Astarte likes to know as much as possible," says Madam Fortuna, in a voice I just caught.

"Astarte must be content with my conviction. Madam, I have brought a dear friend a long distance. Mister Prosser"— he sure wasn't calling him Marshal, and I knew he hadn't when he'd introduced him—"is waiting to appreciate your art. The art which you have claimed, but have not yet begun to demonstrate."

"I'll do my best, Professor."

I sat forward. Could hear her creaking and rustling, through my curtains, and could hear everybody else doing this too.

In a low voice Madam starts crooning. She'd not done it when I'd had the two-bit reading. This was the real business. Sounded like a wind calling between a couple of gaps in rock, hitting one, then the other, on a double note. It was pretty rich. Made me in my darkened place feel real strange, even a bit as I'd felt that night on the Jerseyville road, running with Letty and feeling a blood mist around my motions.

Then I could make out a few words shaped by the windy voice. "Come forth—oh come, from the place where all is new—break through this air, thick with shadows of the past— come forth, appear to us, oh friend of Professor Allan—be with us as you were once in the flesh, show among us and be seen and heard."

She started raising her voice then. I wished she wouldn't. Somehow it made gooseflesh pop out on my arms as though I was taking a cold bath against the delights of the flesh as formerly represented by Sally Lou Loudermilk. I opened my curtains a crack again.

Could just make her out, now, with everybody else sort of framed around her, all looking hard and on edge, even Milt Farley seeming taut as a bow, and her eyes as they looked straight at me, but not seeing me over the candle flame. The crystal seemed to burn like hoarfrost.

"Come forth! Oh, come, man-spirit! Appear!"

Well, right then the professor gives a great wonderful gasp, saying, "Carl!"

It's my signal, and Miz Amily's. I almost didn't move fast enough to get my curtains thrown aside and duck down behind the chair below the picture I'd painted, before Miz Amily had the magic lantern lighted and beaming through the dust motes of the library on the painting. We'd arranged the light to show just right, with a low blue and viridian-colored slide in it that made the picture seem to have launched itself from depths of blue-green space.

To them out there it must've hovered like something just appearing from the deeps of hell, fresh from the Styx.

"Carl, oh, Carl, what have they done to you?" groans the professor. "Murdered Carl Einsner, returned to say who did the deed!"

He was more than half a great actor. Right then he could have given Joe Jefferson, in *Rip Van Winkle*, a great run for his money. I'd seen Jefferson five or six years back and had mar-

veled at him till I got thrown out of the theater for having
sneaked in.

I edged myself around a bit, lying behind the chair, to look
up and appreciate my own painting of Einsner. It was rotted-
looking, he was coming toward you with his mouth half-
open—rotted lips, the way I'd once seen them in a dream at
the mill while Letty slept alongside me—and his eyes turned
up and blood flowing from the wound on the back of his head
got around in front, smudging his jowls. His hands were out
toward you, the arms foreshortened, as city painters say, the
hands claws grabbing at you and hanging on to life even
though they were purpled and dead.

Those hands looked like hooks curving to grab anybody
who stood on the dock of life and snatch him to Lethe, like
grappling hooks set to dig deep in a bale of humankind. But I
was really sort of amazed, myself, at the eyes—they were the
worst. Didn't think anybody'd wish to buy that painting, as
Senator Margate had bought his—till he decided it didn't do
him justice and gave it back to me for use as a sample, which
had made the professor mad, that year before—but I was even
a smidge proud of her.

Now in the library, I can see when I turns my head and
looks up through a forest of chair legs, Madam Fortuna,
Letty's mother, has her head back and all at once she screams.
Same second, Harkins jumps for her. Puts an arm around her,
as though he'll do battle with everybody for her. He's saying,
"We didn't kill the old fool! We didn't kill him! Maybe we
went there, maybe we were both in the house that night, but
we didn't lay a finger on him!"

She's rearing around to him, I'm on my own feet now, the
painting is hovering there like sour fire, and she's yelling at
him in a tone like a bittern's, "Hush up, Loogan, it's a trick!"

But it's too late. I expect she's always partly believed in what
she did, even though she gilded it considerable, the way most
people in any profession, no matter how cheating, get to believe in it. And I expected Loogan was just as caught up in it
as he was in juggling plates, even though he'd never been
whittled out to do that. Milt Farley was saying, his voice cut-

ting across the rest, "That's where you went in July! Back to your husband's—"

I step out, drawing the curtains shut on the painting. I look across at Letty's mother. A handsome woman, affrighted as she is. And mad, too. She's been tricked; she believed in her own art a few seconds too long to stop Loogan from saying what he's said; now it's far too late. As the professor turns up a lamp's flame, making everything blazy, she stares at me and her mouth is strong and accusing and she points and says, "There he stands, came to me bold as brass for a reading, turned the professor on me, there stands the man, him and his friends are trying to put it all on us . . . ."

United States Marshal Tom Prosser cut across all that. Did it without raising his fog-washed voice much. "Mrs. Einsner. Sit down and be quiet. All of you, please do the same. Mrs. Einsner, I know you were at, or near, the farm of Carl Einsner, on the night of July twenty-eighth, last year. I know you were there, Harkins. I don't believe you were, Farley. Sit down. I want reasonable explanations. And of course true ones."

They sat, and he stayed sitting where he was, waiting. His white cuffs glittered against the black coat-sleeves. His head was a round ball of frost and rime on the coldest night in January.

"That is better," he said. "That's far better. Now. The job I do may not be important, but it is important to you. So I shall introduce myself again, with my official title, before I ask you to proceed." He did. When he said he was a United States marshal, Loogan Harkins's small moustache jerked like a worm on a leaf.

Twenty-Six

IN A FEW BREATHS OF TIME, while things got quieter and while
we all kept eyeing each other in the strong lamplight in here
now—with the draperies flung back again from the windows
and the second day of the new year shining in with just a
touch of chill in its teeth—Letty's mother started talking.

Once in a time Tom Prosser nudged her to go over something again, or to remember something he thought she
might've left out, and when he did, he seemed with his white-
haired hands to be squeezing the truth out, as if he'd been
wringing a washrag.

But for the most part he didn't cut into what she said. I
liked looking at her even while I was leaning forward to pick
up all she said; I liked the duck-egg brown of her skin, this
close, and the way she wore the filmy, slightly gaudy clothes
she had on today. Her wide shoulders, and the hollow of her
throat and a pulse going along one side of her throat, and her
hair puffing under the gilt-and-scarlet turban she had on.

She said, ". . . tell you why I wanted to go back there to the
farm that night. We were playing in Hornbeck only twenty
miles off—guess you know that, Mister Marshal—"

His steady eyes said he knew it.

"—one, I wanted to see Letty after all the years. See what she'd grown up into. Other reason, I wanted to see if she still had that money, if the jingle was still there. Jingle, cash, dicker-dockers, coin, Mister Marshal. Loogan and I've never had enough of it. I'd got the money from my uncle. Dexter Follope. Nursed him for Bright's disease just before he died and one day he gave it to me—had it in his mattress—and I kept it from Carl all the years we were married. Guess you think I was cruel and nasty, going off with Loogan—never mind. Shows you didn't know Carl. Figured Letty would get along . . . nice little child, kind of a nixie, off by herself always—proud little child."

Prosser didn't move. Just dropped in with: "Who was your uncle's lawyer, Mrs. Einsner? Mr. Follope's?"

"Oh. Why. Wayde Mitchell—he did all the lawing around that part of the country. He's a habit around there, like scrapple." She leaned forward. "See what you mean . . . he could have known about the money. That it was missing from Uncle Dex's bank, anyhow; and he probated Uncle Dex's will." He looked at her, still waiting, and she went spang on: "Loogan didn't want to go. Liked the idea of maybe getting some of the money back—if Letty'd let us have it and if she wasn't already married and gone off. But he was scared clear through. Well . . ."

Harkins shifted on his chair. Screeled around and looked away, then back. He was sweating like a silo in August.

She cast him a glance, patted his knee, and says, "Don't wet your britches, Loogan. Time to tell some truth. We didn't murder a soul and you know it. All right, Marshal. We got to Jerseyville on the forenoon of the twenty-eighth—Milt had give us a couple days off. Stayed there at the inn in the nooning and nightening. Talked to some drummers—windmill man, rock-salt man—they told me Letty was still the pride of Carl's farm, had a reputation for being offstandish with men though she was pretty as a pigeon's egg. So that night we set out, in the same buggy we'd hired back in Hornbeck. I suppose you've checked all that . . ."

Tom Prosser nods, getting folds in his white throat.

She goes on—voice isn't mystery-cloaked at all now, just flat and plain and country. And rich, like Letty's.

Looking at Loogan, I wonder for a blind flash of time what she sees in him, but then I can see there's something, after all; wasn't he better than Carl Einsner? I can see they've grown into each other, even if the roots were acid, after all these years.

". . . Drove out along the road, dawdling. Got to the farm maybe quarter till twelve, ten till. I don't wear a bosom watch. Everything was hushed-down as a dead owl. Hoped Carl'd be either asleep—he done a lot of log-sleeping—or out on one of his night walks around his acres—he done a lot of that too, when I was married to him. Wanted to see my daughter by herself. Had a difficult, God's own time dragging Loogan out of the buggy then to go up the path to the farm. We—"

But this time Prosser hit the edge of the table lightly.

She stares at him.

"I beg your pardon. Did you hear or see anything out of the ordinary then, Mrs. Einsner?"

"Mmmmm. Let me think. Yes! Little trace-jingle noise from the side road—not the main road, off to the side. Figured some farmer'd put a couple of animals down there to wait while he done some mighty late weeding. Didn't think much of it, tell the truth. Then when I finally prized Loogan loose from the buggy and the horse had started to crop around, the horse rears up. Went back to quiet him and moved him back from the grasses in the ditch alongside the road and see there in the moonlight a touch of red on the grass. Could be where a hawk's killed. Know it was blood, Marshal, because I stooped over and touched it with a finger and looked at it—the finger—in the moon-slash, and even smelled it."

She stops again. Then: "You think I'm too sharp a rememberer, Marshal? Have to be in my line. See a bit of hayseed on a man's hat you know he's a farmer; ink grubbed into fingers you figure some kind of clerk. Though there's a lot more to it than that, Astarte comes through once in a while—" She gazed at the crystal ball. "We went up to the house. Door was ajar— always is left off the latch around there. Good, I thought; Carl's out prowling his acres and patting his full belly and telling himself he's a fine farmer. I steps in the front room—parlor—Loogan right on my tail; I'm just about to call out, soft, for Letty—heart's in my mouth—when I see Carl. He's on the hooked rug there."

She swallowed, and touched Loogan on the knee again. Milt Farley coughs; then says, "Sorry."

She says, "I touched him. Made sure he was gone. When I straightened up I saw a touch of light coming along the hall off the parlor from the door to my old room. Took a couple of steps that way then went into the hall. Loogan stayed where he was. Talk about a petrified man! Well; I went along the hall to the crack of the door that was open and looked in. Didn't touch the door, just put my eye to the crack. The plank in the floor was up—saw that first—then shifting my eye a speck, I could see Letty. Wearing a red velvet dress . . . fine-looking woman, not my height and never will be . . . but fine. Had on a little gold brooch of mine I'd give her years ago, gold with flowers etched on. She was putting the money in a car-petbag—that'd been mine too."

Her eyes were in-turned now and she was looking closer at the crystal ball. Seemed full of some kind of sorrow she couldn't speak, the eyes fixed. "Why didn't I call out? Go in, and take her in my arms—I'll tell you why. Came to me all of a trussle—all over me—there were too many years between us now. She was still my blood and my baby, but I didn't know her and, Lord, she wouldn't want to know me—a fortune teller? An Indian-giver coming back begging for a handout of what I'd rightfully give her? No sir! Loogan and I'd get along—I went back down the hall, way I'd come, to the front room—parlor. Loogan was shaking. Shaking, you never saw it, palsy ain't in it. He'd leaned on the mantel and knocked off one of the candlesticks and it'd rolled near Carl. I—"

Tom Prosser made the slightest motion, but now she looked away from the crystal ball and at him.

"Did it also come to you, perhaps, Mrs. Einsner, that your daughter might have killed your husband?"

Her chin dropped square and firmed. Looked so like Letty on the instant.

"It did, sir. So the less I knew of it, the better for her."

He nods.

"Isn't much more to tell. We got back to the path, then to the buggy. Loogan kept babbling—" She turns to Loogan and puts a finger on his cheek, as you would a baby's. Took it off. "Poor Loogan. Harder on him than on me. He kept saying loud enough, 'He's dead, he's dead,' and all I could do was pack him back in the buggy. He was still saying it then. I had to drive. We went hell-for-leather back to Hornbeck that night . . ." She licked her lips. "Neither of us ever spoke a word to Milt about it, and even if he had thoughts, he was nice enough not to ask. They don't come better than Milt."

Prosser says like a soft bell tolling, "And when you read or heard that this young man, Applegate, had been accused of the murder and was wanted for it, didn't you think of coming forward and telling what you knew? Mrs. Einsner?"

She bridled and could have been Letty. Herself, as ever was.

"And have to say what I'd seen, Mister? And get Letty mixed deep in it? No sir! I'm not a civic dutier anyhow, and I didn't know the young man—beg your pardon," she says across to me, "but it's true—"

"Well, you know me now," I says. "Hello, Mrs. Einsner."

"Hello yourself, and good luck to you." She moves around facing Tom Prosser again. "Did appear queer to me about the reward coming from Wayde Mitchell—according to the prints and the posters—and funny Letty wasn't mentioned much in the prints and not at all in the posters, but if I thought anything about that, I thought Mitchell was just pulling some kind of his fox-strings. I'm not a worrier by nature—Loogan does that for both of us. I say what you can change, change, what you can't, forget."

She gave a healthy sigh. Blew out the candle—it wasn't needed anyhow—back of the crystal ball. While the smoke trailed up she said, "There's the nub and nut of the whole thing, Marshal, and if you want to ask me more call me Jane. I don't like the name Einsner, never did even a week after the wedding. And I've got a thirst, water or wine, I'm not particular."

I got a peculiar urge to ask her, in the small silence now

around the table, if she had a little butterfly-shaped birthmark on her belly like her daughter. Didn't figure I'd ever ask it, it was something you couldn't just work up to naturally. But I was curious, and all of a sudden I knew I liked her a good deal.

"Thank you, Jane," says Prosser, very fog-voiced, very easy. And cold as an ever-unmelting icicle.

Then Miz Amily got up and said, "I have a thirst on me too and I'm going to decant some elderberry wine and nobody's stopping me, Tom Prosser," and nobody did.

It was getting later now, night at the windows turning to shiny teak-black and reflecting us all in the long library, and when Miz Amily brought the wine back she brought food with it; Milt Farley was about the only one who didn't pick at his. While Jane Einsner had talked Farley had looked just nut-jawed and defensive of his friends, but cool, too, and understanding about what they'd done. He ate with a hearty appetite, and once he looked across at me and winked. As if he didn't care what I was, murderer or not, he was being friendly to a man in a pickle.

Meantime Marshal Prosser sat thinking, didn't say anything, took a sip of his wine, sat thinking and brow-ridged longer, and I thinks, Maybe he's just going to rise up—when he gets up—and shoot us all, the way Big Harpe and Little Harpe used to do back around the Natchez Trace when they got tired of people.

But no; and he wasn't through quizzing, not by a sight.

He roused up out of his thoughtfulness, turns to Farley, and, if you've seen somebody carving a basket out of a peach pit and reaching down to get the bare essentials, you've seen somebody work the way Prosser did now.

He quizzed Farley about how long the two, Jane Einsner and Loogan Harkins, had been gone from Farley's Balloon Ascension while it was playing in Hornbeck—*exactly* how long, he wanted to know. Though I figured he already knew that from what his operatives had found out, and was only re-checking. He asked Farley why, since he must've had a few ideas, *he* hadn't come forward to the authorities and told them.

Farley gave him a cool look for cool look. "Because they're my friends. Been with me a lengthy time. They work as well as they're able to work. Mister—Marshal—there's a saying in the trade, on the road or working, wherever you are, you don't go out of your way to know your neighbor's business. You can talk about his pitch but not his personal life." He was crisp as a Baldwin apple, that man.

Prosser stared at Farley a long while, then asked a few more questions and wound that up. Says, "I respect your personal guardianship of friends. I deplore your lack of cooperation with the authorities, and thank you."

You could have scattered him like sawdust in an ice house and he'd have lowered the temperature in July.

Then he wheeled to Loogan Harkins. "And now, Mister Harkins."

Well, all Harkins had to do was back up what Jane Einsner had told Prosser, but it was a terrible job for him to get it all out. I saw what she'd meant by saying he shook in times of stress, and he perspired enough to salt down bacon. Was glad he wasn't juggling, he would have smashed up the library. Yet I could feel something strong—a willingness to call it just the way it had been, not just a backing up of what Jane had said—through his squirming and low-toned answers. Once the professor came over and handed him a silk handkerchief, which he used to pat down his brow with gratefulness. It was a good deal later still by the time U.S. Marshal Prosser was through with Harkins. And it was even as though truth, or a few pieces of truth, were settling down among us and we didn't have to be so on edge as we'd been at the start of all this. I don't exactly mean we were all sitting around cracking old Abe Lincoln jokes.

In the sizable silence while Prosser is just sitting there thinking again, Jane Einsner says to me, not too soft but for me only, "You been good to my daughter, Mister Applegate?"

"Fine as I can," I says. "I'd like the chance to try it again."

Lower, she says, "You didn't kill Carl, did you?"

"Ma'am, I've been saying it so long that even if I did, I might think I didn't. But I didn't. That's flat."

"You got a hawkish look—like you could kill somebody if the time was right; but seeing you near up, I kind of doubt it. That was a terrible trick you played on me and Loogan. If he didn't have a heart like a bull, he'd have expired. Can see why you were doing it, though, and you got my forgiveness. You're Pisces, ain't you?"

"Don't know, ma'am. I came from an orphanage, and before that, didn't have any known birth date except the year."

"Pisces. I can tell. It's the floater-artist kind, and it would go good with Letty—she's Scorpio, level-headed. Some time I'll do a real ball-reading for you free as air."

"Astarte the crystal ball, you mean," I says kind of fast.

She looks at me closer, then smiles a trifle.

"Pisces, I knew it. And with some devil in you too."

About that time Prosser makes a slight noise and I look over at him. He says, "Come with me, Applegate," and I followed his big, slow, black-and-white self across the room where he picks up that drab old valise with the brass lock, and then he gestures again, come along, and this time leads me back into the end alcove, both of us brushing through the still-shut curtains, and he lights a small lamp back in there—pictures of Greek warriors marching around its shade—and motions for me to sit, and squashes himself down in a chair opposite me. Puts the valise on his lap, snicks it open, and damn if he didn't say, "Tell me the whole story again, Applegate, as thoroughly as you did the last time, please."

I cleared my decks and started in. Felt once more that, altogether, something among us was aiming at a bigger truth. And Tom Prosser was guiding us toward it. I doubted that he was the usual U.S. marshal. That was his job, but he took it the way a good painter takes his craft, preparing the canvas careful and using just the right egg in his paint if he needs it—not too much so the surface'll crack in five years—and not so much enjoying it, maybe, as being true to something that made him do it. I figured Milt Farley was the same way. You could tell he loved balloons, and so respected them, and treated them like it.

When I'd finished—he kept looking at those papers while I talked—I was dry as winter husks, and he just stares at me.

For all I knew he thought I was guilty as scarlet sin. He shut the valise and got up and brushed aside the curtains. I walked out with him. Everybody stood around or sat around, eyes turning to him. The professor's quiff of hair seemed to bristle like the sail of a ship under a following wind. Jane Einsner leaned forward, lips open; Loogan, at her side, gave a long deep sigh; Milt Farley sat upright and ready for anything; Miz Amily stirred and her pince-nez flashed. Prosser didn't speak a word for a time, but you could tell he was ready to.

Then he says, "Ladies"—meaning Miz Amily and Jane Einsner—"gentlemen." More or less meaning the professor, Milt Farley, Loogan Harkins, and as an afterthought, me. "There will be some extra guests in this house tonight. I refer to Mrs. Einsner—I am sorry, Jane—and to Mister Harkins. And of course there'll be Applegate and myself. In the morning we will make arrangements to travel." He drew in a pondering breath. "Jane, and Harkins, and Applegate, and I will be going to Jerseyville, Pennsylvania. I shall not explain why, except that there are things there which I must see for myself. And I want all of those I have named, those in my custody, there and on the spot, along with some others whom my operatives will have brought together. Harvey"—to the professor, as everybody hitched around and started staring—"you didn't start this, but you have compounded it. You, and many others. So you will now do me the courtesy of getting ready to go to the telegraph office with some communications. I'll write them in a moment. Some are to my operatives in Mullin's Gap, some to my men near Jerseyville, one to my man in Solomon, and a few to Washington. And, you'll prepare to put these extra guests up tonight. Amily, I am sorry—"

"Lord to John, we've got enough room," she says.

"Thank you." His eyebrows came down. "Jane. Harkins. Applegate. Bear in mind that you are suspects. You have been rounded up. Conduct yourselves as suspects until the case is closed."

Jane Einsner says, quiet-voiced, "Can Milt get us some other clothes from the pitch? These duds ain't fit for travel—"

"Yes, if he wishes." He turns. "Mister Farley, I regret taking these members of your troupe. But I'm taking them. I hope I can bring them back as free people with no stain of suspicion on them. But I don't know it. As for you, you aren't in custody."

Farley's jaw slanted up, blue eyes sparking. "I'll get your duds, Jane," he says.

Prosser swept on. "Harvey. You don't deserve it, but you would never forgive me if I didn't make the offer, and for some reason I still value your friendship. If you promise to put no further strain on it, you may come along."

The professor beamed. "Tom, thank you. You are a true Athenian. You—"

"Then you and I and those whom I've named will take train tomorrow for the nearest point to Jerseyville. Please see about tickets first thing in the morning."

Flat and powerful and cold as Arctic breathing. Not a soul there giving him an argument. For it had gone way past arguments.

Milt Farley was still staring up at him. "It'll take you some days to get there. It's a rattle-boned trip."

Prosser turned his gaze to him, a berg, maybe, noticing a seal nearby.

"I have already told you, Mister Farley, that I'll bring back your cohorts. If they're not guilty, and I can prove it. And as swiftly as I can."

"Aw, I didn't mean that." Farley stretched his tough legs and got up. "How about a quicker trip?"

The professor was hopping around near Farley. I could tell he knew what Farley meant, even if he pretended he didn't. He said, "Are you Bellerophon, sir, do you propose a ride on the winged horse?"

"Not exactly that, though she's winged," says Farley. His fingers when he stretched looked like bits of whipcord. "I mean my balloon," he says. "She'll carry six if need be, and she'll get you there fast, with luck." He stands up. "And frankly, I want this cleared up, 'cause it reflects on me as much as it does my friends, in its own way." He stood staring at Tom Prosser. "I don't like liars and lying," he clips at Prosser. "No more'n you, I think. Even when they're necessary. I can take you faster'n you've ever gone before."

The professor's almost busting.

But he looks to Tom Prosser.

Prosser says, "It might speed up matters a great deal. Let me think it over for a moment."

Professor Allan plucks Prosser's sleeve. "No, no, Tom," he says. "Don't think it over. Snatch the fleeting moment. Take him up on it now."

I'd never heard the professor's voice with quite that break in it. Miz Amily shook her head and said, "Go on, kill yourself, you've tried often and hard enough," and flaps a hand at him and goes off in a corner to stare out of the window into the late black night.

I caught her reflection in there, and she caught mine. She shrugs and gives a small ghost of a smile.

Twenty-Seven

THEN WHILE THE PROFESSOR and Tom Prosser got their heads together over the raft of instructions Prosser was writing out to be telegraphed various places—mostly, I gathered, to his lawmen around Jerseyville—and Jane Einsner and Loogan Harkins got *their* heads together kind of tight-woven in thoughtfulness, I chatted with Milt Farley. He didn't seem to mind spinning words with a possible criminal. He just seemed to want to get all this over with, and he was waiting for Prosser's word as to whether or not we'd travel by balloon or by the steam cars.

I tells him I've witnessed his balloon ascent in the field, not long before, and he says he remembers me in the crowd. Then I asks him why he slips bags of sand when he's coming down—that I'd always thought you did that when you were shooting *up*.

He's happy to explain anything about his craft. "You throw out the sand if you're landing too fast. Can throw it out if you're coming too near earth when you're in flight, too; or in danger of landing in a flock of trees, or in a body of water.

But in just them exhibitions, the valve-work gets a little chancy. You may let a little too much warm air out, or not enough. So you balance your landing with the bags. Valve slipped in my fingers the day you saw me—does it, somewhiles—and I had to trim up my position with the bags."

He tells me how the valve works, letting out about as much air as you can feel the balloon needs, for lower travel; and how the bags back up the valve in such cases. We're talking away nine to the dozen when Tom Prosser, the professor at his shoulder, looms over us. "Mister Farley," says Prosser, "I have decided to take you up on your splendid offer. The United States Government will compensate you for your expenses. I suggest now that you leave and prepare everything for morning. No need to come back here tonight; you can pack bags for Mrs. Einsner and Mister Harkins and they can pick them up in the morning before we leave."

Milt Farley, bronzed and fit, is on his toes. Says, lifting his head a slight bit, eyes afire, "That's all right about the bags, and it'll help not to come back any more tonight, because I got a sight of work to do seeing everything's shipshape for a long flight. Jane," he says to Jane Einsner, "tell me what you and Loogan want slung in, and I'll pack it for you."

She says she will. But Farley's not through. "Marshal Prosser, I ain't taking a cent from any goddamned government's got U. S. Grant and his highrollers, thieves to a man, at its head. I rode with Moseby's raiders for two year, and I don't forget easy—just the way a lot of people in this burg don't forget the siege of Richmond. I've got nothing against you, personal, but I couldn't take government-tainted cash. I'll do this, and do it for my old friends and fellow workers who're in trouble through a stupid mistake of their own. If that's agreed, we've got a compact."

Tom Prosser went a little pink under his white, then nods. "So be it. Accepted."

"And now," says Farley, all business, "I'll get things in order. All of you!" He takes charge and stands there with all of us looking toward him. "Bring a barrel of water, some liquor if you so desire; bring heavy coats. Going to be cold up there for part of the journey. A small barrel, Professor Allan—we can always throw it over if it weighs too much, but let's start out right. Be obliged to you too, Professor, if you'd bring along grub."

Miz Amily is listening hard, preparing to act. From time to time she throws the professor a look as though she's hard put not to call him a childish-minded old gentleman, but she's going along with the fixings, and after a time she heads for the kitchen. I can hear her starting to cook in there. Professor calls to her to rummage in the attic and see about those bear-skins he inherited from his father, to get them out of moth preservative and bring them down and shake them out, and she answers with a couple of hard licks on the edge of a skillet on the range. All through us, even the faces of Jane Einsner and Harkins, there's a kind of anticipation now.

It kept growing while Farley took even more charge. Then he said good night and took the rig he and Harkins and Jane had come in, back to the field to prepare for morning. Got Jane's word on what she wanted him to pack for her and Loogan. Said we had fair wind conditions and that the wind went from west to east and could even carry us at 10,000 feet, at times, if we were lucky, at a ripe old clip. Says to me, while he's standing in the front doorway, "You're able-bodied, Applegate. More so than these others, except for Loogan. If I need your help I'll sing out and depend on it. I'll instruct you while we're en route."

I says I'll be proud to assist. He claps me on the shoulder, gives me a cool blue-eyed look—cool as Letty's when she's being uppity.

"You're all calf-brained when it comes to flying, but I'll get you there. Promise it."

Then, muttering to himself about how he's heard the New York *Graphic,* a newspaper, is plotting to send up a monstrous balloon for the world's record later on this year, and how this good journey will give him just the chance he needs to get a trial-run jump on them, he hurries out. Shortly after that, the professor, moving like a Greek spear if a Greek spear has tufty yellow-white hair and bright eyes and swirls around a good deal, goes out to telegraph the sheaf of messages he's holding in one fist. And Miz Amily asks me to go with her to the attic and she lights my way up the steep stairs at the top of the house, and after bludgeoning our way among what seemed like a hundred horsehair trunks—she says one of them's full of old love letters from girls to the professor: "He was a rip in his youth," she opines—we get the bearskins he's been talking about. There's plenty of them, and they smell like camphor to the heavens. We come downstairs, I staggering under them, and spread them out in the library.

Tom Prosser tells us—Jane and Loogan and me—there's no possibility of complete escape, even if one of us or all should think, now, of leaving the house during the night. For he's informing Washington just what he's doing, and there'll be considerable ruction about it and the word will go out to every community about it.

That doesn't bother me, and it doesn't faze the plans of Jane Einsner and Loogan Harkins, because by now none of us is wanting to leave.

There's a million and three questions I want to ask—all hanging in my throat, and at tongue's tip—but Tom Prosser isn't in any mood to be asked them. If he ever was. I don't know how he thinks he's going to prove—or unprove—Jane and Loogan's story, and I don't know what he's going to do about my story, and Letty's, and I don't even know if Letty will be there in Jerseyville, but it'd take the *Monitor,* or even the *Merrimac,* to break through his wall of sheet ice . . . and still he's got his own ways of working and I respect them. Just the way I respect Milt Farley, though I do keep hoping his balloon is made of the stoutest silk and that that basket is a fortress.

When the professor came back from his errand—he must have purely overloaded the man at the telegraph key—we all, except Miz Amily, tried on those fustian bearskins. They still had quite a mob of fur on them, though they were worn off in scattered patches.

We looked like five bears that'd seen hard times for a spell of years, peering at each other from under the capelike heads of the bears draped around our own heads. I figured the citizens who looked up and got a good gaze at us wouldn't be believed, when they told the story, for all their lives long after that. Loogan told us Farley had his own aeronaut outfit for the high ascents—it was of leather and allowed him to move nimble when he so desired.

After a time we shucked out of the bearskins—I believe even Tom Prosser liked putting his on, though you couldn't read it from his mouth or eyes—and Miz Amily showed Jane and Loogan to spare beds which she'd turned down for them. Then Prosser and the professor sat talking a long time in the study, Prosser chiding the professor for what he called his multiple muddling with the law, the professor taking it easy and not resenting it, but once or twice looking up at me with his eyes shining like he was Icarus himself, preparing to fly to the sun on the morrow, and I was Daedalus, or maybe the other way round. Then Prosser went up to bed, with a parting exact-zero gaze at me; says good night to me, same temperature; and Miz Amily comes in the study and says she's got Country Captain chicken all readied for the next morning, and wrapped in linen, and that the small wine barrel is full of sweet water and has a bung in it.

"And," she adds, standing there gazing at the professor, "if you all crash and your moldering bones are found in northern Virginia sometime in the far future, I'll say good-bye to you both now. Harvey, I've been with you for thirty-one years come this spring, but this is your ultimate escapade. I swear to John." Then she marched over and kissed him, her pince-nez sparkling. Kissed me, too. Rears back. "Oh, I'll be up betimes in the morning, to drive you all down to your possible doom. If God intended man to fly he would have give him not just wings, but the stomach for it."

While she went out, and the professor picked up his stir-about and started mixing us toddies, meantime reciting something which he said was by a man named Anacreon, about the gods on their journeys, I kept thinking what she'd said about the stomach, and thought she'd probably be proved right. I hoped to have the chance to tell her she was, or wasn't, in a future time.

Twenty-Eight

NEXT MORNING when we drove through the upraised canvas
flap onto the field there was no kite flying, no banner advertising Farley's Balloon Ascension; it was too early to get the wits
straight, but I guessed all of ours were in prime sharpness.
Miz Amily was doing the driving; we had plenty of gear to
unload from the rig, and pass in a line of passers made of me
and Loogan Harkins and a small boy who was helping Farley,
and Farley; we got the wine barrel, full of water, stowed away,
and the hampers of chicken and cake and latticework pies Miz
Amily had fixed for us. I thought while we got the stuff
stowed away that at least we all had a chance to die with full
contented bellies.

When we had all these in the bottom of the basket, which
Farley told me was supposed to be called the gondola—and I
decided that might be some compensation, too, to know its
right name when I fell out of it—we waited while Loogan
Harkins helped Farley get the fire started in the stove. We
stood around and stamped our feet and flapped our bearskins. The professor passed about a flask containing fairly

warm toddies, which everybody—including Miz Amily, who said the waiting put her teeth on edge, and including the small helping boy—took a nip of. Sun wasn't up yet but it was showing light rose at the rim of the horizon and spreading out like fingers across the field, around our feet.

As the balloon started filling up and crackling a trifle in the cold with the warm air spewing into its inside, Jarhinda rolled her eyes and Miz Amily had to take a firm grip on the reins and settle her down. "Terrible thing to expose a prize mare to in the prime of her days," she complains. "Settle down there, ma'am—easy, easy now!"

Then before long, just as the sun really topped the rim of earth, the balloon stood up huge and ready above us, and Farley yelled to me to get in, tossing me a guy-rope whose other end was tethered to a stake in the ground. So, gripping my end of the rope, flapping in my bearskin, I climbed over the gondola's edge, while Loogan did the same thing, holding a rope's end too, on the other side. Loogan says to me to just keep a steady grip on it but not to haul on it because at this point that will tip the gondola. So I kept that sort of grip and in the shrewd lively air wondered if birds ever pecked holes in the skin of the balloon. There was a flock of birds chattering in the new air not far above us. Jarhinda whinnied and backed off but Miz Amily held her. Next inside came Jane Einsner, bear-head waggling on her own head, and Loogan helped pull her up and over and in and stow away their bags. I'd noted that once you were inside this so-called gondola it was a sight more capacious than it appeared to be from outside. At least we weren't lumped in like sprats in a barrel. Next came Tom Prosser, Farley, outside, cupping his hands to give Prosser a heel up. I must say Prosser kept his dignity even half-disguised as a wild grizzly from the Far West. Next came the professor, oopsy daisy, over and in. From what I could see of his face behind the bear-grizzle robe that hung over it he was as excited as though he'd just invented everything here and was about to get a medal from the world for having done it. There was a good steady strain on the rope I was holding. Now, last, here came Milt Farley, in his leather suit that he

hadn't worn for just the small ascent in the regular performance the day I'd seen him; he had on a leather cap with a
long bill like a flying duck's, too. He says, "Professor, you
move over there, let's distribute weight as even as we can—
you, Mister Prosser, the other side, and you, Jane," to Letty's
mother, "there. Loogan, move a foot to your right—don't let
go that rope, you butter-fingered fool!"

I guessed I was all right where I was. I'd brought along my
paint and canvas sack with most of my belongings and a couple of small good canvases, rolled in it; I might be coming
back or I might not, but I wanted something to work with in
the meantime. Farley hadn't bade me throw it out so I figured
it could stay. Marshal Prosser had the traveling bag he'd come
to Richmond with and the scuffed old valise and the professor
had a hand-grip. Far as I could see, Jane Einsner hadn't
brought along the crystal ball. But we had a sight of weight,
including coal for the stove.

Farley wrapped a lashing of light strong rope around the
mouth of the balloon, which was small for the towering size of
the balloon's shape above it, not closing the mouth but fixing it
so it hung just above the hot stove, doing it neat and tight and
quick. Then he calls to the small boy to let go of the rope the
boy had tight hold of, on the ground—and the child lets go
and as he does, Farley tosses him a coin. Farley says, "Now,
Applegate—Loogan—" and we tensed. "Cast off together
when I say to."

From where I'm holding my rope-end I can see Miz Amily's
face lifted into the full swash of the morning. She's still holding the reins tight and Jarhinda is quivering. But above us,
sending a thrum of feeling through our feet and bodies in the
gondola too, the balloon is quivering even more than any
horse could—I think, again, of those horses in that picture,
those Greek chariot beauties. All at once I want to yell out like
I'm a child myself and seeing something wonderous for the
first time in my days.

"Now!" shouts Farley—and Harkins and I lets go of our
ropes, together.

Well, I want to tell you—we all went up so fast it was like
being jerked into the air.

One second there was Jarhinda below us, rearing and then settling and backing up, and Miz Amily called "Good-bye, good-bye! Bon voyage!" as she sawed at the reins; the next she was fifty good feet below us and getting smaller every second as though the earth itself was pulled out from under us and we were shooting too far from it ever to grab onto it, by a tree or a bush, again; and Farley is reeling in the rope whose other end the small boy has held steadying it, on the ground, and we're still rising as he drops it on the gondola floor.

There's a sharp rush of wind, feeling it has snow crystals in it, all around my face; I look up and there's the balloon, on a slant, moving to the northeast; look down, and there's our own shadow under us, trailing across Richmond like a great bird's shadow being pulled by time; over the rooftops, over the downtown sector, over the warehouses, over the streets where early-getting-up people are pointing but are now too little to see in making out their features. The professor is chortling, waving; he's shouting something I can just make out, "The sea, the sea, the wine-dark sea!"

Though we're not going in the direction of the sea, he chants it; I know just how he means it. For the whole air and its new rhythm around us, and the great tugging of the balloon, are all part of a fresh voyage to the sea of the air. Beside me, Milt Farley isn't even smiling, but he looks satisfied. He's studying some charts he holds in his thick-gloved hands. "The current's right," he says. "Make it by nightfall if not before, at this clip." Has to shout a bit to make himself heard.

I says, "Wish I could paint this!" Circles an arm around. "All this!" I meant the air and all the ground.

It's all so big. All the land. Water-ribbons are twinkling under us now. Air's sharp as ice. With ice in it, filling the eyes and making you rub them. And the land getting bigger and broader, checker-patched with winter farms now outside the city, with the long dark rows of earth where tobacco plants will grow again come the spring. The balloon upward-rushing, and sailing east and north in the hands of the wind. The gondola vibrating with it like the secret bones of a bird.

I didn't feel a hair uncomfortable. Hungry, in truth. After a time we came right up through clouds and then out of their

tops, mist around us quick and cold-bathing even through that
swaggling bear fur we wore, and as we sailed along over the
clouds, the whole upper air filled with sunlight that burned in
the eyes and that made a song in the marrow, I thought it all
looked this way every day to those geese—the geese of the
kind Seven and Letty and I'd heard and seen going south, that
autumn night before.

About noon we hit the rain. It was freezing. Came up like it
had seen us and pounced on us, though truth was, we'd run
into it. Black around it as Tophet's hat, a blue-black with some
lightning jigging at the edges, and the rain itself in long rods
that swashed you over and tried to soak you through before
you had a chance to get set for it.

Farley hollered through the pelting, "We'll be out of it in a
minute!" But the whole gondola was rocking like a boat on a
bad sea. I've seen the boats go out from Marblehead, Mas-
sachusetts; never saw the real old-time whalers, not even the
clippers, but I'd seen the dories with the fishermen, plummeting from wave to wave and riding them so you never thought
you'd see the boat again from one wave-crest to the next. This
was like that, with the rain hissing like a flock of angry snakes,
like what the professor was shouting were, "The Euroclydon
winds!" Just had to grit your teeth and stand it. Rain that
made your chin want to vanish into your lower belly, wrinkling everything in you.

Then we were out of it, just the way Farley had promised,
and sun was soaking all the doused bear fur and we were
steaming; the professor sat on his traveling bag, eating
chicken real joyously, and passing a wing to Marshal Tom
Prosser, and one around to me, and a thigh wrapped in linen
to Jane, and one to Loogan. Farley took a chunk of breast. He
flipped the wishbone over the rim, and watching, I could see it
fall a long time behind us, lifted by the same air currents that
were moving us at a rate so fast I wouldn't even have wished
to try to gauge it.

Then, a bit later, we weren't traveling so fast. And except
for the light murmur of air in our ears it was right quiet; now

we could hear each other, see each other, and I thought how I expected each of us was marveling, deep in his person, that he was here. As if we happened to be an island of the only people in this whole world. Made everything more precious, everybody look more like his or her *self*.

About this time, Farley says to Loogan and me, "Smarten up, now! This here lull gives us the chance to route our course a little more!"

Then for about an hour he showed me how to pull on one of the guy ropes leading down to this gondola and holding it up, so that the balloon dipped down on that flank; Harkins was doing the same thing. It was delicate work, pulling and waiting for Farley's direction to pull more, or pull less—keeping an angle to it, now, so we would travel faster in one direction than in another. Farley had a compass out, and was studying it as he barked out his orders.

By and by he says, at my shoulder, "Recognize the land?"

"Mister Farley," I says, "I've never seen it from this side up, this far up. Makes me think we're all bugs crawling."

"You get used to it. That's Maryland down there—"

"Sure don't look like a map," I says. "There's no division of color. Ought to be sudden pink, or green."

He grins. "We'll go lower later. We've missed the Alleghenies. Get high upreaching currents from them—cross-winds, too. We cut across just a couple of spurs, they didn't bother us." He leans beside me, compass in his palm. "Gets to a man, that's a fact. Got to me in the war; like I said, I was with Moseby, but one day I see an observation balloon, and I've never been the same since. And this old girl's a living and a way of getting free. One and the same time."

Free, thinks I: somehow I'd forgot until right then what we were traveling for, where we were going. I looked up. Sun was touching the scarlet and blue and white triangles of the tight, fleshed-out silk; we could've been some kind of plant life attached to a bulbous extraordinary grape.

I looked over at Tom Prosser. He was looking down, standing in his given position, the professor sitting in *his* given position on the traveling bag at his feet. The professor was snooz-

ing a bit, but half-smiling. Prosser wasn't smiling. He was
studying out the land below, what could be seen of it. He
hadn't forgot for a nick of time just where it was we were
going, or why.

Pretty soon after that we went lower, and while I helped
Loogan ease up and then tighten on the ropes that kept us on
our course, at the direction of Farley, I started mulling over
the country down there. It was Pennsylvania now, and dark
and bright, both, in the cloud-scud that was now above us.
Like watching a great animal flicker in and out of beautiful
purple and fawn and sienna and turgid shades of shaley gray,
an animal whose hide was the earth, and kept rippling under
us in motioning ease.

I thought of Sara the elephant, of Magnusun, Tad Ainslee,
Sir Alpheus Merry. Thought, close, of the Dabneys, with particular thinking of Penelope. I'd already said a soft full-blown
farewell in my mind to all Richmond, including Sally Lou
Loudermilk; now my thoughts drew tight to where we were
coming, to Seven and the Darlings. And always to Letty.

Tom Prosser had seen me watching him at intervals. Now
he shifted around, jaw out full, and deigned to speak to me.
"Applegate, we will have a reception at the Einsner farm.
Wayde Mitchell—"

"Think you know how I feel about him," I says.

"Yes. That is my point. Wayde Mitchell, Sheriff Wheelman,
Rafe Gondy, Soames, Abraham Tatum, all of them. My operatives are holding them there. And Applegate, no matter how
you feel, please don't speak to them or show your indignation.
The same goes for you, Jane—and Mister Harkins."

I nods. Jane says, her fine hair—Letty's but darker—blowing back from the bear-headed cape, "Don't know any of 'em
but Mitchell, in any case, Marshal. And never had much to do
with him."

Listening to Prosser, I'd let my guide rope slip a trifle. Farley nudged me, rough. "Straighten up there! Keep your mind
on your work!"

The professor had come awake, and was canting a bright
eye up at Tom Prosser. "I should rather imagine there's been

considerable pother and publicity around Jerseyville," he says.

For a second Prosser isn't going to answer, then his heavy shoulders turn and he frowns and says, "I suppose so. My men keep those things as quiet as they can, but they have been working for quite a while there, and some things always slip. Yes, there may be reporters. And the general public." He didn't look as though he always smiled on the doings of the general public. "I shan't let them interfere."

This time I kept my rope steady and one eye on Farley when I talked. Had to ask, finally; even if Prosser heaved me up and cast me down to earth as useless ballast.

I say, clear and quick, "Letty going to be there?"

"Not," he says, finally deciding to answer this one too, "unless I need her there. At present I don't. Her statement is enough. Enough for now. If I find it isn't enough, later, I'll have her brought from Solomon."

Through the wash of aching—damn, I'd thought she was going to be in Jerseyville—I thought, Anyhow, it was good to know she was in Solomon, not at the inn in Mullin's Gap.

I cast a glance at Jane. She was standing looking down over the edge of the stout wickerwork, her hands on the scroll it made at the rim. Knew she felt sorry she wouldn't be seeing her daughter right away, too, though I didn't believe she could feel any worse than I did. Then, I figured she might not feel bad; remembered what she'd said about the years putting a wall between them. Reached over and patted her hand. She gave me a flick of a smile. For another second's grace of time she looked just like Letty to me, and I vowed if Letty and I ever got together again—maybe that was in the cards, maybe not, but this time I was playing out the hand—I was going to cherish her up strong, pass through her orneriness and plumb to the center of her soul. Chances are that can't be done, all the distance, by any men and women on the earth, but it could be sought for.

And there was a sight of joy in the seeking.

Dusk came on the land below us, the land slipping along. The green hills and the big farms appeared. We were lower, Farley was fiddling with the valve. He was on his toes now, near dancing, anxious and watchful. The warm air came out with a hissing that was steady. He shut off the valve. We were all watching him, Harkins and me still holding the guide ropes the way he'd said to do. Harkins had been busy feeding the coal stove.

We were all holding our breath as if it was a big part of the balloon.

We went skifting, dappled in shadow, like a dark moon over the pitiful little collection of feed stores and grain bins and jail and inn and notion stations that was Jerseyville. I remembered coming through there the norning before I'd lighted at the Einsners'. Jane Einsner, still Mrs. Einsner even if her husband was dead, was gripping the edge of the gondola now so hard her fingers were off-white, the blood numb in them.

Down below us people could see us now. A man on a wagon, looking up from a cut in the flank of a field, shaded his eyes and seemed to cower down and back and his horses whinnied, you could just hear it. A woman came running from a farmhouse, her apron tiny but flapping, and cried out; you couldn't make out the words but it sounded like something about the earth's ending.

It didn't seem funny at all now, not in the least, that we looked like wild bear-headed creatures to all of them. It was warmer; just a trace warmer; I threw back my bearskin, and at the same time the professor was shrugging out of his, too. Had his black cloak on under it, and his wide-brim riding hat on his head.

Then, dead ahead below, I could see the Einsners' place. "Damn it!" says Farley. "Let out too much. We'll knock hard if we don't lose altitude slower—" He whirled to Harkins. "Tip out a bag on your side, Loogan!"

Harkins got a bag tipped up and ready. He'd shucked his bearskin too. The bag teetered on the gondola's edge. Harkins looked around to Farley for the sign. We were dashing close to the ground now. Last sun flared and in it I could see a clump of the Einsner cattle all looking across the darkened field at us.

"Now!" says Farley, and the bag went spinning down.

We bobbed a little on the air, like treading water.

Then we started down again a good deal slower.

Then we were bumping along, bouncing, the gondola basket on edge, everybody thrown together, and beside me Farley was cussing and then getting guy ropes in his hands, and pulling on them, and almost at the same time reaching for the little valve, getting it, and air was rushing out of the balloon again. Finally it was all over and we were straight up but with part of the balloon draped into the gondola, feeling smooth and chill to the hands, and Farley saying, "All right, nothing's ruined. Gondola took a knock—"

He looks around. "Everybody all right?"

We'd been banged a little from the dragging, but we were in fair shape.

I pushed back the layer of silk shrouding around me, and Farley said sharp, "Don't manhandle it! Treat it easy as a spiderweb!"

"Yes sir," I says, and he nods.

He says, "Applegate, I live right. You don't hit this close every Monday."

He'd done everything he'd promised. He climbs out, I'm out right after him, Loogan Harkins is out, and then we all give a hand to Jane and the professor and to Tom Prosser. Prosser is still wearing his full bearskin. The balloon is collapsing around the other side of the gondola; Farley is running around there now, with Loogan, staking down its outriding ropes and keeping it safe. Tom Prosser throws back that odd bearskin from off his head and draws himself up to full-chested attention. I look and see where he's staring, and here comes a whole ripe contingent of people, all racing and yelling in the dusk. The cows had had sense enough just to be scared.

Twenty-Nine

THE MAN IN THE LEAD of all the other people pounding up to us carried a sixteen-shot Henry repeating carbine from the war; so did a lot of the other men who were working with him. They were marshals, like Tom Prosser, I guessed, but working under him. I decided Prosser was about the chief marshal of the world, for all I knew; anyhow, they kowtowed to him and the man in the lead came to a smart salute, the rifle in one hand, his star sparkling in the dusk.

The other marshals, behind him, held back the crowd. I could see people strung out all along the pasture and extending clear down to the Einsner farmhouse. And rigs of all kinds drawn up outside the fences. But there were ropes stretched around the farmhouse itself, boxing it in; and there were more marshal guards down there keeping the crowd from ducking under the rope.

Just like the whole affair was a free entertainment. Which it was, free, I mean—but if flocking to see who might've done a murder entertains you, then you've never been accused of one you didn't do.

The man in the lead snapped out, "Daggart reporting, sir."

Tom Prosser nods to him and asks for his report. They stepped aside from the rest of us. Loogan Harkins and Milt Farley were laying out the collapsed balloon. It made a lovely pattern of scarlet and blue and white over the pasture. The professor nudged me. "Chin up," he says. "Tom has everything in hand."

"Yes sir," I says. "That's been pretty plain from the first time he showed up in Richmond. But all I know right now is, it was fine sailing to here—but now we're here I feel like I'm nearabout as bad off as I was before. Not a bit of it your fault. It's just fate."

"You're having a letdown after the *hubris* of flying," he said. "The exaltation of it. Buck up, Luke—we are nearing a solution, and whoever did the deed is approaching his or her nemesis."

I said I'd buck up. I asked Jane if I could carry her traveling bag for her. I had my paint and canvas sack on my back. She said, "I appreciate it. But I think I need somethin' to do with my hands. We've got to pass along past that crowd there." She was sort of drawn up, flashing the crowd down in the pasture and around the house a tough look; she stood queenly, and straight as six o'clock. I could see where Letty got a lot of her stubbornness from.

After a bit Prosser, trailed by the young marshal called Daggart, slewed around and stumped back to us. "We will go straight to the house," he said. "Pay no attention to the crowd. And remember: when we get to the house, no communication with the others now in custody. Absolutely none." He was foghooting that almost direct to me but taking in Jane and Loogan too.

We all nods.

Then the whole bunch of us go moving down-pasture to the house. One of the marshals walked along with Jane and Loogan. Another one, also with a rifle, walked in back of me. The professor swung along near us with Milt Farley. Prosser walked at the head of us with Daggart; Prosser's head was up and his chin was slicing snow out of his path and his eyes had that flare in them.

The professor says to Milt, "Congratulations, Mister Farley. It was a complete triumph."

"Except I damned near broke a hole in the gondola," said Farley. "I've got to do some work on that valve. Someday—" he jerks a thumb at the night sky. "Someday the air'll be full of floating craft. People skimming through it in record time, moving all across the continent, Professor Allan. Getting from one place to another so fast they beat the clock."

"O brave new world," the professor hums behind his teeth.

We moved down across the wintering grasses, past the cows which had forgot all about chewing what there was to chew in those drying grass stems, and made our way through the thronging watchers and went under the ropes and up the front path to the house. Around us I heard somebody say, "There they go, the killers, look at 'em, Eb! They cut off that poor old man's neck with an axe."

I wanted to whirl around and take some issue with that. But the professor nudged me again and Marshal Tom Prosser gave me a look fit to freeze a smithy fire and ignored them, so I ignored them too. We went in the house.

Felt strange being in it; here was the front room, with a couple more marshals on guard. One of them steps to Daggart, who was just a bit in front of us, and salutes, then salutes Prosser as Daggart stepped away, and says, "The others are in the kitchen, sir."

I guessed he meant Mitchell and Wheelman, Gondy and Tatum and Soames. Couldn't keep myself from looking toward the kitchen down at the end of the near hall. The door was shut. I felt my hands get cool and my fingers want to ball up. It wasn't that I exactly wanted to see a one of them, but I couldn't help the mad rising in me.

I took off my paint and canvas sack and slung it on a sofa. Gave me something to do.

Prosser went along with this young marshal to the kitchen, while Daggart stayed with us, not exactly pointing his weapon at us but keeping it handy, like. Before the kitchen door swung shut after Prosser—I couldn't help looking that way

again—I caught a glimpse of Mitchell, though he didn't see
me; he didn't have quite the powerful oozing look he'd borne
when I first saw him, but was appearing crease-browed and
thunderous; I figured he'd had a hard time lately, and was
glad. He was squatting on a kitchen chair. There were plenty
of marshals guarding back there, too.

In here with us, Daggart says, "Please make yourselves comfortable. Sit down and rest."

I sat on the sofa, Jane and Loogan on a couple of high-
backed rockers, all looking at one another edgewise. In the
front doorway, the door standing a little open, the professor
looked out into the night, at all the lanterns and all the crowding out there. Milt Farley leaned on the mantel. There was still
only one pewter candlestick on it, I thought they'd probably
taken the other one for a piece of evidence.

The professor is saying to himself, "What a wonder a mob
is. How unlike a god."

I agreed with him there. I could feel something in those
people out there, who must've represented about the full pop-
ulation of Jerseyville, and a lot more of the country roundabout, that was nearly tastable on the air. It was something
that gets in children sometimes, is born in many, maybe in us
all. The thing that makes them torture a stray dog or marvel
to see a man strung up by the neck, in the sacred name of justice, and his life going out of him while they hug themselves
and congratulate themselves that *they've* kept the law. I always
want to ask somebody just what the hell the law is that it can
take any life at all.

Could tell the professor felt like that.

But then he'd felt like that his life through. Some do.

Seemed a horrible while, with minutes ticking away like sand
grains, one and by one, but it couldn't have been much later
when Prosser and a couple more marshals came back in from
the kitchen. Farley stalks over to him. "I hope you set a guard
on my balloon, Marshal. Some of these gawkers around
here . . ."

Prosser looks at him hard and tired. "There is a guard

mounted to protect your balloon from unauthorized med-
dling, Mister Farley. I too am concerned about it. For the no
doubt selfish reason that Professor Allan and I will rely on you
to get us back to Richmond in it." I noted he didn't say Jane
and Loogan would be going back. Or just what I'd be doing.
He was an old dogged man and he wasn't giving away an inch.

"Daggart," he said, "bring the box . . ." And Marshal
Daggart reached down behind the sofa and came up with a
metal box. At first I thought it was my strongbox—it was
about the same size, and my heart gave a whole turn. But it
wasn't. While they set it on a chair and opened it, showing a
couple of magnifying glasses and things like that in its top
tray, I was remembering how Letty had sat over there, right
where this detecting box, or whatever it was, now sat, in the
warm afternoons when I'd first sketched her. Tom Prosser
took one of the magnifying glasses out of the box, and then he
went to the doorsill, frowning a little at the professor.

"Harvey. Please move away from the sill-board."

"Of course, Tom. I had no idea—" The professor skips
aside and smiles. But Tom Prosser didn't smile; he knelt down
on the floor and crawled along beside the sill-board, looking as
if he might be studying the habits of ants. Careful about it as if
everything he saw had to weigh in his mind down to the tiniest
fleck of a carat. Outside the crowd was murmuring, back of
those ropes and protecting marshals, and here in this room
everything was so quiet we could near hear one another's
thoughts.

Crawling a whit of an inch at a time over the sill, Tom
Prosser looked like the rear of Sara the elephant, except he
was wearing black, and Sara wore her gray wrinkled comfortable hide.

Then he says, "Here," just as though he'd discovered a small
error in bookkeeping, and snaps his fingers up to Daggart.
Daggart handed him a short knife with a bright blade. The
professor was bending over Prosser now, getting a little in his
light, and Prosser says only, "If you please, Harvey."

Says it patient past patient, cold as a bell clapper on winter
midnight.

The professor got back out of the way.

Tom Prosser stooped over even farther and scraped with the knife blade at something between a crack of the sill-board. Then he got up off his knees, still purposeful as a slow-rising machine, and took the knife blade and scraped whatever he had—I couldn't see—in between a couple of sheets of clear glass that Daggart held out to him, and then he draws Daggart aside, just beyond the door in the dark. They had a powwow out there.

Daggart says sharp at the end of it, "The other sample is back with Slooman and Sykes, sir, I'll take this," and runs off, but not so fast he wasn't carrying those glass plates like diamonds.

Prosser came back in. He says, "We will spend the night here. In the morning we will move ahead again."

The professor says, "And in the morning will the case be unperplexed?"

Tom Prosser barely looked at him. "Solved is the word we use in the service."

He turned to me. Thrust his white head forward from those bowed shoulders. "Applegate, step out here a moment with me. Arnold"— he pointed to another marshal who'd come out of the kitchen with him—"come with him."

It was cooler outside the door. Prosser says to me, Arnold hanging at my shoulder, "Arnold will take you out to the sleeping shed. I want you to spend the night in the loft. Wait until twelve o'clock or a little after before you go to sleep. During that time, listen. And tell me in the morning if you've heard anything out of the ordinary. Anything at all that differs from what you heard when you were preparing to go to sleep on the night of July twenty-eighth, last year."

I said, "I don't carry a timepiece."

Arnold said, "I do."

I cast a glance out toward the crowd back of the ropes.

Prosser noted it. "We'll clear most of the crowd out of there. Though I imagine they'll be back in the morning. But when they are gone tonight, with allowance for the time of year— the autumn carries sound better than the summer—when they are gone, conditions for hearing from the shed loft should be much the same as they were that night."

"Yes," I said. There was about the same lack of ground wind in this night, I thought.

"Do you understand, Applegate?"

"Not much," I says, "but I understand what you want me to do."

He nodded to Arnold then, Arnold nodded to me, and we went back in the front room and I picked up my paint and canvas sack, and Arnold steered me down the hall and out through the kitchen. It was just a big cool bricked Dutch kitchen, as always, but now here sitting on chairs lined up in it, like frogs on a log, with more marshals standing guard over them, are Wayde Mitchell, and Rafe Gondy, and Wheelman, and Soames from the livery stable, and Abraham Tatum from the inn in Mullin's Gap.

I only had one worse time of holding myself in, in my life— you'll hear of it later—but right then it was all I could do to keep from swarming over every one of them, left and right, and they even knew it. They batted their eyes at me, and all seemed a mite frozen, as though they'd worried considerably, these past days, and were putting a razor-edge on their worries now. In a flick of a glance I could see Wheelman wasn't wearing his sheriff badge any longer. Noted, in the same flickering-around look, that in spite of Wayde Mitchell's crestfallenness—even his flowered vest, this time something with asters on it, looked frazzled—there was still that sneaking powerful expression, saying, real strong, he knew something I didn't know. I'd have given a lot to jump over the intervening marshals and hit him, but Arnold prodded me, and I just took a good grip on the canvas sack and kept walking.

Out in the night again it was good and fresh, and our footfalls crunched over the dark ground under the watching starlight. Could hardly hear the crowd from here. Arthur Fillitch, one of the hired men, came along then with Phil Rambler, another of the hired men, driving a clutch of the cows home from pasture in the darkness—they should have done it a lot

sooner, they were going to have a long time milking, tonight—
and I says, breezy-like, "Hey there, Arthur!"

I supposed they'd both been enjoying the excitement of the
crowd, and joining in. Didn't look to me from the general appearance of the farm that they were doing a very good job
keeping it up now Carl Einsner was gone. I wondered if
Wayde Mitchell was still giving them their pay, as he'd said to
Letty he was, or if now he was in the government's hands, they
were just riding along to see what happened next. The house
itself had looked moppish, as though it needed a good hand in
it for cleaning. Over everything I kept wondering just how
Letty was, over there in Solomon about fifty miles north; how
she felt with a guard on her, too, waiting to either arrest her—
and maybe the both of us—for the murder, or to finally let
her go.

Arthur Fillitch walled his eyes at me like a horse shying, but
not as neatsome about it as Jarhinda.

This marshal, Arnold, marched me along past the herd of
cows and the barn towering against the night, and around to
the sleeping shed, and then up the stairs.

We went past the window looking out on the stairs where
Letty had called me from that hot night. It was tight shut now.

I says, "He wants me to tell anything special I hear."

Arnold nods.

"Well, the window was open that night."

"We'll open it," says Arnold. He wasn't being mean; he just
took his job serious and cut through anything to do it, the way
Tom Prosser himself did. We went in the loft. It was a shade
frowsty, from not being aired; but the dry alfalfa made a good
scent again, as we opened the door, and then here came the
cats, taper-eyed in the half dark. The biggest one stropped itself around my legs, twining in and out, and I says, "Hello,
Job," bending down to scratch behind his ears and smooth his
back. They had a hole in the back of the loft they could get in
and out to visit the barn by.

Arnold and I worked on the window to get it open and finally it came up with a screech.

"I'll be right there on the stairs," Arnold told me.

"Doing your duty," I says. "That's reasonable."

He cradled his Henry carbine a bit. "Doing my duty," he said, and went out.

I shut the door and in the stipples of moonlight coming in through the open window—and with all the cats now purring around me—got my paint and canvas sack open, and felt to see that the paints and the few canvases and the rest of my belongings had survived the balloon. They seemed to have done all right. Near the window, just below it, I could see Marshal Arnold sitting there, could make out the glisten of his star in the half dark. I thought of Rafe Gondy. Arnold wouldn't be that simple to fool, he probably wasn't that much enamored of his own face as sketched by Lucius Applegate.

But that was all right because I wasn't planning on busting out.

I played with the cats for a long time, a game of you spar with me, I'll spar with you, but don't claw me; that cat Job got right up on his furry heels and sparred, he looked like a dockhand in New York. Then I got tired of that and just sat a spell, fondling the cats meantime, and feeling remarkably wide-awake and fit for anything.

Seemed a lot later than he said it was when Arnold says outside the window, "It's two after twelve." Saw him put his watch away, and says fine. "Haven't heard a thing out of the ordinary," I says.

Nor had I.

While I'd fooled with the cats I'd kept listening, and there had been just regular night sounds. Now, down below, one of the hired men was snoring; figured they'd finally done all the milking. Out in the night, mostly clear silence, even clearer than it had been that July night. Not so full of insects and tree frogs, but with its own cooler noises. And now even the far murmur of the crowd all gone.

I stripped down to drawers and stretched out in the alfalfa straw. For a little I regretted not grabbing one of those bearskins, which we'd left back in the gondola, and bringing it with me, because it was cool on the arms, legs, and back. Wondered how Letty was sleeping. Didn't think I, myself, would get a thimble of slumber all this night long, but I didn't want to freeze dead while trying it. But then the cats came around me, snuggling in, some of them still making that eternal bee sound.

I shut my eyes and listened to the ticking of the straw and the cats.

It got later and I still wasn't asleep. Marshal Arnold was smoking out on the stairs. Smelled like fairly good tobacco. I was half-minded to ask him for a seegar. But didn't do it. Opened my eyes, though.

Now the cats had stopped bumblebee-buzzing.

A frame full of moonlight picked out the straw and part of the loft floor.

Don't know what I expected. Maybe I expected Letty to come up the stairs in that blood-red dark-burning gown.

It didn't happen.

After another section of time I rolled over on my back. Could still hear, listening as Prosser had directed me to do, even if this time I had some alfalfa in my ears. The cats rearranged themselves around me after I'd stirred them up. But this time they didn't make a sound.

Then not meaning to, I went to sleep. Holding the whole night of strangeness and mystery in me like a puzzle behind my eyes.

Thirty

WHEN I WOKE up the marshal named Arnold was shaking my shoulder. Not hard. And it was already early morning light in the sleeping loft. Behind Arnold was Tom Prosser. I figured they'd both been up all night. Prosser showed it the most. You could have fried his eyes and they couldn't have been harder.

"I hope you slept well, Applegate," he says. Maybe he didn't mean it as lofty as it sounded. Or maybe he did.

I says, "Did so, thanks," and got up and started dressing. I wore the dove-gray outfit with the blue facings the professor and Miz Amily had got me for Christmas. And the palm-leaf hat. I took my long razor in its case out of the paint and canvas sack, hoping I could shave soon. Wasn't going to answer Prosser till he asked me about what I'd heard. I could be stubborn too. Then when I turned around and saw his tiredness—him standing there like a big sack of weariness, bound-in with purpose—I says, "Well, I didn't hear anything out of the ordinary. It was just about like it was the night Einsner was killed."

"Thank you. That is helpful."

Couldn't see how, but took it for granted. I kept on dressing, waiting for him to say something else. The cats sat looking
at us for a spell, then vanished through their hole on their way
to the barn. Outside I could hear marshals' voices calling to
each other here and there. I looked out of the window and
down below there was Professor Allan, hands hugging to his
body under the cloak, stomping around in the morning cool.
It was a day fresh as a harbor with a wind blowing into it.

Prosser had noted my razor. "You can shave and have coffee at the farmhouse. Come along."

I cut an eye at him, and preceded him and Arnold down the
outside stairs.

Under one arm, the Henry carbine under the other, Arnold
was carrying my paint and canvas sack. So I decided they
weren't going to take me back to the sleeping loft again.

When we'd gone part of the way across the barnyard, I said
I'd have to go use a privy, and Prosser nodded; he stood with
Arnold while I went inside. That privy had some crevices in it
and out of them I could see the professor come up and talk to
Prosser, and then Milt Farley joining them, with his leather
suit and his leather duck-billed cap; I heard them talking.
Farley said, "Well, you should've joined me, Professor. It's
good sleeping in the gondola and there's room. I put a couple
of them bearskins over me and slept like a baby."

When I came out the professor said, "Good morning,
Luke." He came to me and shook my hand. Sort of wrung it. I
could tell from that that he wasn't as sure of things as he'd
seemed the night before when he urged me to buck up. But
he wished to hearten me. I could smell coffee on the air. We
walked across toward the farmhouse together with the others
behind us. "I'll admit to moments of doubt," said the professor.

"I'm still having nothing else," I says.

I knew Prosser hadn't told him anything. Figured he
wouldn't have told his mother, if she was alive, or his wife, if
he had one, anything when he was working on a case.

Professor frowns. "There's so much in doubt. I am beginning to see—have seen for some while, to be sure, that a case

of murder has more facts—and facets—than any other crime. It is not neatly laid out, as in, let us say, Poe's "Gold Bug." There are factual infidelities in it—as many as Heliodorus offered Meleager. It's a chancy thing—if I had it all to do over again I would call on Tom Prosser immediately, and scuttle my own inclinations."

"If I had it to do over I'd leave here the night before it happened," I said.

But that wasn't true. Even if I'd known it was coming I wouldn't have ducked away from it because that way I wouldn't have got to know Letty and live with her. I says to the professor, "You've done more for me than one man usually does for another, so no matter which way it comes out, don't you ever feel bad. All right, Professor?"

"Nonsense. You would have done better for me. Sometimes I wish you were older—you'd have made an able officer in the war. Under either flag."

I thanked him for that. Out in the pasture where we'd landed the balloon was laid out catching the dewy light. Another couple of marshals were guarding it. I could see now they had to, because around in front, past the ropes spread around the whole front of the farmhouse, a good many people had gathered again and would soon be a milling crowd.

There was a peppery scent of winter herbs and that coffee and the smell of too many people coming from the kitchen when we approached it from the back way. Marshal Daggart came out of there, and stood talking to Tom Prosser in an undertone. Arnold went in the kitchen door. Through the window I could see Mitchell and Gondy, and then Wheelman and then Soames and Tatum. I supposed they'd slept in there as well as they could. I supposed everybody who was in custody had slept as well as they could. Around the corner of the house with another marshal directing them came Jane and Loogan. Loogan looked considerably the worse for wear, frazzled at the rims, but Jane had her head back and was wearing a fox-red scarf and her shoulders swung a little. She could wear clothes with the brightness and grace of Letty, carry them that way, though she was a larger woman. Gave me a

smile and a wave. I waved back. Arnold came back out of the
kitchen with a basin full of water that'd been heated on the
range. I took it from him and set it on the bench where he'd
put my pack and looking into a scrap of mirror nailed up
above the wash-bench I washed and shaved the best I could.
Felt better when I'd finished. I shoved the razor in its case
back in my pack and says to Arnold, "I'll carry the pack. It's
too much like people doing things for the condemned man,
otherwise."

He ducked his chin. "Fine with me."

Then a window came open and another marshal handed
out a pot of boiling coffee. And some tin cups. We stood
around sipping the coffee for a spell, not talking to each other
much in the cool. Except for Prosser who kept on conversing
soft with Daggart.

Then still another marshal, they had the place swarming
with them, came driving a wagon from the barnyard side. Had
a couple of Einsner's grays hitched to it, and the near gray
had a stone in the frog of its right front hoof. You could tell
the way it favored it. I said as much, to Arnold; he nods and
speaks to the marshal on the wagon seat, and the marshal gets
down and with a small knife digs the stone out, while Arnold
holds the grays steady. Light was moving across the whole
yard now, and I stood there watching it pick out the wintry
trees and that place where the path went down to the creek
where I'd often bathed in that hot July at night after I was
through working on Letty's portrait for the day.

When the stone was out of the gray's hoof, Tom Prosser
jerked his chin to the wagon. And he said, not loud, just foghooting and heavy, "Please get up in the wagon. We're going a
little way down the road." He ushered Jane Einsner and
Loogan Harkins up to the big wagon, and after a second I
hopped up after them. They had their bags with them, and so
did the professor and Milt Farley, who followed them up in
the wagon bed. I figured they'd been told to bring them, but it
didn't feel the bright clear way it had felt when we'd all loaded
into the balloon's gondola. The marshal driving the grays was
back on the driving seat. Then, escorted by two more mar-

shals, Wayde Mitchell and Rafe Gondy, Wheelman and Tatum
and Soames trailing them, came out and were ordered to get
up in the wagon. I had the wild thought that maybe Tom
Prosser was going to take us all out on a forest path and get
rid of us. The professor had plumped down beside me. We all
started out of the yard.

When we came out at the flank of the farmhouse, people
pressing against the ropes all yelled and started toward us.

Daggart says crisp and loud to Prosser, "Can we keep them
back with arms, sir?"

Prosser glinted his eyes to the crowd. "If they approach so
near they interfere with our business," he says. "But we *cannot*
keep them from the road; it is public." I looked back where
his eyes were moving. People of all sizes and ages were starting toward us, after us, along the road. The night had been
cold and the mists were just sunning off the road's dust. We
were moving south, away from the direction Letty and I'd run
on the night of the killing. The people came after us, some of
them on foot, as though they'd spied gold for the taking.
Some got in their carts and wagons and buggies and such.
Pretty shortly we were the head of a traveling serpent, trailed
by them all. They seemed to swell in numbers even as you
watched.

With the new sun on my eyelids I rode the joggling wagon
and thought how strange it was to be riding along with powerful Wayde Mitchell, and all his cronies, as though all of us
were haring off to a husking bee. Except there wasn't anybody
singing and cutting up, and there weren't any banjo players or
mouth-harp experts. For some reason I thought of that first
trip home to the mill clearing from Solomon, with Seven playing the mouth-harp in that lonesome easy way. Even if we'd
had any music with us now it couldn't have been heard because of the caterwauling and speculation of the crowd tailing
us.

Then we were at a place where another road crossed this, and
where chestnut trees arched over both that road and this and
let the light through in sun-dribbling flickerings. The side

road was just a path leading down across the meadows, hard-
looking in the brisk air. The chestnut branches still met above
us, like skeins, and with their leaves on would have shadowed
the road completely. The driving marshal pulled the wagon
off to the side and he got down—he had a carbine too—and
Arnold and Daggart got down, and so did the other two marshals who were riding herd on Mitchell and those other people. Prosser got out, slow and firm as a glacier doing it, and
handed down Jane; then everybody was getting out.

Prosser gave the nod to the two marshals with Mitchell's
bunch, and they moved around between all of us and the
mob. Out in front of the mob a young man came running
around one of the carriages and got so far up to us he was
stopped only by a carbine thrust near his face. He said he was
from a Philadelphia paper and had to know what was going
on. Prosser moved over to him and said, "Yes. You'll know, in
good time."

"But I've waited all night," says the reporter.

"Yes," said Prosser. "Some of us might have waited even
longer."

He turned away.

Then with those marshals still keeping the people back in
the road—you couldn't have got a goat cart around them if
you'd been traveling north or south—and with Arnold and
Daggart moving along with us, Prosser led us all to a point
where the crossroads met; there was a spiny hedge here with
bits of dried-Jimson weed and bloodwort showing below it.
Prosser looks tired as the last man on a battlefield when he
clears his throat. He raised his voice to fill the daylight but it
couldn't have been heard from farther along the road because
the crowd was making too much noise for it to be.

Under the light freckling down through the bare-muscled
boughs of the great chestnut behind him Tom Prosser looked
like a white bulldog finally finding his place to bite.

"Applegate. Jane. Mister Harkins. All of you. I don't intend
to give you all the steps by which I have arrived at my conclu-
sions. I'll give you the bare bones and they will be enough."

I was glad of that, no matter what it was going to be.

"Briefly, your stories hang together. I mean yours, Jane, and yours, Mister Harkins. And yours, Applegate, as compared with Letty Einsner's statement. They hang together because there is blood in the crack of the doorsill back at the farmhouse. That is fortunate. While I can't be sure that it belonged to Carl Einsner—there is yet another patch of blood on the rug where he was found. So it is reasonable to assume he was carried into the house. But this was already obvious—that he had been carried in there, after receiving the blow that killed him out here. It was obvious from your story, Jane—and from Mister Harkins's corroboration—that, if the story was true, it is what must have happened."

He'd plunged his weighty hands in the pockets of his black coat and stood swaying back and forth in the sun-dapples.

"As Jane and Mister Harkins know, I visited this place, which is roughly where they said Jane discovered the blood trace—which was not, I think, a hawk's kill—I visited it last night, with them." He flapped a solid hand, white knuckles flashing, then rammed it back in his pocket. "We used that wagon, and those horses, and we made a great deal of noise. Yet, from the sleeping loft—at about the same time of night Applegate had mentioned in his statement to me, under the same conditions—neither Applegate nor Marshal Arnold heard anything out of the way. Nor did any of my men in the farmhouse. So there we have two points. The blood on the doorsill and the fact that the farmhouse and barn and sheds stand far enough from the main road so that it is possible to make a great deal of noise out here, wagon-noise, horse-noise, and remain ignorant of it back there."

My mind was racing faster'n my blood. And *it* wasn't slowing down. But I couldn't still see where he was going.

"So now we come to another point. The jingle of trace chains which Jane said she heard down that side road . . ." Didn't take his hands from his pockets now; just nodded his snowy head to the side path across this main road. "She said she heard it after she and Loogan had gotten down from their buggy."

He cleared his throat again. I thought he wasn't enjoying

himself at all. He was just ramming through to the end of it. Down the road to the north, the marshals holding the people back spoke something that rang out sharp.

Prosser didn't attend to it, but goes on, "She said two other things, as well. Perhaps she didn't think them of much account, but she remembers well, and she included them. Fortunately. One was that Carl Einsner was sometimes prone to take long walks—perhaps admiring his splendid acreage—at night. The other was that when she and Mister Harkins came back to their buggy, Mister Harkins was babbling. Saying— loudly, she said—what was it, Jane?"

Jane had her shoulders back, her eyes were narrowed and cool and waiting. She says, "Loogan was sayin', 'He's dead, he's dead,' and it was all I could do to load him in the buggy and head back to Hornbeck—"

"Thank you. That will do." He was looking deep at me, nobody else. Stared back, waiting. "Applegate made still other observations. Repeatedly, and borne out by Miss Einsner's statement. He said the riding lights were out on the Clamber Trust wagon. He said, further, that Mister Gondy seemed to be in a high state of nerves."

I couldn't keep from nodding back at him.

He was still looking straight at me now. Out of the corners of my eyes I could half-see Mitchell, standing there chewing his lip, his flowered-aster vest heaving; could feel the others with him, kind of edging forward.

Tom Prosser says, "My men had eliminated the hired hands. They had eliminated Mister Mitchell—though he will serve a sentence for other sorts of manipulation, the obstruction of justice being the foremost. But for the night in question he has a firm alibi. Now. Who else was known to be in the vicinity that night? Who, half-drunk which seems to be his natural manly state, was driving horses breakneck along this road—"

I could hear Mitchell breathing, his belly rising and falling like the balloon with tricky valve work. And I couldn't help looking over past him at Gondy. There he stood, a wisp of straw in one corner of his mouth, eyes shadowed by the hat, big body kind of aware and awake, now, and his boots fouled because he never had cleaned them. His nose was a slab of unbeauty.

Couldn't help feeling sorry for him either. Just a dash of sorrow. He hadn't ever caused me any real trouble except for that time when I'd crashed the so-called jail in Mullin's Gap; you could feel the trouble smoldering in him but for all his cheese-paring ways about pictures, he was a biddable man.

And Prosser was going straight on, walking over toward Gondy as he did, and the others, Mitchell and Wheelman, Tatum and Soames, were pulling back from Gondy. "That night, racing along here to do fifty miles to Mullin's Gap—not a great parcel of miles for one night, but you like fast driving—didn't you hit a man walking alongside the road?" He was real close to Gondy now. "Hit him either with a trace chain or with part of your lumber wagon, in the back of the head? Didn't you get out and, in a kind of panic, tell yourself instantly that if he were found *in the farmhouse* no blame could be attached to you? Didn't you tell yourself that it was late, that you stood a good chance of carrying him to the farmhouse and leaving him without anybody seeing you, because of the hour? Didn't you—a large man—carry him, a heavy man, up the path and into the parlor, and"—Prosser was as close to Gondy as you can get to a man without touching him—"and *drop* him on the rug?"

Gondy was shaking his head; he'd started it slow, but now it was fast and faster.

Prosser's eyebrows went tangling into winter forests.

"No candlestick killed him. Harkins, in his fear and trembling, inadvertently knocked the candlestick from the mantel after he and Jane had found the body. You left him in the parlor. And then didn't you run back down the path from the farmhouse, here to the road, and hear the sound of buggy wheels coming from the south, and, rather than be discovered in the vicinity—they were in sight almost before you knew it, I think—drive your wagon down into that path across the road? Where, in summer, leaves would screen it well? And didn't you watch while Jane and Loogan Harkins brought their buggy into full sight, and drew it up here in the grass, and got out and went up the path to the farmhouse? *And,* wait for them to come back?"

That icy flaring was in Prosser's eyes. "I can think of only one reason why you waited for these visitors to come back."

Even though you could see most of the truth now from Gondy's gray-blue none-too-clean face, I wanted it all to stop. It's terrible to see a man break down when he hasn't got any more guts in him than that. Or when he's carted it around with him so long it just leaks out of his eyes and falls into the roadway.

What the hell *was* he—nothing but a hard-drinking driver who'd made a mistake. That was all. Nothing like the creature Mitchell was . . . but it went right on.

"You blew out your riding lanterns. You couldn't be seen. You waited for Jane and Harkins to come back. Why?"

Then finally Gondy's saying, in a blurting voice, "Because, God rot it, Marshal, when I lugged him in the house he wasn't dead yet! Hadn't meant to hit 'im—couldn't see till I was right on him, the way the road dips back there. Takin' him in the house, I'd figured somebody'd find him, mebbe nurse him!" He batted air from around his hat, as though a bee swarm was roaring there, but there wasn't even a fly. "And when I come back here and heard buggy wheels, was just time to duck my wagon outa sight 'fore they see me! They left their buggy here, didn't drive in to the house, figured from that they'd be out 'fore long! I hung around to see 'f when they come back, they'd drop a word about him bein' dead or not. And that fella—" He was near shouting at Loogan. "That fella, he's bawlin' that the critter *was* dead!" He was still pointing to Jane and Harkins, whose tiny moustache seemed about to leap from his lip. "So when they'd skallyhooted on down the road north a way and I see they'd took the side cut west to Hornbeck way, I got back in my own wagon and came outa the side road yonder, and next thing I know, just when I'd got to a good rumble of speed, there's that Applegate, or Lester, or whatever he's calling hisself now, and his woman, and he scairt t' Jesus outa me . . ."

He stopped, and Prosser took an elephant-slow step back.
Says, voice disgusted and mad and as sorry as I'm feeling,
maybe even almost as sorry as Gondy's feeling, "And afterward, when Mister Mitchell—" He took one glance at
Mitchell, and anybody but Mitchell would have looked away
then. "When Mitchell came around, putting his plot
together—and at any time in between—did you say one word
about what had really happened?"

Couldn't see Gondy's eyes. Head was too low, hat over it.

The head shook, back and forth.

Prosser was even quieter now. "No, you didn't. Your crime
is manslaughter. Concealing it all this time isn't going to help
you . . . Daggart."

"Yes sir."

"Arrest this man. Rafe Gondy. And arrest Mitchell—and the
rest of them . . . conspiracy to obstruct . . . you know the
forms."

He turned away as if he was sick to death of it. There wasn't
anything looked like triumph in him.

Down the road to the north the crowd was whooping it up.

They could see, all right, while Daggart and Arnold
marched Rafe Gondy and Wayde Mitchell and the rest of that
bunch over to the side, and stood guard on them.

I stood with things spinning around me, thinking, while
Letty was up at the loft window getting me to run off with her,
Jane and Loogan were coming back down the path. While I
was in the front room finding Einsner, they were getting in
their buggy. While Letty and I were cutting down the road in
the moonlight to the creek, Gondy was pulling his wagon out
of the side road and getting set to put miles between him and
here where he'd—even if not meaning to—killed a man.
Time, I thinks: it can confound you forever or be your good
friend.

But the best friend I'd had, out of all, was that downturned-
mouthed, snow-headed plugger, U.S. Marshal Tom Prosser.

The marshal who'd driven the wagon was looking back,
shading his eyes. It was getting warmer. I figured I'd been
right to wear my palm hat against the sun. But I figured more

than that. For now the wagon-driving marshal calls, "Sir!" to Tom Prosser. Prosser looks around, and we most of us do.

Down the road, the people are pushing the marshals backward. Making a boil of dust and flurry.

The professor's been shaking my hand, though I didn't feel much like it. Milt Farley has too. Jane Einsner pats my shoulder, and I pat hers. But now we stop all this, and all of us, everybody here, just stands stony, watching the crowd coming toward us.

From under his cloak the professor draws a weapon I didn't even know he had with him. An old-style single-action cap-and-ball revolver that I'd bet he used to certain purpose in the Army of Northern Virginia.

He edges to me close. Says, most under his breath, "Put up your bright swords or the dew will rust them!"

I guess it was from a book. Not likely Wordsworth, but maybe Keats, but even more possibly, Shakespeare.

Thirty-One

THERE WAS SUCH RELIEF in me I didn't even worry for a flash
or two about the mob's coming toward us. Everything had
happened so flat and hard after that long time of worrying I
couldn't even feel it simmer through to the core of me yet. I
was a free man, and yet I didn't feel that way; I just stood with
the professor while he pointed his cap-and-ball revolver at the
crowd and I even felt like I wanted to smile, sort of weak-
mouthed, in this moment.

But then I saw Tom Prosser draw himself up tighter and
firmer, his mouth disgusted, and he knocked the professor's
arm aside and said, "There'll be no bloodshed!"

"I want none, Tom," said the professor. "But they'll go for
Gondy and the others, can't you see? They saw your marshals
arrest him, they believe—"

"I know what they believe." Both Prosser and the professor
were talking awful fast. "But I'll talk to them."

I thought he'd better do that quick. The crowd, that reporter from the Philadelphia paper in the lead—I expect news
people think they have to make news sometimes—was pushing

right against the chests of the marshals with the carbines who'd been set to keep them away from us.

I've said I don't paint flocks of people but if I ever painted that I'd like to get in the red-eyed hungry look of even the children being dragged along in that mob, and the way they churned and jabbed forward, and the way they were yelling. They were mindless and it even showed on their ochre-touched faces and through the pockets of their beings and in their hands. Each looked as though he or she wanted a crawful of blood. Right down to dumpy little women and leathery-handed farmers; some of them had weapons, too, if you can call pitchforks and clubs any kind of weapon, and I guess you can. Somebody in the lead was yelling about "Vengeance, saith the Lord!" and a woman was shaking her fist high above the multitude and screeching that she'd have the blood of the killer of dear Carl Einsner. I figured, in a sparkle through my head, that I'd bet a lot of these people had been mulcted by that old Carl Einsner, that Jane-beater, I'd bet they'd been rooked seven ways from Sunday, but did that matter now? You'd think he'd been their king of this community, from the way they were howling.

Something turned over in my gorge, like I was about to throw up. But I just kept on backing along with Prosser and the professor and Jane and Harkins and Milt Farley and our marshals and their prisoners. Then the mob was damned near level with the back of the wagon, and the grays were nerved up and shifting and about to run away for all they were being held by the marshal who had the reins, and sudden-like Milt Farley hoisted the big carcass of Tom Prosser up to the rear of the wagon and Prosser held up his hands.

About this time, the professor decided he'd shoot off his cap and ball. It made a fine sound and a puff of smoke. That cut down the enthusiasm of the crowd quite a bit. The reporter fell back into somebody's arms, they all stopped so fast. The professor had shot his weapon into the air.

Prosser cut a glance down at the professor, and the professor looked cool-eyed back and shrugged as though the piece had gone off by accident; then Prosser, hands still lifted, and looking a mite like a much heftier Moses addressing his people about the tablets, turned to the crowd. They stretched such a long way you couldn't see around the first curve in the road.

Tom Prosser started speaking in a voice that was still fogged and rough but now had turned to a great bell chime too, swinging in the morning, and what he said just about shook the last few burrs off the chestnuts twining over our heads. I've heard thunder in my time—a lot of people-thunder as well as the natural kind—but he outdid it. And it all came out so wry and disgusted and empty-feeling for the whole human race it made you shrivel up under it and wish to die or at any rate hide yourself rather than go on listening. It must've reached the very last child in that crowd.

He tongue-lashed the crowd for being there. He explained what had happened—a man's taking a walk in the night, down beside his acres on the road, and he's hit by a wagon going buckety-clip toward the north, and then the man who hit him is a fool and a coward, because he knows the man he hit isn't dead yet, but dying, but doesn't even try to give him aid and succor. He carts him into the house, where he's found a little later by some people who're here only because they're driven by greed, and when the wagon-driver hears one of those people saying the man he hit is dead, he rushes off in the night saying nothing about it—letting others carry the brunt and blame for months. But even so, says Prosser, that man's not a patch on the man who took advantage of his friend's death, to try to get his acres and his money by pretending to protect the dead man's daughter and by finding a scapegoat for the murder, and working by himself and not telling the law about it at all. Prosser laid it out clear and clean. He drew a parallel between the people in the mob, who now wanted to lynch Gondy, or otherwise harm him, with all mobs everywhere, and then with Gondy and Mitchell themselves, and with Jane Einsner and Loogan Harkins. And then with me and Letty, for running off that night when we'd, separately, found the body of Carl Einsner. He started to make my ears burn and I felt like hanging my head along with the rest of the crowd, and maybe did. He made us all feel like whipped dogs. Nor did he spare the professor. He claimed that friendship wasn't friendship when it set out to defeat the law, even though the law might sometimes be ponderous and foolish-seeming.

He said it was all we had, and even though small men tried to divert it for their own purposes, it had to keep aiming at justice or we could all go back to what he called the dark caves of night.

He laid into Wayde Mitchell again. I'd rather've had a jail sentence a year or longer than to've been Mitchell and listened to that. He laid into the men Mitchell had used, his quashing of Letty's part in it at my expense, for his own purposes. And by this time nobody was looking at anybody else—we all kept looking at the ground, or in the air, or anywhere but at each other.

Then he finished, hands not raised now, and he said, "Dear God, we've come through a war half-split apart and bleeding, and if we don't have sense enough to heal ourselves and be honest one with the other, black and white and in between, red and brown and yellow, then in another hundred years we might as well throw up the country and go off and drown ourselves in the sea, like so many lemmings." He looked down at the professor. "*Man,*" he said. "How like a god indeed, or gods. Christ help us."

Then he got down from the wagon.

Some of the crowd just went on back to the farmhouse, those that hadn't brought their rigs this far to get them and drive, draggle-tailed, home. A couple of the reporters stayed around to get the details and Tom Prosser gave them to them. They looked a little mashed-down in the spirit, too, for reporters.

Milt Farley came over to me and says, "Well, it's over, Applegate."

"Not for me," I said. "I've got some unfinished business up the line," and I gestured north, fifty miles or so north if the truth be told.

"That's right," he says. "You've got that mill and that woman to worry about." He'd heard the whole story by now, in scraps and patches.

"The mill ain't a worry," I pointed out. "It's just *there*."

"It's why I never married," Farley says. He pulled at a pocket of his leather ballooning coat. "The balloon's my old lady, I expect."

I had the thought then, which I'd had in forms before, but never quite this strong, that a limner such as I really ought'n't to be tied down either; that now it was over, as he said—though nothing like that could ever truly be over—it'd be good to hit the road, to move south again, maybe all the way to Florida, where they have all these palm trees and the air's silky and you can paint up a hurricane if you can get the strength in your lazy-going, weather-affected spirit to do it. But somehow I couldn't think of doing that.

"Women," says Farley, looking at a sun spot dancing in the dust down the road where all those boots of the mob had been. "I wish I had the answer to 'em."

"I'm still seeking for it," I tells him.

He sounded for just the slab of a second like Jericho Dabney. But Jericho'd been wrong about Letty, after all. And there she was, up there in Solomon. I'd heard Prosser telling Daggart he wanted to get off a telegraph message to his man in Solomon as soon as possible, telling him to tell Miss Einsner what had happened, and that she didn't have to worry now; but for the time being she might still be worrying, I thought, about whether she'd be clapped in jail and maybe hung later, and maybe even worrying about me. Figured she was doing somewhat of that last.

I looked over at Rafe Gondy who was sitting on the ground. He was beside the road just studying the world. He'd come close to being mob-taken and he knew it; it was in his face; it wasn't a smart face but it wasn't craw-dabbed with evil either. Just a face, now sweating and gray and even pinched.

Wayde Mitchell and his crew, if you could call Wheelman and the rest of them any kind of crew, had drawn off to the side a little.

All were still being guarded by the marshals.

Now I could hear the professor apologizing to Prosser. He'd apologized some, back in Richmond, but this was the full guns. Professor Allan wasn't a man, I think you've gathered, who apologized to many people all his born days. But he was doing it now, with ribbons. Sounded handsome, what I could make out of it.

When I judged he was through, I moved over past Milt Farley and Jane and Loogan, to Tom Prosser. I said, "I'm sorry too. Sorry I acted like such a skittery young fool in the first place, leaving the farmhouse that night when what I shoulda done is go for help and justice and then come back. I'm sorry from the middle of my belly, and I thank you for all you've done. You got a way of going at things that's a correct way of getting on in life, for a man. I'm obliged."

Wasn't much of a speech but I meant it all and it had tones that went above what the words said.

Prosser looked at me and didn't smile—he never did—but nods that he accepts it. "And now, Applegate," he says— "Daggart, you and Arnold come along with us; we'll move along to the Jerseyville jail; get those people back in the wagon—and now, Applegate, I'll fill out the papers you'll have to have to prove you're a free man. I have papers that will apply to Miss Einsner on this score, too. Will you take them to her? Deliver them?"

"Yes sir," I says.

He squinches his mouth a trifle. "There was nothing deductive about this case. Only facts, put together a certain way— with a certain instinct. You would be surprised how many cases are solved that way." A flicker went over his solid white face. "And how many aren't," he said.

"Auguste Dupin is a charlatan," said the professor, sad.

We had all our gear in the wagon; time for us to climb up too, along with the—felons, I guess the name is. Mitchell and Gondy and Tatum and Wheelman and Soames were going to the Jerseyville jailhouse, Prosser said, and he also said he wanted us to come along to have a bite at the tavern nearby when that was over. He told us he wanted a final word with us, too. While the rest of them were climbing back in the wagon, Milt Farley muttering how everyone who was going had ought to get a good start back to Richmond, because this weather might not hold—I stared up at their faces and didn't even see them clear. For I was thinking, I'm not J. P. Lester, or George Rose, or Andreas Artifact the Quick Limner, or even Delevan Gainsborough anymore—I'm Luke Applegate.

Good powerful feeling, for what it was worth.

I got in then and we sashayed behind those lumbering grays along the road to Jerseyville. I sat beside Jane. She said, "Lord, I feel full of bubbles. Just that light 'n relieved. Marshal was right . . . I deserved the rough side of his tongue. It was mainly money drew me back around here that night. But poor Loogan, he was just in my wake, so to speak. Still . . ." She looked out at the peaceable part winter-bare country passing by. "Still, I'm glad I saw Letty."

Tom Prosser turned around from where he'd been sitting, head sunk down, battered old valise on his lap. He said, slow, "Jane, if you would like to go north before returning to Richmond, I will arrange it. If you would like to see your daughter, and this time, have her see you . . ."

She shook her head sharp. "Too late, Marshal Prosser. What was between us is gone. I long ago betrayed it."

Handsome-faced, a ripe woman, she gave me a snick of a smile. "Astarte might get us together some other time, even so. Can't tell when roses'll be thrown your way, it's a gamble."

She sat up proud then. Might've been out riding in her landau, surveying the countryside, elegant.

I wanted a little to kiss her.

Milt Farley kept fretting about the weather, he said it could change rapid this time of year. Kept looking at the sky.

The so-called people to be incarcerated sat in the back with marshals sticking close to them.

When we got to a hump in the road about a half mile from Jerseyville, Mitchell calls from the back, a scowful of tears in his voice—sounded like a nanny goat, that quavering and pitiful, "May a ruined man have one last request?"

Tom Prosser turned half his face, like a cliff. "You will not hang for what you have done, Mitchell. Perhaps you should, but you shan't. I have dealt with your kind before. I am afraid, in my soul, that with your knowledge of the law, and your—friends, allies, fellow-thieves?—you may be out of jail sooner than these other men. So," he said, facing square-front again, the back of his neck white granite, "don't refer to any soulful 'last requests.' Not with me."

"Ah," says Mitchell after we'd gone another six or eight wheel turns, "but could you have your driver stop—and let me out—under guard, my dear marshal, and I am not a nimble man, only one of God's creatures, I shall not try to escape—all I wish is to view the grave of my dear friend Carl Einsner. I wish to see his monument again. I had it erected personally, and I should like to see how it is wearing . . ."

"By God, sir, you have nerve," said the professor, wheeling all the way around. "Zeus may not hear you. He pays little attention to whimpering. But beware, sometime he might—and then it would be a miracle if he didn't strike you dead."

"Quiet, Harvey," says Prosser, wheezing and tired. He sat a few more steps, thought, and then said to Jane, "Would you like to see it, Jane?"

She was staring straight forward, like Letty, with a lot of that pride. Feet planted like a dowsing rod's end when it aims for water in the earth.

"No sir. I lived with him a good many years. Each seemed a mountain. I don't favor looking upon his grave now."

I said, "I'd kind of like to see it."

The reason I had for that was pure curiosity. Maybe I wanted to smile at myself inside, too, over the stone Wayde Mitchell would have raised to his friend.

Anyhow Prosser nodded and said, "Stop," and the marshal driver stopped, and we sat there in the road while Wayde Mitchell, with a marshal guarding him like he was a valuable jewel, got down, his belly near snagging on the wagon rail, and then I put a hand out on the iron-bound wheel and jumped down, and we all walked a short way up to the west, where there's a cemetery. An old, small one, with most of its stones chewed away and most of its epitaphs rubbed down by the wind and the rain and the snows of dark winter.

Mitchell was puffing good by the time we got to the stone he wanted to see, past bramble bushes and old blackberry vines and the remains of what would in summer be long thick grass. Was a nice smell in the air like old apples and sun.

The stone stuck up like a column, with three doves on it, rather fat doves—I thought Mitchell would favor that kind— and a couple of bare-tailed cupids, twining hands. The stone was raw-looking and some of the information cut in it seemed to leap out at you: Carl Einsner, foully murdered, O rest, perturbed spirit.

I'd had enough. Mitchell was already soiling the knees of his good pants by kneeling in front of the stone and he was sobbing like the pump of a New York fire engine. The marshal with us was trying to look the other way while still keeping his carbine handy.

Then Mitchell turns around and looks at me. His wet-streaked face changes, all the distance; it's a look of pure hate, no masks on, no glozed words, and I can tell in the jump of the second that he still wants Letty, wants the money, wants everything, and even thinks he'll get them. Not only that, it's the look of somebody who knows something I don't, a piece of valuable pure gold information. All in the puff of time.

He goes back to sobbing, then, and I turn and walk back down to the wagon in the road, hearing the no-nonsense marshal tell him to get up now and come on; but I can still hear him blubbering as the marshal gets him to his feet.

If I'd stayed any longer there I'd have busted him. Not for the peculiar look, but just because he needed it so bad. And I couldn't forget the look, either.

Thirty-Two

JERSEYVILLE WAS A SANDY, SHADOWY PLACE, not much account as I'd thought when I first traveled through it and then later when I'd seen it again from the balloon. But it did have a jail, considerably better than the one in Mullin's Gap, and an inn-tavern where you might be poisoned but hardly ever on purpose. Jane Einsner and Harkins and the professor stayed at the tavern, ordering up some food and drink for us at Prosser's behest, while the marshals prodded their prisoners on back to the jail, and I followed along with Prosser. I waited outside the front steps of the place while Prosser got all the official business done of locking up the prisoners; I kept peering into the jail from time to time and seeing that when the cell doors clanged shut they clanged on a special cell for Gondy, and one for Mitchell, with Wheelman and Tatum and Soames being thrown in together, looking like sorry bags of wool somebody had cast aside in a warehouse.

Milt Farley was standing in the road outside the jail projecting up at the sky with his chin in his hand. He looked like a tough bird yearning to return to its native element. I thought

to myself how he had a good life as long as the valve of the
balloon didn't completely quit on him one day and let him
down too fast and kill him.

After a time Tom Prosser came out and gave me a look of
puzzlement. "Why aren't you with the others?"

"Thought I'd like to say good-bye to Gondy."

"Well, that would be permissible. Even commendable. As
long as you don't stir him up. He's had a hard few days."

"I don't intend to bother him."

He said all right, so I went in and walked down to the line
of cells. They were stinking quite a bit. The marshal at the
front desk nodded to me; he'd heard Tom Prosser, I was just
a visiting friend now.

I looked into Gondy's cell. Could hardly see him for a second; he was hunched all the way at the back. He was staring at
the floor. I said, "I'm sorry you done it. I'm even sorrier you
didn't speak up sooner, but I can see why not. A man's neck's
a peculiar and lovely possession with him. Anyhow, Marshal
Prosser says you won't be stretched for it."

He looked up at me. I had a pencil stub and a piece of
paper in my new clothes. I took them out and said, "The last
two sketches I done of you were kind of meanly meant. I'll do
one that favors you, that's just like you."

"How's come?" he says, scrannel-voiced.

"I just feel bad about you," I said.

He nods. While I sketched, making it just exactly like he was
and leaving out any personal feelings, getting in the hooked
nose all right but not doing any Phiz-Dickens work, he talked
about how he'd never aimed at hitting anybody, let alone Carl
Einsner, with the wagon that night. It had just happened; he
wasn't a murdering man, he said, unless his own life was
dangered. I wasn't so sure of that, but I was sure he'd never
meant to do what he'd done; he hadn't even known Carl Einsner, he always just used the roads for streaming fast as he
could from one point to another on his lumber route. Some
way, though, he looked to me like I imagined those real killers, who joyed in blood—such as Simon Girty, who slew mul-
titudes of people and burned them at stakes and spat in their

faces and laughed while they fried—might've looked. He had
that rough-cut image. I handed him the sketch and he took it
where a sluice of light fell through onto it and looked from it
back to me. "I'm obliged."

"You're welcome, and no charge, and I wish you luck anyhow," I says, moving on.

I peered into the next cell. Wayde Mitchell was sitting in
there spraddle-legged with his plump hands on his knees. I
was just peering casual; didn't mean to stay. He gets up and
moves over to the bars on my side. Looking at me sort of
sidewise, first with that same mask-off look he'd had for that
single instant of time in the cemetery, then coming over
smarmy, then muttering, "Give my greetings to her. For
you're going to see her."

He meant Letty, no doubt about that.

"What you want me to do, praise you up to her?"

"Ah, just say hello to her, lad. Say hello to my little butterfly,
my little Letitia."

Jesus. I thought quick, sick inside, of the birthmark—the
little butterfly-shape—and where it was on Letty. But then I
thought, maybe he doesn't mean it that way. Maybe it's just
something he's remarking. Still, it was, now, just like it'd been
in the cemetery; I wanted to reach through the bars and grab
him by his silk flowering tie and pull, hard. But I didn't, I
turned around and went out of the jail. Tom Prosser and Milt
Farley were walking toward the tavern. I followed them. I was
thinking that I'd bet this mob Prosser had held back in the
road this morning had been a lot like the mob that at the start
of the war had burned the Carrolls' main house and that had
driven them from the clearing. I didn't want my feeling
against Mitchell to be like a mob's. I just shoved remembrance
of him away from me for the time being, the way you'll put a
hating idea away to chew on later.

In the tavern we all sat around a table together and ate and
drank a little while Tom Prosser filled in dents anybody was
wondering about in the case. He didn't tell all—he never
would, his business wasn't our business—but he did mention

some of the pile of work he and the others had done in the past month, keeping tabs on Mitchell and those people and finding out about Jane and Loogan, tracing everything. He told me the Einsner estate would go to Letty after a while, but that right now just the hired hands would be paid out of it, to keep the farm working. He said he'd be in official touch with us, writing to us in either Solomon or at the mill, about later developments. He said he'd had one of his men telegraph a fellow-worker in Solomon to call off what he called surveillance of Letty. He gave me the papers saying Letty and I were bird-free.

When we'd all nibbled away for a spell, Milt Farley popped to his feet and said, "Folks, we can't tarry here any longer! I sure don't want to start for Richmond any later'n we can help it, and there's still a deal of preparation to go through. Suggest we go now."

The professor nodded. "It has been a royal and sufficing expedition," he said. "Luke—" He didn't grasp my hand, now, he only stared at me. "I am a foolish man, mad with much heart perhaps, very often. But I hope you'll forgive me for that."

"Forgive?" It was my turn to stare at him. "Didn't it come out all right? Haven't I got a whole skin?" I leaned forward. "Say good-bye to the Richmond girls, special to Sally Lou."

"Ah, Luke." He was getting up, swirling his cloak about him. "Sometimes, I believe man can still achieve an Athenian civilization, than which there was nothing more beautiful. But then again I wonder."

"Sir, I don't know about that kind of civilization," I said. "All I want is to do what I have to without getting too chastised for it."

While we walked out into the sun, I told him I wanted to pen a note to Miz Amily, for him to kindly take back with him. He said he would be glad to take that honorable woman a missive, and that it was a rare day when I wrote one, so he'd be all the more happy to. I went to the wagon and jumped up inside and got out my paint and canvas sack; kneeling there, I wrote a note to Miz Amily all right, saying I loved her, which I supposed I did, at least in the way you love a friend like that. And in with the note I put money enough to cover all the professor's running around on my behalf. I didn't have anything but the envelope itself and some spirit gum, though I'd have liked to seal it with wax. Anyway it was tough-made and I didn't think the professor would open it till it got there. Otherwise he'd have cast the money back in my face. He was very dauncy that way. After I'd put the money in I noted I still had a comfortable amount.

About then, a little dark man who'd been occupying a tavern table not far from the one we'd had, drew up below the wagon in a two-wheeled cart, made of wicker something like the gondola of the balloon but a good deal lighter. He had a thin face like a sharp razor and blackberry-currant eyes. He chirps up to me, "You the man they freed?"

"Yes sir," I said. "I'm that very man and it don't cost a copper to see me."

"I'm not inquisitive. I saw that mob working back there and I stayed away. Don't favor large groups of citizens. Heard something of the way the big marshal called them down. Approved of that. All I'm saying is, if you're traveling to the north I'm going there now. You and some Injun boys and an old man run the mill up yonder there, don't you?"

"We did last autumn."

"That's where I heard of you. And of course I heard considerable more when everybody was on the lookout for you. All I'm offering is a ride. Get tired of talking to the horse."

"Mister," I said, "I'll jump at that. For the others are going back by balloon."

"You don't have to spin stories to me, Mister Applegate."

I laughed. "It's true though. It's the way we came here and the way they'll go back. That's all right, I'll explain while we're on our way to Solomon."

"Don't go straight through Solomon, but I can let you out near. I've got an appointment farther up, into New York; got people there waiting for my healing powers."

Oh my Lord, I thought, I always get connected with people who either want to shell a crowd or got strange powers.

But I was gladsome about his offer, so I flipped down and went back to the professor and Milt and Tom Prosser and Jane and Loogan Harkins, and put the envelope in the professor's hand reminding him it was for Miz Amily, and telling him I *would* write later on, to him, without fail. Then there was a clutch of hand-shaking going on—it seems all people can do when they're parting—they don't just turn and walk off. I planted a good buss on Jane's lips. She looked high-spirited and fit for some great crystal-balling. I didn't know what to say to Prosser except to try thanking him again, but he grunts and waved that off; he was a man hated extra fuss. I told them I was going on north now, since the opportunity had come up; they all understood; in the sunlight that was slanting toward noon it felt a fine time to journey.

"Don't let the fox gnaw under your cloak," said the professor. "You are many things but not a Spartan."

"I don't aim to let a fox gnaw." I knew the story. "But I'm afire to see Letty . . ."

I stopped. I was, but at the same time in the back of my mind I was a worried fool. He could see a little of that. I stepped back, then whirled on my heel and went back ahead of them to the wagon. While they came on toward the wagon I got in the sharp-faced small man's cart, hooking my paint and canvas sack down from the wagon's tailboard where I'd left it.

He spanked the reins and we pulled out. Looking back, I saw them all now getting in the wagon, the professor, Tom Prosser, Jane and Harkins, Milt Farley, and I waved till I thought my wrist would drop off my hand. I was still waving, and feeling I wished there could be words you could sling at somebody at a time like that, but there never are. There is never time to say them all. And if you had time to say them all there wouldn't be enough words.

I kept looking back as we curved out into the main road. They were all in the wagon now. We clacked along behind the old horse for a spell. Up ahead came the hump in the road with the cemetery off to one side. You couldn't see that ugly monument from the road at all. The rest of the cemetery was just still and choked with its brambles. We got down the road to the chestnut trees. You couldn't see the Einsner farmhouse from here.

Remembered how Prosser had said while we were still in the tavern that he surely did think Mitchell would get off soon, if not scot-free, then fairly light for all the manipulating he'd done. Prosser'd been ice-eyed about it; it reflected on the law, and the law was Prosser's breath, old bones, and heart's beat.

We drew closer to the Einsner land. Marshals were still standing around the mouth of the farmhouse road, quite a few of them. The rope was still up. I figured Prosser would dismiss all these other marshals, as he'd already left Daggart and Arnold and some others at the jail in Jerseyville, as soon as the wagon got back here. Clumps of people were standing around the collapsed balloon in the pasture; marshals were still there too, keeping them from getting too close. The bulk of the cows had moved off down toward the hollows and the creek.

I says to my friend driving the wicker cart, "See? There's the balloon. And we did arrive here in it. They're going back all the distance to Richmond in it."

He didn't stop the cart but he slowed up. Stroked his nose a little. "Man ought to stay out of the air," he says. "It'll bother the birds no end. Man's an earth-creature, dependent on the land and the sea for his good."

We drew on past the farm. Presently I says, "Sorry, I didn't get your name?"

"John Gingler. Profession, herb doctor."

I should have known that from the scent of roots and herbs rising from under the blanket he had over the rear of the cart.

"Seventy-six, and hale as a forest oak. But I'm not bragging," he says. "I might've been that way without the herbs. It's them I cure with 'em makes me feel good."

He went on spieling. Guess he didn't have anybody much to speak to on his journeys except those he cured. Turned out he was bound for upstate New York along the Hudson, to a group of families there believed in no other doctoring to speak of, and that he'd been south gathering all he needed for the winter. I settled back, hat brim launched over my eyes, and listened. He was a good little man who believed in all he did the way Seven believed in more than one life for man on the crust of the world. Inside me as I listened I was churning, wishing to make the miles drop by a lot faster'n this horse could ever do it, so I tried to possess my soul in patience as the professor had once told me I had to, and to get a grip on all that wild needing to see the mill, and Seven, and the Darlings, and Letty. Oh, Letty.

Within me in the meantime there was this feeling of sadness—the professor called it *Weltschmerz,* I think that was the word, he said it was a barbarous word but better than the French *triste* to show what happened. All it was was a kind of grief at parting with my friends. Yes, friends. If I'd even seen Loogan Harkins show up beside me I'd have welcomed him. At the same time here was Letty waiting ahead.

So I listened to talk about all the kinds of herbs there are, the ones that'll take down the high blood pressure, the ones that'll perk up the spirit and make an old man younger, others that'll ease childbirth, and even herb doses that'll cure a horse of harness boils and a pig of cholera. Sun was heavy on us in the whole spangled day.

It was about an hour later, we were pulling up a rise past a granite-looking cliff to the east, and the horse for all its herb-doctoring it must have had in the past because of being owned by such an expert, was lugging hard into the collar, when all at once here overhead they sailed.

It was the balloon, as ever was, catching the great light with all its jumping scarlet and deep blue and eye-flinching white, and in the gondola I could see the professor, and Tom Prosser, and Milt Farley with his duck-billed hat and leather suit, and Harkins and Jane. I near turned the cart over. I stood up and yelled and waved my arms. They saw me—they were rising high as they went but they saw me. I couldn't hear what they called out, but the professor was the loudest. His lifted hand made a bright mark like an upward-pointing spear against the sky. Then the whole gloried thing was out of sight against the streaming sun.

John Gingler the herb doctor had his jaw all dropped.

"May be somethin' in it at that," he said, finally.

Thirty-Three

IN CASE YOU'RE WORRIED, the way I was, about that balloon being off its course when John Gingler and I saw it above us—and it was, about twelve miles too far to the north—I'll jump ahead now in what I'm telling and say that I got a letter three weeks later, delivered to Jason Felton's general store, which was also a post office, in Solomon, and saying that they got home fine, if somewhat late. By that time of course the newspapers had word of the re-landing in Richmond of the professor and Prosser and the whole crew, as well as stories of the whole solving of the "murder"—which anyhow wasn't a murder. They lauded up Milt Farley pretty good too. I don't think it was bad for his business. The professor's letter, which as I'm saying I got later, said that life might be a dome of many-colored glass, staining the white radiance of eternity— P. B. Shelley, 1792–1822—but that he had been blessed by looking into eternity itself, and that damn it, why had I dispatched that wad of money to Miz Amily, didn't I have any tender feelings for the feelings of my host and hostess? There was a note tacked on from Miz Amily, too, bidding me write to him and set his mind at ease at his end.

But that was all later. Right now all I had to do was speculate about whether or not they'd make it Richmond-ward; and to count the minutes while they sloughed by and John Gingler kept on talking about his trade.

After a time I managed to go to sleep, and didn't wake up until it was cool evening and we were bumping to a stop beside a little pool of fresh water surrounded by rocks. Gingler said it was time to eat something. He told me too that the pool was a boiling spring and that he intended to get in and refresh himself and I could join him if I wanted to.

So after he'd started a small fire and put some yellowroot tea on the boil, and had fed his horse, we shucked our clothes and entered that spring just as careful as children feeling to see with their bare toes if the water's too hot in the round tub on Saturday night; around us blue gaunt chill shadows were coming down and it was a pleasant if coolish place. But the spring was really hot. We eased ourselves in and down, standing to the belly. I noted that Gingler had a sizable wang for a man of his age, which appeared to be in good condition as well. Some old men's just shrivel up, so I decided there must be something to the way he lived.

All the wonder at having been set free of the charge of murder was finally soaking through to me. Gingler says, "If you want, you can dive down. Gets deeper under the shelf of the rocks, and cooler. It's refreshing that way too, like going from light to dark, sweet to sour, coming into the cool."

I played around in the upper water, still standing on the shelf of rock under me, while he flipped himself up baretailed and paddled downward. After a bit he comes up again, hair streeling over his forehead. "Nature has everything for us," he said.

"Yes," I said. "I'm aware of that—been made conscious of it a good deal in my travels. It's all there to use. Though I confess to a hankering after good meat myself, sometimes, and though I've also seen nature can be a goddamned ornery thing when she so chooses."

"Naturally, she can. She can be a pluperfect bitch. It's why we have to love her."

I didn't know if the people who'd had their homes, and often their lives, swept away in twisters—I'd seen some black ones in Kansas—would be on his side about that. I did know I was enjoying myself now and having a hard time not getting my cock stiff as a board when I thought exultant and forward-looking about Letty. To keep this down, I took his advice and launched myself off the shelf-rock into the deeps.

He was right. The cool overtook you like hands of clean cold moving around you. I kept my eyes open so I could see just a bit of the late sun skifting on the water way above, and stroked downward and felt myself go all cold and chill almost to the gut after that near-steaming heat of the upper part of the spring, and I could also feel the spout of warmth bubbling out between the rocks as it passed over my legs. When I got down deeper there were some fish, about the size of elm leaves, darting around me and looking rosy and green combined in the light. Their green parts were about the color of Letty's eyes and I reached to catch one, but they always flipped away. I tried to paddle myself deeper to see under the rocks but then I thought anything could live under there—any goddamned kind of waiting monster—so I came up again. Seemed a long way up holding my breath.

Gingler was already on shore, dressing. I came out and felt the evening air hit me hard—I wasn't studying any woman-loving now—and rubbed myself down on a huck towel he tossed me, and got dressed fast and combed my hair and sat there smelling the yellowroot tea and the mix of nuts and honey and bread and so forth he was fixing up.

I said, "Hope we can make Solomon by morning."

"Morning's just about it, I don't want the old horse to have to hurt himself." He handed me a tin of his mix. It wasn't bad. Maybe it was being so hungry anything, even spring sand, would've tasted good. It had chives and cress in it too, and other natural endowments supposed to make you glad you were breathing.

I felt rinsed through from that hot and cold bath and when we got back in the cart I kept wanting to drive the horse myself, to get a few extra ounces of speed out of it, but there wasn't any doing that. Stars came out and I wondered how they felt to the people in Farley's balloon—if someday man would whomp him up a balloon sizable and stout enough to whisk him to a star. I hoped so, but it seemed uncreditable.

John Gingler himself went to sleep after a spell, excusing himself first for the fact that he was going to nod off. He said the horse knew the way. I vowed not to, just to sit there with my clothes pulled tight against me now against the chill, but after a time I knocked off too. Then when I woke I could tell it was way late, and Gingler was slowing the horse, if it's possible to slow a horse ambling as careful as that one was.

It was most morning, I could hear roosters trying the air on for size.

Gingler says, "Solomon."

"Where?"

I couldn't make out anything in the mist and faint light.

"Right over yonder—take the cobbled road and you'll be in her by good sunup."

I picked up my paint and canvas sack. "Obliged," I said, "and here's for your trouble, please, Mister Gingler—" I was holding out some cash. I like to pay people when they don't demand it. Makes it happier, some way.

I could just see him shake his head. "Nup. Consider it a gift for bein' a free soul again."

"No sir. That's gift enough by itself. You take—"

He says, "If you insist, but you take a gift in return, then." And in the half-dark he made up a packet of herbs, which I shoved down in the paint and canvas sack on top of all the other things I owned, and then buckled the sack and heaved her on my back and got her settled and ready to go. He took the money. "Brew tea out of 'em or just chew on them during times of doubt and peril," he bade me. "Pleasure having the company of an ex-wanted murderer, sir. Enjoyed your conversation."

I'd enjoyed his, though he hadn't given me time to make much of mine. He started up the horse and I walked off, oblique to him, feeling the cobbles underfoot.

I swung along, the land getting brighter around me, Solomon coming in sight with its church and general store and court-house and houses all shining just in glints of greeting through the mist.

When I got to the roadway, the main one in that town, where the whiskey-cup contest had been held and where I'd last seen it when Magnusun's tents were set up and Sara was doing her stint, I turned and looked around. It wasn't a huge town but I hadn't the simplest idea where Letty was staying. I was glad we'd not gone through Mullin's Gap during the dark; I never wanted to see that place again except maybe to rush through and wave to its gander goose. New light started carving out the shape of the courthouse the way the buildings painted by Joseph Turner appear, when they appear at all, in a mist, with cloudy rose springing behind them, and then I hear a man whistling as he comes along.

It's Claron Prescott, the county clerk, I see as he comes closer, with red face and white hair showing in edges of fresh light.

I step forward and introduce myself—not that I'd had to; he knew me. He says, "Proud to hear you're back, and glad the trouble's over, Mister Applegate."

"Oh—you heard?"

"The marshal they sent here told Miz Einsner. I expect you're looking for her?"

"Yes, you might say it, Mister Prescott."

"Marshal told it around town quite a bit. In case people might still think you were a guilty and hunted man."

"Nice of him," I said, and it was, but I wanted to get a move on the way the balloon wanted to tug itself from the earth as soon as it was ready to rise. "Where's she living, could you say?"

He'd backed up to the courthouse steps. Had a key in his hand and I guess was ready to open the door.

"Go right down past Jason Felton's store, turn sharp and take the lane to the end."

"Thanky!"

I didn't want to be abrupt with him but I was gone fast. I

pounded across the road and past Felton's, where there were signs saying calico bolts were cheap today but which wasn't open yet, and whipped to my right and went down a lane between small houses. At the end facing the lane was the smallest. I could just make out by the richening light a sign on its porch rail; it said fancy sewing was done here, by L. Einsner. I thought, Jesus, God, she's not even gone back and got her swag of money from the hiding place between birches, though it is all hers. I thought a lot of things. Leaped up the barely standing step, hauled off, and gave the door a smart swift rapping.

Thirty-Four

THERE'S A SONG, by a musician named Wagner, with a chorus that goes, "Once again, dear home." A German song. Professor Allan used to hum it and sometimes bust out singing it out loud when he was drawing near his house again after a day spent out of it.

That song was something like I was feeling now while I waited for the door to open. Roosters crowed again; a few sparrows started to talk among themselves in the nearby winter-stark trees.

Then I heard a noise inside, and through the curtains at the side window—it sure wasn't much of a house, just three sizes larger'n a birdhouse, I thought—I saw a glimmer of a lamp. It came closer. I jerked myself back to the door and the door came open.

It was Letty. She was wearing an old dress-robe she'd thrown on; I'd got her out of bed, and her eyes looked at me green as spring leaves but even brighter. Hair was all every which way around her head but she still looked neat.

I stepped in and started unfastening the pack on my back

because you can't take somebody in your arms when you feel like you're carrying around a burden. Anyway I wanted her to get her own arms all the way around me if she so wished.

But right then things started going wrong. Even while I undid the straps and shrugged out of the paint and canvas sack—we were in a kitchen that looked prim and neat in the wavering light of the lamp which she'd set on a table now— even then, I could see her backing up and hear the whisper of her bare feet as she did.

So when my pack slumped on the floor I just stood there and then said, "Didn't you think I'd come back? You think I was going on, on my travels, leaving you here?"

I could barely hear her answer. "I don't know what I thought, Luke."

"There's a good many powers of fact unfinished between us," I said. "One is that money. You know if it's still up there between them birches on the other side of the creek near the clearing?"

She shook her head. Goddamn it, I hadn't meant to ask her about the money at all, I was just making talk, and she must've known it. What I wanted was her.

"Haven't gone up there. Don't study to. Luke, a marshal was here, he said I'm free and you are—"

"Oh, yes, Christ almighty, I've got the papers for you, in case you want to frame 'em," I said sudden and sharp. I was looking at her across the lamp's low flame. It was like it had been in the clearing, in the small house, that night of the heavy rain; but this time we weren't plummeting through to any kind of truth.

"The marshal said he had a dispatch—he said Rafe Gondy'd done the deed—"

"That's right," I said. "But it don't matter now." I drew myself up like a gamecock before it strikes, and maybe that's what she thought I was. "And Wayde Mitchell's in jail too, though the word is he may'n't stay there long. And I find you living here taking in sewing, when you could be living better up at the mill and waiting for me there. And doing the sewing under your own name when you could be using the name

Applegate—Miz Applegate, if you wanted—which would doubtless be easier and get you more customers, the kind of customers that care if a lady's tight-married or common law before they take her their hemstitching. And acting like you're scared of me by backing off and shying—that's what matters."

Then I said, "Good God in Goshen, Letty. It's Luke, not somebody you just have to treat like a china-handed stranger!" I drew another breath. "I know I told you to get out and stay out, back at that jail. I was just worried about you having to give in too much to Mitchell. If you thought I meant it, you'd sure ought to know me better'n that." I was snorting and damned near panting. She looked so nice, sitting over there in the opposite corner by the table. I bent low over the lamp, knuckles on the table. "This is a hell of a way to come at a man when all that's been in the back of his mind the past months had been a sight of you, whether he's painting or sleeping or just awake and prowling. What's got into you?"

Sun was really rising and burning off mists outside. Now I could see her lovely hair as she smoothed it with a hand that looked fumbling and nervous, though all the stuck-out pride was still there in her face, that hickory-nut shape but now a sight paler in color than I'd ever seen it. But the bite was there in her tone.

"Luke, I did what I had to. You know very well whatever I did it was that. For both our sakes. He kept at me and at me— after you'd run off. He was at me more than I'd thought he would be. Turned out he *wasn't* a bowl of mush I could handle by stirring. He'd come to me every night and say he had information about you he still hadn't give to the authorities, and he'd hold it back if I'd be kind to him. He—"

Took a stride across the floor, shaking that little room. "Him? Kind to *him*? You mean Mitchell . . . ?"

Her head was thrown back. She was looking right up at me. I put my right hand in her fine-spun hair, gold and lighter than a bird's nest, and drew her head back and looked down. I wanted to put myself down over her mouth and shut my eyes and sink into her, gradual at first and then faster until I was falling like a balloon dropping out of the sky with no valve

working at all. I shook her head back and forth as you'd shake
a scratching cat, not hurting her, just shaking.

Just touching her warm hair and scalp like that made everything in me start leaping like the light opening up in the outdoor sky.

"Goddamn it, woman—"

"—afterward one night I knew he was just lying—I left him
and came to Solomon—and I set up here as a fancy sewing expert. I'm—" Her voice was joggling a little now as I shook her
head. I stopped it and just let my fingers stay in her hair. "I'm
a fine sempstress and it's a kind town and they think well of
me. I didn't go to the mill or lean on you because I can be my
own person, I can use my own name. It's mine!" Her eyes
were stubborn-proud, flashing like twenty lamps.

Then all at once while she stared at me her face changes
and her lips barely move—just half-kissing open—and she
says, "Trouble is, now, there's something I don't know . . ."

Left my hand in her hair. Says, soft, feeling my brain go
dead and all the strength of wanting her knot up in my backbone, where it's near pain; I says, "What don't you know?"

I was as close to her as though we'd been loving all night
and next day and into another night, and yet I was as far off
from her as though that balloon had taken me to the moon
and left me cold and staring and reamed out of all joy forever.
Way in the back of my head I thought, She's got a right to be
what she must be; she is strong as I am; it doesn't make a
damn if she's had any other men. But I couldn't bring this
thought up to the top, or balance it off with anything else. I
says, "What is it you ain't sure of?"

I let go of her. I hadn't hurt her. Not in the body. I didn't
think I could ever do that.

"I don't know whether or not the child's yours or his. The
child I'm going to bear."

I could hardly get it out now: "Mitchell's?" I says finally.

And she nods. I stepped back. Cold, clear, as cold as Letty
was looking at me now, as if *she* was a locked-in part of the
moon, I thought, it doesn't matter, didn't I fool with Penelope
Dabney, and Sally Lou Loudermilk? All that matters is moving
to her now and saying it never did matter. That the whole rich

truth we've got is not having to fret any longer, any time, about being locked up. That we're here on earth in the same place.

But all these things went away in a wash as strong as a sea wave soaking me through, soaking the heart with brine and hardness and dark forever.

"Jesus." I could see him crawling over her. Her cheekbones caught the ripe fresh-rose sunlight. I wanted to go to her and love her up and say it didn't matter, while she sat there bound and convinced she'd been right. I didn't move a hair or a fraction of it. In my mind I could see him touching her; I wished I'd killed him and was already hung for it.

Then she stood up and came over to me, so close I could make out the pearl-clear texture of her face, that I'd painted once and had started to do again, because it was worth putting in anything I knew of painting and the heart's blood that went with it—it wasn't like one of the Richmond girls, or like a senator, or phreno-portraiture, it was like painting the professor as a gift for Christmas, it was what my right hand and fingers and the deep wrenching in me was meant to do.

But the world was sour as tartar on my tongue and I could hardly talk. While she stood there now her robe fell open and I saw the tiny butterfly mark and remembered in a tide of blackness Wayde Mitchell looking at me in the cemetery that way, and then, later, his look and what he'd said in his cell, "Say hello to my little butterfly . . ."

Came close to hitting her then. Would have hurt her.

She knew it, and stood there daring me to, maybe even wanting me to, her chin up and her eyes straight on mine.

I don't even remember, much, moving then. When you're locked in the rage of ice and know you're going to be, maybe the rest of your life, you don't study detail.

Yet there was still a time when both our stubbornnesses hung there raging at each other and either one of us could have by making a motion or stating one word split the whole rock of them. Of all the hating.

"I'll send you the money," I says. "Christ, He knows I never wanted a cent of it."

I was stooping over and fumbling for my paint and canvas

sack, and for the paper that had her name on it, the freeing paper Prosser had handed me.

Above me, she says, "I don't want the money either."

I stood up and tossed the paper her way, and she just stood still, scorning it; it fell to the floor. "I want you to have it anyhow," I says. "You can feed it to the sparrows. Or take it and give it to Mitchell, when his high influence has sprung him from the calaboose. I hope you gave him a real good time. All he spent on you, trying to get you, laying his snares, he deserved the best time a man could have even in a Philadelphia whorehouse. Though I doubt the girls there would've give in to him without seeing his cash first. What you'd ought to plan to do now, you'd ought to fix to get out of this sewing business and set up with him. Get married, and praise him up for his preachy ways, and play the great lady and loll about the rest of your sluttish life . . . now I'm leaving here and I hope never to see you again, or if I do, to look the other way. They'd have real murder on their hands if I didn't go my way now."

She slapped me then, a good heavy crack across the teeth.

I didn't feel it, and it even came to me in a deep flash that it was what I'd been asking for. In the same second I thought how she'd been convinced she was protecting me, and'd been taken in by Mitchell's threats. And that lying with him was scum she must've hated, being Letty, but she'd done it for my own sake. And then she'd risen out of it; she was being *herself*, which is so hard to be most people don't ever try it.

But even while all this went through me I paid it no attention. The air seemed red before my eyes. As red as my dreams of bloody old man Einsner'd ever been.

I looked at the slope of her belly. Didn't seem tighter to me, but a man can't tell much. She'd ought to know. She pulled the robe in tight and close. That was the only move her small fingers made.

I turned around and crashed out of the door somehow. Out in the day the light was clear and it was going to be another fine one. Outside I stood wrapped in shock for a breath. And not truly even breathing. I wanted her so bad, still, or my body did, I thought quick of wheeling about, going back up that near-busted step, opening up the door and raping her. Then leaving. But it wouldn't have done a speck of good. I've never understood what the raping kind of man gets out of it at all anyhow; I can't hate all women that bad, never could. And through all this, still, something was saying, Be a little fair. Seemed to see Seven's long face, him saying, "It's hard to grow up."

Only thing to do now was walk. I walked. After a spell I got the pack fixed on my back. I went along the lane and turned the corner and went past Jason Felton's store; he was inside and he saw me now, but I didn't feel like talking to a soul. Just went on moving, past the courthouse, and then on the cobble-strip on the other side of town. Then after a time I was on the main road and heading toward the clearing.

It was what you'd term a lively day. Snow just promising faint on the air but the land spreading out and beckoning. Back before I'd ever laid eyes on Letty, or Jerseyville, or any part of that whole landscape, I'd have taken joy in it.

A few flakes of snow fell through the sunlight. A dog from a hill farm came to the brow of the hill and barked down at me. I went straight on, making good time. Clouds covered the sun, then slid away. Now there was just enough snow to start freckling the wintered fields. A cart with a couple of farmers, looked to be a father and his son, came by me, going toward Solomon, and they both waved; guess they knew me as the milling man. I waved back, feeling astonished that I had it in me to do that. Now and then I'd turn and look back. She sure wasn't coming after me. She never would. I'd declared myself, expressed all my feelings, I guessed.

Came to the side road and started up. My boots made crackling noises in the wintry ground. Snow came stronger, the light growing dark blue and strange, making the hill path ahead of me stand out like score marks in a tilting ocean wave. There were the wagon and buggy and other rig marks creased in its iron. I climbed on and up, the path twisting. When I got high enough there were the cows of the Darlings. They didn't look quite so lean as they'd done when I last see them, which I figured was a small sign that the Darlings were doing better. From a point up the path I looked back and down and see all of the road and the side roads to Solomon laid out like a living map. On which it was snowing heavier now. The flakes were getting thicker, any other time I'd have stuck out my tongue and tasted one. Now I didn't feel like I'd ever want to make any more unneeded motions in all my days.

Went on, up the path—there above me was the lip of it. I came up over the edge.

And there was the clearing, the moss yellowed now this late into the time of cold. Juncoes and chickadees stopped flipping their wings in the oaks and the cold bare willows and the pines, and flew a little distance off when I stepped toward them. They made small sounds like touches of questions in the day. Wasn't any other sound but, up at the mill, the wheel moving in the iced brown water.

I was near to the middle of the clearing, heading for Seven's house, when the door of his house came open and Barabbas came loping. He stopped five inches from me and I reached a hand to touch his chin and jaws. He whined in a moderate way. Seven came after him, looking taller than I recalled, because I could see now as he got closer, he was also thinner. Looking at the fine modeling of his cheekbones made me think of Letty's. I even wondered if she was still standing there in that little kitchen, even though it'd been hours now since I'd started out for here.

There wasn't any music, Wagner's or anyone's, around me. Just the birds starting up again now.

Seven took my hand. "We heard. We expected you. Jase and Paul were down in the town; they heard the news and brought it here."

He didn't say, "Where's Letty?"

He didn't have to.

So I had to. I said, "Letty's not coming back here."

"Oh," he says. Just that. Then we went walking on across the clearing. He showed me some new repairs they'd made in the mill-house wall on the west where some old timbers should have been crowbarred out before. Showed me a huge heap of firewood stacked over at one of the main house steps. He talked confident and easy, and didn't ask me a question. After a time the Darlings, David holding his Winchester rifle, Peter and Paul and Jase stepping along the way he did, light as— light as butterflies—came to join us.

Jase said, "We get steady milling. They bring us the dried corn mainly, this time of year."

Like I'd never been away and this was a casual fact to throw at me.

He was wearing the same feather in his dark big-brimmed hat.

"Won't be nobody coming soon when the real snows set in," says David.

Peter and Paul nodded that this was a home truth.

I didn't want anybody to come. I says, "I'm kind of tuck-ered. And I got to get out of these travel-stunk clothes. Think I'll stay in the main house."

"It's all ready," says Seven.

He didn't say, "All ready for you," because I could tell he'd meant all ready for both of you.

I went up there and opened the door. Each wheat sheaf carved into it was getting a little lace of snowfall into its carv-ing. The snow kept on being heavier. When I got in, in that ivory-walled front room, looking at the paintings on the man-tel, the one of the little girl, the swimming boys, the one of the Carrolls, and the good one I'd started on the back of Senator Margate's—the second one of Letty—I could hardly make my-self come in the rest of the distance. But I did, shutting the door. The Saxony wheel still had wool in it and looked ready for spinning. The harpsichord stood waiting. The harp itself, without- many strings, but polished the way we'd polished it, took the cold straight light through the windows. There were all the makings for a fire. In the next room the books looked dusted and shining in their calf. Up the stairs the cool day's light glittered.

Seven and the Darlings had kept the place up good.

I thought, Hating a person after you've loved them is like turning to winter in your brain and body.

I went over to the Daniel Boone rifle on the wall. There above the mantel it was shining and catching spears of the snow-light.

I wished I'd used it long before on Wayde Mitchell.

I took off my pack and sat down to consider. I didn't want to go upstairs for a time. Wasn't till near on dark, with the flakes coming down outside filling the whole sky and the quiet ground, and even muffling the voice of the mill wheel, that I got up and made a fire from the logs and brush and stood watching it catch in the throat of the fireplace and leap up, sending color to all the great room.

Out the windows, through the snow, seemed to me I could see summer butterflies. Those little dark ones. But that was only in my thick head.

Thirty-Five

THAT NIGHT SEVEN CAME OVER. I'd just been sprawled there in front of the fire. He knocked and when I said, "Come in," he stood there in the door with a jug in one long lean hand. Shut the door behind him and walked over to me. Stood there looking down.

He said, "This is rum. I was saving it for a homecoming. You might like a cup or two."

I said, "Maybe it'll do me good."

He sat down on the floor and reached for one of the cups he'd also carried along. The rum smelled ripe and bright, like it had stood a long while and had a chance to consider the sugar cane it came from and the darkness of the earth. Watching it pour in the firelight I thought of Professor Allan talking about libations for the dead, in ancient Greece. I kind of wished I had the good fortune of being dead.

We clinked the cups, when they were full, and then drank.

After a time, then, when the second cup came up as a matter of course, Seven started talking. He gave me a full accounting—not that I wanted it—of all the milling money that'd been taken in since I'd been gone, and an accounting of all the corn meal and wheat flour that had been ground, just about down to the ounce.

I watched the fireshine on the floorboards and the chair where Letty used to sit, sewing or spinning.

After that we had another cup. In all my journeyings I've never drunk much as a rule but this seemed what the professor would have said was an anodyne. I hadn't had thing one to munch on since that herb and nut and honey mix the night before with Gingler, and when I went to stand up I was feeling a mite lopsided.

Seven started talking again in a low, searching voice. This time he wasn't telling me about affairs at the mill—though he did mention that he'd built out a better lean-to for the bay, and lined it with thick straw—but started probing back into the time of his own life. I sat down again, sipping rum slower now, listening.

He told me, in a matter of passing, not making a point of it the way some old men brag on about their age as though reaching a certain age means much, that he was in his nineties, well into them. It surprised me because I recalled having thought of him, when we'd first seen him on that quiet hot July day before, as about sixty-seventy something.

Then he went roving in his talk back and forth in the time of his existence, and I could sudden-like get the feeling that he was like a tapestry of events—like something hanging in the wind displaying everything from the days of the founding of the country and the Liberty Bell ringing out official news, up through the whole Revolution wars and through the war that had ripped the country in half like huge tearing hands. He'd always worked with his own hands, but when he spoke of how his father had been a roof-thatcher in England, it made you believe time was nothing at all—that it just flowed along bearing us on its bosom the way the mill wheel turned in water.

He didn't talk about how he believed we got born many times into the whole spread and run of time, but it was there in his recalling.

Somehow with the fire crackling and hot on my back and in
my bones, and the rum, I was feeling myself float up through
generations and back through them. Letty was with me
through most of them, in one way or another. Seven said with
his voice running on like the mill wheel itself ". . . I'm coming
to the end of this sojourn now. It's just the body wears out,
gets to be too frail to hold the spirit." He took another small
quaff. "Luke, don't let a man's pride blind you to what being a
man really is."

That's as near as he got to talking about Letty at all.

From there he turned the talk to what he knew about the
doings of Wayde Mitchell after the night I'd run off south.

He told me Mitchell had nosed around a number of times,
had come back the night after I'd left, and had gone through
the main house again, with Gondy and Wheelman keeping the
Darlings from killing anybody with their new rifle and the old
one. He said Paul Darling had struck into conversation with
Andrew, the young black barouche-driver of Mitchell's, and
learned how, starting their secret investigation down Jerseyville way, they'd moved up farther north, striking pay dirt
in Mullin's Gap in the person of Soames who I'd bought the
bay from with that large piece of cash. And of course reaching
more dirt with Tatum at the Mullin's Gap inn.

Hearing all this, I thought that I didn't give a snap any
more. I didn't care how it all had happened, how that bunch
of connivers had finally come to Solomon, and heard word of
how we were running the mill up here, and been ready on
that night of the fair to come up and accost us . . . except that
we'd showed up and saved them the trouble. All I cared about
was putting a wall up that could keep out what I was feeling. I
took some more rum, walking away from the fire and staring
out. Snow had stopped. It lay crystal and untouched out there,
in the clearing, and at the mill, and on the roofs of the four
houses, including Seven's and the Darlings'.

All at once, whirling around, feeling stone sober, for all the
drink, I says, "Seven, Letty's coming to live here. I told you a
lie the first time."

But I wasn't talking to any but myself. Sitting with his back against the fireplace stones he was asleep. You could almost see the silver of his spirit through the bones of his face. I went out and shut the door soft behind me.

Went down across the clearing to the horse shed, saw the bay looked better'n she had last time I'd seen her, figured the Darlings had done some riding on her, gave her a whack on the sleep-smelling rump—horses when they're warm smell like man-sweat when man is about to take a woman—and started for the creek where it narrowed.

At the edge of the creek—which was still open and flowing all right, but wouldn't be much longer if the still cold kept up—I stood looking back. There was the print of my footfalls stepping from the door of the main house, and nothing else breaking the snow-glaze. Under the stillness of the light holding the whole clearing the creek itself had slants of green like Letty's eyes—or like they are in a painting called "Hunters in the Snow," by Breughel, which the professor had a copy of in his house. That rare witching green. A snow owl went over the whole clearing, from the mill end down to the path's lip, like a huge extra snowflake left over from everything that had come falling so far. I went to the creek-edge, a little closer, bunched myself, jumped and landed all right on the other shelf; went to the birches and reached in and down. The strongbox was there. Its metal felt like ice, and as slick. After a time I got it open and see everything's there. At least the money lay in the same packets I'd left it in. I shoved the whole affair back. If Letty didn't come with me I'd give it back to her the next day. If she did, this was the best place for it.

That goddamned money. Maybe if Mitchell hadn't suspected Jane Einsner'd once had it, and that Jane might've handed it on to Letty, then he'd never have followed us at all, I thought.

But that was foolish. He'd looked on Letty most of her life as his eventual woman, along with everything else that went with her, so he'd have followed. Some way even here, a long way from the Jerseyville jail, I could still feel him following. . . .

I went back and jumped the creek again, then went to the
horse shed—they'd done a nice tight job of constructing here,
better'n the one I'd done previous—and unroped the bay and
backed her out. Stroked her a little, talking with the rum in
me and with the way I'd always felt about this good horse.
Jarhinda had a better gait but this was a lasting steed. I got
her out, and then backed her into the shafts of the buggy
standing, hood covering the only slightly snowed-on seat, beside the lean-to. If I still had hot rum buzzing in my veins the
cold was driving it out. By the time I got everything hitched I
was starting to shiver. Sucked in my breath and tried to stay
warm by holding the breath as much as possible. But somebody's left an old frayed wolfskin—figured it had come from
the main house—in the floor of the buggy, and when I got
that around me things went better.

At the edge of the path I had to cozen the bay quite a bit
more to get her to dare the path; I got out then and petted
her and talked her down the slippery slope.

Then when we were lower down I got back in. She set her
hoofs against the strain. We came out still lower. Over the
silent fields—looked like they were holding their breaths
against the cold too—you couldn't see anything but moon-
glints and secret brightness. And there wasn't any sound but
the screel of the buggy wheels and the chopping noise of the
bay's hoofs on the trail. Didn't see a sign of the Darlings' cows
now—I figured the Darlings' mother took them in for the
night. Or brought them down lower to her place so they
couldn't be bothered by bear or other ravager.

Then we were out on the road. Oh, it was lonesome. Lonesome as a wolf-howl, lonesome as a loon's call.

To the tune of the bay's hoofs on the frozen road I studied
about how, this time of year, in all times past, I'd always tried
to be in a city or in a fine farming community where there was
plenty of work for my hand and my brushes and the fire and
the soup were good till spring. Sometimes they'd been just
small towns—around here they called them dorps—where
people moved like moles and weasels, living under the threat
of the hawks and owls which were the winter weather, and

kept the stock penned in and gave themselves fat bellies from greasy food to ward off the chill. Other times they'd be places like Chicago, or Memphis, or once New York—where a body could live a different life, one of seeing how the hotels bustled and bloomed and the city regaled itself with sleds and sleighs in the parks under the snow, and there was something brisk and cruel and bracing and lovely in all the air, even while the poor froze under the embankments.

Then I started thinking how she might not come back with me. Had every right in the world not to. I knew clear and full, she'd thought she'd been protecting my skin, not hers, in what she'd done with Mitchell. I still couldn't even bear to bring that up in my mind without it being as if I was tearing out a much-valued tooth by the blood-roots.

I couldn't tell anything, but I flicked the reins and the bay went striding out.

When we got to Solomon it might've been a place tombed for the rest of the century. Nothing seemed to be breathing. Swung the buggy down the main road, and then stopped at the lane. I looked along it. Wasn't any light in that house. I got out and tossed the wolfskin over the sweating bay and went along the lane.

Weren't any footprints but the ones I made now, leading to the door.

Stepped up and was about to knock—I didn't even want to knock loud, now; it would have been like tearing apart silence—when the door opened.

She stood there in something I expected she'd made herself, gray-hooded and caped, with a couple of the capes falling down from her shoulders like gray cloth waterfalls. She had her little velvet-starred bag in one hand, I supposed Mitchell had brought it to her from the main house to Mullin's Gap, in the time before she'd left him. Didn't want to think about that. She looked at me where I was halted with my hand on the air.

Then I pushed toward her. Seeing she wasn't going to move a stroke.

Could feel everything hating in me ball together and try to

keep what I truly wished to say from pushing through, and finally it did get out.

It was as hard coming out as anything ever was to say, for
me.

I've said before how when I'd admitted something to Letty,
agreeing she might be right, it was like birthing a calf, personal.

This was like that plus a good many other feelings.

"Letty, I apologize for acting a damned fool. I don't care
whose child it is."

She stood there like she'd been carved. Except her face was
getting rosy. In that outfit she looked globed and wonderous,
like a vessel holding itself aloof from most things and yet par-
taking of all the joys earth can offer.

I went on, hearing myself like I wasn't really saying it, like I
didn't have the sense to say it. But saying it anyhow.

"I don't give a tinker's damn whose child it is. A child's a
child."

She didn't speak. I couldn't keep talking, not without touching her, so I put out a hand and did that. Cupped her chin,
and pulled her a little to me by it, and smelled her skin-scent
in the chill dark-white around us, and I says then, "A child's a
child. I expect I've give the world a few by-blows myself. I
hope they're all taken care of and grow up with some dander
and meaning to them, without too much grief."

Then she's saying, "Well, Luke, they'll sure-God get the
grief too. But I'd like this one to have as little of it as possible.
Wondered when you'd be back—been waiting for you for a
number of hours. You've been drinking."

"I had a little rum for my blood's sake."

"Never needed rum I could make out." She was lifting her
face, the hair puffed about her ears under the hood. "Never
knew you for a hard-drinking man."

"Here," I says, and kissed her, good and strong, crushing
her up and damned near making her lose the bag.

She sighs a little. "Wait—" and turns and shuts the door.
"I'll have to come down in the next few days and clear up
some odds and ends. And I've got a task of embroidery to

deliver to Miz Reicher, and several other things to do. And I'll
have to turn in the key to the house to the fam'ly I rented
from, and all."

I took her arm. Walking back down the lane to the horse
and buggy we made two new lines of our footprints into the
snow now, hers considerably less full than mine.

"How's Seven? How's Jase and David and Paul and Peter?"

"All seem to be flourishing, thank you," I says. I helped her
into the buggy, whisked the wolfskin from the horse, and
tucked it in around her knees. Small knees, but sufficient; a
small marvel of a woman.

Then I got in and we wheeled about and took the road for
the clearing and the mill and the main house and our life
again.

Except I didn't know if it was going to be a life even now free
of being riddled with worry and damnation and hell and dark.

Because on the way back, with the snow-world around us
making sight itself seem to be a keen pleasure, every time
she'd start to bring up something about Mitchell, about how it
had happened, about how she admitted being a damned fool
for letting it happen, about how she'd overestimated her own
womanly strength—which still, I think, made her the
maddest—every time she'd start bringing up something like
this, I'd sheer away and say, "Let's not speak of it. I'd a sight
rather not."

She couldn't see why not.

"Luke," she says, "we'll have to, soon or late."

"Maybe. Right now I don't want to study it. I want to forget
it."

"You can't forget anything happened in life. We tried that
once, when we said we wouldn't speak any more of Daddy
having got killed—but it all came out anyway."

"Schach! I don't want it to come out with me."

"No, because you don't like looking at things head on. It's
the fool in you. An artist has to see things head on, everything, you must know that."

"I don't know it," I says. "Seems to me a man can just do

himself a lot of good by shutting his eyes and shutting off his ears to certain things. Anyhow, seeing things head on, didn't I make a trip down to Richmond for the sake of seeing things, didn't I come back by an apparatus that could have dashed us all to the ground and rendered us comatose forever, didn't I *see* things clear as a man might?"

She shook her head. "The marshal came to see me said you came back by balloon. Seems to me this professor of yours is just as crazy as most men to spill his life in the pursuit of adventure."

"Goddamn, you're sure laying down a lot of law."

The bay's ears pricked back to listen to us. The hoofs went spang and spung in the snowy road.

Then after a time she shrugs again, I could feel it, she was pressed close to my shoulder, and says, "Well, it wasn't my fault, the way I see it. I was doing my best for you. And it wasn't no fun, it was like having a wrestling match with a catfish."

I turned to her and says, "Letty, shut up. Just shut up now till we've had time to clear all this up and stay together and grow together a time yet. It hurts to do it, Seven told me that once, but I didn't know it could tear the hide off your love muscle and rip you up inside till you were on fire with hate and the devil. Up to the time I first see you, I'm an easy man—I could take a woman or leave her, with comfort and keeping my own soul solid."

"Bosh," she says. "That was tumpish. You didn't even know you had a soul. Were just like my daddy or our hired men or even Mitchell hisself. Just wandering around cadging a dollar here and one there, even though you had your gift, your talent. You got to think about being hurt and learn somethin' from it to get bigger inside. Seven tell you that?"

"Aimed at something like it," I says.

She was tickling me, on the surface, the way a bobber will tickle the water when you're still-fishing. Underneath were all the importances that had to be dragged out of me. I didn't want to rise a bit to that paining but maybe not truly evil hook.

Going back up the side path to the clearing was tough; I left

her in the buggy and got out, every last mouth-swish of rum
drained out of me by now, helping the bay along by pulling on
the reins and slugging on up, inch by inch, and then finally
making the whole path-edge and lurching the whole conveyance into the clearing with a tumble of wheels and a blowing
of air from the bay's nostrils.

She jumped down herself from the buggy, before I could
get hold of her.

"Coulda climbed with you; didn't need to ride, Luke," she
says. And she stretched out her arms to the clearing, the
sleeves or whatever they were of that cloak affair falling like
silky gray wings. She looked to me, in the instant, to be a kind
of snow owl herself, who if she'd wished could have spread
her arms and sailed right over above the big chimney of the
main house, and above the mill, circling in the starlight.

I led the horse across the clearing. Stood then, with her at
the horse shed, rubbing the horse down with a piece of sack-
ing and talking.

"You'd ought not to jump down from a buggy or even a
small-size rock," I tells her.

She stares at me, the eyes three shades lighter than the
pines where they're standing, holding snow down all their
arms.

"I'm not made of sugar; won't melt in rain, won't spill in
tumult."

"I mean the child."

I roped the horse for the night, so it could get at its oats and
bran or whatever was in the trough, and we went back across
the clearing.

Couldn't help putting an arm around her, drawing her to
me, and noticing how her flanks made light ripples like gentle
glossy bubbles under the fine garment she must've sewed.
Asked her, casual, if she'd sewed it, and she said, "Didn't anybody present it to me fresh from Paris. Made it out of a *Godey's
Lady's Book* pattern in Jason Felton's store. Keeps the mind oc-
cupied, sewing, and it's profitable. People were right kind and
thoughtful after I got to Solomon."

"You started to say that before," I said.

"Started to say a lot of things before, but you spewed out all you were feeling, and stopped me. Wish I'd hit you more than the one crack."

We were standing on the top step of the two steps leading into the door. She traced the sheaf-design pattern in the door with a fingertip. I was carrying her bag. I opened the door and we went in. The fire was down to a cat's eye wink. Seven was gone. The rum jug's flanks, and the cups, caught the last coal-eyes of the fire. The room was warm.

She says, low and quick, "It don't hurt a woman to love a man till the child's nearly there. And I got a notion it's yours."

It would be warmer here than in the rooms upstairs. They didn't have fires going yet. I took her over in front of the fire, taking off her hood and cloak, her hair falling down ripe as cornsilk, but brighter, in the low light; and then the whole dress under it. There was nice stitching in it so I didn't tear anything, then there she was, all ripe herself, there she was, waiting. Seemed to me it would be a long fine time till morning.

Thirty-Six

ONE WAY, it seemed a long time then till the spring came to
planish the earth.

Another way, it went by in a twinkling, with days and nights
melting into one another while the weather faired off, and
then got snow clouds in it again, and then faired off again and
finally settled to a hard freeze.

I didn't count the snows, there was too much to do around
the clearing, and in the mill, and in the main house, for that.

In the morning Seven and the Darlings got to dropping in
again for breakfast; Letty would be cooking, using both ranges
sometimes now, and the smells of it filled the warm kitchen
like the ravishing breezes from Circe's isle that the professor
used to talk about. If the day was fine enough sometimes we
went down to Solomon; that's where we started getting the letters from the professor and others, at the post office at Jason
Felton's store. Got to know a good many of the people down
there, and they asked how affairs were going as if they truly
meant it and weren't just talking to hear their mouth-gas. We

picked up the newspapers there, too, and I must say the reporters had bedizened the story of the balloon flight and the
solving of the "murder" with a great lot of fanciness.

About that time I got a letter from Thomas Warren Prosser,
in Washington. Enclosed with it were a lot of other papers,
one telling Letty that she was now full owner of the Einsner
farmlands, and the others documents she had to sign and return. Prosser's letter to me was indited in a square hand just
like he looked, the capitals looking Roman; he hoped I was
prospering, painting, and planting seeds for the future. He
wrote—I could hear his foggy voice through the words when I
studied them—that Wayde Mitchell had, as he'd feared,
slipped the legal leash on a technicality, and would be serving
only a few months of time in jail. He wrote, "Some men have
an obsession about injustice, Luke; they wish to guard it as
other men guard honor. I think you must learn to deal with
such creatures, not by running away, and not by force of hand
or arms, but by vigilance against dishonor and the strength to
rise above it with your own soul."

Gathered from that that he thought Mitchell might cross my
path again. Maybe seeking for that money he now knew had
been with Letty and me all the while. I kept the letter in my
pocket a long while, sometimes taking it out to pore over
again. It got wrinkled. Didn't show it to Letty.

Meantime Letty and I were growing into each other again,
but this time it didn't seem the roots we had were nearly as
sour as they'd been before. That is, they wouldn't have been
except for me.

I'd wake in the night's center and get this feeling in me that
if I could just have Mitchell's fat neck between my hands for a
short spell of time I'd be grateful forever after.

No, it didn't make any difference that it might not be my
seed that had made the swelling of Letty's belly. But it was
whose seed might've done it besides mine that plugged at me,
and deviled me, and made me lie in the nights thinking of all
that had happened and having the night sweats. Once Letty
woke and looked at me while I stood at the window letting the
cold air sweep over my body, then she sits up and says, "You

still got a meaning of resentment in you. I hope it's not toward
me."

"No," I says. "It's just him."

"Oh, poo. Him." She lay back with her hair fanning the bolster. Could just see her in the blue cold northing light of the
night. "Don't you know people like him couldn't mean anything to a woman? If she was a real woman? Don't you know it
wasn't much and now you can just let it blow away and be kind
to yourself?"

"That's the way I ought to be feeling, and the way I'm trying to feel," I says. "But it don't come out like that. It's like I'm
trying to do a good portrait and at a certain point my hand
slips. And daubs. I can't tell you how it is, all of it, but it's
there like a cholera germ in my soul."

"Come back to bed, Luke," she says, patting the bolster.

After a time I went back.

Some days, all the Darlings came in the main house and, with
Letty and I taking turns, we taught them to read. Peter was
the first to learn, and I got the notion he did it through pride
more than anything, more than really wanting to learn. When
I pointed out, with Seven backing me, that by learning to read
they might all finally go to Washington and learn how to sue
to get back at least a thumbnail of those Indian lands their fathers and fathers' fathers had owned, they went to it with
more doggedness and speed.

Started them on such books as *Little Bob ⸻il,* by Oliver Optic,
and *An American Girl Abroad,* by Miss Adeline Trafton, and
Young Folks' History of England, by Isa Craig Knox. Such books
were peculiar as duck eggs in a hen's nest. They just didn't fit
with the calf-bound books in the rest of the library. The folks
in them said their words so nice and staid it was like listening
to a crackle of words that missed the whole plunge and glory
and dark of life. But the boys started getting the words
straight in their heads, and after they'd got them real good I
decided we could begin them on the essays of Charles Lamb.

Afternoons, especially when the light flooded into the front
room, I painted. I finished the second portrait of Letty; it

wasn't nearly as lovely-pretty as the first but it showed more of her, what she was, beneath the paint. She was swelling a little as the weeks passed and January slid into February; outside, the ice came and gripped the pond and stopped the mill wheel. Seven said it did so every year. Sometimes, when it wasn't too daunting a day, I took the Dan Boone rifle from the mantel and Seven and I and the Darlings went hunting far down the creek, where it cut through a ravine a long way the other side of the clearing. We got some rabbit and some squirrel; I learned how to narrow off close and squeeze the rifle and hold it tight to keep from the thumping recoil it could give you, after getting my shooting shoulder black and blue a number of times.

It was sure a wonderful rifle for its time. Sometimes you get the feeling people make something the right way once, and nobody will ever make it better. Down in the ravine was a lonesome and windless place, even when there was a shrewd breeze lolloping along the clearing. Seven said it was a fruitless place to cultivate—we were planning to get a plow and another horse, come spring—because it was too stony. Iced rocks were underfoot every two, three yards; the frozen creek went snaking through them like a piece of frozen lightning.

Some afternoons, too, I wrote letters. I cleared off the satin-wood rolltop desk in what had been the study, I presumed, of Mister Carroll; I answered the professor's letter, telling him I was glad he and Loogan Harkins had took the orders of Milt Farley nimbly enough to manage to assist the balloon in getting back to Richmond, and inquiring about his health and Miz Amily's. I got a letter from Jericho and Penelope Dabney, too, saying they had seen the write-up about Letty and me, and the whole caboodle, in the Montgomery papers, and they surely hoped they might come across me one day soon and that our paths would cross. Didn't ever hear from Magnusun or his crew, though I'd have liked to know how Sara was getting along through the winter's tide.

I purely detested writing the letters, but Letty said I'd ought to do it. She didn't know about the one I wrote back to Prosser, thanking him for his advice. There were business things, too, we had to do, and Letty and I together composed a letter, at her behest, to the authorities handling the farm now, saying that she'd like to sell the farm for a stipulated amount, and didn't ever want to come back there for any reason. I couldn't make much head or tail of the letter we got back from the lawyers after that—but then, lawyers. Turned out finally she had an offer for Einsner's lands, and she sold them and a check came in the post office. We opened a bank account down in Solomon after that, in her name—I sure God didn't want anything like that in mine, might have bound me up so I couldn't paint for a month, was the way I saw it.

The strongbox money stayed in the trees for a long spell; then one day in March—a day with the sun so strong through the strip-leafed birches it made them look like fiery white posts—I went across the creek and brought the box back to the house. That same afternoon we spanked down to Solomon again, and put the money in the bank again in her name.

Then, in the bank, run by a quiet-mouthed fellow in a salt-and-pepper suit and a high collar and a lot of patience, seemed to me, to be sitting there while it was such a challengeful day outside—but then some people like the dim and the dark—Letty says, "I don't want it, I always meant that. I wanted it when I ran off. It was going to set up a life for me. But it's death money now."

I had a hand on her shoulder and was fooling with her hair.

I thought of her mother and her part in the whole thing.

It came to me then: Letty was just like me, some ways. When I'd run off from Clagberts after being at the orphanage, when I was a mousy sprat, I'd had no kith and kin I was ever going to know. Maybe I was a by-blow myself; I'd often felt like it, not that it mattered a curse. Letty'd been born with kith and kin, and was you could say a rich farmer's daughter, but in the other way, she'd never had any father and mother either. But now she knew it, all the distance.

So I said, "Why don't we give the damned thing away? There's plenty besides, and going to be more from the mill when the year opens up again."

There was just a little trade now, in the good days; but it was a famous mill and it had been proved out to be a workable one again.

"There are some fine investments possible in railroads," said the banker, name of Cloughran. He'd overheard us.

He went on, "An influential person like yourself, Mister Applegate, ought to make investments of this kind."

A kind of cold chill went up my spine. Traveled all the distance from ass-cleft to nape.

"No thank you kindly," I said. It was that word, influential, that got to me. My God, a man might as well fold his hands and go lie under a marble slab and pretend he'd never existed if he was going to make himself into that. He could turn into Senator Margate, the professor's friend I'd painted, or into Wayde Mitchell, or into just a piece of smiling granite. I'd seen a good many of the pictures done by influential painters—I don't mean Gainsborough, or other good ones, I mean the six cows in a mead, looking like they'd never breathed, and the daubs of trees bushing out in the background, and the stiff people standing in the foreground. I'd rather be back running from justice than be influential, just so I could hold my own hair on with my own live self.

Says, "Letty, let's send half of it without any name attached to the orphanage I come out of. It was a bit-down place but they tried hard with what they had."

She says good, so I chewed a pen hard till I recollected the name of the place—it had been a sight of years—and then we got the banker to do the business, without mentioning us, with a gold-plated check that would wrap it up. I hope the way they used it, at that orphanage, when they got it, they put up some good pictures—not influentially painted ones—and washed the walls and got some beds felt like more than pieces of grit.

I especially hoped it about the pictures, though I guessed I'd never know.

Then I says, "Now the other half, let's send that to your ma and Loogan Harkins." I'd already given Letty her mother's obligances and good will, as Jane had asked me to; I had a

post-office box address for the Milt Farley Ascension Show in
Richmond, which he'd handed me in case I ever needed his
aerial services in life again.

Letty nods, and says, "I'll write her a note with it." So she
did, and there went the other half of that young fortune in
another gilt-edged check.

Wasn't a bit sad to see it go. Only the banker seemed a whit
downcast. Bankers have to be that way.

When it was on the brink of spring we went to the Quaker
church down in Solomon; the day before I'd spent most of the
hours working with the Darling brothers to help them build a
kind of barn of brush and leftover lumber and such for their
cows, so's they wouldn't have to winter again on the slope or
outdoors near the Darlings' ma's house. Miz Darling, if that
was her name, didn't speak English, or even American; she
was a wizened little woman who sat and watched us, her face
in a thousand wrinkles like some Egyptian goddess brought
out of wrappings, and when I gave her some tobacco she
handed me back some oat-cakes. They did like to remain free
and work for their keep, the Darlings.

Anyhow, I hadn't studied to go churching, and I told Letty
so, and said I didn't want it to be a habit.

She just said she had a curiosity.

Well, it was a nice church—not near as sumptuous as that
one back in Richmond the professor favored, where Patrick
Henry had expounded—and the people were so quiet it
worked everybody some good, the way silence often does.
Smelled good in it, like new wool and folds of other fresh
cloth. It was April now and back at the mill the branch and the
creek and the pond were all quivering with mirth and merri-
ment, with the first dragonflies starting to come and skim, and
the bulrushes and other reeds growing up green and spiny,
and the daisies in the fields around the clearing coming up
leggy. It was nice sitting in that place listening to your own
thoughts and the thoughts of others, like so many calm clouds
reaching up out the open windows and joining the sky's

clouds. Once in a time, some man or woman stood up and said something that had come to him or her while they thought; it was always just level and easy said, no jumping and revelating.

After it was over the people smiled and shook hands some, calling Letty "Miz Applegate," which she wasn't, though from the way she stuck out under the new dark blue gown she'd just sewed—it was made to try to conceal some of her coming child in its drapes, but it couldn't do it—you could see why the people said so. I expect they thought we'd been married right after I homed in from my travels.

To her it didn't matter, saying a few words over the Bible and having a ring on her hand; I asked her about it on the way back to the mill. She studied it over, then looks at me with one of her almost smiles—she near made it, it was a fractional miss—and says, "I'd rather we didn't do that, Luke, not maybe till we're old and shriveled. If we get old and shriveled. If it meant a deal to you—"

"You know it don't," I said, urging the bay to step out faster. The whole earth was showing, winter had peeled away like skin from an onion, the day was full of scents of thyme and even, it seemed to me, myrrh. Though that's biblical. Anyhow the sky was that blue—cerulean—it gets, and it was pleasurable taking breath.

Except for that ball of meanness in my chest, that never quite went away. Looking at her now, I wondered what the child would look like. If it would have anything of Mitchell's fawning about it—if it was his.

My face must have darkened because she sighs then. When we got home to the mill I couldn't paint all day, though I'd been doing a sketch of Seven and had had my hand and the paints ready for the canvas. Through the post office in Felton's general store I also got paints, now, from New York and Boston and other points. And sometimes canvases, though I could usually use just any old solid surface in a storm. Anyhow again, I couldn't paint today; I wandered down into the ravine across the creek, till Seven called me, from the topside, standing up there with spring grasses around him, Barabbas leaning over to look at his side. His voice was soft and faint, yet firm. He looked like the spirit of the daylight up there, so old, so set against the sky.

"Watch out for the snakes," he says. "Wear tall boots down in there this time of year, Luke."

I got up out of there fast. When I was at his side, fondling Barabbas and looking down, I couldn't see any stir around the rocks of the creek, except for the squirming shine of the water, but I never did take a fondness for the place.

Thirty-Seven

IN THE GOOD WEATHER, slanting toward May, we bought a
plow—dandy big bull-tongue, made to work around the dark
craggy Pennsylvania stones—and another horse, this one a
draught animal looked so hard he might've been sculpted
from some of the same stone we hauled. A pleasure, it was, to
work behind him and see his muscles gloze and ripple in the
hot light. We scraped off the whole edge of the path side,
leveling it down so a customer or anybody could get up there
without straining his gut and losing all his animals' wind; it
was a job of days. And meantime the customers kept coming
again—not the way they would once more in the autumn
when they wanted to get all the flour and meal in for a long
winter's waiting, but in bits and pieces with corn to be milled
and with their dried-out winter wheat from the cribs.

We turned off, handling the milling and working to slick
down the path side; sometimes Jase and Paul and I worked at
the milling, while Seven and Peter and David plowed and
shifted stone in a stone boat we'd built; depended on which
bunch happened to be fittest that day for the regular task.

All the work took it out of you, right from the center of you, but all the same, come night, I'd still be restless as a prowling night bird. Seemed there were ants and pismires in my blood, working there and making me itch and sometimes stop and slam one hand into another. I'd move out through the dark after supper—we called it supper, the professor would have said dinner—just unable to sit in the main house where Letty was sewing, and playing the harpsichord, and complaining a little of the heat, which was getting to her in her largened condition, and I'd move down through the clearing with that Daniel Boone rifle in my arms; sometimes I'd rove a long way from the clearing. We'd built more of an all-season barn, now, for the horses and the gear; it stood back of the small house where Letty and I'd lived when we first came here, and I'd slope down from it and through the lush-scented dark and far on the other side of the stream, so I could just hear the water running, then sit on a stone or a log till I could feel the night gather around me. Till I could feel even the small animals come close without much fear as if I'd been a log myself, scarred by time and patient with weather.

Up above I'd feel the breath of the stars, and think about this part of the world swinging through space till it seemed I wasn't even in my own body any more but just a shell sitting there with a rifle in my hands, not killing anything but sort of ready and guarded. I'd feel desperate at those times, with a haunt-colored picture of Mitchell eating right in the vitals.

Maybe Letty still knew about this, maybe she didn't. All I know is, I couldn't keep from it.

Warmish night, second or third day into May now, I got up from beside Letty and slid downstairs, pulling on a pair of pants and some boots, and in the big front room, went to the mantel and lifted down that finger-silking rifle. It was loaded, I kept the powder in it all the time now; and it was dry.

When I got out, all I could feel was the liveness of the trees shadowing moss in the clearing, the briskness and watchfulness of the whole clearing itself. It'd been a sun-beating day but now, at night, was when the whole place truly leaped awake. I skifted down past the new barn with the horses moving just gentle in there, and past Seven's house and the Darlings', and on above the creek, and jumped it.

Then I found a hickory log had fell slantwise above the ravine so the suckers growing out of its flank made almost a chair you could sit back against, and lowered myself there and waited.

I'd come to this place before; sat here many a night, waiting I didn't know for what.

But this night, just about when I was going to get up and make my way back to the house, I thought I see a light. First it was a tiddling glimmer, then a real light, sure enough, from a bull's-eye lantern—most like a firefly at first, then nearer and larger and no firefly. It was moving along the ravine, coming down into it from the backside of the clearing. I couldn't fathom who it was, but it was a funny time for an outsider to show up, the farmers around Solomon, and even from Mullin's Gap, weren't the kind to go sashaying and chicken-thief-moving through another man's territory by deep dark.

Figured whoever it was already knew something of the lay of the land, and thought whoever it was had come through the ravine, this back way, to avoid any of Barabbas's watchfulness, or the Darlings or Seven in their houses.

The lantern-shine got bigger and pooled in wider circles, so whoever held it was picking his way through the ravine, and planning on climbing up my side.

Could have been a lost child, I thinks. Though it wasn't likely. Or a man out searching for a strayed cow. Though the Darlings' cows were all that existed around here.

I leans forward, holding all my breath.

Then, in the lantern's quivering fall, I can see plain enough. And it's Mitchell. He moved awkward, with little steps. He was trying to move careful.

I made real sure. Sure as the air baffled in my lungs.

It was him, certain as God. Nosing about, seeking maybe for the twelve thousand—or seeking for a sight of Letty, she being the most monstrous part of that obsession—nice forthright word—Prosser had mentioned in the letter. Or maybe seeking both—whatever he could gather in his buttery hands.

I felt all the hate, all the darkness he'd caused me and Letty, caused the professor, and Tom Prosser, and dozens on dozens of others, come ramming up through my legs and gut and chest and arm muscles. And I felt, with it, a wicked happiness come rising through the veins, and pounding in my wrists like I was going to paint the best thing I'd ever done, a picture gifted and ready.

I'd gone through a lot of guilt fear in my jail-time, and all that time on the road, running, and that whole time with Prosser and the other marshals. I'd come free of all that, but till now I hadn't known, all in a point, what being mad could be. I watched him, his double chin splashed with upward light from the bull's-eye lantern, his patent leather shoes picking easy around the rocks. I watched and thought of him seeing Letty naked and then touching her. Say hello to my little butterfly, I thought, and I understood that till now I'd never known what murder is.

I hadn't known it could come roaring up rich in the veins and heavy with a smiling, terrible feeling that I'd got to do it now.

I lifted the rifle so the stock sat just right and I could see a glint of moonlight along the barrel, that long bright-dark barrel that seemed to stretch forever till it framed, exactly, what you wanted to blast. I wasn't Daniel Boone, couldn't bark a squirrel from a tree, but I was fair enough this close. I could see him yet plainer as he hoisted the lantern, and my finger started homing on the curve of the trigger.

I guessed he'd stashed his barouche carriage down a back road with his driving boy, Andrew, waiting there for him. Tonight, I thinks, Andrew will have to drive away alone.

Another second and I'd have had him. In the second before it, all I'm thinking is, Well, I'll be ridding the earth of one rotten thing, and maybe be presented with a medal, and even if I'm not, it's only keeping off possible burglars from a man's own land; it will stand in court and I'll go free.

Then, next second, a hand's come up and pushed my rifle barrel aside. It's David Darling. In my ear with no more noise than a leaf makes when it's blown in the dark, he says, "You want him? I'll do it."

I'd had no notion David was following. And he'd saved me.

Saved me from being as bad as Mitchell and worse, from having a corpse on my conscience all my life, and my hand from the blight of slaying a man.

It was meant only to use the Power of the Hand for painting, you see.

I says, very soft too, feeling that weight shift from me and knowing how this's got to be done, still with that mad in me that had to leap out, "No, no shootin'." And I put my long rifle down and then started making my way soft and as quick as I could down upon the rocky slope.

When I got to the bottom of the ravine with those rocks sharp around me everything was a blue green light like a field of cabbage under water.

I moved toward Mitchell, keeping outside the rim of the ring of his lantern light.

Then I jumped him, from the front, knocking him back and feeling his sagging flesh soft-plump-warm under me and hearing the lantern crash and go out in an oil flare and explosion, and then I had him on his back and I took his nose, and twisted.

He's spluttering and trying to speak and trying, same time, to get up; and I'm getting ready to ice him off for a long serious time, so he'll feel it all his days, raising my left hand, not wishing to insult or injure the right one, when, up above, David calls out, and then I hear Seven calling too.

I half-turned and what I made out, in David's voice, froze me stiff.

"Snakes," he says. "Don't *move*. Stay still . . ."

Then above the regular night noises in this ravine, I can hear them moving. The snakes, out at night in the warm, out of their dens between rocks; rattlers like the one Letty had killed that long time ago, moving in the dark all around me. I could hear their dry bodies move over the rocks, and then I could hear a regular rattling, close. They were all over. Filling the whole gulch.

Jesus, sweet God. You can get well after a rattler bite but not after twenty. Or even two. They had a smell, too, riding through the warm air—like crushed cucumbers, but a sight more noisome. They seemed to be searching us out, smelling and feeling the heat of our bodies.

I stayed just where I was, not stirring. Then there's a rifle shot, David's Winchester, I near felt the plowing of the air, it came so close, and from a tongue of rock not three feet from my head, in the slash of moonlight there, a shape the size of a mashed-down Golden Grimes apple disappears, and I can hear thrashing. Then another shot came on the other side of the rock-point, this time not hitting a snake's head but landing near it and discouraging it. The body of the one that'd had its head shot off loops down over the rock, half in light, and in this greeny light it looked mammoth. There's more rattling, that dry heavy buzzing-clicking all around my ears. I'm all over sweat and holding Mitchell firm with every ounce of muscle in me, and yet not moving, myself, but just tight and stiff like one of those Greek warriors about to loose the discobolus in one of the professor's pictures.

Next comes the sound of the Darlings' old rifle, that crazy one they'd won the whiskey-cupping with, and it hit near us; then I heard the noise of Seven's rifle; then there were regular shot-splats, a whole volley as they all shot and reloaded, shot and reloaded. Finally, through this, Seven sings out in his level but very hearable voice, "Now start moving, Luke. We'll keep 'em away as you come. Drag whoever you got down there back a few steps at a time."

I did that. Mitchell weighed more'n any man ought to; pulling him was sheer dead weight. He'd had the fair fortune to pass out.

Slow, then, David and Jase and Peter and Paul and Seven came down into the ravine, shooting as they came, and finally they got to us and helped me pull, and push, and hoist Mitchell up the ravine side, and out.

Then while he lay there I picked up the Dan Boone rifle and leans on it, and caught my breath and my wits.

Seven says consideringly, "We'll clean that ravine out tomorrow, I think it's time."

"You might say it is," I says.

He laughs, soft, sounding so like the wind murmuring in a cave mouth, quiet and above the earth yet fixed to it with pine roots.

He looked thoughtful, at Mitchell.

Mitchell's eyes opened. He isn't crying, just starts to gasp. His eyes roll and meet my eyes, and Seven's, and those of the Darlings.

Jase Darling says, "Can we give him the Mohawk End for Enemies, Luke?" He says it very calm but serious, as if he is asking for a piece of sourdough bread and salt butter.

Paul Darling says, with the same calmness, "Flensing the skin off is a long job. You got to start at the feet." He squats beside Mitchell, touching one of his slick point-tipped shoes.

David says, "Ain't hard when you've soaked with hot water a couple days."

Peter says, "His horses and his carriage are down the back path a way. We could use them."

I'd have bet Seven had had the very hell of a time holding in the Darlings when I'd been on the road and Mitchell and his men had come smousing around here.

I'm feeling quiet. Something's been lifted from me.

I says, "No."

"Well, I'd at least like to have his vest," says David.

I hunkered down beside Mitchell. "Good-bye, Wayde with a y," I says. "Don't come back on these grounds." I was a mite shaky, like some tired judge, but still quiet. "Don't ever even speak to Letty again if you meet her. That's all."

I stood up and told the Darlings to help him down the back path, rimming the ravine. And to see him on his way. And not to do anything to him.

I felt like Prosser. Didn't even want to speak his name anymore.

The Darlings hoisted him up, not brushing him off, just doing it capable. Ringing him, they started down around the back-path way. He was sobbing a little now, and Barabbas was trotting close, breathing at his pockets. That was the last I saw of him except for his vest. It showed up later one morning at breakfast, David wearing it. Then in the following days Jase wore it, and then Paul, and then Peter, turnabout.

I never did ask any questions about the vest. They deserved a little something for their vigilance against dishonor.

Under some situations, I've told myself since, Wayde Mitchell could have got to be President. I've seen some since would curl your back-hair, not a whole body of time removed from what he was. Even voted for a couple, and later marveled that the country kept right on running some way, which renews your faith in the earth itself, a forgiving land.

I was scratched up and while I was putting witch hazel and some neats'-foot on myself—oil and hazel rub you down like gold—by the light of a low lamp in the kitchen of the main house, Letty came downstairs and gave me fits for wandering about and getting myself bunged up in the night's dangers. I just told her we'd been shooting snakes. I thought of the Darlings. I smiled at her. She was so hopping mad she near slapped me for the smile. Kept on fussing a time. Was still fussing when we went back to bed. Went to sleep with her fussing. Does a woman good when she's fat with child to blow off steam like a sawmill getting shut of pressure.

But in the center of the night I woke up. Felt relieved and saved and thankful. I haunched over on one elbow and regarded Letty in the slim light coming up here in our big room. She was sleeping on her back, the bedclothes had shifted down, and her breasts were so full and graceful I couldn't keep from touching the one nearest me. What a wonder, what a marvel is this, I thought. That anything can be so beauty-packed and lifting. I touched the nipple, and soon the nipple came up under my fingertips. Then she opened her eyes, the blue-green wonders, flowers opening in the first day of the entire world. Which is always for flowers and people when they open up.

She said, "You've been on edge for a month and more. You think you can't come into me because of the child? I'll tell you when it's too close for that."

She was whispering, close and warm-moist.

I felt the bulge of the child, the skin tight-packed. Then slow as a clock of the night, I put my hand below, and worked it into her maidenhair, and with my legs moving stripped the rest of the coverings from us. And I felt her Venus mount go warm and yet warmer, and thought, now the fire-heat is coming, the gold of the mountain is rising. She had her fingers around me now, those delicate-as-butterfly fingers, touching careful, slow, and stroking, and I thought about slicking up Penelope, and Sally Lou Loudermilk, and then even of girls, women, whose names I'd all but forgot, and it came over me in a flooding charge, like a dazzling of star's fire falling to cover the earth, and swim in my eyes, and pierce through all the moonlight and wrap us, that this was the joyance of man and woman on earth, ours, theirs, the beginning and· ending. All of it, names didn't matter, it was all in her and pouring from her to me and from me to her.

We went slow as lions licking the sun from their fur, slow as time on the first day when the fern came growing out of the earth above the rocks which were still cooling, and all things, all things alive, moved in our veins and there was a kind of humming and singing, and I thought, if it was even thinking—knew, deeper than thought—that the child was mine now whosever it was in seed.

Girl I knew once—I'd forgot her name too—said, "This is what it's all about." Said it at a time like this.

Then when it was all over the first time, I started kissing her belly where the child might've been stirring by now, and worked my way up to her wet sleek breasts, and into her throat's hollow, and felt under her for that gracious decline just above her hips' swelling, where everything swoops down in a V that moves like the flicker of a brush when it's the only way for the brush to go and make the only right color and light and placement, and holding her so, I hardened again, and again went into her by slipping gradual inches. And after that, wet with sweat and its hot-sun seed-smell, we got up and she moved atop of me, straddling and riding, smiling in the shine of the moon on us under the window, smiling now because this was the Letty of the first and the last and the ever.

After that I hardly ever thought—or if I did, then thought not much and lightsome—of Wayde Mitchell again.

And also after that, I'd stop in the kitchen where Letty was baking bread and just look at her, and she at me, and we'd both feel the humming and the singing. Sometimes I'd just touch her fingers, it was enough, it was everything. It was like the sun on the edge of a baking dish, and a work-pan sitting on a table, or an old chair, well made, soaking up sun on a gallery. It was in all that, everyplace.

Next day Seven and the Darlings and I cleaned out the ravine. Seven said when we got through it still wouldn't be even fit to plow and leave fallow, but decent for walking. We accomplished it by setting fire to all the brush we could lug there and burn, and it went on all day, and was fiery hot work. I didn't mind it because I could paint again, any time, I felt free and quit with the world, on a good-balanced keel with it.

I didn't go ravaging off through the night, looking so peaked and damned that David and the rest had to follow me.

Days went on, the weather just spread itself burning and sweet over us all, and I finished my full portrait of Seven. It's another I won't sell, unless worst comes to worst, which it always can in this vale of soul-making, which is what Mister Keats called the world.

Down into May, Letty wakes me in the early morning and says, "It's coming," and it's like she's angry about it, and anxious, and I rode the bay down to Solomon in the early dawn light even without a saddle, caught a doctor out of his warm bed, and paced his slow horse all the way back, nattering to myself like I'd always made a habit of having these fits. The child was damned near there when we got to the main house, and I felt a sinking in my gut because luck won't always hold, you have to shape it the way you shape a portrait, and sometimes you can't.

In all my travels I'd never midwifed anything, or helped to, except stock, and that's something the same but you don't feel that harsh belly-cutting way about it.

Then it's time for me to go in. She's lying there in the big bed that'd belonged to the Carrolls in the old days, she looks wan but the face is that hickory-nut shape and the hair's wet but lovely, and the eyes green as summer leaves after a swashing rain.

Was considerably lightened, too. Couldn't see a hump anymore, and the bedclothes flat against her over the hipbones.

I kissed her, and nuzzled her up and told her she was a sight that ought to stand in a wall-niche holding a lamp, like that Helen Edgar Allan Poe was aiming his poem against, and she says, "You talk to me 's if I was one of the horses, Luke. Not a horse. Never thought I'd bear a human being."

I says, "Horses aren't in it with you, but anything lovely needs good talk."

Then I looked at the child. Well, who can ever tell who sired a child? It was there, that was all—pretty bright red in the face, like it needed a touch of pure white worked into its skin to get the contours and the values right; squinched up in its sleep, and moist, but not crying. Smelled like milk and nutmeg.

I backed off, and later Seven and the Darlings came in. Barabbas came too, but no farther'n the door. We did the cooking for all, those days, and it might as well all been made of unbolted corn meal because it tasted like it, except when Seven brought some fresh trout which Letty lit into like she was a wolf scouring up after a tough hunt.

Whosever the child was, it prospered.

About a month later, with the corn crop in the fields around Solomon showing bright above-ground and the wheat turning gold and that feeling of prowling and exultance—which the professor says is *hubris,* after which bad will follow, but I never put much faith in that—about a month later, Letty and I are out near the mill in the evening, fireflies are climbing the oaks and pines, fading off in little drifts and falls like tents made of tiny green cold lights, and where we're standing the steady turning of the mill wheel makes a roar that cools the ears.

She's got the child in her arms. Forgot to say it was a girl.

First girl child I ever knew about I'd been responsible for, mine or not.

You could see its eyes trying to make out all the wonder of the mill wheel and to make something of the night, to put it into shapes it could feel and know.

Then David comes out of the mill. Comes to me, and I can tell from his look something's wrong.

I moved apart from Letty and the child—girl name of Araba, Letty says it was a name she'd always favored—and when we got inside the mill David says, "In the loft."

I climbed up there after him. This was the uppermost loft, where Seven liked to sit in the times when the dark was coming and then go on mulling to himself in the dark. I suppose he remembered, in flashes—or sometimes in slow pleasurable half-sleeping scenes—everything he'd ever seen in life, all he'd lived through, the small moments sometimes mounting up as high and lofty in meaning as the large ones. I know I didn't ever disturb him up there, and neither did the Darlings, and Barabbas couldn't climb the ladder.

It was shadowed and cool up here above the water's purling.

Some place above the sound of water was a nightbird, I think a phoebe, singing that mourning song, sounds cool as a river over gray stones on a misty day, in the climbing dark.

But Seven was lying on his back, wasn't sitting and looking out. I went to him and knelt down. I took his wrist. It was warm but the pulse was gone.

All the light he'd had in this earth had dwindled out.

I sat there beside him a long time, then. It was like I could feel all he'd meant in his silent ways for all his years float around me and like I could catch pieces of it, slight as gossamer but packed with truth as my own heart's beating, all I was going to know, in my own self, for much of my own life.

Like he kept telling me these pieces of a fact past the fact of simply being alive and lovemaking and taking pleasure in the morn and lying down at night with joy.

For a couple of seconds there while the dark went from heliotrope through dove-gray to the stillness that brings the fireflies even brighter, I near had the whole thing. Nothing I could paint but something that could get into some of the faces I might be painting.

Then I said to David, "Go get your brothers."

And we buried him, that same night, on the ridge behind the creek and the pond and the mill stream, in that thick dark soil so heavy and loamy it crunches apart in your hand slow when you squeeze it, to a dark-shining lasting powder. I didn't know many words to say, but Letty found a few from a Bible in the house.

I read them out, but I don't think they meant as much as the feeling I'd had in the loft, and still had. It was grieving but it was a going on. The child saw something she liked in the spraddling trees around us and reached her hands for it. That was it, whatever she saw, that meant what Seven was for me.

And for Letty too, I'd say. Barabbas sat there looking out at the air above the new-made grave, a long time, and after a time, too, the Darlings came filing back from their house where they'd gone when we'd got through putting him in the ground, and they sat down on the hummocks aroundabout, with drums in their laps, and started rapping the drums.

They sang with it, only you couldn't make out the full drift of the song, but what it said was clear and true. It was a chanting, and it went on all night—went on when Letty and the child and I were in the big bed in the main house, sounding through the sound of the mill wheel.

Well, making a long telling shorter, I got the real itch after that, and one morning I packed all I had in the paint and canvas sack and tells Letty, "We're going off in the nation now. I've rammed around it all my days, and there's no staying me. I'm likely to get more influential by the day, working here—we'll come back in the fall when the real heavy milling starts, but now the summer's waiting."

Her green eyes sparked, and she reared like a colt, but all the same I think she did it for show, to keep me in my basket.

When she was through making trouble—which she was born to create—she simmers down. "Luke, wait'll I get packed."

"Don't take along the earth," I says. "A man like me always lived light and I don't intend to spoil the feeling."

So she packed a couple of light trunks and boxes, and I got the bay out and washed her down and polished her hide with straw and a curry-comb, and shined up the buggy too. Oh, it was a day, and sudden-like, I could see it all spread out, all the roads through the hamlets and the cities, it was a time the circuses would be moving, and I hoped to see some of my friends in them. It was a time you expected to see a balloon making up above the trees any breathing moment.

I told the boys, and they said they'd keep the fort against all takers, and God knew, they could run the mill right to a fare-ye-well.

So when I'd got everything lashed in the buggy, a lot of canvases and the best collection of brushes and paints and turps and all I ever had, we rolled down the path's lip, which was easy going now. The child looked around with eagerness, sun flecking its face. Had my eyes, Letty's hair, or so I told myself, as though it made a whistle's difference.

And pretty soon we were out on the road, and then whirling past Solomon, set out in the world again, with all its promises and its deathly darks, lonesomeness and amusements and witchery.

Butterflies roved ahead of us, clouds of brilliance in the road. The earth was scented with clover so you could savor it like bread. I turns to the child and poked at its belly where the skin's so soft, and says, "Araba, you all right, Araba?"

Letty, holding her while we spanked along, looked like the figurehead of a ship again, that leaning forward.

Araba laughed when I tickled her, and Letty's hair flew out like true gold in the wind. I thought I'd have to paint them both soon, the way they were now, after I'd started in painting other faces in the nation again, which there were a million of to be limned in honesty, and I was the man who, for an honest fee, would do it.